THE RAVEN'S JOURNEY
BOOK EIGHT

STOLAS

Michelle Lee

BLUE FORGE PRESS
Port Orchard, Washington

Stolas
Copyright 2020, 2022
by Michelle Lee

First eBook Edition June 2021
First Print Edition June 2021
Second eBook Edition May 2022
Second Print Edition May 2022

Cover photograph by Michelle Lee
Cover design by Brianne DiMarco
Interior design by Brianne DiMarco

ISBN 978-1-59092-892-9

For information about film, reprint or other subsidiary rights, contact: blueforgegroup@gmail.com

Blue Forge Press is the print division of the volunteer-run, federal 501(c)3 nonprofit company, Blue Forge Group, founded in 1989 and dedicated to bringing light to the shadows and voice to the silence. We strive to empower storytellers across all walks of life with our four divisions: Blue Forge Press, Blue Forge Films, Blue Forge Gaming, and Blue Forge Records. Find out more at www.BlueForgeGroup.org

Blue Forge Press
7419 Ebbert Drive Southeast
Port Orchard, Washington 98367
blueforgepress@gmail.com
360-550-2071 ph.txt

MORE BY THE AUTHOR

THE RAVEN'S JOURNEY

Book 1: See Me
Book 2: See Me Revealed
Book 3: See Me Go
Book 4: See Me Believe
Book 5: See Me Overcome
Book 6: Hawk
Book 7: Ronan
Book 8: Stolas

LOOKING THROUGH THE SHADOWS

The Underbelly
After the Wreckage
We Always Fight

I S.P.I.

I S.P.I. Mischievous Magic (Volume 1)
I S.P.I. Spicy Sorcery (Volume 2)

SHORT STORIES & MORE

Where Realms Collide
Unnerving Descent
Unnerving Eclipse
Unnerving Wicked
Super: Unexpected Heroes Arise
Rise Reflection
Rise Resurrection
Rise Revolution
Rise Recreation
The Space Between Us
The Pulse (The Haunting of Orchard House)

Michelle Lee on the Web

Michelle on Facebook at
tiny.cc/MichelleLeeWrites

or write to
MichelleLeeWrites@gmail.com

For Jamie
who has always wanted
to be killed off in a book.
May your demonic soul
rest in peace.

STOLAS

Michelle Lee

Chapter One

Stolas slumped wearily on his bed, wondering when his life, or what passed for one now, had gotten so complicated. It was a redundant thought. He knew exactly the day it had happened. It had been the first day he had seen the angel, entirely by chance as well. Nothing had been the same since.

He was over two thousand years old, a prince of Hell, in love with an angel who was now married to the one she is supposed to be with and had given him a vision of his future. His existence could be considered mundane by standards of Hell, yet since she came into the picture, it had been anything but tedious.

He stared at the opulence of his room, artifacts, and trinkets he'd collected over the years. It was all meaningless. The most valuable things he had now was a couple of feathers, a lock of hair, and an extensive spy network. All of it involving said angel. Not something the other princes of Hell could boast about for sure. It wasn't something he should brag about either, not if he were trying to keep her safe.

One of his servants knocked at the door. Stolas thought about ignoring it, but they were only to interrupt him if absolutely necessary. If someone had gotten word that movement was happening, he needed to get topside and warn Airiella if at all possible.

"Come in," he called out.

"Sir, the master, has requested your presence at his residence." The demon bowed deeply.

That didn't bode well. "When?"

"Now, sir."

Meetings with him weren't unusual, but the timing of this was. He didn't think it was a coincidence, but he could hope. Airiella had given him that. Hope. He'd hold on to it however he could. He stood up, dismissing the servant, and looked in the mirror, grimacing.

He was glowing. That meant either something was happening he hadn't gotten informed, or Airiella was upset and reacting badly to something. That vow he had given her was going to bite him in the ass. Princes of Hell weren't supposed to glow with divine light. Especially when being called to talk to their boss.

Since the demise of Bael not too long ago, there have been many reassignments and changes in Hell's hierarchy. The sciences were his thing, and he didn't think that the boss was going to take that from him. But the legions he commanded had grown considerably; those *could* get reassigned.

Stolas waited until the glow faded and then headed out his mind racing. He was one of the few trusted princes now after the boss learned of the deception Bael had planned. Stolas knew he wasn't getting out of Hell. He was one of the fallen by choice. But that didn't mean he couldn't become reassigned or lose his status. Losing status meant losing power and losing his network of spies.

Stolas couldn't let that happen. Not now. Airiella's life depended on his help, not only that, he'd pledged it voluntarily. Breaking that vow could result in another war, and Hell was already overcrowded and miserable without adding casualties of war and the crimes it brought out in people.

Stolas assumed the glowing was due to his warning to them earlier. He found himself oddly attached to them, this group who did a television show about the paranormal. Originally it was just Airiella that drew him, an angel. There hadn't been one on earth in several hundred years.

Stolas had come across her on a beach, after answering a summoning not far from where he'd found her. The draw of power he'd felt called to him, a warm feeling he hadn't felt since before he'd fallen. It had left a taste in his mouth that he'd wanted to explore.

It wasn't until Stolas followed the trail that he knew instantly he'd stumbled across an angel, one that was far different from the likes he'd ever encountered before. Her power was unrivaled. It had a taste and feel to it that he'd never seen on another; redemption.

That was the moment his ordinary existence went sideways. Stolas stalked Airiella like prey, craved her, lusted after her, and wanted to own her. The more he learned, the stronger those feelings got. He didn't care that she had others, this group of people she was surrounded by; they were inconsequential to him.

It was the stalking her that had shown him Bael's

intentions. His deception and thirst to claim the power she held within her body and soul. It sickened Stolas, and it was then he realized his plans were just as disgusting. Stolas chose to protect her and intervened when she became threatened.

His course hadn't altered since, though his motivations had. Airiella was too pure and good to fall. As much as he wanted her, she deserved better. Airiella somehow got through the darkness of his soul and saw him for who he used to be. Stolas learned then that demons and princes of Hell could feel love, real love. Her love changed him.

The depth of emotion she brought out in Stolas astounded him daily. Her propensity for love was equal to the vastness of space. It was infinite. And she gave it freely. Even to him. A demon, a fallen angel, a dark one, a prince of Hell. Her chosen ones accepted it, and him. It humbled him.

He took a deep breath and entered the gate for his boss's house and started up the path. To what, he didn't know but would find out soon enough. Stolas knew the master granted him a lot of leeway in his servitude. Freedom many others didn't receive; however, in return, Stolas is expected to serve and answer the calls of the one he agreed to follow.

Chapter Two

Stolas followed the servant into the study, the more formal of the settings that the master could have chosen. He felt a tinge of fear that the rumors he wanted to dismiss as heresy might be real, and the leader himself was going to make a move against Airiella.

Stolas had only ever known him as Lucifer, though throughout the years, he'd had many names. When referring to him with humans, he usually used Hades or Satan. Those were the most well-known and invoked the most fear, which, if he had to refer to him, terror was often the response he was looking for in those situations.

"Stolas," Lucifer gestured at a chair, "sit."

"To what do I owe this honor?" Stolas kept it formal since there were servants in the room.

"I've been hearing some disturbing things, and thought it was beyond time we had a little talk," Lucifer said, giving him a calculating look. Stolas saw the fear flash in the face of the servant who finished pouring them drinks and fled from the room as fast as he could, the door clicking shut behind him.

"Still using the catchphrase, I see." Stolas crossed his leg over his knee and picked up the whiskey that the servant had poured.

"Eh, whatever works to get them out. You're traveling a lot; I've been hearing rumors that have me curious, that much was true."

Stolas had been friends with him since they were both angels. Lucifer had taken him under his wing back then, feeling sorry for him due to the spite some of the higher castes had sent his way. It was partially the reason that choosing to fall had been more comfortable for Stolas. They had a history, and Lucifer had been his only friend.

Stolas kept his face neutral. Despite the years of friendship and closeness, Lucifer was not someone to be on the wrong side of, ever. Lucifer was still the leader of Hell, and it wasn't a friendly place. "What have you been hearing?"

"How long have we been friends, Stolas?" Lucifer crossed his legs and raised an eyebrow at him. "Did you honestly think I wouldn't notice your absence or the amount of time you spend topside? This new divine light that you seem to be wearing?"

Stolas set the whiskey down. "Did you call me here for punishment then?"

"No. I want the truth, and not some stupid little pissant trying to gain my good favor by ratting you out. Is it true, then, an angel walks among them again?"

There was no point in lying. The divine light was a dead giveaway. "It's true."

"And your allegiance has changed?" Lucifer looked pained at the thought.

"No. I still voluntarily follow you," Stolas

conceded unhappily.

Lucifer sighed. "I can pry it all from your head, don't make me treat you like one of them. Just tell me what I need to know."

"What if I don't think you need to know any of it other than she exists?" Stolas fired back at him. If Lucifer pulled it out of Stolas's head, there'd be no explanations, and it would look terrible for him.

"My oldest and dearest friend, only friend, now sports a divine light, and you don't think I need to know about it?"

"Tell me this, then, friend, are we speaking as leader and follower or as friends?" Stolas knew that sometimes they are the same, and it made him unsure of what to share to keep Lucifer at bay, to keep his vow to Airiella.

"Both. First, as a friend. Second, as a leader, because I find myself amidst a power struggle after the shit with Bael, and don't know where the allegiance lies." Lucifer took a giant gulp of the whiskey and slammed the glass down. "Please tell me you aren't against me."

"I'm not. I'm aware I am where I am because of you. I won't deny that some things have changed, topside, here and with me. I am *not* part of a rebellion to usurp power from you," Stolas offered up.

"So that much is true, then, I take it. Bael wasn't the end of it?" Lucifer sounded both resigned and agitated.

"I don't believe so. I think a few of the other princes believe they can take the throne from you. I've heard the same whisperings you have." Stolas just hadn't been able to confirm where they started, and he was trying.

"Are you one of the ones who believe I have been derelict of my duties?" The blunt question caught Stolas off guard.

"Derelict, no. Tired, yes. I can see the strain on you." Stolas reached for the crystal glass again and took a small sip. "Lucy," he reverted to the old nickname he'd used when it was just the two of them, "things are off-balance. Topside and down here."

"You haven't called me that in over two hundred years." He laughed bitterly. "That can't mean anything good if you are trying to soften the blow with an old endearment. Just give it to me straight, no bullshit."

"The angel is here to restore balance. It's not like it's unknown that we are overcrowded due to the legions that manage to break through because of some idiotic summoner that doesn't know what they are doing. They are wreaking havoc up there. Down here, malcontents are delving into areas and legends best left alone to try and steal the power she wields. Bael's deception started a ball rolling. One, I think we might be powerless to stop. There's a vacancy in your hierarchy that some lower-levels are desperate to fill, while Bael's followers are still trying to figure out how to get rid of you. My suspicion is they are going to try to use the angel to do that."

"This worries you?" Lucifer frowned while he processed the information dump.

"On several levels." Stolas fought back a wave of panic at outing Airiella. His gut was telling him that to keep her safe, he had to reveal her, and it was causing physical discomfort to contemplate it. Not to mention, it made him feel like he was betraying her.

"Break it down for me. My power hasn't faded, even if I haven't been using it much lately," Lucifer grumbled.

"My worry isn't for your power. My worry now lies

in the area of people I care about being hurt." Stolas tried to word it carefully, yet he knew Lucifer would see through it.

"Maybe I should be asking about how this light in you came to be." He sat back in his chair and crossed his arms. A hint of jealousy lined his old friend's eyes.

"I made a vow to her."

"Are you going to explain that?" Lucifer's tone grew hard. "I'm not a nice person, you know this and shouldn't push me."

"Cut the shit. I know who you are. You know who I am," Stolas snapped, instantly regretting it.

"Yes, Stolas, I do know who you are. This situation is no game. A vow to an angel by a demon is an interesting paradox I'd like explained. From where I am sitting, it appears as if we are heading into a war, and I want to know if I have to kill my best friend."

Stolas let his guard drop. "I've already told you I'm not against you. We *are* heading into a war; I just don't know against who. I've been trying to find out. I've created a network of spies throughout Hell, and I still can't get an answer or direction to look."

"I know of your network. I think you've got a leak. About this vow?"

"I vowed to do everything in my power to keep the angel and her group safe. Like it or not, she's needed," Stolas relented.

"I should speak to her."

"No." Stolas felt fear rising. "She wouldn't do it willingly, nor would those around her allow it to happen."

"The angel got to you, didn't she? I recognize the signs of love, even if I haven't felt it for years, except for you. What makes her so special?" Lucifer got up and poured himself another drink. "She's a threat to my very existence."

"She's not. Removing you doesn't restore balance. I can guarantee you that it doesn't mean she would be willing to work with you either. She's different, Lucy. Not like the other angels, we have come across."

"I'll bite. What makes this angel different?"

"She has a magnetism that makes you want to be near her all the time. Her power drew me to her, and I was only in the vicinity of her being. She wasn't even using power. Her voice could rival yours when you used to sing, and people would just fall under your spell without knowing it. It's like you can taste her on the very air you breathe by simply being within sight of her. The very essence of her is pure. It's love personified, in the human body."

"All angels have the power of love. Perhaps she's just gifted with it." Lucifer wasn't swayed by the rare display of emotion Stolas just admitted.

"Look at it this way. Bael noticed her, and he was the very definition of narcissism. He wanted to marry her, steal her powers, bind her to him forever, and take over your position. If she was nothing more than the standard angel, why would he have noticed? The only thing Bael ever cared about was himself, and he obsessively needed to possess her." Stolas held his hands out to his sides in question.

"You have my attention. If you are trying to convince me to keep my distance, you aren't doing an outstanding job. I accept that the angel is different; she did manage to capture your attention away from science. Not an easy feat."

"She didn't just capture my attention; I fell head over heels in love with her. Everything she does is different than any who came before her. I'm only now learning how to predict her actions. Even if the calculated risk means death for her, she does it anyway, in the name of love. To protect others." Stolas sighed as his cold heart panged with the memory of her injured.

"She's died then?" Lucifer paused and looked up at that.

"Several times, came back each time. And each time, it felt like a piece of me went with her. Rage would burst out of me, uncontrolled and wild."

"You released power?" This point seemed to concern Lucifer. "Were others around?"

"Seir."

"Stolas, this is going to sound selfish, and it is. You need to keep your power in check. I can't have the others knowing how much you truly wield. You are my secret weapon. It was fine for Bael to think he was my right-hand man, that his power rivaled mine. We both knew differently. Does the angel know how strong you are?"

"I'm not sure. I think some of the angel's group have an inkling." Stolas stood up and went to the window, looking out across the surprisingly manicured yard for a place in Hell. "Here's another thing, I could never fight against her, even for you. I'm not saying that I would fight against you, I wouldn't. Simply that I won't fight against her, this is the reason I am telling you these things, so you understand that yes, we are looking at war, but it's not necessarily between you and her. I more believe that someone from here is trying to manipulate her into attacking you in hopes that both of you will perish."

"You believe we are merely pawns in someone else's game? You don't think I could defeat her?" Lucifer was shocked by the thought.

"Truly, I don't believe you could. And yes, I do think one of the princes, or more, is playing a game with both sides." Stolas hoped that Lucifer was seeing the bigger picture and listening as a friend right now.

"Then I must insist on speaking to her. An uneasy peace is better to work with than simple mistrust. She has enough power to defeat me?"

"She hasn't even come fully into what she's capable of yet. As it stands, I believe her power is second only to the creator, and she has no idea." Stolas turned back to face his only friend.

"This is dangerous for us. Tell me about this group you keep referring to; they seem to have sway with your angel."

"They do to an extent. If any of the angel's group are in danger, she's reacting purely instinctively, guided by a knowledge she isn't aware of; she's fierce and fearless," he said, awe coloring Stolas's tone even though he tried to keep it neutral.

"Still only human, they can be broken."

Stolas felt the power that Lucifer wanted him to keep in check welling up in him at that statement. He struggled desperately to try and get it in control. He spun in place and strode back to the chair, snatching the whiskey off the table and downing it.

"That's quite the reaction from you. I wasn't suggesting that I would break any of the group, just that it could happen. Humans have many weaknesses, why do you think it's so crowded here?"

"That soul I hand-delivered not too long ago; you remember him?" The burn of the alcohol made his voice husky.

"Yes. Go on."

"He came close to breaking her. I won't stand for it, and I made a vow to her. The creator has tested the angel more than enough. I've educated her a little on our kind, not a lot. I've made comparisons about good demons and bad demons, enough to get her to understand that I am not a bad one, but that pushing me can make that happen." He looked at his long-time friend. "I know better than anyone that you are more on the side of good than bad. Please don't push me on the subject of her."

"I am not good, Stolas. If I were, I wouldn't be in the position I am. My cruel streak is quite expansive."

"I'm aware. I'm also aware that you've only used it against those that truly deserve it. Not against those that do not." Stolas sighed heavily and sat down.

"I've not stopped others from doing it," Lucifer clarified. "I won't push you, my friend. But for me to plan out a strategy, I need to understand my opposition. Since we don't know who is pulling these strings down here, that leaves me with learning about the angel."

"She could easily defeat me, now that she's practiced and honed skills. The four most powerful shamans alive are on her side and have created bonds with her. Not only that, she has five chosen connections, three of which also have a blood bond with her. One of those also carries a mate bond, as well as now having the human matrimony bond. To top that off, she also has an animal and can walk in the spirit world and her own at the same time. Also, part of her group is the Irish priest that has troubled you for years."

"Five connections?" Lucifer paced rapidly along the wall. "That's unheard of."

"The weakest of these connections are stronger than that of the previous angel," Stolas mentioned.

"Why didn't Bael take out the connections? It would have weakened her drastically." Lucifer mused. "In fact, why aren't they targets for whoever is orchestrating things now?"

"She thwarts them every time. Her senses are unparalleled. She wields the elements as if they are part of her soul; they respond as I've never seen. She has the ability of divine justice. Now the gift of sight has been added, and her protective powers are almost impenetrable. I've seen only one get through her fire, and that's her strongest connection, her mate. She is also perhaps the strongest empath alive on earth."

"Ah, this accounts for the change in your soul. You are trying for redemption, aren't you?" Lucifer asked, his eyes sparking with fire.

"No. Initially, upon first sight, that was my thought. It didn't take me long to give up on that. Instead, it is simply enough for me to be around her. She gives her love freely. There is no price attached to it, no expectations. She knows what I am, sees the good in me, and accepts me," Stolas admitted reluctantly.

"Interesting." Lucifer studied him. "You said she has an animal. She's able to shift?"

"No. It's a part of the angel, but separate."

"You think she still has more power to gain?" Lucifer went back to pacing.

"I do. It seems with each new battle she has fought, a new ability has appeared. I'm not saying this to dissuade you because of my feelings for her; I'm saying it to you as a friend because I don't want to see you die. I don't believe you could defeat her. Not alone, and maybe not even then. I gathered from the shamans that they believe this angel embodies all the angels that came before her and the gifts they had."

"If that is true, she would be almost equal to the creator," Lucifer mused.

Stolas grew irritated; he'd already said that. "On a side note, she saw the war coming. Before, I warned her to be careful. She also told me I'd find my partner," Stolas mumbled. He didn't know what to think about that part.

Lucifer laughed. "Maybe she could read my future and tell me how this all turns out. I've given up on finding a mate so that information would be useless."

Stolas bristled. "Enough of this. I'm tired. Are we done here?"

"I want to meet her. I don't need your permission."

"No, you don't. I don't think you would get through. The angel is well protected." Stolas thought of Chrissie and her children and didn't want them to be around Lucifer. He had no clear way of keeping that from happening. "I wish you'd trust me on this."

"I do, Stolas. I see no other way than speaking with her. I've reigned a long time, and while I am weary of it, I don't wish to see the domain fall into the hands of one filled with more deceit than I. I know my shortcomings, but I do see myself as a fair person, despite the fall."

"Give me time at least to ferret out who is behind this; if you cast judgment on the traitor, it sends a message to the rest that crossing you results in severe punishment. If the angel does it for you, it makes you appear weak," Stolas rationalized.

Lucifer sat down and nodded. His skills at strategy were top-notch, but he feared his old friend wasn't quite himself after discovering Bael's treachery. "Two weeks," he finally agreed. "If you have uncovered nothing by then, you will accompany me to meet the angel."

It wasn't a lot, but it was all he had to work with, so he'd do his best to find something. "I'll send word if I learn anything."

The rise of power in the room was unmistakable, and Stolas braced himself for the lashing of the burning energy so Lucifer could maintain his secrets. "Sorry, my friend, I want this to look like I was pissed. I won't direct it completely at you, but the fringes will hit you."

Chapter Three

Stolas dragged himself up to his room with strict instructions that unless Lucifer himself showed up at the door, not to bother him. He was hurting, exhausted, and now worried even more about Airiella and her group. He would be of no use to them if he didn't sleep and recover.

Lucifer was his best friend, but he was also the leader. Stolas didn't fault him for the faux punishment, and it could have been much worse. Thankfully the years of loyalty and friendship held under the strain of the rumors someone had hand-fed Lucifer.

Stolas dug through his stones, looking for the healing ones that still had energy left in them and stripped-down, placing them on his body. He needed to replenish his supply and take these others up to charge again, just another thing to add to his list. He'd worry about it later. He briefly remembered to check with the redhaired spirit to see if she'd heard anything. Then he was out.

He woke up with a start over twelve hours later to hear his name echoing in his ears. The voice sounded familiar, but Stolas couldn't place it. He shook his head and moved the stones to his bag to take up top and got up.

As Stolas was getting dressed, it called out again, more urgently. Something tugged at his memory, but his mind was still sluggish after that energy blast from Lucifer. At the third call, he gave in and followed it, landing in the spirit world with the redhaired ghost.

"You," Stolas mumbled. "Sorry. Feeling a bit out of sorts."

"Airiella is in danger, isn't she?" she demanded, her hands on her hips.

"She is. I'm not sure where it's coming from yet. Have you heard anything?" Stolas felt his adrenaline kick in finally.

"I haven't, but Kalisha has. She said to tell you, Moloch. What does that mean?"

"Moloch?" It made a sort of twisted sense. It was a start, at least. "Where did she hear that?"

"She didn't tell me, just said to get a message to you. Who is Moloch?"

"A demon. Another prince. Don't get entangled with him. I doubt he would come here; there's nothing for him to feed on here. Oh damn," Stolas muttered. Moloch fed on kids, Airiella's group was rapidly filling with them. "Thank you. Please thank Kalisha and try to find out more about what she heard. I need to go warn them."

Stolas popped back home, grabbed his bag, then focused on the unique signature of Airiella's power, and followed it. Stolas appeared in front of Chrissie, startling her. "I have a lead, and the children will likely be targets. Please warn the others."

"Whoa, there big guy. Tell me." Stolas heard Airiella

behind him.

Stolas almost laughed. Airiella wore a tie-dye dress that looked like it came from the eighties. "Nice dress."

"This is Chrissie's idea of funny. What's going on?"

"Have Ronnie research Moloch. That's the only lead I've gotten, and if it is him, he will target the children. Babies, kids, adolescents, unborn babies, he's vile. Moloch was very close with Bael but swore that his allegiance was with Lucifer. I have a lot of work to do on my end, but I thought you needed the warning."

Airiella had paled. "Got it. Thanks."

"Your ghost friend told me. Kalisha sent a message through her. I'm going to work on finding more. I won't let you down. Either of you."

Chrissie put her hand on his arm. "We know, Stolas."

Stolas leaned into Chrissie conspiratorially. "It *is* kind of funny, I'll deny having said that, though."

Chrissie smiled at him, biting her lip. "Go, do your thing before you make me laugh and tell your secret."

Stolas popped over to his secret hideaway in the caves and gathered up freshly charged stones to replace the depleted ones and went back home. "Zane," he called out, exiting his room.

"Yes, sir?" the demon walked out from nowhere.

"I need you to get a message to Lucifer's servant."

"The usual discretionary way, sir?"

"Yes, do not be seen." Stolas scribbled a note on a piece of paper and handed it to Zane. It only read, *Think child sacrifice.* It should be enough for Lucifer to understand he was talking about Moloch.

If he thought about it, it seemed evident; Moloch

and Bael had very similar goals and lofty thoughts about themselves. It had also been one of Moloch's legions that got summoned by Chrissie's in-laws, yet he had denied any knowledge of it. Moloch lied well enough that Stolas believed him.

Stolas paced his hallway, thinking frantically. That could mean that Moloch had something to do with Travis and the attack on Airiella, and Chrissie's son, Rafe. He needed to speak to Lucifer again, but couldn't risk it. If some of the others saw him out and about after his supposed punishment, they would see it hadn't been bad.

No, it wasn't smart to take that risk just yet. He needed to speak with Kalisha. He didn't know where she was or where she frequented. She was skilled at not being found unless she wanted to be. The redhead was simpler to find.

Stolas popped back to the spirit world. "Can you tell me where Kalisha is?"

She jumped. "You're sneaky. I don't know where she is."

Stolas fought back irritation. "Where was she when she talked to you?"

"Here, she found me, then walked away."

"Which way did she go?" the girl was purposely goading him.

"Right into the trees."

"Stolas," the musical voice came from behind him. "Leave Winnie alone. What do you want with me?"

"Information." Stolas turned and tried not to notice how stunning she was.

"The name was all I heard. Purely by chance. I know of him, bad news."

Stolas studied the priestess for signs of deception and saw none. "Do you think you'd be able to find out more?"

"Depends. Who does this benefit?"

"I vowed to keep Airiella and the rest safe. Even if it benefits both sides, does it matter? I will uphold my vow." Stolas was losing patience.

"Yes, you will. Come." She held her hand out to him. Stolas took it, then snatched it back when he felt tingles spread through his palm.

"What is that?" his gaze sharp on hers.

"Magic. It will keep you unseen by those who should not see you."

"Invisibility? That shouldn't be possible for you." Stolas had to admit that he didn't understand a lot about her ways, but she was dominant in ways that baffled him. He had respect for her, though, a lot of respect.

"I don't ask you for your secrets. Just accept my hand and allow it."

Stolas retook her outstretched hand and looked back at Winnie, who was watching them both. "She can see me."

"Naturally, she can see you. The ones who shouldn't are the ones who won't."

"Selective invisibility? Even Bael didn't have that." Kalisha was mysterious. The science of her magic called to him, and he wanted to figure it out.

"I am not a demon. I am not good, but I am not bad."

Stolas looked back over her as she led him into the trees. "Your soul isn't dark."

"Neither is yours."

They were walking over thick underbrush, their footsteps muffled by the vegetation when it should have been crunching and crackling with the sounds of broken twigs. "Where are we?"

"Safe," was Kalisha's one-word answer.

"Safe isn't a place." Despite himself, Stolas was intrigued by her. So much so, that he entirely missed the pile of stones and herbs he coveted.

"Quiet. The veil is thin here. The demons can't see you, but they can hear you," Kalisha's lyrical voice whispered against his ear even though they were two feet apart.

Stolas heeded her warning; he'd be stupid not to. Kalisha had proven herself worthy of his trust, even if he didn't understand the way her power worked. She gracefully lowered herself to a moss-covered spot on the ground and tugged him down.

Less gracefully, Stolas sat and looked around. He was in the spirit world, but he also wasn't. He felt suspended in time. Kalisha hadn't let go of his hand, and Stolas guessed that meant he'd be visible if he did, so he didn't pull his away and instead looked at her.

Kalisha was beautiful in an ethereal way, her dark skin flawless. Her dreadlocks giving her an ageless look, and he tried not to look at her plump lips but found his eyes drawn there anyway. Kalisha loved Airiella, and that was good enough for him. Winnie seemed to trust her, and right now, she had provided his only lead. Mysterious or not, he had to play things her way. Touching her wasn't exactly a hardship.

"They come."

Stolas looked around and saw a few low-level

demons headed directly towards them. He stiffened preparing to fight, but Kalisha hadn't flinched and didn't seem concerned. Invisible, right. He relaxed slightly.

Stolas watched as the three demons dropped to the ground, lifted a door he hadn't seen, and pulled out a stack of papers. They flipped through them, wrote a something down, and conferred quietly with each other. Too quietly, Stolas couldn't hear what they were saying but managed to catch Moloch's name a couple of times.

The demons replaced the papers and added a bundle of something one pulled from inside his clothes. They muttered something incomprehensible to him and looked around carefully before lowering the door and walking away slowly.

Once they were out of sight, Kalisha looked at him. "Twice a day for the last three days, they have come."

Stolas looked back out at where the door they had opened appeared and saw nothing that would hint of a door being there. He'd be hard-pressed to find it again and he'd just seen it. "Is magic concealing the door?"

"Yes, but not magic that I can access. It's your type." She stood, still holding his hand. "Come."

Stolas stood up, and Kalisha led him over to where the demons had been, and he felt it. Demon magic. Strong enchantments for low-level demons like that to have. "It doesn't make sense. They aren't strong enough to hide that door."

"Ah, but what if who is hiding it gave them something to use?"

Something clicked in his head. "Look for a stone."

"I took all the ones I found already. Back there." Kalisha pointed to where they had been sitting.

"Then there must be one inside. I wonder what the demons were writing?" Stolas mumbled, scraping the ground with his foot trying to find a seam.

"Names, places, times, and information they've collected. They watch someone. My suspicion is Airiella."

"She'd know if a demon was near her." Stolas immediately dismissed the thought.

"What if they are using a human?"

Stolas was an idiot. He should have thought of that. "Can you continue to watch them?"

"Yes. The demons have gotten lazier, believing no one has spotted them. Today was the first day they talked. It's why I had Winnie call you."

"You could have called," Stolas told her as she led them back into the place where time stood still. He noticed the rocks then. "Can I take these?"

"Yes, the herbs too. Maybe they will tell you something I can't figure out."

Stolas packed them all in his bag and stood up. "Thank you. You don't need to use Winnie," he repeated. "Just call my name."

"I could. I'm unsure of you, still. The spirits warn me not to lose myself to you."

Taken aback, Stolas stopped. "I wouldn't harm you, Kalisha."

"That is my belief too. I am just cautious until I can decipher the messages of the spirits."

"Fair enough. If I need to talk to you, what is the best way for me to do that?" Stolas asked.

"Come here, to this spot." Kalisha stopped at the entrance to the trees. "You'll not be able to cross to where we were without me. I'll feel you here and come get you."

Mystified by her, Stolas found himself bending down to kiss her cheek, a move neither of them had expected. Airiella was rubbing off on him. Stolas felt embarrassment flood his cheeks. "Thank you for your help."

Kalisha nodded lightly, crossing her arms under her full breasts that Stolas should have been gentleman enough not to notice, and watched him head back out to the clearing. Winnie was precisely where he left her and when he turned back to say goodbye to Kalisha, she was gone.

"Find what you need?"

"I found more questions than answers. It's a start. Thank you. I'll be back, I'm sure." Stolas nodded graciously at the redheaded ghost.

Stolas popped back home and rang the bell he installed, so his staff knew if he was there. He went down into his work area and took his bag back out, dumping out the stones and herbs and placing them on the table. As hard as he tried to concentrate on his task, he couldn't stop thinking about Kalisha.

Chapter Four

Four hours later, Stolas was ready to pull his hair out. He'd done nothing but study the stones, and the magic imbued within them and was just as confused as he had been when he started. Some of the rocks had a simple spell woven into them, and others were intricate with layers of spell work. More than one person worked on these, and the signature was one he wasn't familiar with at all.

Stolas stepped out of his workroom. "Zane!"

"Yes, sir?"

"Please send a formal request for an audience with the master. Cite the need to discuss strange magical signatures. Request the meeting for tomorrow or the next day," Stolas ordered.

"Will do. Anything else, sir?"

"Have Hazel prepare a light dinner. I may come back with a guest." At least Stolas hoped he would.

"Very well, sir."

Stolas gathered up the stones, putting them in a protective bag that would preserve the work he'd done and not let them absorb anything else. He popped out back to the field where'd he'd met Kalisha.

There was no one there, and Stolas felt slightly foolish for coming back so soon after his social blunder earlier. He needed answers, though, and Kalisha might be able to help him. He approached the forest she had walked him into and stood there, his eyes wandering around and landing on a female he hadn't seen before.

Quite transparently, a demon, but Stolas didn't know from which legion. The female demons human form looked vaguely familiar in that he might have seen the female before but not spoken to her. Kalisha wasn't appearing, and he wondered if this demon was why.

The female was watching Stolas; he understood that much. He started to catalog her appearance more carefully, so if he saw her again, he'd know for sure he was being watched. Her hair was dark, straight, and fell past her shoulders. She wasn't overly tall, but taller than the average female. Her skin was pale, and her eyes were flashing between the red of an uncontrolled demon and a dark hue, probably black; thin lips slashed across her face, narrow nose, and sharp cheekbones. No curves to speak of, her body was almost boyish.

Stolas stepped away from the forest and knelt on the ground to pull up a common herb and picked it like that was the reason he was here. He took it apart, pulling the useful parts off and discarding the rest. She had slid behind a tree when he moved, but she was still there. He pocketed the herb and stood up.

He was tired of the game. Stolas headed right for her, and she let out a small sound and, in a puff of sulfur, had disappeared. Not many had the power to port in and out of places at will as he did. Stolas sniffed the air, looking for the magical signature that would identify who she belonged to, but found none, that was even odder. Stolas stood there a few minutes to see if she would return, and when she didn't, he went back to the forest where Kalisha had told him to stand.

This time it was only a matter of seconds before Kalisha appeared and quickly pulled him in, her hand gripping his once again. "Thank you for getting rid of her. She's been there for the past hour."

"Do you know her?" Stolas looked behind him; the clearing was still empty.

"No, but she didn't feel harmless. I wasn't sure if she was after me, or you, so I stayed in."

"Interesting. Is this the only place you can come out at?" Stolas noticed the absolute stillness of the place again.

"No, there is one other, but I rarely use it. This one is more secluded, and Winnie likes to meet me here. Why are you back here so soon?"

"I need your help." Stolas noticed Kalisha still held his hand. He didn't say anything or try to move it; he liked it. "Those stones I collected earlier are imbued with magic that I don't recognize. I was wondering if you'd be able to examine them and tell me anything more."

"I could. Do you have the stones here?"

"No, they are in my workroom at home. I can bring you there." Her hand was warm in his and Stolas had the urge to stroke his fingers over the back of it.

Kalisha paused and gave him a cool look. "You want to bring me to Hell?"

"Only my home. It's protected, you'd be safe there," Stolas promised her.

"Safe from everything, but you?"

Stolas understood her concerns but grew frustrated. "I have no desire to harm you, Kalisha. What can I do to convince you of that?"

Kalisha dropped his hand and crossed her arms. "You are rather old-fashioned, aren't you?"

"In what regards?" Stolas didn't know where Kalisha was headed with this.

"In all of them. You are trying to gain my trust, thank me, offer protection, that kiss on the cheek earlier, and the formal way you ask for my help."

"To be fair, some of those are new traits that you can thank Airiella for; they surprise me as well. Before I knew her, I would probably demand that you come with me to help, but I still would have thanked you and offered you protection." Stolas thought about it. "You are right. Compared to others, my standards are slightly different. If that makes me old-fashioned, then I guess I am."

"It's not a bad thing. I'm just trying to figure you out. I feel off-balance around you."

"I apologize for that. Feel free to ask me anything you'd like. I'll do my best to answer honestly. However, there are some things that I am not at liberty to discuss."

Kalisha uncrossed her arms and retook his hand, that tingle he felt every time she did it came back and was somewhat comforting to Stolas. "I'd only be going to your home, correct? And I'd be free to leave?"

"Correct. You are not a prisoner. My servants are safe, my home is safe." Stolas was wondering what she'd heard to make her think she'd be captive.

"You have servants?"

"I do. The servants are like employees, not enslaved

like some of the others. Their position is voluntary, and I do what I can to keep them safe as well."

"This is why I'm having such a hard time with you." Kalisha squeezed his hand. "You are a prince of Hell, yet act with morals, dignity, honesty, and kindness. Can you see why I'm off-balance?"

Stolas chuckled. "Perhaps one day, I'll tell you my story."

"Why did you kiss my cheek?"

Stolas shrugged. "I'm not sure. It felt right. Would it make you feel better if I admitted that I am just as off-balance around you as you are around me?"

"It would. Though now, I want to know why."

"I don't know why. I haven't had a lot of time to put the thought into it." Stolas didn't want to think about it. He was woefully inept when it came to women.

"Yes," Kalisha took his other hand, "this problem you are working on; very well, take me to your lair, dark one." Her words said with a smile that told him she was joking.

"This might feel weird to you, brace yourself." Kalisha clutched his hands tighter, and Stolas popped them both back to his house and rang the bell, showing her into the workroom. He waited until she had her bearings before he started talking.

"This is Hell?" Kalisha asked, slowly turning around.

"We are in my home, which resides in that realm, yes. How are you feeling?" Stolas gently put his hand on her back.

"I was dizzy, and I'm better now. Thank you." Kalisha looked around at the room, and Stolas wondered what she was thinking.

The room itself had shelves where Stolas had jars of herbs and stones. Another shelf held several notebooks he'd written recipes and spells in. In the center of the room was a large table with a microscope, and the current notebook he was using. The back wall held a counter and sink, with a cabinet on the other wall that held his tools.

Kalisha wandered over and looked closer at the jars with stones in them and ran her fingers over the notebooks. "What are these?"

"My notes over the years. Recipes, spells, notes about things that work or don't work. Maps of the stars." Stolas felt self-conscious as Kalisha scrutinized things.

"It doesn't look like an evil lair a demon should have."

Stolas laughed at that. "I suppose I'm not your typical demon."

"This is true." Kalisha's words sounded more musical than usual, and there was a light in her eyes, making her charcoal color a lighter shade of gray. "You have quite a lot of rare plants in here. And stones."

Stolas walked over to one of the jars that had a small number of stones in it. They were black and rough, a white vein running through a few of them along with metallic glints of a metal not found on earth. He casually set it on his work table.

"It might be safer for you to step back next to that cabinet over there." Stolas pointed.

Kalisha gave him a questioning look but did as he asked, her careful gaze locked on him as he gathered his energy to him, reciting words in a dialect of the demon language known to very few. Stolas wove a complicated spell and imbued it into the stone, leaving the spell open.

"Please, open that cabinet behind you, and find something in there sharp enough to poke your finger, then put only one drop of your blood on this stone," Stolas instructed Kalisha quietly, holding the spell in place.

Again, Kalisha did as Stolas asked, but he could see she had several questions for him now. Probably the same ones he was going to be asking himself once this finished. Kalisha squeezed out a drop of blood on to the stone and watched as it sizzled and burned, disappearing instantly.

Stolas finished the spell, closed it, and nodded to the stone. "Take that. Keep it with you; to use it, hold it in your hand and picture here, or any room in my house, and that stone will bring you here. It will only work for you, and only for here."

Kalisha picked it up and studied it. "Why?"

"I am unsure of what I am dealing with and if it is you who is under observation or me. If it is you, I'd rather have a safe place you can get to quickly then to have you in danger. Be aware; if you step outside my house, you are not protected. Dangers lurk."

"What stone is this?" Kalisha studied the stone.

"One not from here. Remnants of a dying star found several hundred years ago. I found that they work great for transportation spells." Stolas didn't see any point in not giving her the truth.

"You've given a lot of these out then?"

Stolas couldn't identify the expression on her face. "No. Only a few of my servants have them."

Kalisha was seemingly satisfied with that answer and pocketed the stone. "Alright then, why are we here?"

Stolas pulled out the bag of stones. "First, hand me

the tool you used to prick your skin." Kalisha handed Stolas the knife, and he pulled more of his energy to burn the residue of her blood off it; he carried it to the sink and washed it off, replacing it in the cabinet. "I didn't want any traces of your blood lying around. Very dangerous in the wrong hands."

Kalisha looked surprised by his statement but covered it quickly. "These are the stones that you took?"

Stolas shook himself of the thought of wanting to touch her again. "Yes. I have partially deconstructed the spells on them to see if I could find out who had done it. The signature isn't one I recognize, and a few of the spells are quite extensive and layered. There aren't many that I am aware of that can do this type of work with a stone."

"You think I did them?" Kalisha cautiously looked at him, her eyes holding a bit of fire.

"No, that wasn't my thought. Are you able to do spells like this one?" Stolas picked up one of the more complicated ones and handed it to Kalisha. From what he could tell, the spell held a concealment element as well as what he guessed was a booby trap.

Kalisha scrutinized it, and set it down even more carefully. "I can, but it comes with quite a cost. This spell is the work of blood magic. There's a part of this that remembers who touches it and stores the memory for whoever cast it."

Stolas hadn't seen that part. "Are you sure?"

"Positive. The blood magic I can smell. The other part, my senses warned me about, do you plan on destroying this stone?"

"I do now. When I pulled apart the spell, I see the concealment element right off the bat. I also see some sort of trap embedded here, but was unable to tell what the trap was. Is the tracing the trap?"

"No. The caster can activate the trap part of the spell. If what I am seeing is correct, I believe after the caster looks at who touched the stone, the caster could then activate the trap part to harm the person they were after. So if the caster picked this up and reviewed the stored persons who touched this stone, say it was you, and he wanted to hurt you, he could activate that trap spell to go off the next time you touched it."

"Clever." Stolas thought this over. "You said he, is there a reason for that?"

"No. Gut instinct. Whoever did this is cunning and shrewd and does not have good intentions. That could be either female or male, but my senses are picking up a male."

"Blood magic. Not an uncommon thing in Hell." Stolas took the rest of the stones out and spread them across the table. "I am picking up multiple different signatures across these stones, though these complicated ones all carry the same one."

Kalisha looked around. "Do you have gloves?"

Stolas pointed out the cabinet and watched her put them on. Her movements were graceful and precise. She wasted no action on things he'd seen other women do, the swinging of the hips, jutting out of their chest. Kalisha wasn't trying to entice him, but he found himself attracted all the same.

Kalisha examined the stones and moved them into separate piles. "This pile here has hoodoo elements. Simple spells, none that cause harm. Whoever did these have ties to hoodoo."

"How sure of that, are you?" Stolas asked, surprised by that answer.

"Quite." Kalisha pulled out an amulet from her pocket and handed it to Stolas. "Feel the spell on this?"

Stolas held it carefully and looked at the spell work. Simple protection spell, but woven in a way that was similar to the stones she had set aside, but this one also had layers that he figured made it more than a simple protection amulet. He handed it back to her.

"I understand what you are saying." Stolas looked back at the stones she had set aside. "It also has demon magic. I will need to look for hoodoo practitioners in this realm then."

"These here, still blood magic, but very dark blood magic. I get the sense of harm from these." Kalisha gestured to another pile.

"Correct. The intent of these was to kill, but the spell is a directed one. Anyone looking for that door would have gotten killed if that stone had moved. I unraveled that part of the spell, so it is no longer active. How did you move these?" Stolas pointed at them.

"I didn't. Those stones rolled to that spot where you picked them up. I am not sure how you didn't get harmed."

"I have my protections in place against things like this." Stolas was vague about it. He suspected Airiella's light in him had something to do with it. He did have his protections, mixed into a lotion that he put on his hands multiple times a day that neutralized harmful spells like this, as well as tattoos that Lucifer had ordered done for him.

"These other two piles, I think they are the same person. These are simple blood magic, while these more complicated ones require great sacrifice. I don't believe this is hoodoo. If it is, it is a very twisted and dark form of hoodoo that I am unaware of."

"It's demon magic," Stolas confirmed.

Kalisha pulled the gloves off, and Stolas took them from her, incinerating them within his palms and then neutralizing the ash in the sink. There was a curious look on her beautiful face that made him pause between the sink and the table.

"You hide your power," Kalisha said simply.

Stolas wasn't sure how to respond to that and was grateful for the knock at the door. "Enter," he called out.

Zane walked into the room. "Sir, dinner is ready. Will you have a guest?"

"Would you care to eat dinner with me?" Stolas asked Kalisha, nervous she would say no.

"Thank you. I'd like that."

Relieved, Stolas nodded at Zane. "Excellent, sir. I'll have Hazel add a place setting."

"Very formal," Kalisha commented as Zane disappeared.

Stolas put the stones back in the bag and stored them in a hidden compartment in the table. "I've asked them to be more relaxed, but this is what they choose to do."

Stolas finished cleaning up the room, used his demon magic to disinfect any other presence in the room, set his protections in place, and held out his arm for her. "Please, come with me."

Chapter Five

Zane seated Kalisha, glanced at Stolas with a slight smile, and disappeared. The food was already on the table, and they would serve themselves. Stolas didn't like them hovering over him, and he valued his privacy.

"Where does he go when he does that?"

"Does what?" Stolas looked over at Kalisha.

"Disappears."

"Oh, I'm guessing back to his quarters." Stolas held the platter of baked chicken out to Kalisha to take what she wanted. Then he held out the broccoli and roasted potatoes.

"Very healthy dinner. That explains why you are in such great shape."

The comment embarrassed Stolas, and he didn't know why. "It's nothing compared to yours," he replied without thinking. He wildly blushed as he realized the words he'd just said. "I'm so sorry, Kalisha. That was rather inappropriate for me to say. I have no idea what came over me."

Kalisha laughed softly. "That might be the first time I've ever seen your composure slip like that. I liked it. A sincere response."

"I'm always honest with you." Stolas stared at her blankly.

"Let me reword that; a very naked emotion then." Kalisha cut a piece off her chicken and ate it slowly. "This is very good. Tell me something about yourself, Stolas."

Stolas stuffed food in his mouth to give himself time to think of what to say to that. He took his time chewing, and Kalisha smiled as if she knew what he was doing. After swallowing, he said, "In regards to what?"

"Oh, I don't know. Something personal."

"I've held you in the highest respect for years," Stolas admitted shyly.

Kalisha ate her dinner for a few moments. "I don't mean like that. I mean personal. About yourself." She took another bite and Stolas wished he were the tines of the fork sliding between her lips. "How about I start? I have a daughter that no one knows about."

Stunned, Stolas dropped his fork. "You do?"

"I do. I set up an adoption when I was pregnant, with a couple I didn't know, but who were desperate for a child. I never met them; they never met me. It was for the safety of my daughter that it was that way. She'll received a letter explaining the nature of her adoption and birth and who I was when she reaches the age of twenty-five."

"I haven't had a relationship in nine hundred and seventy-three years," Stolas blurted out without thinking it through. That didn't help Stolas's case any.

Kalisha's tinkling laugh captivated him, though he was still embarrassed over his lack of control of his mouth.

"This explains some things then."

Stolas went silent and ate his dinner, trying to form coherent thoughts that didn't make him sound like a bumbling idiot. He was known for his knowledge and intellect though you'd never know it by this conversation.

"What makes you so nervous around me?"

"I honestly don't know." Stolas fumbled around with his napkin before giving up and putting everything down. "I feel like a teenage child; this is not how I normally act. I can assure you of that. I wasn't even like this with Airiella, and I fell in love with her from the start."

Kalisha put her fork down. "Are you telling me that you are in love with me?"

Stolas bit his tongue. He was going to be permanently red-faced around this woman if this kept up. "No, that's not what I am saying. I don't know what I am saying. You intrigue me; apparently tongue-tie me, and I lose brain cells at an alarming rate around you."

"Courting rituals have changed in the past nine hundred and seventy-three years, Stolas." Kalisha smiled widely. "If my boldness doesn't bother you, I would suggest that maybe you have a crush on me."

Stolas stammered; this was humiliating. Kalisha was right; he had a crush on her. Stolas hadn't known it until she said it. Nonetheless, it was true. "Perhaps you are right," Stolas admitted quietly.

"Being of this century, I am bolder than what you are used to; I don't mind. Does this also mean that you haven't been physical with anyone for that same amount of time?"

Stolas wasn't sure who disarmed him more, Airiella, or Kalisha. He cleared his throat. "You are correct in the assumption you are making." Stolas fisted his hands under the table. "Airiella kissed me if you count that."

"I would be lying if I said I wasn't interested. I get the feeling that it makes you uncomfortable to talk about this."

Kalisha was interested? In him? Stolas needed advice. He was so far out of his comfort zone with this that Stolas was afraid he was going to ruin any chance he had to explore something with Kalisha. Stolas hadn't even been aware he wanted to explore it. His body was uncomfortably hard at the thought, and Airiella's vision was playing out in his mind.

"We will take this slow, Stolas. Tell me more about yourself, please. I don't know much about you, other than you fell in love with an angel, and you've made it your goal to keep her safe. That's a goal we share, by the way."

"I used to be an angel," Stolas told Kalisha quietly, trying to will his body to soften so he could stand without it being obvious he wanted to explore *her* body. "Many don't know that Lucifer is my friend. As angels, he was my only friend. When he left, I voluntarily followed as there wasn't anything keeping me where I was."

"Lucifer? As in, Satan?" Kalisha was stunned.

"The same." A crooked smile tilted Stolas's lips. It wasn't him caught off guard this time.

"He doesn't seem to be the friendly type."

Stolas smiled fully. "Depends on what side of things you are on. As I once told Airiella, there are good demons and bad demons. Lucifer falls right in the middle of that. To me, he has always been good. I was never really sure why, but it wasn't something I was going to look away from either. The other angels picked on me to no end. I didn't participate in their pettiness and popularity games they played. Knowledge was my forte, science in particular. That made me different. One day when we were children, Lucifer older than me, I got cornered by a particularly aggressive angel. I lacked the fighting skills others had, and they were trying to force me into a duel. Lucifer stepped in and offered to fight on my behalf. He won, and after that he said I could help him with his studies to make it up to him. I thought that would have been the end of it since he was very well known and liked. His singing voice was the best, in fact, and it was well known he was the Creator's favorite."

Kalisha's face was carefully blank. "This is certainly not what they teach about Satan now."

"No, it's not," Stolas agreed. "I followed him because first and foremost, he was my friend. He knows I don't have the same heart as others, but he made me a prince, elevated my station, and gave me free rein to do as I saw fit. He helped me learn to fight, hand out punishments, do the magic I do, and in return, I keep our relationship a secret as well as the power I wield."

"You make him sound normal."

"He's far from that. Lucifer isn't what the modern-day religions make him out to be. He can be cruel. But from what I know of him throughout our history together, he is cruel only to those that deserve it. For those that end up here because of a gray area, he has much more leniency. Lucifer expects his followers to be loyal, and he punishes those that aren't. He is capable of great evil, it does happen, and it's terrifying. Again, he reserves it for those that truly deserve it."

"I could have easily ended up here," Kalisha confessed.

"No. You are firmly in the gray area, but the gray that you've dealt with is on the lighter side of things." Stolas could see her soul and the colors of it all.

"How do you know that?"

"I can see your soul," Stolas stated simply.

Kalisha shifted in her chair at that news. "I can see yours as well. It's made me wonder why you are here."

"I can be cruel. I have a darker side. You don't get to be here as long as I have and not develop one. I thought at first that Airiella would bring me redemption if I claimed her," Stolas said before he realized what he admitted.

Kalisha's face went hard. "You tried to claim Airiella?"

"No. It was only a thought I had when I first set eyes on Airiella. I could never do that to her." Kalisha's face softened. "I told her that I'd rather be the only dark part of her, in fact," Stolas quickly added.

"You aren't dark, Stolas," Kalisha murmured. Her musical voice wrapping around him, his head was once again dizzy with desire. Stolas stared at her plump lips and wondered what they would taste like if he kissed them. "You are looking at me as if you'd like to devour me," Kalisha said with a smile, "but you aren't dark."

"Tell me about you," he replied instead of admitting he did want to devour her.

"I was born with power running through my blood. I often got asked for things of a darker nature, and many times I provided them. Believing that as long as it wasn't me harming, I was still good; I was merely providing a tool. Later, I began to believe that even providing the tool was crossing a line I shouldn't have crossed. I grew up in Africa. I had two sisters and three brothers; out of us all, I was the only one who got the power. My mother told me some of my ancestors that left and went to the Caribbean also had the power."

"The smell of your power draws me in. Like a river rolling through a forest and all over the bank are wild herbs and flowers." Stolas snapped his mouth closed, realizing he gave away more than he intended to. "The power runs in your family then?" Stolas tried to change the subject.

"It's cute, this shyness that goes against everything I've seen from you this far. I'll spare you and allow the direction to change. Yes, it runs in my family. I believe that my daughter inherited it, but I have been unable to get through the veil to see her. I'm blocked."

Stolas was saved again by a knock at the door. Zane popped his head in. "Sir?"

"Yes, Zane."

"Message from the master for you, sir." Zane walked in and handed Stolas a sealed envelope.

"Thank you. I'll call if I need to send a reply." Stolas pulled the envelope open and saw the meeting confirmed for tomorrow morning. He slid it into his pocket, the distraction enough to calm his out of control desire and tenting of his pants.

Stolas stood up and offered Kalisha a hand. "We can go to the sitting room, the workroom, or I can take you back to your spot."

Kalisha pulled him a little closer, bringing his body flush up against hers. The raging desire was back in a flash. "I think I'd like to stay a little bit if that's okay with you."

"Y-y-yes," Stolas stuttered, his brain shorting out.

"Do you equate sex with love?"

Stolas blinked, then blinked again. He had no idea

how to answer that. "No?"

"Is that a question or a statement?"

Thoroughly tongue-tied, all Stolas could do was lean his head down and capture those juicy lips that had been wreaking havoc on his mind all through dinner. Kalisha tasted like vanilla and some tangy berry. As close as their bodies were, there was no hiding the fact that he was as hard as steel.

Chapter Six

Once again embarrassed, Stolas tried to pull away, but Kalisha held him tight. "Don't move away," she whispered against his lips. "You taste like dark chocolate. For being almost a thousand years out of practice, you are quite good at that."

"Did you enchant me?" Stolas asked quietly.

Kalisha's deep throaty laugh caused his body to react. "No, if I enchanted you, it would have been for more than a kiss."

"Maybe it would be more accurate for me to say that you do enchant me. Was that enjoyable for you?" Stolas had to know.

"Oh yes," Kalisha purred and sucked on his lower lip. "Did you enjoy it?"

Stolas burst out into laughter, his hands falling to her hips. "I am sure that you can feel my reaction."

"I can, but that is one you've been having and trying to hide all night. Lust is easy to smell."

"It's not lust; it's something more, and I most certainly enjoyed it," Stolas told her, unsure of what to do next.

"Come, take me to the sitting room, or somewhere we can get more comfortable." Kalisha grabbed his hand, waiting for Stolas to lead her.

The encouragement was all he needed. Stolas led Kalisha to his bedroom, locking the door behind him. "Please don't think me too forward. I can guarantee privacy here."

"You aren't planning to seduce me then?"

Stolas couldn't tell if she was teasing him or not. "I'm not sure that I would know how."

"I think you are doing well enough for not knowing how. You said this was more than lust, how do you know that?"

Stolas sighed and sat down in a chair while Kalisha settled on the bed. Her being on his bed wasn't helping him. Stolas should have gone to the sitting room, but he knew with her being the first female he had brought here in several centuries, he would get watched.

"Lust is a basic urge. These aren't basic feelings. Sorry, I keep bringing Airiella up, but it's the only frame of reference I have, for example, Airiella; I didn't feel lust for her, it was deeper than that. If she had given me the slightest inkling that she was interested, I would have moved to take it farther. With you, it's not just lust. I can't deny that it isn't there, but it's deeper than lust. If it were only lust, I probably would have made a move and then been done and over it." Stolas's words made him feel guilty.

"Are you telling me that you are interested in me on a deeper level than just sex?"

"I believe I am. I'm saying it badly, but yes." Kalisha rolled to her side and studied his face, the curves of her body begging for Stolas to touch them.

"You aren't saying it badly. Tell me what is between you and Airiella."

"Airiella?" Stolas was startled by her request.

"Yes. If Airiella is your only frame of reference, then tell me what is between the two of you, so I understand."

"I'm in love with her." Stolas said it bluntly. "Airiella loves me, but not in the way she loves Jax, Ronnie, or the others. When she's hurt, I physically ache and have to calm myself forcefully so that I don't go on a destructive streak trying to take down anything related to what hurt her. I've even cried. Every instinct I have wants to protect her and help her. Because of who I am and where I am, it's not possible."

"You have helped her. I know the lengths you have gone to for Airiella. I also know that feeling that way about someone can be very painful when it's not returned."

"Airiella loves me. I've received far more than I could ever give her," Stolas confessed.

"I don't think that is true, Stolas. You've helped Airiella in ways no one else could. You have to win her trust, and you did. Not an easy thing to give for someone like her. If Airiella gives you something, it's because she feels you deserve it."

Stolas looked up from his hands and directly into Kalilsha's eyes. Stolas wanted to tell her that he was starting to have the same feelings for her that he did for Airiella, but he was too afraid to say that. "I've never brought anyone here before," Stolas said instead.

"I'd be lying if I said I wasn't interested in you." Her slow smile burned its way through his body. "I'd also be lying if I said I wasn't scared. Much like the angel, my trust needs earning. Sex and love are two very different things for me. I can have sex and not have it mean anything. I can also love someone without sex. What scares me the most is that I want to see where this thing with you can go. When I'm around you, there is this feeling in me that rises, and sometimes it feels like it consumes me. Kissing you sent shockwaves inside me that made my heart sit up and take notice. I don't know what it all means, because you are right, it's not just lust. I'm willing to start with that, though."

Stolas felt his breath catch, Kalisha had repeated it. "You are interested in me?" his voice came out hoarse and scratchy sounding.

"I am. You draw me to you. I can feel you when you are near."

"That's just my power," Stolas told her, feeling somewhat let down.

"No, Stolas. I feel *you*. Your power is different. I feel that too, but what I feel first is the very essence of your soul." Kalisha closed her eyes, and her musical voice wrapped its tendrils around Stolas, holding him captive. "It drifts over to me and slides over my skin like a soft lovers touch, that familiarity of warm lips against my ear whispering words only meant for me to hear."

Stolas knew what Kalisha was talking about exactly. He'd felt it ever since she had taken his hand and walked him back into her hiding spot. "What is it? This thing between us?" Stolas whispered captivated.

"I don't know, but it's alive. I want to be near you. The spirits tell me, no, and I can't disregard them, but they are selfish, and I know that." Kalisha patted the bed next to her. "Come, lay with me."

It was like a siren call, and she pulled Stolas. Not precisely against his will, more of a feeling Stolas didn't want to fight. He wanted to be next to her; he craved it. Kalisha scooted over across his bed and Stolas lay down on his back, she moved his arm to put it around her, curling her body into his. It felt nothing like it had when Airiella had done it. This feeling was fire, a dangerous heat that felt like it was eating him up from the inside, and he wanted more.

Kalisha slid her hand across his belly, and Stolas stilled it, the sensations were almost more than he could bear. "It's intense," Stolas said quietly. "Like fire licking at my veins."

"It makes me wonder if this is what Airiella feels with her connections," Kalisha murmured seductively.

"If this is what it feels like, I don't understand how they can ever be separate." Stolas's voice was a low growl.

"Allow me to stay," Kalisha begged him. "We don't have to do anything more than this."

"I don't think I have the power to make you leave," Stolas admitted, lowering his head to kiss Kalisha softly. Her lips like a drug, and he a starving addict.

Kalisha peeled herself away from Stolas long enough to strip out of her clothes and slide between his sheets. The sight of Kalisha naked stopped his heart, his mouth went dry, and his body went rigid. He'd never seen anything more breathtaking. Kalisha was perfection.

Stolas carefully got out of bed and undressed, setting his clothes on the chair before taking a deep breath and getting into the bed with Kalisha. Nothing could have prepared him for the feel of her naked body against his. Stolas's entire body hummed with a raw energy that had very little to do with sex and so much more to do with his heart and soul that it terrified him.

"For the first time since I died, I feel like I am right where I am supposed to be." Kalisha's gentle voice and words pierced through Stolas, and he felt tears prick his eyes.

"I don't understand any of this." Stolas's voice was thick. "I'm not sure I deserve it either, but I'm going to be selfish and hold on to it."

Kalisha slid her hand up to his chest, and his heart was thumping so hard Stolas was sure she could feel it. His reactions embarrassed him; he was over two thousand years old, and he was acting like a virgin. Kalisha threw him off, and the confidence Stolas had built over the years came crumbling down.

"Let me touch you, please," Kalisha pleaded. "You are magnificent. Strong and sexy." Her hand was roving across his abdomen, and Stolas stilled it again.

"Kalisha. You make me nervous in ways I am not used to; I am afraid you will find me lacking, inexperienced, and unsure." Stolas's admission was a hard one to make.

Kalisha sat up, her confused gaze meeting his wary one. "You are scared of me?"

"Not *of* you, of being not enough to suit you," Stolas corrected her.

"That is not a fear we share, Stolas. I am quite sure that you are more than enough. But I said we would go slow, and I meant it. I just want to be able to touch you, and I want you to touch me. Let my hands learn your body before my mouth does. I want my mind to be able to map you out, so when we are apart, I remember how each part of you feels."

Stolas groaned. "I may not be able to hold back," he warned Kalisha. "You are intoxicating, and every touch makes me lose a little more control."

"I understand." Kalisha sounded disappointed but lay down next to him again.

Stolas bit back a curse and hauled her on top of him. "Lay on me. Let's start with this." Kalisha felt small on him. She had such a significant presence to her that the size difference between them shocked Stolas. He wrapped his arms around her, his hands landing on her low back, his fingers grazing the softly rounded curve of her backside, a spot Stolas would love to kiss.

Kalisha settled against Stolas, her hands running down his sides, giving him chills, but he didn't stop her. Her ear was over his heart, and in his ears, it was beating out her name, Kali-sha, Kali-sha. All the characteristics Stolas had seen Jax, Ronnie, and Smitty display over Airiella made perfect sense to him. Stolas would fight to the death for this woman.

Stolas ran his hands up Kalisha's back and then down her sides. The soft swell of her breasts nearly undoing him. His hands roamed back up her rounded hips until Kalisha was caged in his arms again. If Stolas kept touching her like that, there would be no stopping him.

Kalisha's breathing eventually slowed, and her body went lax in his arms. Never had someone fallen asleep on Stolas before. It was heady. Half of Stolas wanted to stay awake to just relish in the feeling; the other half of him was exhausted and knew he needed the sleep. Stolas gave in and drifted off.

Chapter Seven

Stolas woke with a start as soon as his brain realized that the erotic dream he was having wasn't a dream. Kalisha's hand was wrapped around him, slowly stroking as she kissed his chest. His body was begging for release, and her touch was destroying any resistance Stolas had in him.

"Let me give you this gift, Stolas. Don't fight me," Kalisha said, her lips pressing against the throbbing vein in his neck.

Kalisha changed her grip on him and his back bowed. Stolas pushed against her hand, his mind weak against the sensual touch of her hand on him. He frantically cupped the back of her head and smashed his lips down on hers as she increased the pace, and his body shuddered.

Kalisha's tongue warred with his in an erotic dance, and his mind blanked out entirely as Stolas came, the release his body needed, granted. Wild moans tore from his throat as Stolas threw his head back, his body bucking as she stroked it all out of him.

The touch Stolas had denied himself all these years was quickly taking down the walls of indifference he'd built around his heart. All undone by the beautiful woman half-laying on him. Hot tears streamed from Stolas's eyes, the vulnerability in him too much to bear.

His seed covered them both, and Kalisha didn't seem to care, so Stolas crushed her to him in a hug, burying his face in her neck as he cried out his shame. Stolas had done just what he had told himself he wouldn't do. He gave in to his urges and selfishly took the pleasure Kalisha had offered him.

What Kalisha didn't know, was in the moment that she wrung the orgasm out of him, Stolas had given her his heart. Kalisha deserved so much better than Stolas, nothing more than a demon. Now, no better than the rest of them that doled out their seed, giving nothing in return.

"Stolas," Kalisha sounded alarmed, "what's wrong? Did I hurt you? Was it not enjoyable?"

Stolas laughed darkly through his tears, though it sounded like nothing more than a sob. "Not enjoyable? I covered us both with proof that I enjoyed it immensely."

"Then you are going to have to help me understand why you are reacting this way." Kalisha was stroking his face softly, trying to console him.

"There are various reasons." Stolas tried to gain control of himself.

"Tell me one." Kalisha paused and looked at him.

"Shame." Stolas's response was immediate.

Kalisha flinched, taken aback. "I made you feel shame?"

This conversation was going badly. Something about Kalisha made Stolas lose his detached persona that he'd crafted so carefully all these years. "Not you. No." Stolas sighed and sat up, dislodging Kalisha from his chest. Stolas fought to get his emotions under control.

"I'm not understanding, Stolas. I just wanted to do something for you. I have no expectations." Stolas could tell Kalisha was trying to keep the hurt out of her voice, but he could hear it.

Stolas didn't know how to fix this. "Can we clean up while I try to figure out how to explain this without sounding like an utter fool?"

"Is this pity you are showing me?" Anger flashed behind Kalisha's eyes, and Stolas felt a swell of energy forming.

"No, Kalisha. Pity is the last thing I would feel for you. Please?" Stolas held out his hand.

Kalisha reluctantly took his hand, her actions and movement wary. "You confuse me so much."

"You aren't alone there. I confuse everyone. It's not intentional," Stolas mumbled, leading her to the bathroom. Stolas turned on the shower and waited until it wasn't icy cold before lifting Kalisha in and following. Stolas stood close to her at first, then unsure of what to do, he backed up putting space between them.

Stolas reached for the washcloth and gently washed himself off of Kalisha, trying not to linger on her perfect skin. Kalisha lost patience with Stolas halfway through and took the washcloth from him. "Are you afraid to touch me?"

"No. I don't deserve to." The shame Stolas felt earlier came rushing back.

Kalisha gave him a sharp look. "Explain the shame."

Stolas sighed again and switched positions with her so he could rinse himself off, so if he cried again, it would be less noticeable under the spray of the shower. "You know why I chose to be here; because of Lucifer. Yes, I made bad decisions that has permanently kept me here, but I also chose not to be like the rest of them."

"What does that mean?"

"I didn't want to be like the others. The ones that got off on lewd acts because they could. The selfishness of using women for their own pleasure, spreading their seed because they felt it was their right, never giving any pleasure in return. It sickens me. That's why there has been no one in my life for so long. The taint of being here wears on you, and I don't want to be them."

Stolas saw the understanding of what he was saying light in Kalisha's eyes. "Stolas, you didn't use me. Unless I am mistaken, you didn't even know what was happening until you woke up. I chose to do that, not you. I wanted to see you lose control, that for me was a gift."

Stolas tipped his head back so Kalisha couldn't see his face. "I apparently, don't have any control around you anyway. I seem to lose myself around you."

"What would you have done if I had stopped?"

"Taken an ice-cold shower," Stolas replied honestly.

Kalisha's rich laugh washed over him, pulling his eyes down to her face. "You aren't like them. If you were, and I had stopped, you would have made me finish. That's the difference. You have respect; they don't. In my eyes, you are not much different than me. I could have easily ended up here."

"I don't deserve you," Stolas told her again, brushing his fingers across her cheek.

"That is for me to decide. Please understand, your reaction hurt me. I understand now, but not at first. I did what I did because I wanted to feel you, the you that you have locked up inside under these layers of detachment; that you in there calls to me, and for a little bit, I got to see him. That's what I need to see to quiet the voice in me that says to stay away. The pleasure and ecstasy on your face were beautiful. There's passion in you, Stolas. It burns hot, and I want to feel it."

Raw, sexual desire ripped through Stolas, a growl erupting from his throat. "I have a meeting with Lucifer shortly. Can I see you later today?"

"You can take me now." Kalisha slid her wet body against his.

"There's not enough time," Stolas told her, sliding his hands down her back and over her rounded cheeks, lifting Kalisha while she wrapped her legs around him. "I want to take my time and ensure that you feel the burn as much as I do."

Kalisha licked her lips. "I'll come back." She unlocked her legs and slid back down him, then bent over and sucked him into her mouth, his breath hissing between his teeth at the sensuous torture. "That was so you think of me."

Kalisha winked at Stolas, stepped out of the shower, and wrapped a towel around her, disappearing back into his bedroom. Stolas turned the shower to cold and washed himself off. He was almost certain he'd be able to think of nothing else but her.

Kalisha was gone when he finished. Stolas got dressed slowly in his customary black pants, a black button-up shirt, and black blazer with the deep pockets. He needed a haircut, but it'd have to wait, though he had liked the way it felt when Kalisha had run her fingers through his hair. It fell in waves over his ears, the dark brown color deep enough to be mistaken for black in the right lighting. His eyes were a dark brown as well, and almond-shaped. Someone had told Stolas before that he looked exotic, but he didn't see it.

He needed to focus. Stolas went to his workroom, grabbed the bag of stones, putting them in his pocket, and going back upstairs to eat some breakfast. "Zane?"

Zane popped in. "Yes, sir?"

"Kalisha is allowed to be here; I've given her a portal stone."

"Thank you for telling me, sir." Zane grinned. "If I may say so, I'm happy for you, sir."

Stolas blushed. "Have Hazel bring me breakfast, please."

"Right away, sir."

Chapter Eight

It became clear to Stolas that he was being followed, which meant his house was also being watched. He was glad that he'd given Kalisha a stone, that would keep her from being seen at least. He made a mental note to let Zane know to be careful.

Stolas rang the formal bell at the gate for Lucifer's for appearances sake. He announced himself and his appointment time which was a matter of record and waited to be escorted in. There were very few trusted people in Hell and Stolas was sure that they all worked for Lucifer or himself.

The servant showed no sign of recognition as he opened the gate and their attitudes were formal with each other while in view. After the doors to the house closed, the servant, Dakota, let Stolas know that Lucifer was waiting in the study, also for appearances sake.

Stolas headed off in that direction and waited while one of the other servants served them beverages and scurried out of the room. Neither spoke until the doors were latched closed and Lucifer activated his enchantments that assured them of privacy.

STOLAS

"That was fast work, Stolas." Lucifer kicked his feet up on his desk.

"We've got problems, Lucy." Stolas wasted no time in getting to the point. "I'm being watched and followed, but I can't tell by whom. Moloch is planning a coup and he has someone powerful working for him." Stolas pulled out the bag of stones and leaned forward to spill them on to Lucifer's desk.

Lucifer lowered his feet and looked with interest at the stones. "Blood magic." Lucifer separated the ones with complicated spells on them right off the bat. "Very dark blood magic. Some of these smell of hoodoo as well."

"It took you a lot less time to figure that out than it did me," huffed Stolas. "I asked a friend to take a look and she was who informed me those there," Stolas separated them, "are hoodoo. I tried to deconstruct the spells on these," Stolas gestured to the complicated ones, "but they are woven in such a way that I wasn't able to."

"Where are these being left?" Lucifer was all business. His relaxed face now held a cold expression that would frighten most.

"In the spirit realm. My friend showed me through this clearing that was strange in itself as it seemed to be in a separate place, but I think it is one of her constructs. Regardless, she told me that she's watched two to three low level demons come twice a day to this clearing. They came while I was there, and they opened a door in the ground that was hiding things. She said that they are notes, times, places and names. She collected these stones that were left in the area. As well as a collection of herbs."

"Well some of these are concealment stones, so that makes sense. She touched these others and wasn't affected?" Lucifer raised his eyebrows.

"No, those she said rolled to where I picked them up from. There's tracking spells on some of them," Stolas warned.

"I felt that. How sure are you that it's Moloch?"

"Certain. I myself heard the name. It makes sense, he was close to Bael and would probably feel like he had a score to settle with the angel and taking you out would be an added bonus." Stolas watched Lucifer's face carefully.

"Does she have children around her?"

"Yes. Several, and pregnant friends." Stolas shuddered to even think about it.

"I've never liked the slaughter of innocent souls," Lucifer spat out. "Do you recognize the signature on any of these?"

"No. Any chance of getting a list of hoodoo practitioners down here? As for these, who do you think would be powerful enough with the intelligence to create something so complex?" Stolas knew he himself would have a hard time creating something like that.

"I'll get you a list. Discretion is going to be top priority here. Also, there's a new soul here, calls himself a dark mage. He's got some interesting power rolling off him and he's already petitioning to be a prince. Strong manipulation skills. I've been watching him, and he has indeed approached Moloch but has not joined one of his legions."

"You think he could be our guy? Did you look into his history?"

"I did. I haven't decided yet if he is or isn't. He does have knowledge about stones, he's apparently summoned you before and you imparted knowledge. Far less than you normally do, and my guess is that's because you sensed his intentions were less than honorable."

"No one has petitioned to join my legions, but I will add him to a watch list. What's his name?" Stolas asked.

"Stone. He has association with your angel as well."

"She's not my angel." Stolas's response was automatic. His brain working furiously to put the pieces together. "If there is a connection to her, chances are he's the one."

"I agree. I want to be certain though." Lucifer put his feet back up on his desk. "There's something different about you today, my friend."

Stolas tried to school his face, but judging the look on Lucifer's face, he wasn't successful. "I'm not sure what you mean."

Lucifer grinned. "Let's start with the fact that you missed a button on your shirt. It could happen, however, I've never seen it happen with you. Then there's the color in your face. You aren't pale, but there is a rosy hue to your cheeks I've never seen."

Stolas felt himself blush. "I'm tired."

"Bullshit. There's a woman. Your angel's prophecy came true then?" Lucifer smiled wickedly. "Did you finally get laid, Stolas?"

"She's not my angel. And I don't believe in prophecies." Stolas totally ignored the last question.

"Speaking of that. We need to set up a meeting with her. I did some research on my own yesterday and there is a very old prophecy I stumbled upon that spoke of one who would be born with the power to destroy me in order to restore balance to the universe."

"Destroying you wouldn't restore the balance,"

Stolas countered uneasily.

"No, it wouldn't. I think she is the one it spoke of. It fits. If Moloch stumbled across it the same way I did, he would have only focused on the part where she has the power to destroy me."

Stolas sat up straight. "You're right. It's very possible she's strong enough to do that. I know without a doubt she's stronger than me. That doesn't tell me why you want to meet with her though."

"To discuss strategy. I don't claim to be a good man, but nor do I slaughter innocent souls. If she can destroy me, she can destroy him. If he's using this dark mage to get to her, she would need to know that too. If your vow to keep her safe means anything, this is your best option. I've thought it over from several angles and I understand why you want to keep me away from her."

Stolas resigned himself to the meeting. Given the new information it was the smartest move. "I'll set it up."

"Good. Now tell me, who's the woman?"

"Why are you so sure there is one?" Stolas hesitated.

"Because I know you. Would it be the friend who told you about the hoodoo?"

Stolas sighed. "Yes."

Lucifer hooted. "I knew it! You lucky bastard. You finally got laid!"

"No, I did not have sex," Stolas ground out.

"I call bullshit again."

"Shut up, Lucy. I didn't have sex." Stolas stood.

"So defensive. She must be important to you. What's her name?"

"Stay out of it, Lucifer." Stolas did his best to sound

stern, but really, he was scared.

"I won't interfere. I do want to know who she is though."

"Kalisha." Stolas heard the pitch change in his voice and winced.

"Well, I'll be damned. You're in love."

"You are damned, look where you are." Stolas sat back down in defeat.

"She's the hoodoo priestess, isn't she?"

"You know of her?" This worried Stolas even more.

"I do. I passed her over. She was murky, but not enough to be here. She's a spirit, Stolas."

"I'm well aware of what she is," he mumbled in response.

"I can offer her a position of power which gives her some safety, but she would be tied to you for eternity."

"She doesn't deserve to be here," Stolas pointed out. "You passed her over."

"She doesn't. It's the only chance you have at a relationship with her. She'd have the same freedoms that you do, and she'd be able to take a corporeal form on earth again. Think about it. If Moloch is having you watched, then chances are he knows about her, and if he gets his claws in her, there won't be much I can do to protect her from him."

"Fuck." Stolas slammed his fist down on to the arm of the chair almost cracking it.

"Not a word I often hear from you. You didn't consider that aspect of this, did you?"

"No, I didn't. I gave her a stone that gets her in and out of my house. Maybe he hasn't seen her." Stolas didn't dare to hope.

"Maybe. Is that a chance you are willing to take?"

Stolas felt like he was being backed in to a corner. "It's a chance I have to take right now. I spent all of one night with her, and *no sex*. It's not like going and offering her a position in Hell is going to go over smoothly. We aren't even in a relationship."

"Be that as it may, you still fell in love with her."

"We aren't having this conversation, Lucy. We need to figure out what to do about Moloch."

"Set up the meeting with the angel. I'll get you a list of hoodoo people, and find out what you can on the dark mage, Stone. I'll do more digging from this end. Our next meeting can't be one on record, send messages through the servants."

"Do you still have the stone I gave you?" Stolas had given Lucifer a stone directly to his house as well. He'd only used it a couple of times.

"I do. That's a last resort. Especially if you are being watched."

"Maybe you should think about doing rounds again. Start dropping in on your princes, enforce some things you've let slide. Reassert your authority," Stolas suggested.

"Not a bad idea. Just think about what I said, if he claims her, I have very limited options on what I can do."

Stolas hated it that he was right. "I'll watch more carefully and if she thinks that she wants a future with me, then it will be something I discuss. I will ask you this favor, if you get word that something is happening with her, let me know. If there is no time, then you claim her."

That caught Lucifer off balance. "You want me to claim her? That ensures an eternity here, and I'm not sure I can. I only get one chance to do that."

"I know. I'd rather her be with you if I can't do it. At least I know she will be safe." Stolas hated the thought of her being in danger.

"Let's just hope it doesn't come to that. Do what you need to do. Stay in touch and be careful."

Stolas nodded stiffly and left the room keeping his composure as he walked out of the house. Once he was outside of the gate, he popped back into his own house and rang the bell then called out for Zane.

"Yes, sir?"

"Find out everything you can for me on someone calling himself a dark mage, goes by the name of Stone. Add Kalisha to the watch list for protection, and be on guard. I am being watched and followed."

Startled, Zane asked, "By who?"

"I'm not sure. My gut feeling is some of Moloch's legion. If that's true, then we are all in danger and utmost caution needs to be exercised. Let the staff know and keep from leaving here unless absolutely necessary," Stolas doled out instructions.

"Sir, I have some friends who have expressed interest in working for you. I can enquire if they would like some security work. It couldn't hurt to have a few people outside watching for lurkers."

"Do you trust them, Zane?" Stolas asked his longtime servant.

"I trust that they want a better quality of life. They are currently unassigned to anyone."

"Then do it. They are not to be told any information on anything that goes on in the house, or on who comes and goes from here. Not until I know that I can trust their loyalty." Stolas wasn't going to back down on that.

"Standard compensation, sir?"

"Yes, there are a few empty rooms in one of the quarters outside. Set them up and watch them. Trial period of thirty days, if they want to stay, they have to swear fealty to me."

"Very well, sir. I'll take care of it."

"Thank you, Zane." Stolas strode off for his workroom and put the bag of stones back in the compartment.

Stolas needed to talk to Airiella, and he was dreading it. Airiella and Lucifer in the same room was not a good idea but Lucifer was correct in thinking it was the best way. Stolas knew enough about his friend that he also understood Lucifer wanted to meet with her to sniff her out and satisfy his own curiosity, as well as plan a strategy to keep himself straight.

Lucifer wasn't a bad demon, but he liked his position of power most of the time and was selfish enough to want to keep it. Stolas knew he'd do whatever he deemed necessary to make it happen. There was also the side of Lucifer that wanted to keep the position in order to keep Stolas safe as well. Lucifer was complicated

Stolas has chosen to fall and follow Lucifer, that was true. He didn't think he'd actually have to fight for the side of Hell though. The thing with Bael didn't really involve him in that the plans had nothing to do with Stolas. This time, Stolas was in the linc of fire if he was being followed. That could mean Moloch was aware of the power that Stolas kept hidden within himself. Which meant, somewhere along the line Stolas had slipped up and displayed too much. Chances are that happened somewhere in relation to Airiella.

Chapter Nine

Stolas closed his eyes and focused on the light of Airiella's being, her energy signature, and popped into what appeared to be an ancient castle. Airiella was near, but no one was where Stolas was. He refocused on her energy and let it guide him. Stolas was indeed in a castle, a large one too, that was filled with massive amounts of negative energy that crawled over his skin like thousands of tiny spiders.

This place had to be driving Airiella crazy. Stolas walked down a hallway and saw a macabre tapestry showing heads planted on spikes and stopped in his tracks, looking around and noting the artwork displayed and then burst out laughing. Stolas was in the castle of Vlad Tepes, or better known as Vlad the Impaler.

His laughter brought Smitty tearing out of a room up ahead, a camera strapped to him. "Shit! Stolas, you scared the hell out of me with that crazy laughter."

"Sorry. I was trying to figure out where I was, and this," Stolas pointed to the tapestry, "was my first clue. Leave it to you guys to be investigating here. Dracula."

"Baby girl! Stolas is here!" Smitty called back into the room. "Is he truly a vampire?" Smitty turned back to Stolas and asked.

Stolas heard Airiella's laughter, and she walked out. "I should have known it was you. You should have seen them all jump when you laughed."

Stolas couldn't help the grin that lit his face. "Tell me you got it on film." Stolas turned to Smitty and shrugged. "I didn't know him."

Ronnie poked his head out. "Sure did. The creepiest damn thing I've ever heard too. Damn-near shit myself."

"I didn't check the time, sorry. If you need to finish what you are doing, go ahead. I can wait."

"Thanks, should only be another hour or so." Airiella grinned at Stolas. "You should follow them around and scare them every opportunity you can."

"Trying to get them back for something?" Stolas smiled at Airiella as she walked closer and hugged him.

"Yep. The guys are making me plan Chrissie's wedding. I suck at it."

"Ronnie, proposed?" Stolas felt like he should have known that already. He had too much going on in his brain.

"You okay?" Airiella's concern broke through his thoughts.

"We need to talk, but I'd rather do it with all of you. I'll just follow behind and be quiet."

Stolas kept to himself and remained out of sight of the cameras while they finished the investigation. Stolas admired Jax for the growth he'd shown and the way he investigated places now. Far less confrontational but a lot more intuition. It must be Airiella's effect on them. They picked up on things Stolas hadn't even picked up on, and

Jax's grasp of the history of the place was spot-on accurate.

As soon as they finished, Jax walked up to Stolas. "Airiella said you needed to talk, mind if we do it at the hotel instead of here? This place is creepy as fuck. Cool because of the history of the place, but still creepy."

"I don't mind." Stolas silently agreed with Jax. The castle was firmly in the creepy category.

The drive back to the hotel was full of excited chatter about the evidence they'd gotten in the castle and how it related to the history of the place. Stolas was sorry he hadn't appeared earlier to witness what they were talking about having seen.

They filed into the hotel, and all went to Airiella and Jax's room automatically, Airiella having already told them Stolas wanted to talk to him. "Do you want the women here as well?" Ronnie asked as they sat down.

"That is up to you." Stolas shrugged; he was on the fence about that.

"I'm guessing this isn't good news." Jax pulled Airiella closer to him.

"No. I don't want to scare the ladies, but I also don't want them to be away from the children," Stolas told them.

"I researched Moloch," Ronnie threw out there. "Is that what this is about?"

"Partially, yes."

"He's a fucked up one." Ronnie pulled his laptop out of his backpack. "He eats children."

"He does. The problem this presents to you all is pretty grave." Stolas looked over at Aedan. "Your children are not safe with him at play." Stolas turned to look at Ronnie. "neither is Chrissie's."

The group went still and silent. "Even more of a

concern for me is your friend's children, the warrior's that were just born, and the hawk's who will be born shortly. Those children not only have blood from Airiella running in their veins, but they are also the children of powerful beings. Moloch will eat them, suck their soul, and gain their magic in the process, to put it crudely."

Airiella bolted up, outraged. "No! Nope! Not happening. How do I stop it?"

"Sit down, love. Let me finish," Stolas requested gently. "I made a vow to keep you all safe, and I will uphold it, including them. First, you need to warn them of the danger, who he is, and what he can do. I am working on things from my end. You all need to be extremely careful and diligent around any demon that appears, as it may be one of his legions. Dispatch them as soon as possible. They are watching you, taking notes."

"What kind of notes?" Smitty asked slowly.

"I don't know yet. What I'm sharing is information I have only found out recently. My best guess would be anything useful that points out weaknesses to hurt you, plans of where you will be in the future, your names, things along those lines. Something is in the works, and Moloch is at the head of it."

"What's his end game?" Ronnie asked angrily.

Stolas hated this. "He wants to take over. Moloch was a close friend of Bael. My intuition tells me that he is using that bone to pick a fight with Airiella for killing him as a tool to start a war between you guys and Lucifer. If he can get you to eliminate Lucifer, he can move into position to take over, and Moloch can dispatch as many legions as he pleases to take all of you out. Moloch is awful."

"Worse than Bael?" Airiella asked quietly.

"Yes. There's a lot more at play here than there was with Bael. *I'm* being watched and followed, as are you. Lucifer is a target, and Moloch is pulling in complicated spell work by unassigned parties to harm those that are sniffing too close to his plans. Someone is calling himself a dark mage that's new to Hell and goes by the name of Stone. He has some sort of tie to you, Airiella."

"Trevor Stone?" Jax's voice took on a frightening tone.

"I'm unaware of the whole name." Stolas furrowed his brows. "Isn't that who used to be on your council?"

"It is," Ronnie confirmed, typing furiously on his laptop. "He's dead."

Stolas felt himself grow faint for a moment as things began to fall into place. "Suicide?"

Ronnie gave him a quizzical look. "Was that a guess?"

"Yes." Stolas suppressed a shiver that crawled up his back.

"Hung himself in his cell before the trial," Ronnie recited.

Stolas stood suddenly. "He wasn't magic." Stolas started to pace, his mind spinning in mad circles as a larger picture revealed itself. "Do you have contacts within the police department that can find out information for you?"

"We don't, but Taklishim might." Jax's body had gone rigid.

"He was behind things when I came into the picture," Stolas said suddenly. "He was already in contact with a demon, Bael. It's not a stretch to think he could have summoned Moloch." Stolas grew sick as the implications hit him. He started voicing his thoughts out loud. "Moloch could have given the power of magic and how to harness it."

"You aren't painting a pretty picture here, Stolas." Airiella stood up and got in his path, halting Stolas.

"It's not a good picture at all, love. We are pawns in his larger game, and we are all in the path on this one. Every one of you, your spouses and children. Anyone associated with you, or with me, and on a larger scale, Lucifer."

"I'm not so sure I should be concerned with the devil as a target." Airiella poked Stolas in the chest. "I am, however, concerned about you."

"I need to set up a meeting between Lucifer and you."

Ronnie and Jax both shot to their feet, while Aedan and Smitty's mouths fell open. "Fuck, no! That's not happening," Ronnie shouted.

Jax stepped up behind Airiella and pulled her away from Stolas. "Why?" Jax asked.

"Better the devil you know," Airiella quoted softly. "You want me to fight for the devil?"

"No," Stolas corrected Airiella. "I want you to fight for you and your loved ones. Moloch is no joking matter, and he's amassing power. He wants to pit you against Lucifer, so you do the work for him."

Jax pulled Airiella back down beside him. "Let me get this straight. You want to set up a meeting between Lucifer and Airiella, to do what?"

"Lucifer would like to strategize. He has no interest in fighting Airiella," Stolas answered.

"You know this how?" Jax continued in a calm tone that in no way matched the look on his face.

"Because he discussed it with me. I argued against it, believe me, the last thing I want is those two in a room together. However, it would be beneficial for both parties to know how they are being played and make a plan."

"He's right," Airiella said softly to the guys. "I hate the idea, but he's right. I'd rather *not* have to fight the devil and all his armies." Airiella chewed on her lip. "That said, I also know you are holding back information from me. How you can know me and what I can do and still not think that I can't feel the emotions you have rolling through you right now is beyond me."

Stolas allowed a small smile to spread across his lips. "We all have a story; you only know a tiny part of mine." Stolas knelt in front of her. "I made that vow to keep you safe, and if I didn't think I could keep it, I wouldn't be here right now."

"I'm not worried about me," Airiella challenged him.

"Ells," Jax broke in. "You are *my* concern."

"She's all of our concern," Ronnie interrupted, "as well as that of the children."

Stolas ignored them all and focused on Airiella. "Do you know what that vow means for me?"

"In what way?"

"If I am unable to keep you safe, my life is forfeit. The light that lives inside you will take me as well. If any of you become harmed because of something I could have done, that is my price." Stolas handed out the information on the powers vows held.

Airiella gasped. "Why would you do something that stupid? You know I'm a magnet for shit storms of danger and trouble."

"It was my choice to make, and I made it willingly." Stolas sat back on his heels. "I've lived a long time and have never come across another like you."

Airiella studied him carefully. "You've met her, haven't you? Something happened."

Stolas blushed. "I did, and yes."

"Who is it?" Airiella demanded.

"Not important right now. I need to know if you'll agree to a meeting." Stolas knew it was a longshot but tried to change the subject anyway.

"Fuck that, Stolas. I do not agree to anything unless you tell me what I want to know."

"If I tell you her name, you'll agree to a meeting?"

"Wait, what's happening here?" Smitty interjected. "What are you talking about?"

"I had a vision that Stolas found his partner, but I couldn't see who it was. I told him about it, and that he needed to be open-minded about it as she played a part in the upcoming war I saw."

"You had a vision about a girlfriend for a demon?" Smitty sounded dumbfounded. It was the same reaction Stolas had had.

"Zip it; he's my friend. It's not like I can control the damn things," Airiella fired off. "Well, Stolas?"

"You'll agree to a meeting?" Stolas pushed back.

"I will." Airiella answered to the groans of the rest of her team.

"Kalisha," Stolas softly whispered.

"Are you saying that to shut me up?" Shock was written across Airiella's face. "I would have seen it if it was her."

"No, angel, she's a ghost. You can't see them,"

Ronnie reminded Airiella.

That hadn't even occurred to Stolas, but he realized Ronnie was correct. "She's had to use magic to get you to see her."

"What happened to her?" Airiella's voice was strangely even. "This puts her in danger, doesn't it?"

"If what you said is true, yes. Kalisha might be in danger anyway if spotted with me." Stolas tapped Airiella's knee. "And what happens between her and I is between her and me."

"What else aren't you telling me?"

Airiella's eyes saw way too much, and there was an odd glow coming from them. "What do you want to know?"

"I want to know whatever it is that you are holding back from me. I can see it on you. This squirming line of color that feels important."

"Lucifer is my oldest and closest friend," Stolas admitted. A deafening silence fell around the room.

Aedan cleared his throat. "I think that classifies as important information."

Now wasn't the time to get into his history with Airiella. "Well, now, you know." Stolas held her gaze and allowed all the emotions in him to come to the surface. "I'm holding nothing back from you. My past is a story for another time. All I ask is that you remember when I told you there are good demons and bad ones."

"I remember." Airiella didn't look away from him. "Legends paint him a certain way."

"I'm here telling you the truth. Yes, Lucifer is the leader of Hell. He didn't get that way because he is soft. I am also telling you that Lucifer does *not* hurt innocent souls and he punishes those that do. Lucifer's punishments are harsh and often very cruel and reserved for those who truly deserve it."

Stolas felt a wave of calming energy hit the room, and he knew it wasn't for his benefit. "I'm trusting you, Stolas."

"We will be there with her," Jax added.

Stolas nodded. "I figured as much. If I can think of another way, I will make it happen, love."

"You are also going to set up a time for me to hear this story," Airiella said firmly. "You better keep Kalisha safe."

"For such a smart guy, this seems like an idiotic decision," Ronnie muttered darkly.

Stolas stood up. "You are all under my protection."

"Not very convincing when faced with the devil," Smitty retorted.

"Would you like to hear a secret?" Stolas looked at each of them, waiting for a nod of acknowledgment.

"Better be a good one," Ronnie countered.

"Hand me your computer." Stolas held out his hand. "Due to the nature of being followed, I will not speak this, nor will you." Stolas let his energy flow through him and out into the room with his words that would bind them from repeating his secret.

Ronnie handed his computer over, and Stolas opened up a document he could type in and wrote: *"My power is only slightly less than Lucifer's. I am his secret weapon. Bael wasn't even close to as strong as I am."*

Stolas handed it to Airiella first, who shared the screen with Jax. Airiella's eyes widened. "Oh, you are, for sure, telling me your story." Airiella handed the computer to Smitty, who shared with Ronnie and Aedan.

"We *all* are going to be sitting in for that story," Ronnie agreed. "I'm deleting this now."

Stolas watched and made sure it was gone. "You'll be unable to repeat that."

"I felt it," Airiella told him bluntly. "Why you wouldn't trust me is another issue. You know all my secrets."

"Now," Stolas ignored Airiella's statement, "the meeting needs to happen soon, but I also want time to gather more information. I will be there, I made that a condition before agreeing to this, and I warned him that you all would be there too."

"Can we do it after Ronnie's wedding?" Airiella pleaded.

"When is it?" Stolas asked.

"In eight days," Ronnie responded. "Feel free to join us, but please don't bring your boss."

Stolas chuckled. "Weddings aren't his thing."

"We don't have to go to Hell, do we?" Airiella said with a grin.

"No, we'll come to you." Stolas fought back a laugh. "See you in nine days." Stolas popped out and went back home.

Chapter Ten

"Zane," Stolas called, ringing the bell.

"Yes, sir?"

"Send a message to Lucifer. Say only: Be free in nine days. Send to Dakota and don't be seen."

"Yes, sir."

Stolas headed down to his workroom when Zane stopped him by a subtle touch of his hand. "What is it?"

"Two of them have offered fealty now and are outside watching," Zane offered.

"How many were offered the position?" Stolas asked.

"Four. One declined, the other is on the fence, and I rescinded the offer. Something smelled off to me."

Stolas nodded. "Are you wanting me to do this now?"

"I'd feel better if they swear in sooner rather than later, given the circumstances."

"Very well, lead me to them." Stolas followed Zane and reached in his pocket for a stone imbued with truth magic. Stolas's estate was one of the larger ones, which had been a point of contention among some of the other princes, Lucifer had only stated that Stolas needed it for the herbal gardens which benefitted them all.

It wasn't true, it was blatant favoritism, but the downside to that was when it came to punishment, Stolas had to dole it out the same as he did for everyone else. One of the many reasons Stolas stuck to not breaking too many rules, or at least where he could get caught doing it.

Zane took him out to the back of the property where the gardens were. Several greenhouses of herbs that were no longer findable on earth flourished and grew there for Stolas to make his remedies and have a supply on hand. Stolas kept Lucifer supplied with many things that would protect him as well as heal him and their staff.

Before they came to the greenhouses, Zane stopped, and two low-level demons melded out of the shadows. "Sir, this is Sam and Volt."

"I understand you'd like to swear fealty now instead of after a trial period?" Stolas asked, his tone firm.

"Yes, sir," they both replied.

"May I ask why?" Stolas was listening to tones and inflections.

Volt stepped forward, keeping his eyes cast to the ground. "May I speak freely, sir?"

"Please do."

"I have heard that you treat your staff with respect and fairness, which is unheard of here. It is true, I made bad choices and wound up here, but I can't say I have a desire to be beaten and tortured for the rest of eternity."

"Understood. Are you aware of what the terms of fealty are?" Stolas was surprised to hear that unassigned demons knew of how he treated people.

"Loyalty or death, sir," Sam answered.

"You are both willing to patrol the grounds and keep those from entering that should not be here?"

"Yes, sir," they both replied again.

Stolas smothered a sigh. "It's not necessary for you to keep your eyes to the ground. I'd rather be able to look in your eyes and see the truth myself. Some view keeping your eyes down as a sign of respect. To me, it's unnecessary. I don't care if you like me or not. If you are swearing fealty, then you know the consequence of breaking that vow." Stolas shifted his weight from one foot to the other. "Do either of you have any questions about the positions? Or myself?"

"Do you allow us to use magic to perform our job duties?" Volt asked, raising his eyes.

"Yes. If someone comes on this property, use any means you have to detain them or stop them if you feel they mean harm to yourself or anyone here or are trying to sneak in. Is your name an indicator of the magic you possess?" Stolas asked pointedly.

"Yes, sir. I can use electricity."

"Zane is the head of all employees here. If he issues an order, I expect it followed. Zane also will have any information you need to perform your job and has the authority to solve issues should any arise. You will report directly to Zane daily. He will show you where you will stay, and he will go over meals and any other compensation. If I am not here, Zane is in charge. Is that clear?" Stolas recited out the rules.

"Yes, sir," they both replied.

"Any more questions?" Stolas reached in his pocket for the stone.

Sam raised his eyes. "Sir, are you able to heal?"

"I may be able to help; do you have an issue?" Stolas looked over at Zane with a question on his face, removing his empty hand from his pocket. Zane appeared shocked by the question.

"I was injured before coming here by a recruiter for another prince." Sam lifted his shirt and showed a gaping wound along his side.

"Who was it? Why did they do it?" Stolas felt the anger in him bubble up; this was the exact behavior he deplored.

Sam hesitated before responding, and Volt stepped in to answer. "It was one of Moloch's legions. He was questioning us both about our powers and how we can use them in a fight, sir. My power is a little easier to figure out because of my name, but Sam's isn't. When Sam didn't respond fast enough, the hunter slashed Sam with a knife coated in something."

"A hunter? Or a recruiter?" Stolas wasn't surprised that it was Moloch. What did surprise him was that Moloch had people out recruiting for a fight; this was farther along than Stolas had thought.

"He was a hunter that was recruiting specific skill sets from what I could tell, sir," Volt answered.

Stolas stepped closer to Sam and examined the wound. On closer inspection, he found it seeping and infected. "Sam, does this only hurt here, or are you feeling it everywhere?"

"Everywhere, sir," Sam said quietly.

"Zane, please go to my workroom and grab the black wound bag for me," Stolas said curtly.

"Yes, sir."

"I'm well enough to take the vow, sir," Sam said, dropping to his knees. Volt quickly followed suit.

"Very well. Sam, take this stone, hold it in your hands and give me your vow." Stolas reached back in his pocket and pulled out the stone and handed it to Sam, letting his magic wash over Sam.

"I vow fealty to you, Prince Stolas, from now until the end of time. If I should break this vow, I accept the term of death and eternal damnation." The stone started to glow red, proving Sam was speaking the truth, and the magic Stolas let loose sealed the vow to his soul.

Stolas took the stone back and handed it to Volt. The process repeated and vows accepted by both demons that now bound them to Stolas.

"I vow my protection to you both so long as you follow orders." Stolas sealed the deal and motioned for them both to rise.

Zane, who had returned while the vows were happening, handed the bag over, and Stolas instructed Sam to remove his shirt. Stolas prodded at the wound a bit, and the stench of poison wafted out.

"Sam, you may become sick," Stolas told him, "whatever cut you had poison on it." Stolas grabbed one of the containers from his bag and generously smeared it over the wound as gently as possible.

Sam winced and gritted his teeth together, beads of sweat popping up along his brow. "Is there anything I could do to help him?" Volt asked.

Stolas glanced at his new servant and appraised Volt. "Did you kill who did this?"

"No, sir. Just stunned him enough to knock him out."

"Then beware, he will be looking for you." Stolas handed Volt the container. "Keep applying this to the wound until it seals shut." Stolas dug around in his bag and found a general healing mix. "Mix this in water and drink it," Stolas told Sam. "It will help kill off whatever has started to circulate through your system."

"Thank you, sir." Sam briefly smiled.

"Why did you hesitate to answer?" Stolas was curious about the act that had gotten Sam the wound.

"I knew they'd want me, and I didn't want to join them," Sam answered honestly. "My skills are strength and speed, sir. Useful for fighting."

"So, they never found out?"

"No," Volt answered for Sam. "After I shocked him, I grabbed Sam and got away."

"I see. Your skills would be useful to them as well. They'll be looking for you for revenge as well as to add you to their team. My guess is if they capture you, they wouldn't be gentle. I'd suggest you patrol back here where it's harder to spot you than upfront."

"Yes, sir. We also both possess skills in being unseen and blending into our background," Volt informed him.

"Notify Zane immediately if any of Moloch's legions or Moloch himself show up around here," Stolas instructed them both. "I suspect someone is following and watching me. I want to know by whom."

"Yes, sir," was the unanimous response.

"For now, get settled, eat, and plan out how you two will work this. You can either start tonight or tomorrow morning. Let Zane know your plans. Sam, if there are any changes to the wound, tell Zane immediately."

Sam nodded stiffly, Stolas could see he was in pain but chose not to call attention to it. If they broke their fealty vow, Stolas had every intention of carrying through with death. Stolas was good to his employees, and working here was a privilege most condemned to Hell could only hope for as a sentence.

"Sir," Zane said quietly. "I think you have company."

"See to them." Stolas turned. "I'm heading back."

Chapter Eleven

Seir, I'm surprised to see you," Stolas greeted his friend.

"Something is amiss out there," Seir told him, stepping inside.

"I feel it too. What do you think is happening?" Stolas hated the deception, but he had no idea who he could trust. Trust being a loose word among demons.

"I'm not sure. It's dangerous, though."

"What isn't dangerous here?" Stolas shrugged his shoulders.

"It's more than that." Seir paced a bit in the entryway. "I could swear someone was following me the other day."

"Really?" Stolas didn't have to feign surprise this time. "I've noticed the same thing."

"There's a feeling I can't shake that things are unstable. It makes me nervous." Seir paused to settle his gaze on Stolas. "You don't seem exactly shocked by that."

"I'm not. I believe something is happening. I just haven't put it all together yet. Another prince is making a power play."

"Who?" Seir started pacing again. "Now that you say that, it makes sense. He'd be looking for allies and tailing the rest of us to look for weaknesses."

Seir was never very politically inclined or interested in status or hierarchy. The simple fact Seir noticed let Stolas know how far things had gotten. "I'm not sure who. My best advice is to stay alert and take steps to ensure your safety."

"Do you think there is a danger to us?" Seir looked worried about that.

"I do. I, myself, have hired some security for here."

"You trust unknown demons?" Seir's tone was wary.

"They took a vow of fealty; if they betray me, they die permanently."

"My servants didn't take a vow," Seir commented offhandedly.

"I didn't require it, they offered. It also tells me that things out there are worse than we thought. One of them got injured by a hunter acting as a recruiter because he took too long to answer a question about his skills," Stolas informed Seir.

"Who was recruiting, and for what?"

"They told me they were looking for specific skills for fighters. That tells me someone is building an army. I have my suspicions on who it is, but nothing concrete," Stolas hedged.

"If I had to wager a guess, it would be Moloch. He's been different since Bael was killed. Speaking of that, if there *is* going to be a war, it may be against your angel and not to take power here."

"She's not my angel, but yes, I've considered that as

well. I've warned her."

"I can't say that I would be pleased to fight against her. I rather like her." Stolas chuckled darkly at Seir's response and leaned against the wall. "She's involved in this, somehow, isn't she? The look on your face gives it away."

"I can spout off all the theories I have, but they are only that, theories. Aside from not knowing the who-to-trust part of all this, I lack proof."

Seir looked affronted. "You don't think you can trust me? I put my own life on the line helping her when she needed, and her human friends."

"It's not you that I don't trust, it's everyone. I'm not singling you out. The only thing I can tell you with absolute certainty is that we are heading for war." Stolas sighed.

"If you are sure of that, then I fight on the side you fight for; are you with the angel on this?"

"I'm not against her." Seir had always been a friend to him. "Come with me to my workroom. We can talk safely there."

Stolas led Seir back through the house and down the stairs to the workroom. "Zane," Stolas called out.

"Yes, sir?"

"I need absolute privacy. No one near this room while we are in here."

"Understood, sir."

Stolas closed the door and wondered how much he needed to say for Seir to be satisfied and back off from asking questions that he didn't want to answer and put Lucifer in a tight spot. Stolas sighed again. "I think you are right. Moloch is who I believe is behind this. I think it's a lot more complicated than a simple war."

"How so? War is pretty complicated already if you ask me."

"He's targeting Airiella and her group with demons. Moloch's pitting her against Lucifer. My thoughts are that Moloch is going to use Airiella to try and fight against Lucifer to take him out so Moloch can move into position."

"Devious. It does sound like something Moloch would do. So the recruitment is for what?" Seir asked.

"I told you, I haven't figured it all out yet. There are pieces I am missing. Everything I have discovered thus far has led me to these conclusions. Have you heard anything about a new soul down here calling himself a dark mage? Going by the name Stone?"

"Yes, I have. Stone has not joined a legion yet, but popular opinion is it will be Moloch's. You wouldn't fight for Lucifer? That's treasonous."

"I would fight for him, but not against Airiella or her group." Stolas was hesitant in answering.

"Puts you in a tough spot if a war does happen."

"It *will* happen. I need to talk to Airiella still. I'm trying desperately to get indisputable proof. Moloch has covered his tracks well." Stolas wasn't going to reveal that Lucifer had already discussed this with Stolas, nor was he going to show the stones, or the hidden cache.

"Is Airiella strong enough to defeat Lucifer?"

"I don't know. Moloch, I think she could beat." Stolas wondered if Seir knew about the old prophecy that Lucifer had found. Stolas didn't want to bring it up, plus Seir didn't realize of Stolas's real power.

"I will fight alongside you, whichever side you choose to fight on. I really would hate to see Airiella get hurt. She's quite remarkable and fierce. Easy on the eyes as well." Seir was a playboy through and through.

"Hardly the point, but I appreciate the support. Keep your ears open for information. Either on Moloch or Stone. Both would be helpful."

Seir gave him an odd look. "What do you know of prophecies of old?"

"Not a lot. Prophecy isn't something I ever put a lot of time or thought into; why?" Stolas felt his heartbeat pick up.

"There is one about a being with power equal to the Gods called into creation to balance out the divide."

"Wouldn't that make that being a God themselves? It seems contradictory to me." Seir knew far more than Stolas had given him credit for, a mistake he wouldn't make again.

"This is one you should know considering that you know so much about the stars." Seir laughed.

"The science of the stars," Stolas corrected.

Seir shrugged. "I'll see if I can find it for you since that's my thing. To me, it seems our mutual friend might fit that bill. If that's the case, your guesses will probably pan out, and this is something far more powerful than we could imagine."

"For Airiella's sake, I hope it's not. I've never wanted to be wrong more." There was a knock at the door, and Stolas turned, halting when he remembered that he wasn't supposed to be interrupted.

"It's time for me to go, anyway." Seir headed to the door. "I'll be in touch."

"Watch your back, Seir," Stolas reminded him and pulled open the door to see a disheveled Kalisha.

Chapter Twelve

Seir gave Kalisha a curious look but didn't linger and made his way out. Stolas looked at Kalisha in concern and led her to the kitchen, he poured her a cup of water and handed it to her. Something had shaken Kalisha, and her usually calm composure was now nervous.

Stolas hadn't spoken other than asking if she was hurt, to which she had merely shaken her head. Stolas waited until Kalisha drank some water and sat down. Once she calmed enough to stop shaking, he tried again.

"What happened?" Stolas reached for her hand and held it between his own.

"Trevor Stone is here," Kalisha whispered.

Stolas froze, it was valid then. The Stone that called himself a dark mage was Trevor Stone. He didn't have magic, though; something was definitely at play here. "Did you see him?"

"Stone found me. He was following me. He waited until Winnie left, then cornered me." She trembled again. "Trevor's different. Unmistakably insane, and so malevolent it was repelling."

Kalisha could have the information Stolas needed to tie this all together. "Death often changes people, especially ones that find themselves down here." Stolas tried to play devil's advocate. "Start from the beginning. Tell me what happened, you are safe here with me."

"I'm not. I'm not safe anywhere." Kalisha stood abruptly.

"Kalisha, I promise you; you are safe here. I can guarantee it. However evil Trevor Stone is, he cannot beat me."

Kalisha dropped back into the chair as if all the strength in her body gave out. "I don't live here; Trevor will get to me out there. What happens if he kills me in this form?"

"I will end him," Stolas promised Kalisha, steel in his voice. "One thing at a time. First, I need you to tell me everything that happened, so I know how to proceed from here. Give me a moment." Stolas retook her hand.

"Zane," Stolas called out, his voice harsher sounding than he intended.

Zane's appearance was almost instantaneous, and he looked frightened. "Is everything okay, sir?"

"No. Please notify the staff, including the new ones, that we are now on high alert for trouble and to proceed with utmost caution. All defensive measures are to be put in place immediately."

Zane's eyes widened slightly, and he nodded his understanding. "Right away, sir."

As Zane left, Stolas focused his attention back on Kalisha. "I'm all yours. Tell me what happened."

Kalisha met his gaze, her own unwavering, but wary. "You know the clearing where you met Winnie at?"

Stolas nodded. "I was there, turning to go back to my space when I felt that prickle that alerted me to danger." Kalisha pointed at an amulet on her wrist. "It burned me, and I froze. I didn't see anything at first."

Stolas moved the amulet away from her skin and saw a scorch mark on the stone's bottom. "This burned out," Stolas said, startled.

"I've never had that happen before, not even when Bael killed me. It took a few minutes for me to move again, then he came out from the trees. He was cackling like a lunatic; his eyes were red like he was burning from within."

Stolas felt a little of his contained power trickle out and tried to dampen it, so it didn't frighten Kalisha. "He sold his soul." Stolas stroked his thumb over her hand. "The red eyes like that, he's tied himself to a powerful demon and somewhere, something went wrong with it."

"Bael. He summoned Bael before Airiella killed him. He was working with Bael. He has power now, and it's vile. He smells putrid," Kalisha started to babble. "It's like a stale ashtray that's overflowing that a cat peed on, then a drunk person vomited on it."

"Kalisha, look at me, breathe slowly. That's it, go slow," Stolas spoke softly, trying to soothe her. "He can't get to you here." Kalisha's description made him want to laugh, but it wasn't funny.

Kalisha started to calm down, and once she wasn't breathing hard anymore, she spoke again. "How is that possible? He never had power before."

"He told you he summoned Bael?" Stolas himself was trying to work this out.

"His exact words were, 'Bael was summoned and saw in me a worthy vessel.' That's what he said."

"We are missing something here. I don't think Stone summoned Bael, but someone in his presence did. Bael didn't grant powers to those who summoned him, even with a sacrifice. He only granted powers if he thought it would further himself. I'll need to do more digging on that," Stolas thought out loud. "Keep going."

"He said that I helped bring his downfall upon him, so he was going to destroy me but would use me first until he tired of me." Kalisha trembled again, and Stolas couldn't stop the power surge that tore through him.

Zane appeared immediately, worried. "Sir?"

"It's fine, leave me," Stolas ground out, waiting for Zane to leave. Once Zane was gone, Stolas pulled Kalisha closer to him. "Finish your story, and we will talk more about the options you have."

"He was out of his mind. He went on about how he was joining forces with the most powerful and that soon everyone would learn to respect him. He said that he would bring down that bitch once and for all and everyone she loved would go with her." Kalisha went still and turned her steady gaze on Stolas again. "He's talking about Airiella, isn't he? He hated her. From the moment he saw her, he hated her."

"I don't know who he's talking about, but if I hazard a guess, yes, Airiella would be who I would say. Did Stone mention any other names?" Stolas was having a hard time staying calm.

"No. Trevor kept talking about how everyone was trying to woo him on to their teams because of how strong he was."

A few more pieces of the puzzle fell into place. Lucifer needed to know these things. "Is that all?"

"No. While he was there, I wasn't able to move, it felt like there was an invisible box around me that was pressing against me. All I could smell was death, and my ears started ringing so loud I thought they would bleed. Everything in me panicked." Kalisha took a deep breath. "That was when Taklishim and Onida showed up."

"The warrior was there?" Stolas couldn't have been more stunned if Kalisha had slapped him.

"Not the whole time, they showed up then. Maybe I was sending distress signals; I am not sure. Taklishim sent one of his shadows at Trevor, and it freed me. Onida told me to go, and I ran. Trevor saw where I went. I think my little haven is no longer a viable place for me to hide. I stayed there until I calmed down enough to leave and come here. I'm sorry, I didn't know what else to do."

"You did exactly the right thing," Stolas murmured, his mind a blur. "I don't understand why he came after you."

"When Airiella interviewed for the position with the show, our task was to evaluate her skills as an empath. Stone was to evaluate her mental state and give a recommendation to the producers on if she could do what was needed, which was help get that energy out of Jax. Airiella walked into the room, and Taklishim declared her a raven before anything even got started. That's when there was a change in Stone."

"A change as in how?" Stolas wondered if the man had been dabbling in summoning already or was involved with someone who was.

"Trevor purposely started to be snide in a subtle way. The rest of the process, Trevor was just flat out an ass to Airiella and the rest of us because she had us all firmly believing in Taklishim's assessment that she was far more than an empath. When Trevor spoke to each of us individually, it was more of the same. With me, Trevor tried to convince me to see that Airiella was emotionally unstable, and he got openly hostile with me for not agreeing with him."

"Openly hostile?" Stolas needed more clarification on that one. He wanted to be sure of what Stone had done to Kalisha to plot out how to retaliate best.

"From that point on, any suggestion I made during council meetings or votes, or on any communications Trevor tried to dismiss, or disprove, or ridicule. If I saw Trevor in person, he was outwardly friendly when others were around, but as soon as no one was within earshot or sight, he got aggressively angry."

"He put his hands on you?" The fury boiling up in Stolas became hard to contain.

"Not how you think. Trevor would walk into me on purpose, things like that. He'd make lewd sexual references, talk about how his family was slave owners."

Stolas stood and paced, trying to calm himself before he let out a blast of energy that would call attention. "It sounds to me like Stone had already been in communication with a demon. Those are characteristics I would associate with a lower level demon. The pettiness and anger would be something they would pass on easily, paving the way for larger things."

"I can't speak on that. I avoided Trevor as much as possible after that. Afterward, I started to believe he was behind some of the attacks that happened with Jax and his team." Kalisha shifted in her chair to watch him pace. "Why are you so sure I am safe here?"

"For one, no one knows you are here. Two, nothing short of another prince would dare to try to attack me on my home soil. Three, I'm stronger than any of the others; four, I have protections in place. Five, Lucifer wouldn't tolerate an attack against me. Those are just to name a few." Stolas had counted the reasons off on his fingers.

"Is Trevor possessed?"

"I don't know. I haven't seen Stone. I will find out." Stolas kneeled in front of Kalisha. "I will also keep you safe."

"So, you've said. I don't see how." Kalisha's hands gripped his shoulders, and she stared at Stolas with those eyes that unraveled him slowly.

Stolas stood back up and ran his hands through his hair. "How much do you know about demons and our ways?"

"Not a whole lot. I know what you've told me, and what religion says about you. Why?"

"You can always swear a fealty vow to me, and at that point, you fall under my protection, but it also classifies you as a servant to me. I have no desire for you to be a servant. To anyone." Stolas faced away from Kalisha, suddenly afraid to speak Lucifer's thoughts on claiming her.

"That's it? That's my only option?" Kalisha's voice took on a higher pitch making her sound hysterical.

"No. I'm just trying to figure out how to word this without sounding like I'm insane," Stolas admitted quietly, still not looking at her.

"After seeing Stone the way he was, I'm willing to give you a little leeway on that score."

"You know how Airiella has her connections?"

Stolas started and then stopped because it wasn't precisely the same thing.

"Yes, go on."

"If I claim you," Stolas winced at the words, "it sort of creates something like that between us. My power would transfer to you and vice versa."

"Why are you afraid to tell me that?" Stolas hadn't heard Kalisha come up behind him. "That doesn't sound so bad."

Stolas turned to look at her, the truth blaring in his eyes and tone. "It's for eternity, Kalisha. It's binding, and it means you'd be here in Hell with me. I don't know that I could condemn you to that."

Kalisha backed up from him, fear evident in her eyes. "Are those my only two options?"

"Lucifer can claim you as well. I've asked him to if something were to happen to me, and you needed to be safe."

Kalisha did look horrified at that thought. "No. Out of the question."

"You also need to be aware that another of the princes or a higher power demon could claim you without your consent. It's underhanded, but magic exists that would force you to agree even if you didn't want to."

Tears sprang to Kalisha's eyes, and Stolas hated himself for it. "It doesn't sound like I have a whole lot of great options."

"You don't have to choose any of them. Even without those, I will still do everything in my power to keep you safe," Stolas promised Kalisha.

"How? By following me around and watching me every day? That doesn't sound feasible to me."

"You have the stone. Anytime you feel unsafe, just come here. If I'm out, you only need to call me or wait for me to return, and I can go check your area to make sure that it's safe."

"Living my afterlife on the run," Kalisha stated. She gave him a calculating look. "May I ask a personal question?"

"Of course," Stolas agreed immediately.

"You'll answer honestly?"

"I have not lied to you, Kalisha. I don't intend to. Ask." Stolas stood still and kept his eyes on hers.

"When you talked about claiming me, for a moment, you sounded as if you wanted to. Then just as quickly, you sounded abhorred by the idea. Which is it?"

"Both," Stolas answered instantly.

"Well, that makes things so much clearer now, thanks." Kalisha almost smiled. "Is there an upside to this claiming?"

"For me, yes. I'd get you and get to share in your power and share mine with you. I'd be able to protect you and not worry about your safety. I'd have a companion for eternity. For you? In my own opinion, no. I'd be tying you to me and this place. My powers could be a bad thing for you; maybe you wouldn't like how they feel. You could decide you hate me, and then you'd be stuck here miserable with no end in sight."

"Tell me how I'd be protected."

"If you were bound to me and anyone tried to harm you, I'd know. I'd have free reign to destroy the individual's soul or issue any punishment I saw fit. The reverse is also true if you were wondering. As a prince, the laws that govern me would then govern you as well, which also means that Lucifer would be able to offer protection or punishment if anyone were to break those laws. Since Lucifer is the greatest friend I've ever had, I fall under a different category for him than the rest."

"But in return, I'd end up serving Lucifer as you do and live out eternity in here in Hell."

Stolas cupped her chin. "Yes. Though trips to earth would be easier for you as you'd be able to take a human form there."

Kalisha's eyes lightened. "I'd be able to see my daughter? She'd be able to see me?"

"Correct. However, if your daughter has your powers, she'd probably know that you were a part of Hell. Your soul wouldn't change, though," Stolas told her softly.

Kalisha looked thoughtful and turned away from Stolas in what he could only guess was contemplation. "Would you have to sleep with me?"

Stolas sucked in a breath at her question and tried not to let the sting of rejection color his tone. "I would *never* force myself on you, Kalisha. That is not a fear you should ever have with me."

"You misunderstand me, Stolas. It isn't a fear, it is a desire." Kalisha's words washed over him. "Do you care for me?"

Her blunt question forced Stolas forward until he was right behind her. "I do," Stolas answered honestly. "More than I thought possible."

"I find myself in a similar boat as you then." Kalisha turned into him. "As much as I don't want to, I trust you."

Kalisha cared for him. Her admission rang in his ears, sending his pulse skyrocketing. "I find you irresistible," Stolas whispered and slowly captured her lips.

"Likewise, demon," Kalisha purred as he pulled away. "How many are you allowed to claim?"

"Only one. Ever."

"That's good. I don't want to share." Kalisha pulled his head back towards hers. "Claim me."

Chapter Thirteen

Stolas pulled back, momentarily stunned. "Are you sure that's what you want? It's not something we can just go undo later."

"I understood what you told me, Stolas. I'm not a fool."

Kalisha took his hand and led Stolas through the house. Kalisha didn't know where she was going, and she pulled him into the first room she found that had a place to sit. It wasn't one of the rooms Stolas usually used, but Zane made sure they were all cleaned.

Kalisha pulled Stolas down next to her on the loveseat. "Do you not want to do this?"

Stolas thought about it, hard. All his hang-ups over it had to do with condemning Kalisha to Hell for the rest of her existence. "I feel like you are getting the short end of the bargain on this." Stolas caressed her face.

"I did pick up on that." Kalisha leaned her cheek into his hand. "I don't think you are seeing me clearly. My soul is almost the same color as yours. If doing this doesn't change my soul, really for me, all that's changing is where I reside, and I am assuming the fact I won't have any other romantic relationships other than with you. Do I have that correct?"

"That's not all that would change." Stolas shifted to face Kalisha fully. "Your power would change, and you'd be able to feel me on a different level than you are used to; it would be something similar to what Airiella and Jax feel. I'd know if you were hurt, angry, or unhappy, and you'd feel the same. You'd also be changing allegiance to Lucifer."

"The only one of those points that cause me to hesitate is the last. The rest doesn't strike me as bad. Is this moving faster between us than I thought it was? Absolutely. Are the spirits yelling at me? Again, absolutely, but with them, I believe that their reaction is one of fear because I wouldn't need to call on them with your power. They are greedy and do love their offerings."

"Kalisha." Stolas paused. "I don't want you to regret it."

"Why do you think I will?"

"You'd be stuck with me." Stolas wanted so badly to tell Kalisha that she had his heart, but fear kept him from saying it. He'd had one sexual experience with her and lost his heart, what did that say about him?

Kalisha's laughter was light, and the sound made his heart skip a beat. "I certainly don't see it as being stuck with you. I more see it as you are a choice I am choosing to make, which I wouldn't do if I didn't care for you. I think it would take me years to unpeel all the layers of you and learn them. And more importantly, I want to learn everything about you."

"Why?" was Stolas's desperate answer.

Kalisha studied his face, and Stolas didn't know

what expression she saw, but her face softened even more. "You've been honest with me about everything, correct?"

"Yes. I have not lied to you." Stolas felt himself nodding and tried to keep still.

"Why are you in love with Airiella?"

Taken aback by the question, Stolas could only look at her for a few moments while he gathered his thoughts. "That wasn't a question I was expecting. I will answer you. Airiella's full of love and life. The love she has for everything drew me to her; it was the one thing my life was devoid of."

Kalisha smiled and nodded. "I don't think you are alone in feeling that way. Now, tell me why you care about me?"

Stolas paused at the wording since Kalisha didn't know he fell in love with her also. Stolas cleared his throat. "If you want total honesty from me, then I suppose I should say that I fell in love with you too."

Astonishment lit Kalisha's eyes. "You love me?"

Stolas dropped his eyes to his lap. "I do. Does that change your opinion on this whole situation?"

Kalisha took a deep breath before asking, "Is this because of what happened this morning?"

"Yes and no. That is more of a complicated answer. Was it the act itself? No."

Kalisha nodded at Stolas. "No, it doesn't change my opinion on you claiming me. It does solidify it. Tell me this then, why do you love me?"

"You challenge me, make me feel, I get tongue-tied around you and nervous. You are full of life, rhetorically speaking, since you are a ghost. You are intelligent and seem to understand me on a level most don't. You are wonderfully complex and stunningly beautiful." Stolas let the words fall from his lips in a rush, feeling oddly vulnerable, even saying them.

"Why do you think I wouldn't feel any of those same things for you?" Kalisha asked him gently. "If I didn't, I certainly wouldn't want to learn everything about you that I could. As for why I want to learn about you, it's for the same reasons. When I look at you, I don't think Stolas the demon. I think of you and all that you are inside. The intelligence and the way you think, your need to protect Airiella and me, even Lucifer. Yes, the rest of my existence is a long time, but I think spending it with you would be anything but boring."

Stolas felt overwhelmed. Airiella and Chrissie were the first in over a thousand years to think he was a good man. Hearing Kalisha speak what she had almost made Stolas feel exposed. She unraveled him strand by strand, and he didn't know what to do about it. "I just want you to be sure; this isn't something to take lightly."

"How did it feel when I slept on you last night?" Kalisha asked him softly.

Stolas groaned at the memory of it. "Like paradise."

"Did it feel like that because a naked woman was on you?"

"No, because it was *you* on me. We could have remained fully clothed, and I would have felt the same way. I've had others throw themselves at me and never had a single reaction. Yet around you, everything inside me crumbles." Stolas almost winced at how that sounded to his ears.

"I'd love nothing more than to take this slow with you and savor every moment before we do the claiming. We don't have that kind of time; it seems. It may take me longer to admit love, but I can tell you already, Stolas, I care for you much more than I have for anyone in a long time. If that is enough for you, I am ready and willing. There is something special between us, and I'd be a fool not to want to dive into that. As I've already told you, I'm not a fool."

Stolas hauled Kalisha on top of him as he leaned back against the arm of the love seat. "You took down those carefully crafted walls inside me like they were cardboard, and you were a class five hurricane."

"I've been called many things, being called a hurricane is a first." Kalisha smiled and kissed him. "How do we do this?"

"We have to do it in front of Lucifer," Stolas admitted. "I'll have Zane dedicate one of the extra bedrooms for you."

"Why? Wouldn't I share yours with you?"

"You don't want your own space?" Their noses were about an inch apart, and her gray eyes were hypnotizing him.

"To sleep? No, I'd rather be with you."

Stolas swallowed; he wasn't sure he'd be sleeping a lot if Kalisha were with him. His body was wound tight already from how she touched him. Stolas wasn't about to deny her request. "I feel like I should warn you that I'm not a hearts and rainbows type of man," he voiced his last warning.

Kalisha's warm laughter soaked into him. "I don't want hearts and rainbows. I want honesty and genuine feelings. I'm happy with you the way you are, Stolas."

"Are you ready to meet Lucifer, then?" Stolas

wondered if she noticed the odd rhythm his heart was beating.

"If that is how we need to do it, then yes, I am ready."

Stolas stood up, lifting Kalisha in the process and setting her gently on the floor. "Zane," he called out.

"Yes, sir." Zane appeared in the doorway.

"Kalisha and I are headed to see Lucifer, to complete the claiming ceremony. From here on out, she will be here in this house and my equal. Can you please notify the staff and see to it that her word carries as much weight as mine does?"

"Very well, sir. Welcome, ma'am." Zane bowed to her slightly. "Whatever you need, simply call my name, and I will appear."

"Thank you, Zane." Kalisha smiled.

Chapter Fourteen

Dakota, could you please let the master know that Stolas and Kalisha are here for a claiming ceremony?"

"Yes, sir. Please wait here a moment." Dakota opened the door and let them in. If Dakota was surprised by the sudden appearance and announcement, he hid it well.

Stolas kept his hand on Kalisha's lower back, unwilling to not be touching her outside of his home. Until the claiming happened, she was still in a great deal more danger than she would be after it. At least with the excuse of the claiming, Stolas would have an opportunity to share with Lucifer the things that Kalisha had told him.

A few minutes later, Dakota appeared back in front of them. "He'll see you in the study, sir."

"Thank you, Dakota." Stolas pushed against Kalisha's back, leading her to the study. He knocked once and then entered, closing the door behind him. Lucifer grinned widely from behind his desk, and Stolas felt the swell of power in the room and knew he'd made it soundproof.

"I'm pleased you took my advice, Stolas, though I didn't expect it to happen so soon."

"That should tell you that things are moving fast." Stolas moved his hand and took Kalisha's. "May I introduce Kalisha? Kalisha, this is Lucifer."

"Stunning. I can see why you want to move quickly on this." Lucifer's voice changed to the enchanting one. "It's a pleasure to meet you."

"Lucy, knock it off," Stolas warned him. "The room is now soundproof, so anything you say is between us," Stolas told Kalisha. "The voice thing is just him being a jerk, I'm afraid."

"Voice thing? Was that what that tingle I felt was?" Kalisha cocked her head sideways and looked at Stolas with a somewhat confused expression.

"Interesting that is all you felt." Lucifer stood and came out from behind his desk. "Are you wearing protections?"

"Yes, I am. One's that I have made," Kalisha answered.

"Formalities aside, Stolas, did you tell her everything that this will entail?"

"He did," Kalisha answered for Stolas. "I'm aware that I have to pledge allegiance to you as well, I become a permanent resident down here, we share our powers and that this is unbreakable."

"And did he tell you about the relationship between him and myself?"

"Yes. Not the nuances and specific details, but enough for me to understand that it's not the same relationship that you have with others and that you are close."

Lucifer chuckled. "Close. Nice way of putting it. Due to the nature of our relationship, I'm afraid that I would have to ask another vow of you. One of silence. It would be binding."

Stolas hadn't even thought of that. "I could do one," Stolas offered.

"No, my dear friend, it would have to be me. However, I do believe that if you didn't find her trustworthy, you wouldn't have told her what you did or be going forward with this little ceremony. Shall we get that part over with then? I'm assuming you have more to tell me since this is happening."

"Please, let's do this," Kalisha stated.

"Very well. Stolas, you start. Kalisha, use what he says in the beginning and only change the wording at the part of the laws, and allow your powers to be open. I have heard some say that if you hold back, it can be painful when mixing."

Stolas looked at Kalisha, the woman he was about to tie himself to for the rest of time. "Kalisha, in this realm and all others, I claim you to be mine forsaking all other interests. From this moment forward, I share my soul with you, and my powers, the laws that govern me, will also govern you. The protection that Lucifer offers me, will be yours, should anyone try to break this bond or bring harm to you the punishment will be severe. You are mine, and I am yours."

Stolas felt his powers rise through the room, waiting for the vows Kalisha would speak. "Stolas," she began, "in this realm and all others, I claim you to be mine forsaking all other interests. From this moment forward, I share my soul with you, and my powers, the laws that govern you will also govern me. The protection that Lucifer offers you, will be mine, should anyone try to break this bond or bring harm to me the punishment will be severe. I am yours, and you are mine."

Stolas caught his breath as Kalisha's powers slammed into him and he settled into hers. It was heady and exhilarating both. Then Lucifer's magic stole over them both, binding the vows to him. "I, Lucifer, ruler of this realm, accept the vows given by Stolas and Kalisha as they claim each other. Kalisha, you are now bound to Hell and the laws I have set in place. I accept responsibility for you and your wish to claim each other."

Stolas felt a burning sensation on the inside of his wrist, a searing hot flash, then nothing more. He heard Kalisha gasp and saw her look at her wrist. Stolas's eyes widened as he saw his name burned into her skin. He yanked up his sleeve and saw her name burned on his.

"Did you not know of this part?" Lucifer sounded surprised.

"No, I didn't. I'm sorry, Kalisha, I would have warned you of that had I known." Stolas felt awful about it too. It had hurt.

"It's fine. I don't mind. I'm assuming this is so it is obvious to others?" Kalisha asked quietly, running her thumb over the raw skin.

"Correct. Now for the vow of silence. I'll need some blood for this." Lucifer handed her a small knife. "A finger prick will suffice."

Kalisha gripped the knife and poked her finger, the blood welling. Stolas held her hand still for a moment, knowing Lucifer had to speak his words.

"Kalisha, by punishment of death, do you swear to hold any information regarding the relationship between Stolas and myself in secret? As well as the power he wields and information we share in this room?"

"I swear." Stolas let go of her hand, and she held the drop of blood out to Lucifer, who took it and pressed it into his wrist, sealing the vow.

"Welcome, my dear. You are quite powerful on your own. How did that feel, Stolas?"

"Exhilarating. It will be harder to keep this power hidden."

"The beauty of this is it's easily explainable by the claiming now. If someone catches wind of whatever you can't hide, you can say it's the combined power of the both of you." Lucifer sat in one of the chairs and crossed his knees. "Before we begin, let's celebrate." Lucifer smiled and called for Dakota to serve them drinks.

After Dakota left, Lucifer sat forward. "The room is sealed once again. Let's hear this new information."

Stolas let Kalisha tell her story and watched the play of emotions that crossed Lucifer's face at the news that Bael might still exist inside Stone. Lucifer wasn't happy about it, and his power reverberated through the room, pressing them down into their chairs.

"It shouldn't be possible," Lucifer roared. "Stolas, I don't think it's only Bael in there. The magic in those stones feels more like the work of a couple of people. What are the chances that he summoned Moloch as well?"

"I don't know. I'm not even sure that Bael survived any of what happened. It could be only his powers that transferred, but I've never heard of that happening either.

With what Kalisha told me, it became apparent that she was in danger, as well as anyone else associated with Airiella."

"Any chance of moving that meeting up?" Lucifer slammed back the rest of his drink.

"No. It's fine. I asked that the guys research Stone and those he came into contact with," Stolas informed Lucifer.

"I don't need to remind you how important it is that we stop this plan. If Moloch comes into power, you and Kalisha both will be in grave danger. I won't be able to protect you. All that power you hold will then be his to command you to do with it as he sees fit."

"I'm aware, Lucy. Beyond that, it means you would die, and that just doesn't work for me either." Stolas closed his eyes for a moment. "She can defeat them both, you know. It might come at a cost to her, and I don't know that I'm comfortable asking her to pay that."

"She'd die, wouldn't she?" Kalisha looked between the both of them.

"Quite possibly," Lucifer admitted. "Not as much of a concern of mine as it is his."

"It's a concern for me as well," Kalisha told Lucifer harshly.

"There's more, Lucy," Stolas started.

"Why do you call him Lucy?" Kalisha interrupted.

"It's a nickname an old girlfriend used to call me when we were kids." Lucifer smiled. "He overheard it, and it stuck. He's the only one who uses it and can get away with it. It's more a term of endearment."

Stolas chuckled. "Moving on, Seir came to see me today. Someone is following him as well. He, himself, suspected Moloch and asked me if I'd noticed anything. He also recalled the prophecy you mentioned as well and related it to Airiella."

"Seir? Of all the princes, he seems like the least likely to have fallen prey to this. What stance will he take, do you think?"

Stolas shifted uncomfortably. "He said he would fight on whatever side I fought on. Lucy, that puts me in a weird spot since I won't fight against Airiella or you. You need to work on your princes and find who your true allies are. Up there, it would be easy to fight against them on her side, without you in the picture. Down here, it would be easy to fight on your side without her in the picture. If you both are there, no side is safe."

"Seir is loyal to you and her both?"

"Seir helped me with her after Bael, and after that soul, I brought to you. I needed transport services. Seir's fond of her."

Lucifer sighed. "You don't make my life easy, my friend. Anyone else?"

"No, Airiella's only met us two. To be more specific, she's met other demons, but has dispatched them all."

Kalisha set her glass down on a table. "It sounds to me like we need to figure out a way to keep this war separate then. He," she pointed at Lucifer, "needs to stay down here if something is to happen with Airiella, or, if he has to come up, then he needs to figure out how to fight on her side against them. I'm assuming it wouldn't be as easy as her coming here to fight against the rest for you."

"Correct." Stolas gave her a crooked smile. "Airiella coming down here is something I've done my best to keep from happening."

"I need to start thinking of the political ramifications if I am fighting on the side of an angel of light." Lucifer drummed his fingers against the arm of the chair.

"What if this isn't as complicated as you think it is?" Kalisha asked him.

"Explain your thoughts," Lucifer demanded.

Stolas shot Lucifer a look at his tone. "Ease up, Lucy."

"I apologize for my tone; I did not mean it to sound so harsh."

"Accepted. My thought is this, if it's known that there is unrest and a coup is getting staged, it won't get questioned that you joined forces with an angel of light to fight against the one that is trying to start a war that will leave the world devastated and take your throne. The enemy of my enemy and all that. Your fight isn't with her, at least not right now."

"This is true," Lucifer hummed.

"Let's cross that bridge when we come to it," Stolas hedged, uncomfortable with the thought of them even fighting near each other. "I'd rather keep them separate, if at all possible. While I don't necessarily believe in prophecies, if she is the one in yours, I don't know that her power wouldn't react by your mere presence. If I can avoid damage to either of you, that is my preferred route. Political ramifications aside, what Kalisha said is correct. You could send loyal legions to help defeat Moloch if it came down to it without having to be there yourself. You showing up is going to give it a lot more attention than if you didn't."

"The flip side of that is me not showing up, allows

others to believe that I am unconcerned with acts of treason. I'm stating that I'm aware of it, and it isn't tolerated by showing up to handle it."

"That's true as well," Kalisha murmured.

"There is no easy answer to this. I've thought of little else." Stolas took a drink.

"Kalisha, I hope you understand how truly remarkable this man is," Lucifer said quietly. "He is my one friend, and while we don't see eye to eye on everything, he knows the real me. The cruel me, and the kind me I am with him, and he loves me anyway. Enough that he followed me to this dismal place. I'm afraid you will see a different side of me when this plays out, but please remember, I will always look out for him."

Startled by the unexpected words, Stolas stared at his friend. "We are all different things, to different people," Stolas returned.

Kalisha intertwined her fingers in his, and Stolas pulled up their hands to kiss her fingers. "I understand, Lucifer. I wouldn't be here right now if I didn't see who he was."

"Let's recap." Stolas wanted to change the subject before she undid him in front of Lucifer. "Stone has a possible connection to Bael and Moloch and is set upon destroying everyone he believes played a part is his downfall. Moloch is recruiting for an army. We've found evidence that supports an uprising we believe Moloch is a part of with plans to pit Lucifer against Airiella. Seir, myself, and Kalisha are getting followed. Twice now, this old prophecy has gotten referenced. Bael and Moloch were close friends. Someone has been utilizing hoodoo magic."

"There's quite a few of those strings that lead to

Moloch," Lucifer pointed out. "I think it's safe to say that Moloch is behind this, even without concrete evidence. Let's also not forget that I am meeting with the angel in seven days now."

"Wait; what?" Kalisha asked, swiveling her head back and forth to look at each of them.

"*We*," Stolas pointed between him and Lucifer, "not him. We are meeting with Airiella. If we can gather enough proof that Lucifer isn't behind this, we can rest assured that she won't voluntarily come after him and instead leave the fight with Moloch. This scenario helps me knowing that two of my closest friends won't try to kill each other."

"Will I get to join you on this?"

"I'd rather not. The less, the better off we are." Stolas squeezed Kalisha's hand. He'd tell Kalisha later she could meet with Airiella the day before at the wedding.

"Here's another thought, do you have someone that could try to penetrate Moloch's forces and give you information?" Kalisha thought out loud.

"It's not quite that easy. If someone has sworn a fealty vow, the individual wouldn't be allowed to speak against Moloch. Since he's trying to do this behind the scenes, chances are he requires anyone he recruits to take that vow. So even if we found someone to send in, they wouldn't be able to tell us anything," Stolas explained.

Lucifer stood up. "I'll start rounds with the princes tomorrow. For now, let's just keep digging. Go home, you two. I need to find a willing bed and relieve some tension." Lucifer grinned wickedly.

"If I have my way, I'll be doing the same." Kalisha grinned back.

Stolas blushed and stood up. "Have fun, Lucy."

"I like her, Stolas. She's got fire. We'll be in touch." Lucifer waved his hands and Dakota came back in to show them out.

Chapter Fifteen

Stolas came out of the bathroom and saw Kalisha on the bed, staring at her wrist. They were both healed already, and the names were black. "Do you regret it?" Stolas leaned against the door frame between the rooms loving the way she looked on his antique four-poster bed with the crisp white sheets.

"Not at all. I was noticing that if I touch your name, I can pinpoint exactly where you are in the house and what mood you are in." Kalisha looked up and smiled. "I was hoping for frisky, and instead, I found nervous."

Stolas's pants were still on, though they were unbuttoned and loose around his waist. At her words, he was instantly hard. "Check again," he replied huskily. "I can feel it when you touch it."

"Oh," Kalisha sighed, "I can work with that." She pointed at his state of undress. "And *that* is an amazing look on you."

"Have patience with me; this is all new for me, and I want to make you feel amazing," Stolas admitted as he stripped. He slid into the bed next to Kalisha, ignoring the compliment that he didn't know what to do with but made him ridiculously pleased that she found him appealing.

Kalisha moved and straddled him. "Just touch me already."

Stolas slid his hands around her waist and up her sides, pulling her down to him, latching on to those juicy lips. The taste of vanilla and berries flooded his senses again, and he rolled, pinning Kalisha under him. "If I let you take control, this will be over way before I'm ready for it to be over."

"That just means we get to start over again." Kalisha wiggled against him, making him groan aloud.

"Hold still," Stolas murmured against her neck. "I'm going to taste all of you."

Stolas did just that. Worked his way down her body, paying particular attention to the places that made Kalisha gasp and moan, the areas she held still for, and the ones that made her arch into his mouth. She tasted divine, and he could have happily spent hours between those legs.

Kalisha was pulling at him, her body trembling, so Stolas gave in and kissed his way back up to her lips. Her eyes were glazed, chest heaving, and he loved it. Loved knowing he could do that, bring that look to her beautiful face and undo her in the same way she destroyed his defenses.

Stolas was determined to go slow and drive them both crazy with passion, yet he feared his body would betray him the moment he sunk into Kalisha. He tried to control his breathing, but she stole his breath with each kiss, and when she wrapped her legs around him, he was lost.

Kalisha was guiding him into her, and Stolas was

helpless to stop it. When he drove his hips into her, the pleasure was so intense he felt like he was going to blackout. Stolas needed to slow down; he didn't want to miss one second of this.

He sat back on his heels and held her hips still. "Give me a moment, my love," Stolas begged her. She was tightly sheathed around him, and every time Kalisha tightened her muscles, he groaned. He ran his hands up her belly and back down, using his fingers to work the little bundle of nerves that drove her wild.

Kalisha cried out again, and he couldn't wait anymore. Stolas's body took over, and they were both lost to the rhythm. Their cries mingling, a sheen of sweat covering them, their gazes locked on each other. She was magnificent as she came around him, driving him right over the edge with her.

Stolas rolled, bringing Kalisha on top of him, so he didn't crush her with his weight, his body still buried in hers as he gasped for breath with her sprawled out on his chest. This gorgeous creature had claimed him, wanted him, and consumed him with her fire.

When Kalisha's breathing was under control, she propped her chin on her fist and looked at Stolas with a smile. "For being so long out of practice, you certainly performed well."

Stolas chuckled. "Not as well as you think. I planned to go slow, that went out the window pretty quickly." He draped his hands over her hips. "I have no control with you."

"Control is overrated. I'll take wild passion with you like that any time. I feel like my body is singing." Kalisha moved and dropped a kiss on his chest.

"I feel lucky, which is at odds with everything going on around us. You do something to me, Kalisha, I don't know what it is, but I love it," Stolas growled and lifted her for another kiss, his body finally slipping from hers. "Let's clean up." Stolas stood with ease, supporting her weight with his arms and carried Kalisha to the bathroom.

"Glad you are carrying me, I'm not sure I could walk right now." Kalisha's dark cheeks flushed with a rosy tint, and her smile was slow and sexy.

A strange mix of emotions hit Stolas as he turned on the shower. "Did I hurt you?"

Kalisha's husky laugh had his body reacting again. "No," she caressed his face, "my legs feel like wet noodles."

"Is that a good thing?" Stolas wasn't sure how to take it.

"Very good." Kalisha clutched at his arms as she stepped in the shower. "Come on, get in."

Stolas stepped in, and Kalisha soaped up her hands and ran them over his body, down over the length of Stolas and cupped him, a wild moan tearing through his throat as Kalisha massaged him. Stolas was shaking under her skillful hands, his body still starved for touch and affection.

It didn't take Kalisha long to bring another shuddering orgasm out of Stolas. It felt too good for him to be embarrassed, and Kalisha looked happy that she did it. Spent, they cleaned each other up and crawled into bed wrapped around each other and slept.

Chapter Sixteen

Something woke Stolas. He kept his breathing even and noticed that Kalisha was still asleep, their limbs tangled together, and her warm body pressed close to his. Stolas opened his eyes slowly and saw a glow in the room and tried to place it.

"Stolas," Kalisha said softly, "you are glowing."

Stolas cursed under his breath. "I think it means Airiella is in danger. She didn't call me."

"Do you need to go check?"

"No. I'll wait until one of them calls me. That must have been what woke me up. I didn't mean to wake you. Go back to sleep, my love." Stolas absently stroked Kalisha's back and arms as she drifted back to sleep, the slow rhythm of her breathing lulling him back to sleep as well.

"Stolas," he heard Kalisha saying softly. "Stolas, wake up."

There was something in Kalisha's tone that told Stolas he needed to listen, but the feel of her against him was more substantial. He just wanted to feel it a little bit more before discovering whatever new disaster awaited them. He didn't know how long they had slept, and he didn't care.

"Whatever it is, it can wait. I just want to lie here for a bit," Stolas murmured, holding Kalisha tight. Her body perfectly molded to him. Heaven might deny him, but this had to be the closest thing to it.

"Sweetheart," Stolas felt her kiss his chin, "whoever is on the other side of that door is about to break it down, and I am very naked. Since I don't know how you feel about others seeing me this way, I felt it was in the best interest of everyone to wake you up."

Stolas bolted awake and was at his dresser in a flash, pulling out one of his shirts and tossing it to Kalisha. "What did we do with the blankets?"

"I was trying to figure out the same thing." Kalisha pulled the shirt over her head and put a pillow over her legs as Stolas pulled on a pair of exercise pants. He checked to make sure Kalisha was decent before flinging open his door.

A startled Zane was there. "I'm sorry, sir. Seir is downstairs and in a bad way."

Stolas froze. The angry words died on his lips. "What do you mean, bad way?"

"He's injured, sir."

"Shit." Stolas turned and saw the bedding bunched up halfway under the bed. He picked it up and tossed it on the bed. "How bad?"

"It's not good, sir."

"Can you get him to one of the extra rooms?" Stolas needed to get dressed.

"I have him in your study, on the couch, sir."

"I'm on my way. Send a message to Lucifer through

Dakota that Seir's injured," Stolas ordered.

Zane bowed. "Right away, sir."

"I'm sorry, my love. Not how I pictured our first morning together being." Stolas changed into more appropriate clothes. "I'll have Zane get you clothing. Better yet. You tell Zane what you need, and he'll get it. But, I rather like how you look in my shirt."

Kalisha laughed. "We'll have the rest of eternity together, right? Go, do what you need to do. I'll talk to Zane."

Stolas crossed the room to her. "Is it ridiculous that I want to spend the day here with you?"

Kalisha wrapped her arms around his neck. "No. I'd like that too. We will get a chance."

Stolas kissed her, his tongue tangling with hers. "I'll see you soon, my love." If Stolas didn't leave the room now, he was doubtful he ever would. He closed the door behind him and raced for the study. Zane already had the medical bag in the room, and Stolas found a very bloody and broken Seir on his expensive leather couch.

"Seir! What happened?" Stolas asked as he kneeled by his friend, wondering where to start.

"Moloch happened," Seir managed to get out between swollen and bloody lips.

Stolas cursed again and mixed up a bottle of water with some of the healing mixes he had made. Stolas held it to Seir's lips and helped him drink as much of it as he could. He pulled out a container of salve to help with the pain and smeared it on Seir's lips and gums.

"I can't heal the broken bones, my friend, I'm sorry," Stolas apologized.

"Stolas, I have called my healer to come here," he

heard Lucifer say from behind him. "Who did this?" Lucifer's tone was cold and hard, and the energy radiating off him was dark and extremely dangerous.

"Moloch," Seir managed to get out again.

"Give him a minute, sir. The pain salve hasn't quite kicked in yet." Stolas spoke formally.

Stolas saw Kalisha come in behind Lucifer, fully dressed and concerned. "May I use your workroom?" she asked Stolas.

Stolas glanced at Seir, who had his eyes closed again, and he moved over to her. "You don't need to ask. What's mine is yours," he told her gently.

"I'm going to make him a protection charm if you don't mind."

"Use my power as well as yours, make as many as you can," Stolas told her.

"How do I use your power?"

"The same way you use yours. Just feel for mine, it will have a different signature, call it to you, and infuse it along with yours. The added power should make them unbelievably strong."

"Will do. How many should I make?"

"Make them for all of Airiella's team and spouses. Seir, Lucifer, yourself. Zane will get you whatever you need."

"You have a supply of stones down there, correct?" Kalisha glanced nervously at Lucifer, who was standing over Seir, his power almost suffocating.

"There is. Use whatever you want. I'll come to check on you in a bit." Stolas gave Kalisha a quick kiss and turned back to Seir. Zane walked in with the healer behind him, and Stolas moved out of the way for him.

"This needs to fucking end," Lucifer growled in his ear. "Moloch attacked another prince, openly. He's declaring war by doing this. The princes are under my protection."

Seir's screams of pain pierced the air as his bones shifted back into place, making them both wince in sympathy. "If this is his intent, I don't think anyone is safe. Did you get any other information from Seir?"

"Not yet. Why would Seir come here instead of to me?"

"Probably because of the salves and whatnot I have. Seir knew I'd send for you." Stolas hoped that was the reasoning at least. "I wouldn't read too much into that. Did anyone see you come here?"

"No, I used the stone." Lucifer's stance was aggressive, and the energy that was rolling off him was making the healer nervous. Lucifer knew it too. Stolas could see him trying to calm himself, but he was too angry. "I can't let this stand."

"And you shouldn't. Let's map this out. If you just react, it could go badly. We need to be strategic," Stolas reasoned.

"Your angel is probably in danger, you know."

"She's not mine," Stolas replied automatically, then stiffened. "Last night, something awakened me, and I was glowing." He looked slowly at Lucifer. "He's topside."

"Moloch is topside," Seir called out. "That's where he was going. He doesn't know where Airiella is."

Lucifer and Stolas were at Seir's side in an instant. "What happened?" Lucifer demanded.

Seir glanced apologetically at Stolas. "Go ahead, he knows everything I know," Stolas told him.

"I sought the prophecy I was telling you about; I told you I'd get it, and I did. Only I ran into an issue named Moloch." Seir shifted painfully and pulled a folded piece of paper out of his pocket and handed it to Stolas. "Moloch was after the same thing." Seir pulled out a feather that stopped Stolas's heart mid-beat. "I think he wanted it to look like Airiella did this to me."

Stolas felt a wave of power that was dizzying tear through the house. "What was that?" Lucifer looked at Stolas wildly.

"Kalisha is making protection charms," Stolas explained, hoping Lucifer would understand she was using both of their powers. "She'll bring one up for you and Seir when she finishes."

"Did you claim her, then?" Seir asked weakly.

"I did. Last night," Stolas acknowledged with a smile to cover his fear over Airiella.

Seir sat up as the healer moved away, bowing low to Lucifer before bolting out of the room. "Moloch took the prophecy; what I gave you was what I copied down right before Moloch got there. He had a legion of demons with him. Moloch ordered them to finish me when he saw what I was holding. He left the feather."

"Moloch assumes you are dead then?" Lucifer asked, eyeballing the feather with interest.

"I don't know if he does or doesn't. Moloch took off, telling them he was going after the angel, join him when they finished. He got one punch in on me," he pointed to his face, "planted the feather, then the legion swarmed me. It took me a minute before I could pop out of there. If they told him I disappeared, Moloch would know I'm not dead and will also assume that I reported the attack. If they don't tell him, then maybe luck is on our side, and he won't expect us."

"Us?" Stolas looked at him blankly. "You are in no shape to fight."

"There are too many of them for you to take on alone, even with the master. Even with *her*."

Lucifer drummed his fingers on his arm. "Strategic," Lucifer mused. "We do nothing until we know if he knows Seir is alive or not. No one knows I am here; we could use this to our advantage. Does he know where the angel is?"

"Not that I am aware of," Stolas told Lucifer. "He's not a tracker and will have to search for Airiella. If I had to guess, Moloch would be near her home, and she is not there. How he obtained the feather, I haven't the slightest idea."

"That meeting needs to happen sooner rather than later," Lucifer said firmly. "Unless you want to put her at more risk than she already is."

"I'll talk to Airiella today." Stolas swore under his breath. He was about to put the warrior in danger along with his new family, and Airiella wasn't going to be happy about that.

Kalisha walked in a few minutes later and handed a stone to Lucifer and another to Seir. "Keep them on you. They won't protect you from a physical beating. However, it will reduce the damage. And they will protect from a magical one."

"Shit, this is a strong stone," Seir murmured. "I apologize for my language, my lady."

"No apologies necessary." Kalisha waved it off.

"I'm putting you on the list to allow in," Lucifer told

Stolas. "Talk to who you need to talk to and get back to me. Kalisha, thank you for this." Lucifer held the stone in his hand. A nasty gleam in his eye as he reined in his anger again. "I hope that you made one for yourself."

"I did."

Lucifer popped out, and Stolas looked between Kalisha and Seir. "Have you two met?"

"No." Kalisha stepped forward. "I'm Kalisha."

Seir kissed the back of her hand. "Seir."

"Are you feeling better now?" Kalisha stepped back to Stolas's side, and his arm automatically went around her.

"Healing isn't a fun process down here. It would have been unbearable if not for the stuff Stolas gave me. Once the pain dies down, I'll be fine."

Stolas turned and grabbed another bottle of water and mixed more of herbal mix he used to dull pain and handed it to Seir. "Drink it down; it'll help."

"Are you going to go see Airiella?" Seir asked Stolas.

"I am. I have no way of knowing if Moloch knows where Airiella is or not. Do you think his army reported you disappearing?"

Seir shrugged. "They looked pretty terrified of Moloch, so I would guess no so that he doesn't know they failed, but I could be wrong. If Moloch was after this prophecy, he is for sure looking for her."

"By her, are you guys referring to Airiella?" Kalisha interrupted.

"We are," Stolas told Kalisha softly. "Did you make stones for them?"

"Yes," Kalisha confirmed, narrowing her eyes at him. "I'm going with you."

"I expected that you would, my love. Seir, anything else I need to know?"

"The mage was with him, Stone."

Stolas felt his blood run cold. If that was true, and if Stone had Bael's power, Moloch could track Airiella. "Stay here as long as you need to. Zane," Stolas called.

"Yes, sir?"

"See to anything Seir needs, Kalisha and I will be out."

"Yes, sir. Would you like the security report before you leave?"

"Did anything happen?" Stolas turned to look at Zane.

"Someone is watching the estate, sir."

Stolas swore again and looked back at Seir. "When you came here, did you go to the front door?"

"No, I popped right inside. No one saw me." Seir struggled to stand, but Stolas motioned for him to stay put. "Lucifer is pissed, be careful."

"Rest, Seir. We may need your skills later."

"I'll be back later this evening if that is okay with you. Right now, I'd like my bed."

"Whatever you think is best for you, just keep that stone on you and watch your back. If you stay here, you are somewhat protected," Stolas pointed out.

"Fine, point me to a room." Seir winced.

"Sir, allow me to take you there." Zane stepped forward and popped them both out.

Stolas grabbed Kalisha's hand and tugged her to him. "I'd hoped we would have time for you to practice with my magic today before any of this came up."

"I'll be fine. It took me a moment to get used to it

147

when I made the stones, but I know how to access it. I'm a fast learner, so we'll do it on the fly. I'll be solid again when we go to see Airiella, won't I?"

"You will," Stolas confirmed. "I can lock us in on Airiella's signal and appear wherever she is as long as she is conscious. If something like what happened last time happens and drugs mask everything, we would need to fall back on a tracking spell, as you did for me before."

"Is that a concern this time?" Kalisha's brow furrowed.

"I honestly don't know." Stolas wanted to know how Moloch got one of her feathers.

"Well, I can tell you that my power fuels yours to a degree I've never felt before. I thought the room was going to burst into flames."

Stolas smiled. "We felt it up here too. Lucifer didn't know what was happening."

"Did I give away your secret?"

"No, not really. Seir knows about me claiming you and would assume the extra power is from you. Seir still doesn't know the extent of my abilities. It won't be a secret anymore if we have to fight, but that also means that I need to practice with my skills since I spend so much time keeping them hidden." Stolas leaned his forehead against hers. "Our schedule is looking pretty busy, my love. I'm sorry."

"I don't mind. Let's go see Airiella; I want to be able to hug her."

Stolas cringed for a moment. "Shit."

"What's wrong?"

"Airiella doesn't know about the claiming; she's only going to see that you are a demon now. I don't know how she will react to that. I didn't even think of that, I'm sorry."

"Stolas, stop apologizing for everything. We'll take it as it comes. Airiella doesn't react badly to you, does she?"

"No," Stolas admitted.

"I'll be with you, and we will be able to explain together. Don't borrow trouble."

Chapter Seventeen

Damnit! That better be you, Stolas!" he heard Airiella mutter.

"It's me, love, relax," Stolas called out.

Ronnie poked his head around the corner, and his eyes lit up as he saw Kalisha. "Am I seeing things?"

Kalisha laughed. "No, I am here."

"Fuck, ouch. Seriously? Ronnie, you better not be screwing with me," Airiella growled as she came around the same corner Ronnie had. "Kalisha!"

"Brace yourself," Stolas warned as the angel barreled into her.

"How? Wait, I don't care," Airiella amended as she hugged Kalisha.

"Airiella, I am so happy to be able to hug you again," Kalisha murmured.

"Why is she a demon?" Smitty's voice came hesitantly from down the hall.

"I don't care, she's here, and I can hug her." Airiella grinned. "Scratch that, I do care, were you hurt?"

Stolas grunted. "You think I would hurt her?"

"Not you, but someone else could have." Airiella crossed her arms and glared at Stolas. "Explain."

"It was my choice," Kalisha said gently. "He is for me like Jax is for you."

Airiella's jaw dropped open. "Well, shit. Congratulations?"

"How about you tell me why there's demon blood on you," Stolas interrupted as he zeroed in on Airiella.

"Because some of your bastards were up here trying to cause issues during our investigation," Airiella retorted. "Not only that, I think a demon possessed my friend, the one who was my wedding photographer, Jamie."

"What happened last night?" Stolas pressed Ariella. "I was woken up by something, and I was glowing. Was it because of your friend?"

"Well, it wasn't the night for me." Airiella grinned for a moment. "You should have been doing something else other than sleeping. I didn't know about Jamie until he showed up here."

Kalisha laughed. "Stolas did that too. We aren't here for that." Kalisha reached in her pocket and pulled out several stones. "Replace the ones you have with these. They are much stronger, and you all are in a lot of danger. Tell us about your friend."

Airiella took the stones and shot a look at Stolas. "Hold up." Airiella handed a stone to Ronnie and one to Smitty. "There are a lot more stones here," she pointed out. "The others are coming."

"For the rest in your group," Kalisha told her.

Stolas saw a very weary Jax coming down the hallway. "Jax, are you feeling alright?"

"I'd probably feel better if I wasn't fighting demons

on very little sleep, much less, ones that were at my wedding." Jax tried to smile but failed. "Are you two married now?"

"In my world, that would be a comparable thing," Stolas told Jax.

Jax slid his arm around Airiella and looked at Kalisha. "Are you happy? Was this what you wanted?"

"It was my choice. Stolas is a remarkable man."

Airiella handed Jax a stone. "Let's hear it, Stolas. What shit storm is about to descend on me now?"

"Moloch is looking for you," Stolas cut right to the chase. "Moloch tried to have Seir killed not too long ago. Did any of the demons you were fighting escape?"

Airiella gasped. "Is Seir okay?"

"He will be, love. Did any escape?" Stolas repeated.

"No," Ronnie answered. "Including her friend, Jamie."

"Where is Aedan?" Stolas looked around.

"One of the demons got a good hit on his leg, he's tying it off now," Jax responded.

"Where?" Stolas snapped to attention.

"Third room down the hall on the left," Ronnie told Stolas.

Stolas took off running, pulling the container he'd thought to bring with him at the last minute. Aedan looked up in surprise as Stolas barged into the room, the bottle already open. Aedan's leg had a large gash across the thigh, and blood was soaking through his pants.

"Stolas, I didn't expect you."

"Put this on the wound. Liberally." Stolas held the container out for Aedan.

"The timing is good. This wound hurts like a bitch."

Stolas helped Aedan stand and supported his weight back down the hallway to the rest of the group. He settled him next to Airiella on the steps of what Stolas assumed was an old hospital. He could smell traces of the black plague in the air. "Where are we?"

"Italy," Ronnie answered.

"The meeting with Lucifer needs to happen as soon as possible. With the attack on Seir, and Moloch, here, searching for you, the time has run out. Moloch has an army of demons with him, and you are drastically outnumbered," Stolas spilled. "Clearly, he knows a lot about you if he got to one of your friends."

"Can Moloch find me?" Airiella asked quietly. "You always seem to know right where I am. Can he do that?"

"Trevor Stone is with him." Kalisha reached forward and took Airiella's hand. "Trevor might be able to find you."

Jax's face froze. "It's true then, what you thought about Trevor?"

"Trevor attacked me," Kalisha told them. "He's after anyone and everyone he blames for his downfall. Not only that, he now has access to magic."

"Ronnie, were you able to find anything out about Stone's stay in prison? Who he had contact with, anything like that?" Stolas hoped Ronnie had been able to find something.

"His cellmate called himself a Satanist and summoned demons all the time," Ronnie told them bluntly. "I don't know if he was successful or not."

Not the news Stolas wanted to hear. "The cellmate may have been successful based on the power that Stone is now wielding. Bael's power may have transferred to Stone, or maybe it's Moloch's. The worst-case scenario it's both."

"Fuck!" Airiella roared. "Can't I have a little downtime to at least have a honeymoon with my husband?" Airiella stood and pulled at her hair. "I had to kill a friend! Jamie was only on the fringes of my life; Moloch shouldn't have been able to get at him. Killing demons is one thing; killing a friend that has been taken over by a demon is totally different. Jax had to stab him with a blessed knife, and when that didn't work, I had to light him up with electricity! Damn it all, Stolas. Why?"

Jax reached up and pulled Airiella back down next to him, kissing her cheek. Stolas felt somehow this was his fault, even though he knew it wasn't. "Can one of you please get ahold of the warrior and tell them all to be on the lookout, I suspect that Moloch went to your home to find you. If so, that puts all of them in danger, especially since he has infants."

The look of horror that crossed Airiella's face sent Stolas's heart plummeting. Whether or not this was his fault, he was the one that put that look on her face. "Stolas, why are you feeling guilty?" Kalisha asked him quietly.

"It's not just them, love. All your friends here, make sure they all carry stones." Stolas reached for Kalisha's hand and squeezed it, not wanting to answer that question in front of them.

Kalisha handed over the rest of the stones. "There are enough for the children as well."

"What will they protect against?" Jax asked.

"Magic of any kind. With our combined powers, I believe a physical assault can still happen, but this will probably reduce the amount of damage you sustain," Kalisha explained. "This means, if you are in the crossfire of Airiella or Stolas firing magic at a demon, it will not harm you."

"That's handy." Smitty studied the stone in his palm that he would give Jillian.

"Come to the hotel tomorrow, I'll meet with your boss then," Airiella replied glumly.

"Thank you, love. Now for the warnings," Stolas began, and Airiella looked up at him sharply. "Do not enter a verbal agreement with Lucifer of any kind. Period. Demons use verbal acknowledgments for their gain. For example, if I were to use magic and ask if I could talk to you again, that magic would bind itself to you, allowing me access to speak to you whenever I want. Agree to nothing. If in doubt, look at me. Lucifer might be my friend, but he is still the ruler of Hell, and a master manipulator if he chooses to be. Do not make aggressive moves against him, as he can use that as an opportunity to attack in the name of defense. I'm not saying he will, but it opens the door for it. Because of my stance on fighting against you, I do not believe he will, but I'd rather you know ahead of time."

"You display none of these traits," Airiella said.

"I am not a ruler. You also need to be aware that Lucifer's voice is a weapon. When he infuses his will and magic with his voice, people tend to fall under a spell that compels them to do whatever he asks. I have no idea if it will work on you or not, but it will certainly work on the rest of you. Also, every single one of you needs to work on putting your walls up around your mind. Airiella, this goes double for you. Lucifer can dive right into your mind to find the information he seeks. He can also alter your reality or memories to suit him. Don't give him an open door."

"Why are we meeting with him again?" Aedan asked, alarmed.

"We are fighting a common enemy," Airiella spoke softly. "You aren't painting a good picture, Stolas. I agreed to the meeting for you. If these things you speak of come to pass and Lucifer tries any of this shit on those I love, I can't promise not to be aggressive or react."

"I know, love. I don't know that Lucifer will try any of it, nor believe that he will, but as I said, I'd rather you prepared. Lucifer knows that I will not stand against you, and he knows I have vowed to protect you all. He values my friendship, but I am also aware that all rules go out the window when it comes to war."

"Will his magic work against us with these stones?" Smitty asked Kalisha.

"I don't know," Kalisha admitted.

"Most likely it would, but I don't know that for sure either. If it does, it will probably be a diluted version. There are safeguards in place when using demon magic for protection, and they usually don't work against Lucifer. With Kalisha's magic in there as well, I can't be sure. We haven't tested them against him, and I doubt we will have time," Stolas told them.

"Do you still want us all there for the meeting?" Jax spoke up.

"Yes," Airiella answered firmly. "I want everyone where I can see them and know they are safe. I'm not budging on that, Stolas."

"It's fine, love. I agree with you."

"Is Kalisha going to be there as well?" Ronnie asked.

"No," Kalisha answered for Stolas. "He told me already I wasn't coming to this one. Which is fine as I am going to use the opportunity to make some more charms that we can use defensively."

Stolas looked at her in surprise. "Brilliant idea." He squeezed her hand again.

"What else do we need to know?" Smitty sounded alert but looked exhausted.

"For the meeting? Nothing. Use me as a guide. If I interrupt and answer for you, accept it, that means it's for your best interest." Stolas tried to think of every avenue he could.

"What does his magic feel like?" Ronnie wanted to know.

"Painful," Stolas answered. "It's heavy and deadly."

"Mine might not be heavy, but I can be just as deadly," Airiella warned. "I won't tolerate aggression from him any more than he will from me."

"Trust Stolas," Kalisha begged Airiella.

"I do," Airiella promised.

"I won't let anything happen to you, love," Stolas promised her.

Airiella's eyes were sad when she looked up at him. "Stolas, I don't think anyone can keep me safe, as much as they want to."

Sadly, Stolas agreed with Airiella, but he would do his best to make it happen. Tears stung his eyes at the look on all their faces. They were looks that told Stolas just how much this one woman had been through already; looks that told him the lengths they would go to to keep it from happening again.

Jax started to say something, and Airiella silenced him with another glance. She glanced back at Stolas. "I'll extract this promise from you as many times as necessary. If it comes down to it, you save them over me. Promise me." Airiella held Stolas's eyes.

Kalisha gasped and looked at him. "You can't do that," she exclaimed.

"I have to, my love," Stolas told her quietly. He looked back at Airiella, his tone grim. "You know how I feel about this."

"I know. But if someone has to die, I'd rather it be me who at least has a chance to come back. I can't live without any of you, so I want to hear no arguments from anyone." Airiella's voice was quiet but firm. "I already know you will, Stolas, so give me your words and your demon magic that make it all real, just in case one of these stubborn but well-intentioned men tries to go around me to change your mind."

"Damn it, angel," Ronnie snarled, his face tormented.

"It's not negotiable, Ronnie." Airiella cast her eyes down, and Stolas unintentionally squeezed Kalisha's hand too hard. Her gasp let him know, and he released it immediately, looking over at her.

"I'm sorry, my love," Stolas whispered to her. Kalisha's eyes filled with tears as she gazed at Airiella, silently begging him not to make this promise.

"Just do it, Stolas." Jax's voice carried to him, the pain in his words evident. "She won't relent, we all know it."

Stolas closed his eyes, the all too clear memory of Airiella's screams, pain, and dying fresh in his mind as he knew it was in all of theirs. Stolas would rather promise to save them the agony of seeing that again, but he knew he couldn't, knew she was right.

"I promise you, Airiella." Stolas let his magic swell around the words, "that if it comes to it, I will save the lives of those you love before attempting to save yours."

Airiella let out a sigh, and Stolas saw Smitty pull her down to his lap and hug her, his shoulders shaking. "Thank you."

Kalisha buried her face in Stolas's shoulder and turned her back to the group. "He might promise that, but I don't," Kalisha said quietly.

"My love, she includes you, Seir, the warrior, and his family and all the rest in that promise. I've already promised you safety. If that means I have to remove you from the situation, I will. I'm not sacrificing you, neither will she," Stolas told her in a low voice the others couldn't hear.

"You can't let her die, Stolas."

"Airiella's stronger than me, my love. It's also part of the vow I made to her to keep them *all* safe. She didn't make me promise not to save her, just that I had to save them first. Nor did Airiella specifically make me promise not to enlist others to help. You asked her to trust me, and she does, now you need to trust me as well."

Kalisha nodded slowly and turned back to face them, her face streaked with her tear tracks that made him want to unleash all of Hell on Moloch, so he didn't have to enforce that promise or see tears on Kalisha's face again.

Smitty stood, handing Airiella to Jax and walked down the hallway, Aedan and Ronnie, on his heels. "I'm sorry, Stolas. I can't be alive if they aren't. Whatever it is about me that makes me so different will die with them. If I know they are here, then I have a reason to come back."

Jax made a choking sound and tried to move to follow the others, but Airiella held him in place. Stolas wished there was a way to communicate with Jax, all the loopholes the promise he made has so that Jax understood Stolas would do everything he could to make sure it didn't happen. The problem with just voicing it was that Airiella would make him reword the promise.

"They aren't mad at you, Stolas," Airiella told him. "They aren't even furious at me. They just don't like it."

"I know, love. I don't like it either. Do you understand why they feel that way? Put yourself in their shoes and imagine seeing what they have to witness watching you die, or even simply getting injured. I understand why you extract the promise from me, but I also understand their viewpoint. I've seen it, and it was the worst thing I have ever witnessed. It broke something inside me, love, and I don't have the same ties with you that they do. Be easy on them, shit, be easy on me," Stolas said roughly.

"If this Moloch is bringing the fight to me, I will do what is necessary to keep them safe."

"You need them, love. We can't win this fight alone. Even with all your power, they have the numbers to overwhelm us. You need to let them help and trust in them as they trust in you." Jax gave Stolas a grateful look. "Wasn't that part of your wedding vows to Jax?" Stolas felt like an ass for bringing it up.

Airiella glared at Stolas in response, then seemed to cave in on herself. "Fuck, I'm an asshole. I'm sorry, Jax." She tucked into his side. "I can't lose him, Stolas. My heart beats for him."

Kalisha stepped forward. "You won't lose him. I believe in you, Airiella. We will get through this, all of us, together."

"What time tomorrow, love? Time works a little

differently for me than it does here," Stolas asked.

"How about I just call you when I'm ready?"

"I will only agree to that if you aren't thinking of telling me you'll never be ready, and that's why you won't call for me."

Airiella laughed. "I hadn't even thought of that, but it does sound like something I would do. I just want to make sure that everyone can get some sleep and food in them beforehand. Pretty sure after meeting the Devil, none of us will feel like eating."

Stolas studied Airiella's face, and seeing no signs of a trap, agreed to wait until she called for him. "Go finish your investigation. Oh, wait. Call the others back out here, please."

Airiella gave Stolas an odd, look but soon they reappeared and stood loosely in the hallway and looked at her. Even Kalisha was giving him a look. Stolas raised an eyebrow at them, and they finally moved and went to stand near Airiella.

"In case there are more demons here, I'm going to test those stones now. Who wants to be a guinea pig?"

"I'll do it, Stolas," Kalisha told Stolas.

"You can't, it needs to be one of them," Stolas told her.

"Then you damn well know it will be me." Airiella stepped forward to an armbar from Ronnie.

"The fuck it will, angel. How far do you think you can push me in one night? Do your fucking blue fire around these guys. I'll do it." Ronnie was angry. Out of all of them, Stolas figured that Smitty and Ronnie picked up that this fight would be more dangerous than all the ones before.

Stolas watched Ronnie go back to the hallway and

stood there alone, his body tense. Stolas looked back at Airiella and patiently waited while she argued with Ronnie in her head. Soon the blue fire appeared around them, and Stolas let his magic well up inside him.

Ronnie's face changed slightly. He could feel the pressure of the magic, and Stolas wasted no time and let it flare out. The energy backlash took Ronnie right off his feet and hurled him backward down the hall, but Ronnie's fighter instincts took over, rolled, and landed smoothly, none the worse for it.

"It worked, there was no pain," Ronnie said tersely and walked off again.

"Give me a minute, please," Stolas said to them all and went after Ronnie.

Stolas found him in one of the rooms and approached slowly. "I get it, Ronnie."

"Then why'd you do it?" Ronnie growled out.

"Can she hear you right now?" Stolas waited.

"No, I shut her out," Ronnie confirmed.

"I did it because Airiella's statement has a lot of loopholes that I can workaround. Please trust me in saying that I will do everything I can to save her as well as all of you. My promise to Airiella says nothing about enlisting help. I will get her out of there if it comes down to it. The only thing I can't get around is the vow I gave her on her wedding day included all of you. With her promise on top of it, I have to save you first. It doesn't mean I let Airiella die. Work with me, please." Stolas reasoned with Ronnie.

"Level with me, man." Ronnie crossed his arms, "how much worse is this than the other times?"

"It's worse," Stolas admitted. "But we aren't alone. I can't fight Lucifer, and I can't fight Airiella. Nor will I. We must work together on this, as much as you guys and Lucifer don't like it, it's the only way this will work. We have a common enemy. This fight won't be like it was with Bael. Yes, he showed up with a legion, but that legion is small compared to what Moloch will bring. With Bael, we also didn't have Lucifer."

"Doesn't matter what we do, he's coming, right?"

"Correct. Despite my doing everything I could to keep Airiella off the radar down there, she's too bright. This plan completely caught me off guard, and we are still uncovering it. I'm doing everything possible to cover all contingencies. That promise wasn't to piss you off."

"Airiella won't admit it to anyone but Jax, maybe, how hard all this is on her. She jokes and tries to play it all off, but when she's asleep, and her guard is down, we all know the truth. You'll see the truth of it tomorrow on her face. She'll have dark circles under her eyes because I can guarantee you, she won't sleep now."

"I wish I could change this, Ronnie. Believe me. I wish I could change it and make it go away. Please, just trust me." Stolas didn't know what else he could do.

"Trusting you isn't the issue, man." Ronnie sighed. "You better not let me miss my wedding."

Stolas cracked a small smile. "I wouldn't dream of it."

They walked out to see Airiella and Kalisha huddled together, and the other three guys were sitting on the stairs. Jax stood up. "We'll see you tomorrow, then." Jax held out his hand, and Stolas shook it.

"Ask Ronnie what I told him about that promise. Try to get some sleep, all of you. Including her." Stolas nodded at Airiella.

"No promises from me, but we'll do our best." Jax gave a tight smile.

Stolas went to pull Kalisha from Airiella, and she threw her arms around him. "Don't let me down, Stolas."

"Have I ever?" Stolas kissed the top of her head.

"Not yet. Something feels different this time," Airiella told him, worry in her eyes.

"You are right about that." Stolas tapped her chest. "Whatever it is in there that makes you so special, believe in it. I know I do. In fact I've staked my own life on it."

Airiella stared at him, and Stolas could see that she was getting ready to argue with him, but he grabbed Kalisha's hand and popped back home before her words could get out.

Chapter Eighteen

Zane," Stolas called out as they popped in.

"Yes, sir?"

"How is Seir?" Stolas ignored the glare that Kalisha was giving him.

"He's sleeping, sir."

"Anything else happening?" Stolas questioned.

"No, sir."

"Send a message through Dakota. Tell him the meeting will be tomorrow. I don't have a specific time; she will call me."

"Through normal channels, sir?"

"No. Don't be seen." Stolas turned to the angry woman next. "What did I do?"

"You just left without giving her a chance to talk."

"I know Airiella's arguments already, Kalisha. I've been down this road with her before. Airiella's fuming right now; I can guarantee it. I didn't lie to her. I staked my life on her. I've already told Lucifer I won't fight against Airiella, and nor will I fight against him. If forced to choose, my life will be forfeit either way."

"You didn't need to tell her that!"

"Yes, I did. I don't lie to Airiella. Just as I won't lie to you, if Airiella needs a reminder of what's at stake, I'll give it to her."

"What happens to me if you die?" Kalisha whispered.

"Then everything I have goes to you, and it becomes up to Lucifer to decide if you take my position or not," Stolas replied, confused.

"I'm not worried about that, you giant ass! I'm worried about you!"

Understanding women wasn't Stolas's strong suit. "If I die, you'd feel it, but you'd survive."

Kalisha stared at him dumbfounded and then flounced away in a huff. Stolas stood there, silently wondering where he'd gone wrong. He honestly had no clue.

"For someone so smart, you're an idiot," Seir said from behind him. "Wasn't trying to eavesdrop my friend, but it was hard not to hear the yelling from the other side of this door."

"What did I do wrong?" Stolas asked Seir. He'd take any advice he could get.

"What *didn't* you do wrong? Technically you answered Kalisha's question but didn't listen to her tone or see her body language. Have you not been in a relationship the entire time you've been down here?"

"No, I haven't." Stolas shrugged.

"Kalisha doesn't want you to die because she loves

you. Not because of any other reason than that."

"Oh." Stolas wondered why Kalisha didn't just say that then.

"Hasn't the angel taught you anything?"

"How do I fix this?" Stolas asked.

"Learning to listen to the emotions behind the words would be a good start. What else have you learned about what's happening?"

"I'm taking Lucifer to meet with Airiella tomorrow. How are you feeling?" Stolas gave him a cursory look over.

"Tired. Not ready yet, but if you need me, I could pull it off."

"How much defensive magic do you know?" Stolas was trying to think ahead.

"Not a whole lot. I could do it in a pinch if I had to. I'm a lover, not a fighter."

Stolas shook his head. "Do you think I'm that much of a fighter?"

"No, but you certainly aren't a lover either if you haven't had a relationship the whole time you've been here." Seir snorted.

"Fine, I get it. Kalisha is going to stay behind for the meeting. She said she is going to work on some defensive magic. I figured if you knew some, you could help. If not, no big deal. Kalisha's pretty powerful on her own."

"If that little surge from earlier was any indication of Kalisha's power, you are right."

"That was the result of both our powers combining," Stolas hedged.

"Kalisha must have had power in life." Seir shifted his weight with a wince.

Stolas pulled out the pain salve from his pocket and

handed it to Seir. "Put some on your gums and over the injury."

"Will it dull my senses?"

"No, just take the pain away." Stolas watched while Seir lifted the legs of his pants and smeared some over his shin. "She was a hoodoo priestess in life. The most powerful one that lived."

Seir raised his eyebrows. "Wow. Nice find. Kalisha's got the power of the Gods of old behind her then. I could probably find a book or two she could use if you want."

"I'll leave that up to Kalisha. I'll probably need your transport skills in the upcoming days. Airiella extracted another promise from me," Stolas admitted, defeat lining his tone.

"Save the others before you save Airiella?" Seir asked with a smirk.

"Good guess. I didn't point out the loopholes."

"Better that you don't. Airiella's smart enough to remember to correct that next time. Has she seen any sign of things up there?"

"Airiella was fighting demons when we appeared. None escaped, and they were ash by the time I got there, so I couldn't see where they were from." Stolas ran his hands through his hair, making it messy.

"Don't tell me where she is. That way, if caught again, I can't tell them, and they won't be able to see it."

"Don't get caught again," Stolas warned.

"The less that know, the better off we are. You know it's true, and I'm not offended by that. I'll hang around here for the most part if you think I need to; otherwise, I'll go home."

"I think you are safer here. If Moloch wants to know

if you are dead or not, home is where he'd look for you first. I'm not saying you can't go there, just that it's safer if you stay here."

Seir yawned. "If you finished pissing your woman off, I'm going to go back to sleep. It's been a while since I've taken a beating like that."

"I'm truly sorry for getting you involved at the beginning, Seir. If I hadn't, you would have been safe."

"Eh, I also wouldn't have gotten to meet a charming angel and be her knight in shining armor, which was a nice change of pace. I don't fault you, Stolas. I will ride your ass if you don't fix things with that beauty you managed to snare."

Stolas let out a breath. "First, I have to figure out how."

"You're smart, you'll figure it out eventually." Seir laughed and closed the door.

Stolas made his way to the kitchen and found Hazel putting the finishing touches on dinner. "Perfect timing. Can you serve it in the dining room, Hazel? Maybe light a couple of candles? Women like that, right?"

"Some women, do, yes, sir."

"By any chance, would you know if the one here does?" Stolas tried not to sound hopeful, but he figured she saw through his ruse.

"I don't, sir. Sorry. She's only been here a day."

"I've already managed to make Kalisha mad, and now I need to try and figure out how to fix it."

"My advice, sir? Apologize, and mean it. Learn from it."

"Sage advice, Hazel, and I'll follow it. Hopefully, the candles and a good dinner that I had nothing to do with preparing will help." Stolas was going to be lucky if he made it through the next month without alienating Kalisha at the rate he was going.

"I'll take care of it, sir." Hazel turned and opened a cupboard and pointed to a package. "The last advice, sir, chocolate."

Stolas smiled at that. "Thank you, Hazel."

Stolas set off to find Kalisha, and she was in the last place he figured she'd be, his bedroom. Kalisha was on her back on the bed, staring at the ceiling. Her posture was tense, but her face looked sad. Stolas sat down next to Kalisha on the bed, took her hand, and stroked his thumb over the back of it.

"It got pointed out to me that I may be smart, but when it comes to you, I am an idiot. I'll gladly concede that fact, and I can only hope that you'll accept my sincerest apology and help me understand my mistake."

"Zane called you an idiot?" Kalisha almost smiled at that.

"No, not Zane. Seir."

"I like Seir." Kalisha rolled to face him. "Do you truly not know?"

"I sincerely didn't. Seir told me you were upset by the thought of me dying because you loved me. It never occurred to me to think that, because you were open with me about not being in that place yet. Aside from that, I'm hopeless when it comes to relationships. I've never really had one, much less than for all eternity and with someone I wholly loved."

"You love Airiella, and you have a relationship with her. Just as you do, Lucifer," Kalisha pointed out bluntly.

"Airiella is committed to Jax and the other guys.

Lucifer is the closest thing to a brother I've ever had. You, my love, are entirely different from both of them."

"How am I different, Stolas?"

Stolas tried to do as Seir suggested and read Kalisha's tone and body language, but he was as lost as ever. The only thing Stolas could think to do was use a comparison. "You saw today how the guys reacted to the promise. Did you notice Jax, though?"

"The crushing weight of Airiella's words on Jax? The devastated look on his face? The way Jax didn't argue with Airiella even though he wanted to? Yes, I saw it."

"That's how I feel about you. It's different than how I feel about Airiella. When Airiella said that she couldn't live without them, my only choice was to grant her the promise. If the reverse situation were true, I'd extract the same promise from someone else about you. It has nothing to do with sex or being starved for touch the way I starved myself. It's about how you make me tongue-tied, how I forget the most basic things around you. The way my heart races when you smile, and the way I wanted to light Hell on fire to make sure you never shed tears the way you did earlier."

Stolas stroked Kalisha's face, mesmerized by the contrast of his skin on hers. "It's easy to make comparisons to Airiella because she's the only other person I've been in love with, and when the two of you are side by side, I find I'd still choose you given a choice. The love I have for Airiella is different. I thought it was all-consuming until you touched me the way you did the other morning. The touch may have been sexual, yes. But it also woke me up."

"You aren't as bad at this as you think you are." Kalisha leaned into Stolas's touch. "I might not be able to say the words yet, because that is my fear, I do feel them though. Seir was right about that. I express my feelings better through touch than I do words."

"Well, you have me beat. I'm not good at expressing my feelings at all. I promise to learn." Stolas stood up and offered Kalisha his hand. "Hungry? Hazel has dinner ready."

Kalisha stood up on her own, but then took Stolas's hand anyway. "If Stone hadn't done what he did, what course do you think you and I would have followed?"

"I'd have figured out a way to be around you more. I'm slow about this stuff, but I was aware of the draw I had to you. Caught me unprepared, too." Stolas was sure about that.

"You believe then that Stone just sped things up and that this would have ended up this way anyway?"

"I haven't put that much thought into it, but yes, I do believe it. I'm not prone to falling in love, or there would have been a string of failed relationships behind me." Stolas kissed Kalisha on the top of her head. "If this is too fast for you, say so. I'll take this at whatever speed you want."

"The speed we are going is fine. It just will take some getting used to by both of us." Stolas led Kalisha down to the kitchen and held her chair out for her and then seated himself. "The candles are a nice touch," she said and she winked at him.

"After dinner, we can go out and practice using my magic if you'd like," Stolas offered.

"Where would we do that?"

Stolas thought about it. "Is your place visible to others?"

"No, but I'm not sure it could withstand your magic, either."

"Then we'll pay a visit to Lucifer. He can shield us from prying eyes," Stolas thought out loud.

"Can't you do that?"

"To an extent, yes. I haven't tried it since our powers combined, but if you are more comfortable here, we will stay here and do it," Stolas conceded.

"I am more comfortable here if you don't mind."

"Not at all." They ate in silence for a bit, and when they finished, Kalisha stood and started to clear the table. "My love, Hazel, will do that."

"I can do it, too. I'm not entirely comfortable being waited on hand and foot, either. Don't argue with me, Stolas."

Stolas snapped his mouth closed and assessed Kalisha. He'd let Hazel know it had nothing to do with her skills or either of them being displeased with her. Kalisha's movements were graceful and strong. Stolas had no idea he'd be staring after Kalisha until she came back in the room and cleared her throat, an amused smile on her face.

"See anything you like?"

Stolas blushed and looked down at the table. "I have no idea what to say. You told me to stop apologizing, so I don't want to say I'm sorry. You just mesmerize me. I was thinking about how powerful and graceful the way you move is."

"Oh." Kalisha came closer to him. "You can say things like that. No one has ever told me that before. You are so different from the other men that have been in my life I feel just as much of an idiot as you say you do."

Kalisha sat down next to him. "Did you love your

daughter's father?" Stolas couldn't help asking.

She took a few minutes before answering. "I thought I did. I'm not sure now. It doesn't feel the same way it does with you, but I suppose it wouldn't. You don't love different people in the same way, as you pointed out with Airiella. On a young and naïve level, I suppose I loved Adeben. It devastated me when he left, choosing another person over me. My power made him insecure, Adeben wanted to hold power in the relationship, and I could no more change that about myself than you could have changed falling in love with Airiella."

"He's a fool if he left you by choice." Stolas was glad he had though.

"Maybe. If Adeben hadn't, would I be here right now? I try to look at things that way. Because of him, I chose to learn more about my power, embrace it, and give my daughter up for adoption so that she could have a normal life. It brought me to the council that introduced me to Airiella, and even though I died, it brought me to you. I can't be sorry about that, can I?"

Stolas took Kalisha's hand and held it against his rapidly beating heart. "Do you feel that? That's the effect you have on me."

Kalisha leaned forward and moved her hand, kissing the spot her hand had just been. "Degataga told us once that Airiella was the most unlikely angel to have ever existed. Dega wasn't wrong. I think you are the most unlikely demon to have ever existed. Everything you do is to help others. You aren't so different from Airiella. Just where you reside."

Stolas was about to argue that point vehemently, but Kalisha silenced him with a kiss. His soul bore plenty of stains. Maybe far less than others, but they were still there, and Stolas knew it. He let it go because lost in Kalisha's kiss was where he wanted to be right now, and he'd take it.

Chapter Nineteen

Feel the way it moves when you have a hold of it. Notice the flow is slightly different than yours, but you can meld them together for more power. Now visualize what you want to do," Stolas told Kalisha. Seir was standing closer to the house but watching them practice.

"Do you want me to release it since we have an audience?" Kalisha asked Stolas quietly.

"Yes, just not full power. You aren't playing with all the power right now; you only grabbed hold of a small part of it."

A few feet in front of them, a rock exploded into thousands of smaller shards. Stolas thought it wasn't a terrible defensive move. It wasn't an expected one, and if Kalisha directed the shards, it could be quite useful.

"Is that what you were going for, my love?" Stolas watched Kalisha's face.

"Mostly. It's not something people expect to happen during a fight. I'm trying to think outside the box and of ways that I can catch them off guard. If someone had been standing there, instead of letting the shards fall, I would have sent them at whoever I was fighting with a force strong enough to penetrate the skin."

"I like it. It can also happen from a distance, which could effectively keep you out of range from physical fighting. Your imagination is your limit for those kinds of moves. Now try something different, see if you can feel the energy of the air around us, or the ground under us," Stolas guided her.

"Yes, I can feel those, I just didn't want to go crazy playing with them in front of your friend."

Stolas smiled at Kalisha. "Do something small like make a breeze go around my head," Stolas instructed her. "He won't notice that unless you try to blow my head off."

Stolas felt the air around him stir. "For me, that is easier than the exploding rock," Kalisha replied with ease.

"I also have the same power Lucifer does at getting in minds. It's one I rarely use, and one that doesn't work against the ones I want to use it on."

"Airiella?"

Stolas chuckled. "Correct. Sometimes I wish I could see just where Airiella's train of thought is going when she does things that make no sense to me."

"You want me to try on you, or Seir?"

"Seir, he knows I have this power. He might not expect it you to use it, though. Mental power is a little trickier; you'll have to feel for Seir's signature and sort of use your mind to caress it gently. The trick with this is you want it to be unknown. If you just force your way in, it can get used against you."

"I can feel Seir, but there aren't any openings."

"It won't work, Queen," Seir called out. "I'm protected, remember?"

"Oh, damn. I forgot about that," Kalisha commented. "Why did Seir call me Queen?"

"No idea." Stolas shot a look at Seir. "Seems like you know how to in theory at least, but Seir was aware, so you'll need to work on being more gentle."

"Ok, so can you only work with air and ground, or can you work with all elements?"

"I don't have much luck with water. Fire I can do." Stolas held a fireball in his hand.

Kalisha mimicked him and turned to throw it at Seir, who caught it and tossed it back to her. "What do I do now?"

Stolas caught it. "It doesn't burn me. For you, I'd rather not test that boundary. If they get thrown at you, use the air to either stop it or turn it back around like a giant ping pong ball. Redirect it or hold it until you see an opening to lob it. You can also feed it to make it large or shrink it to make it nothing." Stolas fizzled it out.

"What about what you did back there with Airiella?"

"I just call those energy blasts. I let my power well up into me, leaving it wild and giving it the intention to either kill or hurt. In that case, it was to kill demons. Then once it's at a level I think is sufficient, I push it out hard. The stone you made absorbed the killing intent, and only pure energy hit Ronnie. That is usually my go-to defensive move. Since my power is more than others, it's effective."

"If it's effective for you, it would be effective for me, right?"

"Yes. It takes a little to recharge after that. Since I've only really used it against two or three demons at once, that's all I've tested it on. With an entire legion, I don't know that it would work. It would take out some at full power, but I doubt it would be all of them. Then I would be powerless until the expended energy had a chance to recharge."

"How long would it take to recharge?"

"For me, probably about ten minutes. Lucifer has said if I tap into the energy around me, I can get it done faster, I just haven't ever needed to, and that isn't something we can practice right now."

"I had a minor healing gift," Kalisha told Stolas. "With our combined power, do you think I would be able to heal?"

"Good question. If you had it before, then it's still there. I don't know if it grew or not. Seir healed, so we can't test that on him." Stolas pulled out a knife and sliced his hand open. "See if you can heal it."

Kalisha gaped at Stolas but took his hands in hers, and he felt the warming energy seeping into him. The bleeding slowed, and very slowly, the wound closed. Stolas could see it took her effort to make it happen, and Kalisha probably used up a good chunk of energy to do it.

"Well, I can do it, but it didn't happen very fast."

"In an emergency, all you'd need to do is stop the bleeding. Good work, my love."

"How about you do not do that again? What if I couldn't heal it?"

Stolas pulled her closer. "I would have used one of my remedies and been fine." He kissed Kalisha lightly. "How do you feel about using our magic?"

"I'm fine with it. It's nice not to have always to encase it in a stone or a charm. But it's given me several ideas of defensive stones I could make and hand out. I believe that Airiella would be able to explode them, as well as you or me, and release the magic contained within. Kind of a double whammy. The stone shards exploding outward as well as the magic contained within being set free."

Stolas couldn't help the laugh that bubbled up inside him. "I don't know if I should be impressed or scared."

"Both? I just want to be able to contribute as much to this fight as I can. I'm not good with physical fighting, but as you said, these work at a distance." Kalisha wrapped her arms around Stolas.

"Seir said he might be able to find a couple of books on defensive magic for you to go through if you'd like," Stolas told her. He didn't want Kalisha near the fighting at all, but he couldn't see a way around it.

"Really? That would be helpful. More knowledge never hurt anyone." Kalisha tipped her chin up and looked at Stolas. "Was it just me, or did the guys around Airiella seem a little more than normal to you?"

"They did, but I noticed it at the wedding. I think it had something to do with the vows we all gave Airiella. It certainly made their life force stronger. I didn't have a whole lot of time to sit around and study them."

"Next question, what does Moloch look like?"

"In his demon form, Moloch looks somewhat like a large bull. He would be large, have vicious sharp horns, and look like he was burning. Moloch used to have wings, not sure if he still does or not. In the human form, I have seen Moloch as an older man, though, still large and very strong. I've also seen him as a younger man. Moloch's size will be what gives him away. He is large," Stolas described.

"You are large, Jax is large, Ronnie is huge. Define large to me."

"I would say closer to seven or seven and a half feet tall and double Ronnie's size in demon form. Moloch would be able to pick you up in one hand and crush you. In human form, still larger than Ronnie."

Stolas saw fear in Kalisha's eyes. "What are you in demon form?"

Stolas smiled. "Either an owl with long legs or a raven."

"Like Airiella?"

"Bigger than Airiella's raven, but yes." Stolas pushed Kalisha's hair back behind her ears.

"I'm not sure if I'm happy about that, or would rather you be something terrifying enough to scare Moloch away."

Stolas tried to paint a picture for Kalisha. "Imagine you are sitting outside, like at a park, and there are ravens in the trees. Would you know you were in the presence of a prince of Hell, a demon that has enough power to take all the life from the park with a single flick of his wing?"

Kalisha shuddered. "Utterly terrifying thought. Moloch would be harder to hide. I see the distinction."

"There's a reason I blend in and have the power I do. Moloch is strong, no doubt about that. I am stronger, and I can blend in where Moloch can't. In either form."

"I wouldn't say you blend in exactly. You are too good looking." Stolas blushed again and became reduced to the tongue-tied version of himself Kalisha brought out in him.

"You don't think you are handsome?"

"I can't say I've ever really thought about it," Stolas answered her honestly.

"You and Lucifer both look like walking sex. It's

unfair. Come to think of it, Airiella's men are the same way."

"Walking sex?" Stolas spluttered. He had never gotten called that before. Lucifer probably had, but not him.

"The first time I saw you, my first thought was how does Airiella collect these absurdly sexy men. My second thought after learning who you were, was that demons should be ugly." Kalisha grinned at Stolas. "I'm ridiculously happy that you aren't, but it wouldn't matter to me if you were. It was what was in here," Kalisha tapped on his chest, "that pulled me in like a magnet."

Stolas had no idea what to say to that and told her as much. Stolas led Kalisha back to the house and met Seir at the door. "She's good with her magic," Seir acknowledged.

"Even he's got sex appeal." Kalisha nodded at Seir, then turned to him. "Stolas said you had a couple of books I could look through."

"You think I'm sexy?" Seir grinned at Kalisha, turning on his charm.

"Yes, not as sexy as Stolas, sorry. Books?"

"I can go get you a couple if you'd like, but it looks like you don't need them."

"It wouldn't hurt for me to go through them. If it's not a bother to you, I'd like to borrow the books." Kalisha reversed the charm Seir was using on her and channeled it back at him.

"Not a bother to me at all. I'll pop out and retrieve the books. They'll be on the table here for you when you come down." Seir popped out.

Stolas leaned over and picked Kalisha up, tossing

her over his shoulder. "Woman, stop calling other men sexy. I'm not used to this jealous feeling, and now I have the urge to take you straight to bed."

"Get moving then," Kalisha said. "This view is enticing," she teased him, patting his ass.

Stolas took the stairs two at a time and shut and locked his bedroom door, enacting the sound seal he had put on it. "Now, what should I do about this jealousy?"

"You aren't going to do anything, you are going to shut up and let me prove to you that you are the only one I want," Kalisha murmured in Stolas's ear as she pulled his clothes off.

"Is that how this jealousy things works? So, if I made you jealous, I'd have to strip you and prove you are the only one I want?" Stolas asked for clarification purposes.

"Not exactly. If you made me jealous, I'd be furious and mean, and then I'd have you in whatever way I wanted. I would make sure that it was so good that it canceled any thought of others that had been in your mind. Afterward, I'd probably cut you off from sex as a punishment, with only the reminder of how good I am to keep you warm." Kalisha yanked his pants down, and Stolas stepped out of them, helping her.

"Seems unfair," Stolas gasped as she wrapped her lips around him. Kalisha stood up and kissed him.

"I'll get mine; don't you worry about that. Right now, I just want to taste you as you tasted me." Kalisha pushed him back on to the bed and straddled his legs. "Do I have a reason to be jealous?"

"Never. Only you have ever made me react like this." Stolas clenched his fingers around the blankets under him as she made some movement with her tongue that almost sent him flying off the bed it felt so amazing. "Kalisha," Stolas groaned.

"Shh, let me do this, Stolas." Kalisha cupped his balls and stroked her fingers behind them, his eyes rolling to the back of his head. "Remember, I express myself through touch. Give me this gift." She kissed over his belly button.

"Will you allow me to return the favor?" Stolas grunted out as she sucked him down again.

"Yes, now hush." Kalisha went back to work, and Stolas lost all ability to think.

Chapter Twenty

Stolas woke up and stretched; his muscles pleasantly sore, and his mind calm. Kalisha curled into his side, one of her legs thrown over his hips. In all his years Stolas, had never imagined the pleasure Kalisha gave him was at all possible. Now he couldn't imagine not having her here with him.

Stolas tried to slip out of bed without waking Kalisha, but those beautiful cashmere eyes opened, and all thoughts he had about getting out of bed left his mind. Stolas rolled over and settled himself between her legs. "Good morning, my love," he said and he braced himself on his elbows and took possession of her lips.

Kalisha moaned and arched up into Stolas as someone knocked at the door. Giggling, she pushed him. "Go on, get the door."

Stolas stood up, tucking the blankets around every bit of Kalisha's skin that showed before pulling his pants on and flinging open the door. "What?" Stolas barked at a started Seir.

"Am I interrupting?" Seir grinned at the look on

Stolas's face. "Are you learning anything, Stolas?"

Stolas growled, deep in his throat. "What do you want, Seir?"

"Lucifer is downstairs," Seir said with a smile. "He doesn't look nearly as satisfied as your lady does."

Stolas heard Kalisha laugh. "Stolas is a swift learner," Kalisha called out.

Stolas blushed and pushed Seir out of the way as he closed the door. "Take your time," Stolas told Kalisha. "I've got to get down there."

"I'll be right behind you." Kalisha crawled out of bed and went straight to the bathroom. Stolas heard the shower turn on and briefly thought about joining Kalisha, then deciding the ribbing he'd get from both Lucifer and Seir might not be worth a quickie. Stolas would rather take his time, and if Lucifer was here, that means time wasn't something Stolas had.

Finished dressing, Stolas headed downstairs and found Lucifer in the dining room talking with Seir. Lucifer looked up at Stolas as he walked in. "No call yet?"

"No, what time is it in Italy?"

"Early afternoon," Seir answered. "Damn it. I didn't want to know where Airiella was at."

"Then you shouldn't be sitting here," Stolas snapped.

Seir laughed. "See how grumpy Stolas is when you interrupt sex?"

Lucifer howled in laughter. "I must admit, this was worth it."

Stolas sat down, and Hazel brought him in some food. "Why are you here?"

"Figured it was easier to wait for the call here than

send messages back and forth."

"Airiella was fighting demons when we saw her. None escaped, and they were ash by the time I got there, so I couldn't see who they belonged to." Stolas felt his heart quicken as Kalisha walked in and sat next to him.

"Seir said you practiced with magic last night, Kalisha. How did it go?" Lucifer took a sip of whatever was in his cup and waited for her to answer.

Kalisha thanked Hazel for the food and took a bite of the frittata, groaning, "This is so good. It went fine; thank you for asking."

Stolas had gone utterly hard when Kalisha groaned, and his unfinished business from the morning came right to the front of his mind. Stolas loved it when she made those sounds. He was now thinking of everything he could do to get more of those sounds out of Kalisha. Stolas was so distracted he hadn't even heard Lucifer or Seir talking.

Kalisha elbowed him. "Stolas? You in there?"

Seir cackled, "I know exactly where Stolas is."

Stolas blushed again as Lucifer joined in the laughter. "Unquestionably worth it. I have never seen Stolas like this. It's tempting to send them both back to his room."

Stolas saw Kalisha's cheeks turn rosy and happily smiled that he wasn't the only one blushing now. "Twice now you've interrupted things I'd rather be doing. What did you ask?"

"If you were satisfied with Kalisha's knowledge of magic," Lucifer repeated a broad smile on his face. "Honestly, I reworded it; my original question was if you were satisfied with Kalisha. I already know the answer to that one."

"Kalisha's already quite handy with magic, and now she has a good handle on mine," Stolas responded.

Kalisha broke out in delighted laughter. "If you had seen the look on Seir's face when you said that you'd understand my laughter," she responded to Stolas's questioning look.

Stolas went back over what he said and didn't get it. At Lucifer's laughter, his mind switched gears, and Stolas blushed again. "You two are children."

Seir grinned and slid two books across the table to Kalisha. "Here you go, Queen."

"What's with the Queen?" Kalisha asked Seir.

"It suits you. Powerful, smart, beautiful, and Stolas snaps to attention every time you are around," Seir joked. "Stolas also said you were a priestess, I improvised."

"Are you staying here with Kalisha today?" Lucifer asked Seir.

"That was my plan, sir. Do you need me to do something else?"

"No, I'd rather you were here with Kalisha, so she isn't alone. If you have anything to offer with the angel, I'm welcome to hear it, or invite you to the meeting."

Seir was startled by that, as was Stolas. "I can't think of anything right now. I do think the less of us that go, the better off we are. We leave a definite signature that would be easy for Moloch and his legions to pick up on if they are in the area. We already know Moloch has trackers with him."

Stolas wondered if Lucifer was testing Seir and decided to let it go. "Seir, would you be able to teach Kalisha a few self-defense moves?" Stolas asked.

"Sure. I don't know much, Queen, but I can show

you a few."

"Is it necessary?" Kalisha asked.

"Yes," Lucifer answered for them all. "I'd like one of my guards to work with Kalisha as well. Seir can oversee it or take a lesson with her."

"Shall I send a message with Zane for one of the guards?" Stolas asked, slightly uncomfortable with the situation. Jealousy was rising again.

"Not necessary, I brought them with me. The guards are outside. I've put an illusion over your property so that it looks as if no one is here." Lucifer looked over at Kalisha. "No magic, just physical defense."

"Understood," Kalisha answered Lucifer nervously, standing to take their plates back to the kitchen. "Excuse me."

Stolas watched Kalisha go, confused. "Read the body language, my friend," Seir told him.

"I'm trying. I don't understand." Stolas felt frustrated by his lack of experience with women.

"She's scared," Lucifer told Stolas. "Go talk to her, but I'm not budging on this, Stolas. If you want to keep Kalisha safe, she needs to learn physical defense."

Stolas nodded and followed Kalisha into the kitchen. "My love, what's wrong?"

"I'm fine, Stolas." Kalisha sounded anything but fine.

Stolas turned her to face him. "I know you aren't; I just don't know why. Fill me in, please."

"I'm not strong. Physical things tend to intimidate me unless we are talking about sex. I'm pretty damn sure Lucifer wasn't talking about one of his guards teaching me about sex." The thought of one of the guards sexually touching Kalisha in a sent fury through Stolas. "Calm down; we are just talking."

Stolas took a deep breath in. "Lucifer's right in you need to learn it. If you exhaust all your energy in magic, there is nothing to fall back on if something comes at you. Even a few skills can mean the difference between life and death. I'm aware if that Airiella is on the scene, she will keep you safe, but if she isn't, I'd rather you know a few moves." Stolas kissed Kalisha. "Don't say you aren't strong, because you are."

"If you think I need to, then I will. Physical violence just intimidates me." Kalisha wrapped her arms around his neck, standing on tiptoe. Stolas bent and lifted her, setting her on the counter in front of him, bringing them eye level.

"We'll dive into the reasons for that later. Part of this claiming is you can draw from me what you need. In this case, since it's a fear, draw some of my clarity to you. Distance won't matter for this, and you don't have to. Use what you can of mine if you feel out of control, or the fear is too much. It won't hurt me or drain me."

"Do you trust the guard?"

"I don't know who he will use, but I trust that Lucifer will not do anything to harm you as it would harm me. Lucifer's protected me all these years, and he has no reason to stop. If the guard goes too far, simply tell Seir, and he'll stop it. Or blast the guard with magic." Stolas kissed her again. "Strength doesn't come from here." He squeezed her bicep. "It comes from here." He tapped Kalisha's head, then her chest. "The scrawniest person can easily take down the brawniest one by thinking quicker. You are strong, my love. You render me useless all the time."

Kalisha laughed. "Not useless, just pliable, and a lot of fun to play with."

Airiella chose that moment to call him. Stolas stiffened. "Airiella is calling." He kissed Kalisha, fast and deep. "Be good, my love."

"Be safe." Kalisha kissed him one last time before Stolas pulled away.

"She called." Stolas strode back into the dining room. "Let me go first." Stolas handed Lucifer a stone. "This will bring you to me with no signature."

Lucifer stood and nodded once. Stolas focused on Airiella and answered her call, popping in outside a hotel room door. Stolas was irrationally nervous now; he knocked softly and waited. Jax opened the door, a strange smile on his face.

"Sorry, man, you know how she is," Jax offered as a way of explanation as he moved and allowed Stolas inside.

Stolas didn't understand at first, and then he heard music playing loudly and remembered Airiella's affinity for it, so Stolas listened as he walked in and felt all the tension in him drain out in an instant as he started laughing. "Is this the song lyrics I inadvertently quoted while you were in the hospital?" Stolas asked Airiella.

"Yep. Seemed fitting. Maybe for both of us. Where's the Big Bad?"

"Lucifer's coming." Right as Stolas said that he felt the pressure change, and Airiella went rigid.

"Demons," Airiella said, her body starting to glow, all of them lighting up along with her at the danger.

"Calm down, it's probably Lucifer," Stolas tried to tell Airiella.

"There's more than one, Stolas."

STOLAS

Stolas felt a swell of magic in the air, and the door opened, startling Jax, and Lucifer walked in with two guards behind him. Stolas should have known. He moved to stand between Airiella and Lucifer. "I didn't agree to a meeting with several demons," Airiella snarled and then looked at Stolas. "Why does he have to be handsome?"

Unsure of how to respond, Stolas looked between the two. Lucifer looked completely enthralled by Airiella, and she was glowing bright, her innate powers flaring to life in Lucifer's presence. A blast of air had Jax moved behind Airiella from where he was standing near Lucifer, Airiella clearly not liking that positioning.

"Hello, my dear. Airiella, isn't it?" Lucifer finally spoke stepping closer, and Stolas could hear the magic in his voice.

"Lucy, don't," Stolas warned. Too late, though. Airiella's wings sprung out from her back, and the blue fire was immediately around all her team and family, including Stolas. It shouldn't have surprised him that Airiella would try to protect him, but it did.

"My dear, you far outnumber us, let us agree to a truce. If you don't harm me, I won't harm you, what do you say?"

"Love, remember what we talked about." Stolas hoped Airiella could hear him; this was a trap. If Airiella agreed to it, she wouldn't ever be able to harm Lucifer without risking her own life.

"No deal. Lose the demons with you, and I'll drop the fire, and we can talk."

"They are merely here for my protection, that is all," Lucifer tried again.

"You have Stolas. Lose the demons." Airiella's voice

was hard, and Stolas could hear the anger in there.

"Let me out, love," Stolas tried again, and slowly the fire around him diminished, and he could see them both. The guards behind Lucifer had their magic ready to fire. "I'm offering a compromise. Dismiss the guards, if Airiella or one of her group tries to harm you, I forfeit my life, and if you try to harm any of them, my life will be forfeit anyway."

Lucifer's jaw dropped open, and the blue light in the room flared so brightly he had to close his eyes. "Very well, back home," Lucifer told the guards. "I hope you know what you are doing, Stolas."

Stolas felt a stinging sensation burning on his chest, and he hoped he knew what he was doing too. He had zero doubt Airiella could end him. Stolas knew she wouldn't risk hurting him by attacking Lucifer. He also knew Lucifer wouldn't end his life or attack Airiella unnecessarily, knowing Stolas would have to protect her.

"We will have words about this, Stolas," Airiella growled.

"I'd expect nothing less, love," Stolas replied wearily, rubbing the spot on his pecs. As the rest of the flames lowered, he saw most of the others rubbing their own chests. Stolas fought the urge to check and looked back at Lucifer, who had an odd expression on his face.

"Interesting song choice." Lucifer smirked and stepped farther in the room, standing closer to Stolas than Airiella. "I'd say it's a pleasure to meet you, but if I'm honest, you are a little scary."

Stolas heard Ronnie snort and smothered his smile at the look on Airiella's face. "Ditto," Airiella told Lucifer, not offering her hand.

Lucifer looked at Stolas. "Fuck, I hate it when you are right."

"Ditto again, but what is Stolas right about?" Airiella crossed her arms, her wings still blocking the others from Lucifer.

"Stolas is right about you, my dear. May I sit?" Lucifer gestured to the chair next to him.

"Go ahead." Airiella's wings disappeared, though the glow remained. "What about me?"

"Please, sit and relax. My guards are gone, and our mutual friend here has put me and you both in a very awkward situation with his little compromise. No one is at risk from me, and since you just declared the generals in your army, they have no reason to be afraid."

"What?" Stolas and Airiella both stared at Lucifer.

The faces behind Airiella were just as confused. "Stolas, you are telling me you can't see the powers she just gave them?"

"No, I can't. Please explain." Stolas brought his hand to his chest.

"Exactly. Remove your shirt and look," Lucifer told Stolas. "Ladies, feel free to remove your shirts and look as well," Lucifer joked. At the angry look of the men, Lucifer replied, "I was kidding. You all were rubbing your chests, if I am right, you all carry a mark there now of some sort."

Stolas didn't remove his shirt, but he pulled it away from his skin and looked at his chest. Lucifer was right; he had a mark. Stolas looked back up at Lucifer, who gestured for Stolas to take it off. Ronnie had already peeled his off and was staring at the symbol that fell to the left of a large tattoo snaking across Ronnie's chest.

Both Chrissie and Airiella moved to touch it, and

Airiella looked to Jax, who shrugged his shoulders. Stolas had seen that his mark was different from Ronnie's. Stolas unbuttoned his shirt and exposed his chest to Lucifer, who didn't seem the least bit surprised.

"See the difference?" Lucifer asked Stolas.

The set of wings on his chest differed from Ronnie's in that one of the wings was black; the other was a duplicate of Airiella's wing. "What does this mean?"

"It means you should learn your prophecies, my friend." Lucifer smirked at Stolas. "You are sworn to both sides. Unless I miss my mark, and I haven't yet," Lucifer reminded him, "you have a good shot at going back up if you were to die."

Airiella walked up to Stolas and traced her fingers over the mark, a strange tingle running through him at her touch. "I did this to you?"

Stolas pressed Airiella's hand to his chest. "You already knew I would fight for you, love."

Airiella whirled back to Lucifer. "Since you are the only one here who seems to know what the fuck is going on, why don't you stop smirking and explain it?"

"Fierce. You were right about that too." Lucifer grinned at Stolas. "I always knew you were different, Stolas." Lucifer looked back at Airiella. "The threat of my position being so close to you brought out some new powers, I believe. In doing so, those that are loyal to you have now been declared generals in your army. Stolas, this was in the prophecy Seir brought back to you. Did you not read it?"

"No, I didn't even remember I had it," Stolas blurted out. Airiella looked like she was about to lose her mind. "I've never put much belief in them."

"This one seems to be playing out exactly as foretold." Lucifer stood. "My dear, could you bring your wings back out?"

They sprung out of Airiella's back, knocking over a lamp on the table, her eyes were wide, and she had gone pale. Jax and Ronnie both flanked her, the glow between them getting brighter. "No!" Airiella cried, pushing them away. "Lucifer's fine. Don't come closer, if you got powers, who the hell knows what they are and if they will react to Lucifer; Stolas, the giant dumbass, put himself in the line of fire. Stay back."

Ronnie sat back down, glaring at Stolas, while Jax silently stood behind Airiella, his hands on her waist. The wild look of panic that had come across Airiella's face started to ease. "Why do you need to see her wings, Lucy?" Stolas asked.

"Lucy?" she half-smiled.

"Don't think you can get away with calling me that." Lucifer's tone had gone cold. "It's a name reserved for Stolas only. I am sure he trusted you enough to tell you that we are close."

"He did. I wasn't making fun of you, either, so back off." Electricity crackled in the air.

Stolas sighed; this wasn't going well. "Wings?" he reminded Lucifer.

"Do you know why they are both black and white?" Lucifer asked the room.

Smitty answered, "Taklishim told us it was because she is a balance of everything."

"Angel, please come sit down before Jax has a stroke," Ronnie interrupted.

Stolas glanced over in alarm at Jax, who was visibly

shaking the closer Lucifer got to Airiella. "Love, please. Jax isn't going to leave your side, and he's having a hard time not reacting."

The words sunk in, but instead of sitting down, a wall of flames went up behind Airiella, shielding the rest from Lucifer. "Jax can pass through it, but none of the others can. Baby, please go sit down," she told him. "I'll join you in a minute."

"Not happening, Ells." Jax walked right through the flames Stolas couldn't even come close to touching. Stolas had broken out in a sweat.

"You are the one she married, correct?" Lucifer was using his magic again. Stolas didn't think Lucifer even realized it, or if he did, Stolas wasn't sure what Lucifer was trying to get to happen.

"I am, and as her husband, mate, connection, bonded, where Airiella goes, I go."

Stolas knew the control Jax had to be exerting was beyond anything he had done before, and Stolas was impressed. "Airiella! Take this damn wall down right now!" Chrissie yelled. "You tattooed my chest; you owe me the decency of being allowed to see whatever bullshit you are pulling."

"May I see your mark?" Lucifer ignored the rest and spoke only to Jax.

Airiella narrowed her eyes. "Why?"

"He will be different than the others," Lucifer answered simply.

"So? Why do you need to see it?"

"I don't need to. I want to." Lucifer looked at Stolas. "I can't help it. I like her."

Stolas felt a measure of fear hit him, instantly he

knew it came from Kalisha. "Kalisha is scared, is something happening there? Ask your guards."

"I am guessing Kalisha was marked as well and just noticed it," Lucifer responded, a detached look in his eyes. "I am sure that hers is not like yours, it will be one-sided for your love."

"Stop, Lucy. You know my stance."

"I do." Lucifer tapped his chest. "It's also marked on your skin." Lucifer stood down and sat back in the chair.

Airiella dropped the wall of blue flames, and Stolas saw every one of them standing behind Jax. "Fucking hell, guys, sit down. Stolas is not the enemy, and I don't want him hurt."

Aedan pushed Jax out of the way, picked Airiella up, tossed her over his shoulder, and strode back to the couch, flinging her down. "If you want us to stay put, then you stay put. Shit. Listen to us for once!"

Smitty grinned and clapped his hands as he settled down next to Jillian. Chrissie and Ronnie were shooting daggers at Airiella. Stolas stepped in. "We aren't getting anywhere with this. For the life of me, I can't figure out why I agreed this was a good idea."

"What is this prophecy?" Airiella got control of herself, and Stolas felt her energy flare-up in the room, Lucifer visibly starting at the feel of it. Each person in Airiella's group relaxed and Stolas himself, felt her love filling him.

"Amazing." Lucifer studied Airiella, then shook his head. "That shouldn't be possible, yet it happened."

"Prophecy," she said again.

Lucifer began to recite:

There is one who will come to be, that can walk

through any world.

Faced with war, she will create an army, and upon meeting her foe, her powers will be unfurled.

Armed with powers from Heaven and Hell, difficult choices she must make;

she will take life, yet give it as well, though not one will exist that she can't bend or break.

She will see the balance restored, and choose who will be spared;

be it both, or one, Devil, or Lord, the truth of it all will be declared.

The words dropped like a bomb and reverberated around in Stolas's head. "Prophecies are up for interpretation."

"You are correct, though this one seems unavoidably clear to me." Lucifer sounded resigned. "Upon more digging before coming to you, I found another reference to what I can only imagine is her, as well as you, Stolas."

"What?" Stolas turned stunned.

"Listen:" Lucifer pulled a piece of paper out of his pocket and read the short prophecy.

She will take no sides –

On raven wings, she will ride.

An army she will build, her powers shared and disbursed.

All who oppose her can be killed, and her army shall never be cursed.

"You never belonged to me, my friend. Yet you stayed. You have a role in this, and while your part in this is open for interpretation, the rest is pretty cut and dry. Neither side is exempt from the angel's power. She has both in her and is the balance between us. Simply put, she decides who lives and dies."

"I'm not God," Airiella said weakly.

"No, you aren't though you could kill him if need be. Same with me. And this is why I am here. I do not doubt in my mind these are about you. You fill every aspect of them both and more. I cannot claim your soul for killing any of mine, nor shall it be held against you from the divine side. You are the most powerful being in existence. It's an odd feeling for me, yet also freeing."

Stolas wanted to find words to argue against the prophecies, but he couldn't. "Are these prophecies literal?" Chrissie asked.

"As Stolas said, they are open for interpretation. Is there a specific part you are wondering about?" Lucifer no longer had any magic in his tone. It was as if voicing the prophecies took power from him.

"No," Airiella said firmly. "I refuse."

Lucifer chuckled at that. "You don't get a choice, my dear, but I can understand your stance on that."

"How does anyone expect me to choose who lives or dies? I am not a judge, jury, and executioner."

"Your army is the executioner," Lucifer told Airiella. "They carry out your orders."

"Absolutely not!" Tears sprang to her eyes. "Why are you here? To beg me not to kill you?"

"No, my dear. I am here to help you figure out how to defeat Moloch. This war is because of him, not me. Regardless of lore about me, I don't kill innocent souls, nor do I manipulate those who are innocent to make them do bad things simply to claim them. I do bad things to those who choose to do bad things. I enjoy doing bad things to bad people; it is why I am what I am. I am good at it."

Airiella looked at Stolas, her face raw and filled with emotions Stolas couldn't even start to name. "I can't do this, Stolas."

"I don't want to say this, but I think Lucifer is right. It's being thrust upon you whether you want it or not. It's not a burden I would ever ask you to shoulder, and it hurts me how this hurts you. I'm sorry, love."

"For what it's worth, I too am sorry. I know all too well the consequences of what you must take on. Fuck, I truly am sorry. I know that we are on opposite spectrums, for this instance at least, we fight a common enemy." Lucifer honestly did sound sorry and contrite, which shocked Stolas right out of his stupor.

Stolas walked over in front of Airiella and kneeled before her. "Whatever comes, you aren't in this alone, love. Remember our talk. You need to let us help you. Whatever designated us as your army is for a reason, and I believe we will share the burdens with you."

Stolas saw the fire behind the pain in Airiella's eyes. "Whatever chose them, also just put all of these people that are my life in a direct line of fire. How am I supposed to live with that? Knowing that because of me, all of them, you included, can be hurt or even killed?"

"If I may, I can speak to that," Lucifer said gently.

Stolas stood back up but gave his oldest friend a warning look. Airiella was on a delicate edge, and if that fire took control as Stolas has seen it before, the entire building could crumble around them. Airiella felt backed into a corner, and her fight instinct was kicking in.

"Stolas is the only living being that is close to me, that I can honestly say I love. I did everything in my power to protect him while we were angels, including beating the shit out of others to keep him from simply being bullied because Stolas liked books and found one particular angel pretty. When our war happened, and I fell, I had hoped Stolas would finally be safe as most of those that opposed him fell from grace with me. Their souls bore their marks of cruelty plain for all to see. It was my one hope in all that shit that Stolas would finally be safe. He was so different from the rest of us assholes. Then Stolas voluntarily left, and that hope came crashing down around me."

"Lucy, your guards," Stolas warned, knowing they could hear.

"They can't hear me; I took care of it." Lucifer looked back at Airiella and continued speaking. "That became a mark on my soul that I could never erase. Because Stolas loved me and followed me simply because of that, because Stolas wanted to make sure I had a friend, I wear it proudly and do everything I can to keep him safe. His little compromise earlier was well played; Stolas knows I won't do anything to hurt him, just as he knows you won't either. I gave him a position of power, wealth, and status and burdened Stolas with secrets that could hurt him, all to keep him safe. While at the same time, Stolas was doing the same for me, though I often didn't see it. Seeing him here with you, now that it has all come to this, has made it clear to me, this was Stolas's choice to make all along, and I need to honor it, however much I don't like it. If any of those that now carry your mark choose not to help, that is their choice. It is also their choice if they choose to help, and you need to honor it. If I could go back to when it all started and tell Stolas not to follow me, tell him of the shit and chaos that would happen down the road, what do you think he would say to me?"

"He'd do it anyway," Airiella answered quickly. "Stolas has a good heart."

Stolas bit his lip hard to keep a hold of the emotions that started spinning wildly out of control. "I'm not a good person."

"Bullshit, Stolas. Everything you've done has been on my orders. If there is a stain on your soul, it's mine to carry. Soldiers in war don't go to Hell because they followed orders, and people died. It's no different." Lucifer looked to Airiella. "It was clear on that, what they must do in the war, is not a burden they will get judged for, and it is their choice to do it or not do it just as it is your choice whether or not you let them help. If I had turned Stolas away because I was angry that he followed me, what would you think the outcome would have been?"

"You see it your way, Lucy, I see it mine." Stolas blinked slowly. "No need to sit down and tell you my story now, it seems." Stolas tried to regain control of the situation.

Airiella ignored him and focused on Lucifer. "A variety of things could have happened if you turned Stolas away. As your friend, it would have weighed on Stolas, and he would carry that pain and loneliness. Stolas wouldn't be the way he is now."

"No, he wouldn't. Stolas would still have a good heart underneath it all, but he wouldn't be who he is. It wasn't up to me to decide who Stolas was or what he could be. I simply gave him the tools at my disposal and let Stolas make his own choices and stayed close in case he needed me."

"Baby girl, these are words I never thought I would

say, but the Devil is right." Smitty leaned forward to look at Airiella.

"Let's not say that then," Airiella tried to joke. Jax pulled her on his lap and held her. "What's our next step?"

"If you are asking me to make your list of those who need to die, I am more than happy to do that." Lucifer smiled at Airiella.

"Not what she's asking," Ronnie growled out.

"Stone is with this Moloch?" Smitty asked.

"He is," Stolas answered, sitting back down but keeping a close eye on Airiella.

"Then for sure the fight will come to us," Jax said slowly, his fingers entwining with Airiella's. "He has a score to settle with me."

"You'll need to individually figure out what powers you now have and work on using those skills to perfection. I see Ronnie being particularly helpful in this with his fighting background. Use the strategic skills you possess in identifying the next strike coming for you and utilize the skills best required to defeat it." Stolas felt the pressure building in his head and rubbed at it absently.

"I wish I could provide a timeline for you, but the prophecies didn't come with one. Moloch is here, somewhere on earth. He has an army of his own with him, as well as Stone, who we believe possesses some sort of tracking ability. I will have legions at my disposal that I can send to aid you, but the chances of them following your orders will be slim. Stolas, myself, or Seir will need to be present."

"Seir is involved in this too?" Mags asked.

"Seir recovered, I believe," Lucifer added as an afterthought. "Seir's specific skills could be quite useful, and he has volunteered to be on the side of the angel."

"Bet that chaps your ass, doesn't it?" Airiella fired off.

Lucifer laughed. "I really can't help it; I like you."

Airiella looked at Stolas a moment before looking back at Lucifer. "You honestly aren't going to ask me to spare you, are you?"

"I'm not. If it's my time to be done, then so be it. Just get rid of Moloch first."

"Tell us more about Moloch," Jillian demanded.

Lucifer gave Jillian a cursory glance. "Stay away from him. Those babies' you ladies carry are at considerable risk if Moloch is near. He feeds off them, takes their lives as if it was an appetizer to snack on before sacrificing children as the main course. For those that have abilities, Moloch drains their powers first, taking them as his own before sucking down their soul. His realm has been the worst level of Hell for the worse offenders. Moloch is cruel beyond measure, and those who deserve to suffer, do so horribly at his hands."

"Did you say, babies?" Ronnie zeroed in on the one thing Stolas had picked up on too. "You said ladies and babies, as in more than one."

Lucifer gestured at Chrissie and Jillian. "Correct."

Ronnie yanked Chrissie into his arms. "Fuck. Are you serious right now?"

Airiella stretched out her hand and put it on Chrissie's belly and gasped. "Yep."

"How do we keep them safe?" Ronnie demanded his eyes both wild with fear and excitement at the same time.

"Kalisha," Stolas answered. It was the only thing he could think of as a solution. "She carries my power now and is deadly in her own right. We have Kalisha stay with them and the children."

"You said something about your power being great before or something like that. What does that mean exactly?" Airiella looked back at Stolas.

"When we were young, Stolas's power was wild and uncontrollable, making him the butt of jokes as Stolas couldn't control simple things. They all failed to realize Stolas's power was so incredible that his young body couldn't contain it all. Head to head, Stolas could probably take on Moloch and sustain non-life-threatening injuries. His power is second to mine. By claiming Kalisha, all the power she held is now shared with him, making him about equal to me. If Kalisha is left to protect them and the children, the odds are quite good that they will all be safe."

"What the fuck? Why wouldn't you tell us before now?" Smitty almost shouted.

"He couldn't," Lucifer answered for Stolas again. "Stolas was bound to me to keep it secret. When he told me he made a vow to the angel and all of you to keep you safe, the divine power of that vow canceled out the binding in regards to you all. Stolas still can't tell others."

"That prophecy said she could give life," Chrissie broke in. "Is that why I am pregnant?"

"It's open to interpretation." Lucifer fell back on that explanation. "Unless you haven't been sleeping with your betrothed, the answer to that can simply be sex."

"We are not discussing our sex life with the Devil," Ronnie stated. "How will Moloch fight? Does he have a preferred method?"

"Dirty," Stolas answered. "Anything goes. He'll use magic, physical brute force, weapons, whatever is easiest for him. Moloch will seek out your weak spots and put everything he has into it, including a legion."

"Sounds fun," Ronnie snapped and closed his mouth.

"What will kill him?" Aedan asked.

"Her." Lucifer pointed at Aireilla. "Or me, possibly Stolas. If you want to make sure Moloch is completely dead, it needs to be her as she has the power of the divine as well as my power."

"No pressure, or anything, right, Ells?" Chrissie took Airiella's hand.

"Can we please have all future communication go through Stolas?" Jax asked.

"I'm agreeable to that. Being around you makes me itchy." Lucifer smiled at Airiella. "Aside from everything else, I wanted you to hear it directly from me. I am not out to hurt you. Your very existence is a marvel for me, and truthfully a little scary knowing she can kill me, and at best, I could probably only hurt her." At the hard look from Stolas, Lucifer added, "Not that I will."

"The result we are all looking for is an end to Moloch. If he were to be in power, the fall of humankind becomes probable," Stolas told them.

"Essentially, that is correct. Hell would run unchecked. Moloch would suck the power from everyone he saw as a threat. I shudder to think of what would happen if Moloch obtained mine or Stolas's power. If we stop him, by stop, I mean kill, one of us can take command of the legions and demand fealty or dispatch them." Lucifer stood. "Any other questions?"

"What was Stolas like as a child?" Airiella asked with a small smile.

"Scrawny." Lucifer grinned and looked back at Stolas. "I sincerely like her." Lucifer looked back at Airiella. "Forgive me for not shaking your hand, but your skin is crawling with electricity that is snapping loudly in my ears, and I have no desire to be burned."

Stolas looked at them all. "Loudly call if you need me; otherwise, I'll be in touch."

"Stolas, wait," Airiella called to him and stood up. "The raven wings don't have to be you; maybe they reference my raven."

"It's possible, love," Stolas said quietly, "but I think it's referring to me. It's fine. I'll gladly carry you. Be safe. One hint of trouble, call me."

"You be safe." Airiella stood on tiptoe and kissed him, then wrapped her arms around Stolas, hugging him. "Nope, not scrawny now."

Stolas blushed and left the room, finding Lucifer waiting in the hallway.

Chapter Twenty-One

K alisha launched at Stolas the moment he appeared back at home, Lucifer chuckling behind him. "Oh, how my world has changed in such a short time. It used to be women threw themselves at me, now I am shunned by them all."

"Shut up, Lucy," Stolas growled.

"Stolas, I have wings on my chest," Kalisha babbled.

"Me too, my love. I'll explain it all; it's fine," he said and he kissed her on the head. Stolas turned back to Lucifer. "Since when are you so free with explanations about everything?"

"It's odd when your angel speaks; I feel compelled to tell her the truth about everything."

Kalisha laughed hard. "Jax calls Airiella Siren because of that."

"Shit, Lassie." Lucifer's rarely used nickname for Stolas came out. Lucifer only used it in his most vulnerable moments. "Airiella's it. She's the one in the prophecy. I can feel it simply by being around her. The angel could end me."

Kalisha looked at Lucifer, a gentle look on her face.

"She wouldn't. That's not who Airiella is. She would never hurt Stolas in that way, nor would she want to even in retribution."

"Kalisha's right, Lucy. Airiella doesn't even like killing the demons she does kill. She's called herself a murderer for it."

Lucifer dropped into a chair as Seir walked in. "Never in my entire existence have I been more aware of my mortality than in the angel's presence. I damn near wet myself when those blue flames erupted everywhere. Those fuckers are potent."

"Airiella threatened you?" Seir misunderstood what he overheard; shock spread across his face.

"No. The angel powers in Airiella reacted strongly to Lucifer's presence, and she went into protect mode," Stolas explained. "Those rings of fire went around everyone behind her, including me."

"Lassie, I thought for sure when those flames dropped, you would be nothing but ash. They burned me, and they weren't even around me." Lucifer rubbed his hands over his face. "By the way, you make a boneheaded move like that little compromise again, and I'll beat you myself."

"It was a calculated risk. There was no way Airiella was going to let any of them take a chance of hurting me."

"How did you know I wouldn't go after them?"

"Airiella wouldn't have let you," Stolas answered honestly. "You truly saw powers in all of them?"

"Every single one of them. Bright as can be."

"You going to let me in on this conversation?" Kalisha asked.

"Me too?" Stolas had forgotten about Seir

momentarily. "I'm feeling a little left out."

"Need a drink?" Stolas asked Lucifer.

"Quadruple shot of the strongest of whatever you have."

Stolas went and poured them all drinks, and they sat at the dining room table, Lucifer exhibiting signs of genuine fear and Seir watching him nervously. Stolas filled them in, Lucifer adding details as he saw fit, and by the end, both Kalish and Seir were just as stunned.

"That's awful!" Kalisha cried. "Do you have any idea of how much Airiella has been through already?"

"I do, my love, Airiella's shared some of it with me, and other times I've witnessed, or seen the aftermath."

Seir hadn't said anything but had a pensive look on his face. "There was a second prophecy? Any idea when these got declared?"

"Before I became who I am. The prophecies predate us, and yes, I found another. Quite buried, but it was there all the same."

"Can you repeat it?" Seir asked.

"Repeat them both, please," Kalisha requested. "I can guarantee you that Jax, Ronnie, Smitty, and Aedan are all dissecting these word by word, and I intend to do the same."

"Very well." Lucifer shrugged and recited:

There is one who will come to be, that can walk through any world.

Faced with war, she will create an army, and upon meeting her foe, her powers will be unfurled.

Armed with powers from Heaven and Hell, difficult choices she must make;

she will take life, yet give it as well, though not one

will exist that she can't bend or break.

She will see the balance restored, and choose who will be spared;

be it both, or one, Devil, or Lord, the truth of it all will be declared.

"The second one reads:"

She will take no sides –

On raven wings, she will ride.

An army she will build, her powers shared and disbursed.

All who oppose her can be killed, and her army shall never be cursed.

Seir had written it down as Lucifer recited it and stared down at the words on the paper in front of him. Seir's face was blank, though Stolas knew he was thinking it through. Kalisha reached across the table and pulled the paper from Seir.

"That can walk through any world. Does that mean Airiella can walk here? We already know she can walk in the spirit realm."

"That is my take on it," Lucifer said when no one else spoke. "Stands to reason, Airiella would be able to walk among the angels as well."

"Did Airiella know that?" Kalisha looked at Stolas.

"Not that I'm aware of; I didn't know Airiella could come here."

"Does the foe in the next line refer to you?" Kalisha looked at Lucifer for confirmation.

"I can't be certain. The meeting with me caused Airiella to mark her generals and gave them powers. While we are not always on the same side, I don't know that I would call Airiella a foe. That could refer to Moloch, or

Stone, or both, and when she meets them, more powers will come to her. In either case, part of that line came true today."

"There's no way to tell what choices Airiella will have to make, but in war, everyone makes tough choices, armed with powers from Heaven and Hell. I know Airiella has changed since I was alive, but I still see no darkness in her. None. If Airiella had powers of Hell, wouldn't I be able to see it?"

"I wondered about that myself," Seir piped up. "I don't sense any bad in Airiella."

"Nor did I," Lucifer confirmed. "Maybe that's where the difficult choices come in."

"No, they are there," Stolas spoke quietly, his mind churning. "When she killed Bael, it was a pure reaction to Jax getting injured. Airiella unleashed her powers, and had they all not been wearing the stones you made them, Kalisha; it would have hurt them. It forced the shifters to change. I also saw it when they were fighting what they called Spearfinger. I think the powers of Hell come out when Airiella loses control. She utterly destroyed a large section of the forest. I saw a hint of it today when she was talking. There was so much pain in Airiella's eyes and her voice, but when I looked closely, I could see the fire behind it. I just don't think Airiella knows what it is."

"Wouldn't it still show as dark, though?" Kalisha asked.

"Not if she isn't using that power for dark reasons," Lucifer clarified. He looked over at Stolas. "You think that's what it is?"

"Yes. The couple of times I've had to release energy because I was so angry at what had happened to Airiella, I devastated the land. I didn't connect it until now."

"Stolas, you'll need to work with Airiella on learning to harness it," Lucifer warned.

"Already thought of that."

"We already know Airiella can kill, she's been killing demons and Native American creatures," Kalisha went on. "Can she heal?"

"Not that I am aware of."

"Airiella's friend asked if the giving life was what made her pregnant. It is a possibility since all the females around her have recently had babies or are now pregnant. That one is still open to interpretation." Lucifer shrugged again.

"No one she can't bend or break," Seir jumped in again. "Thoughts on that?"

"My assumption was myself and the creator," Lucifer replied. "Making it clear we are not exempt from Airiella's powers."

"My thought on that was the same," Stolas agreed.

"The last two lines are self-explanatory, except the last statement of all will be declared. It's ambiguous." Kalisha drummed her fingers on the table, and Seir reached over to flatten them. "Sorry. I know you still have a headache."

"This is a total mind fuck for that poor girl," Seir said.

"The second one," Kalisha ignored him, "she will take no sides. In context with the rest, to me, that means she is neutral grounds between the creator, and this one." Kalisha pointed at Lucifer.

"I agree," Seir added, sitting forward. "The rest of that second one is clear. No judgement can get cast on

Airiella or those who fight for her. Or for whoever she chooses to spare or kill. The confusing part to me, is the part that refers to Stolas. I can only assume the raven is Stolas."

"Why do you assume that?" Kalisha challenged Seir.

"It's usually the form Stolas takes when he doesn't want to get noticed up there. Airiella's seen it, and Stolas is right smack in the middle of this with her. Stolas won't fight against Lucifer or Airiella. I just don't know what it means."

"Airiella can't literally ride you, can she?" Kalisha looked up at Stolas, and Lucifer burst out laughing. "I'm not talking about sex." Kalisha glared at Lucifer.

"No." Stolas smiled at Kalisha, smothering a laugh of his own, "my raven can't carry a human, literally. This statement is figurative, I think. Airiella will need me to get her through something."

"The question is what?" Seir said.

"We might not know until it happens. Such is the way with prophecies." Lucifer slammed back the rest of his drink. "Since we don't know a timeline on this, my suggestion is that you three tail them. Spend the time topside, and work with Airiella on her powers, Kalisha can watch over the others, and Seir can transport if something happens. Seir can come to get me, or whatever needed."

"Are any of you going to let me in on the secret you are hiding about Stolas's power?" Seir put his hands behind his head and stared at Stolas and Lucifer. "Come on; you didn't think I would pick up on the power radiating off this one?" Seir jerked a thumb at Kalisha. "I know Kalisha is powerful on her own, but I also know Stolas's signature."

Lucifer sighed. "Do you forfeit your life if you

betray me?"

"Isn't that a given since I am a prince?"

"If that was the case, would we be facing a war with Moloch?" Lucifer countered, and Stolas felt the power swell.

"Point taken. Yes. My life is forfeit if I betray anyone at this table," Seir agreed.

"Stolas is equal to me in power now with his combined power from Kalisha. Before Kalisha, Stolas was second only to me. If Moloch didn't have an army and a deranged psychiatrist with him, I would have sent Stolas after him alone and taken care of the issue. I won't sacrifice Stolas to an army."

"But, you'll sacrifice Airiella?" Kalisha's voice went up an octave.

"My dear, that angel can wipe me out of existence. I'm not sacrificing anything. My trust has to be in the angel to do what's right for those that matter to me. Which is those of you at this table; this trust is not an easy thing for me to give. I will be at Airiella's disposal, and a legion of trusted ones to fight alongside her. Strike all thoughts from that pretty head of yours that I wish to anger someone who can end me. I may not beg the angel for my life, but I am still selfish enough not to want it to end."

"My apologies," Kalisha offered sincerely.

"We can head topside whenever you want," Stolas replied, squeezing Kalisha's hand. "Seir, does this present any problems for you?"

"None for me. I might be able to help you piss Airiella off to get her to lose control," Seir joked.

"I wouldn't want that directed at me," Stolas warned.

"No joke there, Lassie." Lucifer sounded down again. "I do find it odd that the creator hasn't spoken to the angel, only me. So be it." Lucifer pushed off away from the table. "Keep your asses off the radar and stay alive. I think Airiella would lose control if something happened to either of you two." Lucifer pointed at Stolas and Kalisha. "Maybe you too, Seir, I don't know. Let's not have it happen, because you are my only friend, Lassie, and I can't say that losing you would be good for anyone around me."

Stolas nodded stiffly. "The reverse is true as well, Lucy. If Seir is unable to come for you, listen for my call, or Kalisha's. Chances are it will be swift."

Stolas had a deep sense of foreboding about the whole thing, and Lucifer turned one last time. "Use the company card. Spare no expense to keep them all safe." Lucifer laughed darkly. "Words I never thought I would utter."

"Pack a bag," Stolas told Kalisha. "Keep it light, the clothing we can buy as well as everyday items. Pack supplies you think you might need. You too, Seir."

"I've already got one. I went home to grab some stuff earlier."

Stolas nodded at Seir. "I'll be down to the workroom to pack a bag for myself in a moment. I need to talk to Zane." Stolas kissed Kalisha on the forehead. He watched her walk out and saw Seir staring at him. "What?"

"Neither prophecy said whether Airiella would win or not. Did you notice that?"

"I did. The wording is leading but carefully crafted. Airiella's not given me a reason to doubt her, and now's not the time for me to start."

"I'm not saying that you doubt Airiella, but I think

our boss is worried."

"I don't blame Lucifer. Go, get your bag. Zane," Stolas called.

"Yes, sir?"

"Everything is in your hands until Kalisha or I return. Hopefully, both of us. I will be topside. Stay on high alert. We are at war. If Lucifer shows back up here, give him whatever he needs. Do you remember where my important papers are?"

"I do, sir."

"You know what to do if I don't return. I will leave medical supplies in the workroom for injuries. They are all labeled. Do I need to tell the rest, or will they listen to you?"

"They will listen, sir. No one has questioned the authority you have given me. If you'd like me to gather them all, I will."

"Do it. I don't want anyone giving you grief in my absence."

"Just a moment, sir." Zane popped out, and slowly the servants started to fill the dining room as Kalisha and Seir came back in. Once the last servant was there, including the new security, Stolas looked at them all, one by one.

"Zane is in charge from the moment I leave until I return, or Kalisha returns. Is that clear?"

A chorus of yes, sir's sounded throughout the room, a mix of shock and concern on their faces.

"If you are unclear about anything, or if something concerns you, I want Zane to know about it immediately. We are at war, and I want you all safe and uninjured. I do not know how long I will be gone. As usual, if Lucifer shows up here, give him anything he wants. You have free reign to use your magic against those that mean harm to anyone here or the property. Again, stay safe. Dismissed."

Stolas looked at Kalisha. "Give me a moment to grab a bag. I'll be back."

Stolas popped into his workroom and collected everything he thought he would need, and if there was something Stolas didn't think of, he could always use Seir to get it for him. Stolas set out various containers of mixes and salves for Zane should the need arise and gave a last look around before popping back out.

"You got where we are going?" Seir asked at Stolas's appearance.

"I do. Hopefully, the hotel will have rooms for us." Stolas grabbed Kalisha's hand, Seir taking her other, and they left, the deep sense of doom trailing after Stolas.

Chapter Twenty-Two

Stolas knocked softly on the door, hoping they were still there. A sleepy Jax greeted him. "Stolas?"

"Can you tell her I'm here?" Stolas asked quietly.

"She knows," Stolas heard Airiella call out. "You better not have the Big Bad with you."

Stolas chuckled, "I don't. I do have guests, but not that particular one."

Jax opened the door for him, and Kalisha and Seir trailed behind him. Jax was greeting Seir warmly but giving them both odd looks. "I've already called the others," Airiella said as they walked in. "I just assumed that a late-night visit didn't mean anything good."

"It's not bad, Airiella." Kalisha went to Airiella and hugged her.

Stolas waited until the others arrived, noting it was only the connections, minus Mags. "We are here to stay and follow behind you wherever you go."

The startled looks on all their faces were comical. "Why?" Ronnie asked. "Your boss doesn't trust us?"

"It has nothing to do with trust. Believe it or not,

Lucifer is worried about your safety. Both Seir and Kalisha can attest to that. Us being here is to help you and be your link to Lucifer. I'm assuming you all studied the prophecy the same way Kalisha did?"

"You mean we take it apart and try to decode it all?" Smitty grinned. "Bet your ass we did."

"Powers of Hell, you are here to train Airiella, aren't you?" Jax sat on the arm of the chair Airiella was sitting in. "She's already got them, right?"

"I believe so."

Ronnie looked like a board had hit him. "The forest," Ronnie said in wonder.

"Not just that, but the way she was when she took out Bael. I saw a bit of it earlier today. Love, I think when you lose control of your emotions, those powers take over. I can't be sure, but my gut tells me I am right."

"Taklishim thinks the same thing," Airiella admitted.

"I'm here to teach you how to harness them and use them. Kalisha is here to watch your friends and the kids and keep them safe, and Seir is here to help me."

"I heard you got beat up, Seir, how do you feel?" Airiella asked him with a small, sad smile.

"Good as new. Don't worry about me."

"Ronnie, would you be willing to work with Kalisha on self-defense? Probably Seir here too. Shit might as well include me in that."

"Sure." Ronnie looked confused. "You don't strike me as needing it, though. If you are going to be trailing us, then just join us when we work out."

"I don't need the training to use my magic in defense or offense. But physically, I could use some brushing up, too." Stolas shrugged. "I'm not much of a fighter, but Lucifer made sure I became trained."

"So, you are up here for good then?" Airiella asked the three of them.

"Until we are no longer needed," Stolas corrected.

"Meaning after the war is over," Smitty added.

"Correct." Stolas stood up. "We have the rooms on this side of you." Stolas pointed to the left. "I also would like to offer to pay for meals. I know I'm too late to offer to take care of the rooms."

"It's not necessary," Jax started to argue, and Kalisha shushed him.

"Bossman would be paying. Lucifer said to spare no expense to keep you safe, so let him." Kalisha grinned.

"Done deal." Airiella grinned back. "Now, can we pick this back up in the morning? I'm exhausted after the shit Stolas and his BFF dumped on me earlier."

Kalisha stood up and handed Airiella another stone. "Sleep with this near you. It will keep nightmares at bay and allow a good night's sleep for whoever is in the room with you without the fogginess of drugs."

"This right here, this is worth gold." Airiella clutched the stone in her hand.

Kalisha turned to Ronnie and handed him one as well. "Airiella told me what happened and that Chrissie and her son suffer them too."

Ronnie threw his arms around her. "I'm not sure the last time Rafe had a good night's sleep. Thank you, Kalisha."

"If you want to thank someone, thank Stolas and his collection of stones and this power he gave me. That's what made those possible. Regardless, I'm happy to help."

Stolas felt a surge of love flow through the room, and Stolas looked over at Airiella, who was watching him closely. Stolas wasn't sure what she was trying to convey with the look she was giving him, but the love was unmistakable.

"Rest. Knock on the door or call when you wake up and want to eat. We can go out, or I can order room service. Whatever you prefer." Stolas turned to go, wrapping his arm around Kalisha.

"Take care of her, Stolas," Jax said.

"I have every intention of doing just that."

Seir headed off to his room to sleep, despite what he'd told them, Seir hadn't fully recovered yet, the lingering headache still bothered him. Stolas and Kalisha went into their room, and she flopped on the bed.

"I'm almost too awake to sleep, but we need to acclimate to the time zone here. Any idea what we could do that would wear us out enough to sleep for a bit?" There was a broad smile on Kalisha's face when she asked that.

"I have some ideas of things we could do to pass the time; I'm not sure I could sleep either. We could look for a place to practice magic safely. We could plan out ways to work with Airiella on the magic. We can try to track down Moloch." Stolas started listing things off as he stripped.

"Not quite what I had in mind." Kalisha frowned, closing her eyes.

"How about I worship every inch of your body? Is that more what you were thinking?"

Kalisha's eyes popped open to find him nude in front of her. Stolas pulled her up and started peeling the clothes from her body, eventually revealing Kalisha's mark of a general on her chest, right over her heart. Kalisha's eyes glued to his.

"It's different than mine. Why? We are together."

"I'm guessing it's because I am loyal to Lucifer as well as to Airiella. You may have agreed to be a part of that world, but you aren't truly loyal to him." Stolas pulled her arm up to him and ran his thumb over his name on Kalisha's wrist. A low hum of energy passed through them both, and her breath caught.

"Do that again," Kalisha whispered.

Stolas knelt in front of Kalisha and kissed the inside of her wrist, licking it, and her eyes went glossy, a moan escaping between her lips. "My love," Stolas pushed her back, "when you make sounds like that, I lose focus, but damn I love how they sound."

Stolas grabbed her legs and slid them over his shoulders as Kalisha lay open before him. He was going to take his time, and that was all there was to it. Stolas stroked his hands along her hips as he lowered his head and lost himself in the taste of her. Kalisha exploded over his tongue. Over and over, Stolas coaxed intense orgasms out of Kalisha. Before finally giving in to her pleas and climbed up on the bed next to her.

Kalisha straddled her quaking body over Stolas and held him captive in a kiss that told him everything her words couldn't. Kalisha rode him in a slow, languid pace that drove Stolas just as crazy as he pushed her, the pleasure rolling through him in waves he didn't think possible. She touched every part of him.

When they finally lay there, bodies wrapped around each other, Stolas felt overwhelmed by the emotions Kalisha brought out. Stolas finally understood how Jax and Ronnie felt when it came to Airiella. Their reactions to everything that has happened and was happening. And then it dawned on Stolas that it was because of Airiella he was able to feel this way about Kalisha.

It was a gift Airiella had given him. Stolas didn't know how, but he was grateful for it. Centuries of not feeling, and now this. Stolas pulled Kalisha closer and buried his face in her neck and hair to hide the tears that came out of nowhere.

"Sweetheart, what's the matter?" Kalisha stroked his back. Stolas only shook his head and held on, riding the emotions, tremors running through his muscles. "Talk to me, please."

"I don't know how," Stolas mumbled.

"Tell me what's in your heart," Kalisha tried again.

"You. My love for you. How much it makes me feel after so long of not feeling anything. It's all you. The darkness inside me goes away when I'm holding you like this. This love I have for you is incredible and terrifying both." Stolas kissed Kalisha's neck. "It's so deeply rooted in me. There's no space between our bodies, and yet you still feel not close enough. I can't stand not touching you, even if it's just to make sure you are real and here with me."

Kalisha tugged on his hair, trying to get Stolas to lift his head, but the feel of her fingers on his scalp was another sensation he loved. "Stolas, look at me, please. I want to see your eyes. I need to see them."

Something in Kalisha's tone made Stolas move his head, his eyes meeting hers. Those beautiful eyes. The color of charcoal, her dark skin, and black eyelashes framing the orbs in perfect beauty. "I love you," Stolas whispered to Kalisha.

"That's what I needed to see, Stolas. The naked

truth in your eyes. These eyes that are a color I've never seen before, almost like mahogany. When you say you love me, there's a glow in them that tells me its real. When you are angry, they look like a storm cloud." Kalisha kissed him softly. "I do love you, Stolas. Very much so."

Chapter Twenty-Three

Fuck! Stolas, I'm just not getting it!" Airiella shouted.
"Sit down, love. Come here, over by me." Stolas
patted the ground next to him.

"What am I doing wrong?"

"Focus. The times I've seen it have been when your
emotions fly out of control. When you saw Bael hurt Jax,
there was a change in you that was terrifying. The
devastation of that forest where you took out that creature.
Think of the emotions that you felt at those times. Harness
that feeling; I believe that is when the powers of Hell come
out of you. Something in you opens, and that barrier is
down."

"Wouldn't harnessing those emotions just bring out
utter destruction?"

"Not if you harness it. It allows you to feed that
power into what you want to be doing." Stolas felt like he
wasn't doing a good job explaining it to Airiella.

"Will it make me dark?"

"No, love. You aren't using those powers for a dark
purpose. When you allow the two to work together, I
believe you will be unstoppable. You will be what the power

that created you meant you to be, a perfect balance in a world that has gone off balance." Stolas rubbed the back of Airiella's hand, trying to soothe her.

Airiella leaned up against him, and Stolas put his arm around her. "It's scary to think about; I don't want to be unstoppable. I don't want to be the most powerful being alive. I don't want to make hard choices or put those I love at risk simply because of who I am."

A loud explosion sounded in the air, making them both jump. "Sounds like someone has some sort of explosive power," Stolas commented.

"Maybe they are playing with those stone weapons Kalisha made."

"While I'm thinking about it, I need to thank you, love." Stolas kissed the top of Airiella's head.

"Thank me? For what?"

"For whatever gift you've given me over the time you've known me that allows me to feel once again. I know it's because of you, just like I know you can do what you need to do. The love I feel for Kalisha gives me hope and something to look forward to; I finally understand how Jax feels when he looks at you as I keep finding myself looking at Kalisha the same way."

"Your ability to love has always been there, Stolas. All I did was give it a little push; the rest was all you, buddy."

Stolas stood and pulled Airiella to her feet. "We are going to do this, however long it takes. You've got to clear all this other noise out of your head. When you need to clear your mind, what do you do?"

"I go to the ocean, or out in nature."

"We are in nature, and it isn't working. So, we will

try the ocean. Do you want me to take you home?" Stolas suggested.

"No! If there are demons there watching it, looking for me, that puts everyone in that area at risk if I show up there. Let me try music. I won't be able to hear you, though. So tell me what you want me to do. Wait, shit, I don't have my music with me."

"Seir," Stolas called and waited.

"What can I do for you, pretty girl?" Seir ignored Stolas.

"I need my iPod; it's back at the hotel."

"Be right back." Seir popped out, and Stolas felt irritation poke at his eyes but forgave Seir when he appeared moments later and handed Airiella what she needed. "They are coming along nicely," Seir told Stolas.

"What was the explosion?" Stolas asked.

"Aedan was playing with one of those stones Kalisha handed out," Seir snickered. "I must say it was pretty hilarious, and now Aedan's exercising a bit more caution when handling one of Kalisha's creations." Seir popped back out to where he was working with the others to figure out what powers they had to use.

"Love, what I want you to do is first, clear your mind. Once you do that, I want you to feel for the energy of the powers that reside in you. It's no different than when you call the lightning. You feel for it, right?" Stolas asked her.

"Not exactly. At first, I called out to it mentally, asking for help until I learned what it felt like."

"Please don't call out for Hell. Instead, since you know what the other powers feel like, separate those energies until you find one that isn't familiar. Hold on to that energy, and let it fill you, learn the feel of it and picture yourself using it. Whichever ability it is, it should manifest. Then we'll know, and you can put a name to it. If it helps, speak out loud what you feel when you grab that energy, and it might give me a little warning of what's to come." Stolas hoped that had made sense to Airiella.

"Shit, now I'm going to worry about hurting you since I don't know what I'll be messing with."

"You won't hurt me. Face this way, and when you let the energy fill you, picture yourself using it in this direction. If you can, open your eyes and direct it with your hands." Stolas faced Airiella out to the open side of the mountain they were on.

Stolas stood there and watched while Airiella put the headphones on, and Stolas heard the sound of the music filling her hears. Airiella gave him a nervous look but then sank on to the ground and closed her eyes. It took a few songs, but Stolas finally saw her body relax.

Stolas looked around them, making sure there was nobody around. Seir had found a little spot in the Dolomites that would work well for what they needed. Not too far away was another clearing where Seir was working with Aedan, Smitty, Jax, and Ronnie.

They were halfway up one of the peaks, a small river flowing not too far away and behind them, dense forest, in front of them a large cliff, and off to the side, the ledge of where this clearing ended. Stolas felt life in the surrounding forest, but none of the animals were close enough to be injured.

Stolas had her connect to all the elements first in hopes of grounding Airiella, but her nerves came into play the moment Stolas tried to get Airiella to switch to the unfamiliar. Stolas would have to ask Seir to find a safe spot near an ocean if this didn't work.

A few moments later, Airiella's raven landed next to Stolas, and he wasn't sure what that meant. He was about to tap Airiella on the shoulder to ask if everything was okay when the pressure around him changed. A massive fireball flew out of Airiella's hands, slamming into the wall of rock in front of her. The energy blowback was huge, and Stolas barely had time to grab Airiella before flying towards the trees, her wings coming out and wrapping around them both.

As the dust settled, Airiella slowly unwound her wings, and they heard clapping. Seir and Jax stood at the edge of the clearing with wide eyes. Stolas quickly checked Airiella over, though he didn't know why since she'd protected them both.

Stolas pulled Airiella up to her feet, and they looked at where she had hit the side of the mountain with the fireball, leaving a charred black crater with tons of unstable rock above it. "Holy shit! Guess that was a fireball power," Airiella said shakily.

Airiella leaned down and touched the dirt, closing her eyes once again. Stolas stared in fascination as the earth healed what Airiella had done to it, the unstable rock no longer an issue. "Love, that was amazing."

Jax walked over and wrapped Airiella up in a hug when she stood back up. "What was that?" Jax asked her in awe.

"I shot fire out of my hands and tried to kill us by bringing down the mountain," Airiella said into Jax's shoulder.

"We saw the fire and the impact. It was fucking

huge, baby. You did it!" Jax praised Airiella.

"She used one of the powers, yes." Stolas waited for Jax to release Airiella. "We need to work on the others now."

Seir nodded and touched Jax, popping them both back to their clearing. "Did I hurt you?"

"Quite the opposite, you protected me. That was great work. How do you feel?"

"Weird. Kind of excited and terrified both."

"Will you remember what that energy feels like and be able to harness it again?" Stolas asked Airiella carefully.

"I think so. Can we practice that a couple of times, so maybe I don't send a house-sized fireball? I can change how big they are, right?"

"You can. It depends on how much energy you feed into it. Go ahead and practice." Stolas went over and picked up Airiella's music player where it fell when they got blown back.

"Where should I aim? I don't want to aim at the forest; it could start a fire."

"Aim at the side of the mountain. If you are shooting small ones, you won't bring it down on us. Not sure how you fixed that, but it was great." Stolas handed the device back to Airiella, and she stuffed it in her pocket.

Stolas watched as Airiella shot varying sizes of fireballs in different directions at the mountain, and then Stolas grew fascinated as Airiella worked on the distance she could send them. Her strength and power were a sight to behold. Once Airiella agreed that she had a firm grasp on that one, they started the process again.

Airiella went back to sitting with her music playing. Stolas sat next to Airiella this time, and she kept her wings out, one of them behind him, touching him this time. Stolas tried to focus on Airiella's energy to see what she was grasping ahold of, and the next thing Stolas knew he was sitting in Lucifer's study.

"What the fuck, Stolas?" Lucifer growled, looking at them both. "You scared the shit out of me. What's the angel doing here?"

"Uh." Stolas stared back, dumbfounded. "Airiella brought us here. We were working on harnessing the powers of Hell. Love." Stolas pulled one of Airiella's headphones out, "open your eyes."

"Holy shit!" Airiella shot to her feet, starting to panic.

"There's nothing holy about it, I can guarantee you that, but yes, it's still shit. Nice to see you again. Maybe knock next time, so I don't have a heart attack."

Airiella looked wildly around. "I did this?"

"You just proved another part of the prophecy, congratulations. You can walk in this realm as well." Lucifer sat back in his chair, clearly unsettled.

Airiella grabbed Stolas's hand, and he found himself back in the clearing. "You certainly keep things entertaining, love. How did you manage that one?"

"I don't know. I was letting the energy fill me when I felt you trying to connect to me, and I saw a picture of a study, which was where we ended up."

Stolas's eyes opened wide in amazement. "You ported based on something I saw in my head?" Stolas shook his head. "Unbelievable. Okay, you remember that energy signature? Name it and now practice it, but I am blocking you. Before you go exploring the realm of Hell, I'd rather have you be proficient at this ability. Keep touching me, but picture places that you know instead."

Airiella started to shake. "I literally was just in Hell."

Stolas chuckled, "You were, indeed. Practice this before I throw in a curveball to this one." Stolas kept touching her as Airiella ported them around to places she was familiar with, the last being the home of her parents, who were no less surprised than Lucifer had been. Once Airiella was comfortable, she looked at Stolas in question.

"What curveball?"

"Seir can find anything. I want to see if that is something you can do too. I'm not sure how he does it. Seir's able to port right to it. I don't want us popping up in the middle of a crowd, though."

Airiella looked at Stolas thoughtfully for a moment. Suddenly Stolas found himself amidst a bunch of ruins. "Love?"

"Ronnie lost his hotel key, so I was thinking about his hotel key and held on to the energy. Does that mean since we ended up here that it's here?"

"Let's look," Stolas suggested. A few minutes later, Stolas stood staring down at a hotel key card. Stolas picked it up gingerly and called Airiella. "That answers that question. Let's go for a new twist now. Focus on Ronnie and see if you can pick up his signature and port us to them."

Airiella held Stolas's hand, and he found himself standing in the middle of the field with the others staring at them in shock. Seir started howling in laughter. "Travel just got a lot easier, didn't it?"

"Guess where she took us first?" Stolas couldn't hide the smile on his face.

"The ocean," Smitty answered.

"Nope." Stolas let the suspense hang for a moment. "Airiella took us right to Lucifer's office."

Seir stopped laughing. "You're kidding."

"No, Airiella saw the picture of it in my head. She didn't know where it was." Stolas felt a sense of pride for the angel. "She's absolutely incredible."

"By the way, Ronnie," Airiella smiled at Ronnie, "here's the key card you lost."

"Well fuck, I'm useless now," Seir deadpanned as Ronnie's jaw dropped open.

"How are things going here?" Stolas asked, giving Airiella a moment to relax.

"They all have small abilities with the elements, air being the easiest for them all. Jax was able to call the water from the river, and I think Ronnie was able to move a few rocks. We've been working with air a lot as that comes easiest. They've been able to knock each other over with gusts and create whirlwinds with ease."

"You called the water, Jax? That's amazing. That one was the hardest one for me." Airiella went up and kissed Jax.

"Yeah, angel, Jax called it all right and drenched me with it." Ronnie glowered at Jax.

"Retaliate, throw a rock at him," Airiella suggested. "Jax can try to use the wind to knock it away before it hits him. If he can't, he'll learn."

"You are savage." Smitty laughed, slapping his leg.

"Have any of them been able to call lightning?" Stolas asked Seir.

"No. I think that will be uniquely Airiella. I didn't want to push the guys too hard today; they'll be exhausted by all this. I was more working on getting them better control of what they could use."

"No arguments from me on that," Stolas agreed. "We'll let you get back to it."

Airiella ran around and kissed all of them, even Seir, though it was only on Seir's cheek before Airiella took them back to their clearing. "What's next?"

"Are you tired? Travel like that takes quite a bit of energy." Stolas studied Airiella.

"I feel fine. How many more powers of Hell are there?"

"A lot. It's why it's hard for me to say what you'll be able to do or not. If you feel like it, keep going," Stolas told Airiella, releasing her hand.

Airiella put her music back in her ears, and this time she found the new energy quicker, her confidence gaining. Stolas felt the energy build and knew what was about to happen, Airiella was going to release a blast of power, the pure demon magic that was so potent and strong in both him and Lucifer.

Stolas quickly pulled out Airiella's headphones and stopped her. "Do you have a good grasp on that signature?"

"I think so, why?"

"That one has the power to hurt me. Remember those energy blasts I've done, that's what that is. With as much energy as you gathered on that, you could have leveled this area. I'd rather work on that one somewhere more open and with some protection for myself. Also, not with the others so close by."

"That's what I did to that forest, isn't it?"

"I believe so." Stolas stroked Airiella's arm. "Don't be alarmed. I think it's because you are touching me that I recognized that one. I could feel it build, and that's why I stopped you. Categorize that one, and we will practice that one somewhere else."

"That one almost feels like my lightning, but there's a subtle difference to it."

"That's the demon magic. Lucifer and I are the strongest ones with that one. Given that you have outshone me on the rest, I can only assume that this ability will be stronger than mine, too." Stolas didn't want to tell Airiella it could kill him.

"That's the one that will make a difference, isn't it?"

"Probably. How many other signatures do you feel when your mind clears?" Stolas was curious.

"There are several weak ones and a couple of stronger ones. Do you want me to only focus on the strong ones?"

"For now, if they show up to you as strong, then it's probably a reasonable assumption that you should have a firm hold on what they are, so you don't reach for something unknown," Stolas rationalized.

"Okay." Airiella's headphones went back in, and before Stolas could blink twice, Airiella had disappeared.

"Airiella? Love?" Stolas could still feel Airiella's hand in his. Stolas reached forward with his other arm slowly and touched Airiella's body. She reappeared.

"What? Was that another dangerous one?"

Stolas was confused. "Can you do it again with your eyes open and no music playing?"

"I think so." Airiella stared at Stolas, and she disappeared again. "Stolas? Where are you?"

"I'm right in front of you, love. Can you feel my hand?" Stolas asked.

"Yes."

"Hold on to whatever you are doing, but let my hand go," Stolas suggested, moving his leg from touching Airiella's and leaning forward, so her wing wasn't brushing his back.

"There you are." Airiella's voice sounded from around Stolas.

Stolas smiled. "You are invisible, love. With you not touching me, it sounds like you are all around me. I wouldn't know where you were if I didn't know you were next to me."

"No, shit? That's cool." Airiella retook his hand. "When I touch you, you go invisible too."

"Yes, that is pretty cool. I've never known that could happen. I do notice that when you touch me, your voice isn't all around me, it's right where you are, even though I can't see you." Stolas smiled at Airiella's delight.

She let go of the magic and grinned. "I can have so much fun with that one. Oh, Ronnie has some serious payback coming for his little jokes."

"Can you do it again? But completely open yourself to me. I want to see if I can copy that energy. You'll probably feel me since I'll need to free my magic. It might feel oppressive, but it won't hurt you."

"Do you think I don't trust you after all this shit? Do what you need to do, I'm open." Airiella disappeared. "Do you need me to touch you?" her voice came from all around Stolas again. It was slightly disorienting.

"No, but I'm letting my magic go now, brace yourself," Stolas warned.

"Yep, can certainly feel you, but it's not oppressive." Stolas tried to lock on to the signature but couldn't quite get it. "You shimmered."

Stolas reached forward to grab Airiella's hand, but she wasn't there. A giggle erupted all around him, and Stolas smiled. It was nice to see demon magic used for harmless fun. Stolas felt Airiella hug him from behind, and he grasped her arms, the signature still elusive.

"It's okay; you can let it go. It wasn't power I have ever had. I just wondered if I could learn to use it," Stolas told her.

"You did something because you kept flickering."

Stolas would work on it. "How many more strong ones?"

"Two, but one is the one you told me not to use, and there is this other one next to it that is just as strong."

"You don't have to put your music back in?" Stolas asked, a little surprised.

"No, I can see it now. As well as all these weaker ones."

"What does the other strong one feel like?" Stolas asked.

"Hazy. Like smoke, kind of; when I touch it, there is a weird tingle that starts in my chest and a pulling sensation."

Stolas froze. "Don't grab that one." Stolas's voice came out scared.

"What is it?"

"The ability to rip a soul from someone's body." Airiella had Lucifer's power as one of her strong ones. Stolas himself had that ability as did other princes, but it wasn't strong like it was for Lucifer.

Airiella looked horrified. "Why would I need that?"

"We can't practice that one, love. Only you would ever know if you need that power. Label it, and don't ever grab it unless you are prepared to use it." Stolas sounded like a frightened kid and tried to shake it off.

"It would have killed you, wouldn't it?"

"It will kill anyone. If you were to infuse your lightning with it, there would be no coming back, no being reborn. I think some mixture of that is what came out of you when you killed Bael. I only felt the lightning because the other part is something I recognize on my own, and I never thought to look for it."

Airiella grew pale and started to shake, and Stolas gathered her up in his arms and kissed her head. "It's okay, love. You were supposed to have the power. Since you are the balance of all things, that means you can give life as well."

"Can we be done now?"

"Of course, love. Are you going to stop shaking?" Stolas ran his hands up and down Airiella's back, trying to rub warmth back into her.

"I could have killed you." Airiella trembled.

"You didn't. How you described it told me everything I needed to know. And if demons come calling, I'll have you practice that particular power on them. I promise, love, it's okay. You know exactly the ones that are safe to work on and practice on your own, and we'll go through the weaker ones on a different day. You did brilliantly."

Suddenly Stolas was back in the clearing with the others, and Jax was rushing over to them. "I've got you, baby," Jax was saying as Stolas let Airiella go. "He's fine. Look at me, Stolas is fine. We are all fine."

Seir came up to Stolas. "Did something happen?"

"Later," Stolas told Seir. "Nothing happened, but

we'll talk later."

"Practice time is over," Seir announced.

Airiella got sandwiched between Ronnie and Jax, and they disappeared. Stolas gestured to Smitty and Aedan to come over, and Seir popped them back to the hotel. Once Smitty and Aedan left to see to Airiella, Seir turned back to him.

"What was that about?"

"Airiella has the power to rip souls. I stopped her before she grabbed ahold of it, but it's strong. She freaked out when I told her what it was," Stolas explained.

"How strong is it?"

"Strong enough, she can describe the sensations of it as hazy and smoky, with a tingle in her chest and a pulling sensation. For me, with as strong as I am, I only get the pulling sensation when I use that power."

"That's all I get, too," Seir said. "And I can only pull some souls." Seir looked a little shaken by that revelation as well. "That seals it for me, the prophecies are authentic, and I am way more terrified of Airiella losing control than I was before."

"Airiella's got a good handle on it now, and I'm less worried about it, but that was also a controlled environment, and it took a while for her to focus. We still have work to do, but this was an excellent start," Stolas defended Airiella.

"I need a drink. Possibly a woman. I'll see you later." Seir took off, leaving Stolas alone until Kalisha entered the room.

"Airiella is in rough shape," Kalisha said as a way of a greeting.

"I need to call Lucifer." Stolas kissed Kalisha.

"Airiella's extremely powerful. She's shaken by the power to rip souls. Seir was too. We'll let her calm down a bit then see if they want to go for dinner. Need to talk to Lucifer first."

"Not without me, you aren't," Airiella said from behind Stolas. Her face still pale and eyes wide. "I'm not using that power until I hear more about it. I don't care what happens to me."

Kalisha moved and wrapped her arm around Airiella's shoulder. "Stolas was going to call him. Go back to your room. We'll call when Lucifer's here. You need to calm down first before you talk with Lucifer. It makes me nervous having you so raw feeling around him."

Airiella nodded and disappeared. "That's going to take some getting used to," Stolas said with a small smile.

Chapter Twenty-Four

Stolas hung up the phone and sighed. "Group meeting number two. They all are coming except the women and kids," Stolas informed Kalisha and Lucifer.

"I expected no less," Lucifer said dryly.

At least they appeared knocking at the door this time, and Stolas moved to let them in, Airiella safely ensconced in the middle of them all. Stolas snickered a bit. "No one here is going to attack Airiella, relax you guys."

"Habit," Jax replied. "Airiella got pretty rattled earlier, and it brings out the protective instincts in all of us. Should have seen Mags and Chrissie, they wouldn't even let *us* near her."

The guys slowly parted, leaving Ronnie and Jax flanking Airiella's sides and Smitty and Aedan behind her. "It's an improvement, none of you are glowing this time," Lucifer remarked. Stolas shot him a look.

"Are you hungry, love? Would you like me to order up some food?" Stolas asked gently.

Airiella shook her head no and seemed to gulp in the air in big lungful's. Airiella stepped away from Jax and Ronnie and disappeared. "Creepy not knowing what to expect, isn't it?" Airiella's voice echoed around the room.

Lucifer was so startled he dropped his drink, and Stolas bit back a laugh. Then all the rest of the group disappeared and reappeared at the table Lucifer was sitting at, making him jump once again. "Clever girl," was all Lucifer managed to say.

Airiella sat down at the table while the guys spread out across the suite as if they were covering all the room's angles. "What I would really like to know," Airiella started, and Stolas saw her eyes change slightly, a glow appearing in them, "is why you wouldn't tell me about this beforehand?"

Stolas felt it, Airiella was playing with the very power that scared her. Lucifer's eyes bugged out, and Stolas saw Lucifer's soul start to separate. "Love, no," Stolas begged Airiella.

She released it. "I wouldn't have done it, Stolas. Despite the lack of training with it, the same principals apply to the other powers I used. This display was merely a demonstration to go along with the important question of why Lucifer wouldn't tell me about this, at least as a forewarning seeing as how I could have killed you. When you combine invisibility, my lightning, and that ability, no one would ever know I was near. I could end everything and everyone."

Lucifer was visibly trying to get himself under control; she had thoroughly frightened him. "I wasn't sure what abilities you would have," was the only defense Lucifer could muster. Stolas knew it wouldn't fly.

"Yet, you believed I had the power to kill you. It seems to me those would go hand in hand." Airiella crossed her arms. "I'm not sure you understand just how pissed off

I am right now."

Kalisha stood up and went to sit by Jax as if some sense of danger invaded her thoughts. Stolas crossed the room to stand by Kalisha, concerned. Unfortunately, it left Lucifer alone at a table with the most powerful being to walk among them.

"Airiella's fine," Jax told him confidently. "Pissed, but fine."

"I honestly didn't consider it. I should have, but I didn't. No one seems to understand what you can or can't do or how you can do it. I do apologize, it was not my intent, nor would I have put my friend in danger like that," Lucifer expelled in a rush.

"You'd better think quick and tell me any other little surprises that might be in store for me before I start to want to practice on you," Airiella declared.

Stolas couldn't help it, and he did laugh then. Lucifer had never been put in his place before, much less by someone he'd just met and so effectively. Stolas knew Airiella wouldn't hurt his friend; however, she just proved she was willing to push Lucifer's limits of comfort.

Airiella looked over at him. "Tacos, please."

Stolas wasted no time and ordered what she wanted, taking direction from Jax while Airiella stared down Lucifer. As Stolas was hanging up the phone, a crack of thunder that shook the walls tore through the room.

"Fuck, this has been a truly awful day," Lucifer spit out as a white light settled at the table with Lucifer and Airiella. "You choose now to show up?"

"What are you?" Airiella spluttered.

"Meet the Creator, the other half of your powers," Lucifer spit.

"Wait, that's God?!" Ronnie shouted.

Stolas shushed Ronnie, his eyes riveted on the table. "Are you a man or a woman?" Airiella asked.

"I am whatever you want me to be," the Creator answered Airiella.

"Then a woman, there is entirely too much testosterone in this room, and we all know women are the ones who truly hold power."

Smitty snorted then quieted down as a woman now sat at the table, a soft, serene smile on her face. Her hair was a close match for Airiella's, her eyes a golden color not seen in humans. She looked exactly like an angel that Lucifer used to fool around with before he fell. As a matter of fact, the one that called him Lucy.

"This is a bit much, don't you think?" Lucifer growled, his face angry. "You could have chosen to look like anyone."

"Ah, but this is so much fun," she said. "Life needs to have fun in it, don't you agree, Airiella?"

"I'm missing something here," Airiella said carefully, looking between the two.

"It doesn't matter." Lucifer tried to take the high road. "Took your time is coming to this party, didn't you?"

"I came right when I was supposed to. You are doing beautifully, Airiella," she said and she smiled at the angel.

At this, Airiella stirred to life again, a wave of anger surpassing Lucifer's settling on Airiella's face. "Beautifully? There is nothing beautiful about this. My life has turned into a giant fucking circus, the ones I love are now on the firing line with me, and I have to face another demon asshole! What exactly is beautiful about this?"

"For starters, you," she told Airiella calmly. Stolas cringed as blue flames erupted all around them, Lucifer included, and Airiella's body came to life, her skin crackling with the unleashed lightning. Another look of fear was on Lucifer's face, but the creator remained calm. "See? Very beautiful. You even protected Lucifer. I chose perfectly in you."

At once, it all died down, and Stolas let out the breath he'd been holding. A look of sadness replaced the anger that had been on Airiella's face. Airiella's team moved as one, only stopped by Kalisha. "Let her be, Airiella will ask when she needs you."

Jax dug his fingers painfully into Stolas's arm, his need to go to Airiella strong. Even Stolas had reacted to the look on Airiella's face. "Do you have any idea how much it hurts to see that look?" Jax whispered to Stolas.

"I do," was all Stolas could say.

"I know the burden is heavy, Airiella. I know it hurts you. I wish that I could say you won't experience more pain. I can't tell you that, though. I don't know how this will end. The answers all lie within you. Stolas, please come here, child."

Startled, Airiella looked over to Stolas as he slowly walked to the table. Airiella reached for Stolas's hand and clutched it tightly as he stood next to her. The energy Airiella had rolling under her skin tingled against his side.

"Sacrifice is always a part of every life that has free will," she started.

Airiella stood. "I am *not* sacrificing Stolas!" she thundered.

"Love, relax. Let her speak," Stolas told her quietly. Lucifer was watching the exchange with narrowed eyes.

"I'm not asking you to, Airiella. I am speaking to the sacrifice Stolas made in his choices. I was heartbroken to see him go, yet I understood his choice." She reached across the table and tapped his chest where the mark lay. "This is why Stolas is marked the way he is. Stolas could have chosen a different path, yet even the wrong choices he made, Stolas made them for the right reasons. Despite the guilt he holds inside him, Stolas has reacted with kindness, loyalty, and love for those who need it. Now, you have chosen love again, and it's beautiful to see."

Lucifer huffed. "Your choices in this are just as selfish as mine, don't try to act differently. You took an innocent soul and gave her choices and situations that suit your needs."

"I may have chosen Airiella, but her creation wasn't to suit my needs," she said and she looked at Lucifer, her tone cooling. "Airiella has the power to destroy me as well as you. She no more serves me than she does you. That precisely is why she is the chosen one. Her very existence is one of love, and she clearly can see the justice that you and I don't see because of our division. Airiella has chosen love instead of hate at every opportunity. You have never been stupid, Lucifer. Don't start to act it now."

Airiella looked at Lucifer. "Knock it off. For as old as you are, you can act like an adult and have an adult conversation. I heard you out; I can hear her out as well."

The Creator laughed. "Do you not see it, Lucifer?"

"No, I see it. I saw it before," Lucifer grudgingly admitted.

"Stolas is your advisor, Airiella. Stolas is your guide between my realm, this one, and Lucifer's. He's walked all of them, lived all of them, and seen the good and bad in both. It is only through his choice Stolas remains where he is. Stolas can choose where he wants to reside, and I would welcome him with open arms. His role in this is purely for you. Like your own raven, Stolas can be a messenger between the gods and the spirits."

"I have access to your realm?" Stolas wasn't sure he heard that right.

"You always have, child. You just couldn't see it. Kalisha does as well."

Airiella looked up at Stolas, still holding his hand. "I knew you were different." Airiella looked back at the Creator. "Why me? Will I ever get to live a normal life?"

"Your life has *never* been normal," Lucifer choked out. "Could you not tell that by the shit you've been put through? None of which was my choice, I might add. I would never have done that to you."

Airiella glared at him. "Zip it."

"Lucifer's right on that, Airiella. Your destiny is for things greater than either of us could manage on our own. You don't conform to one religion; you've accepted all of this with grace no one else could; you love despite the tragedy, and you can easily tell the difference between right and wrong. If that hadn't been the case, the powers in you wouldn't have manifested. That was my failsafe. Each of those that carry your mark now, they share this with you. Together, that which threatens this planet can be set to rights again. Lucifer has not lied to you about that."

"I haven't lied to Airiella about anything," Lucifer snapped.

The Creator ignored Lucifer, instead, looking at both Stolas and Airiella. "Your guidance will be paramount, Stolas. Even with that, the choices will remain with her.

Moloch will do exactly as you fear if left unchecked." She pointed at Lucifer. "It won't be just you that's ended, it will be me as well."

"Why did Jax not get a mark?" Airiella asked quietly. Stolas jolted, and Lucifer looked intrigued.

"Jax did, Airiella. Like Stolas, his is just different than the rest. You can't do this without Jax."

"I *won't* do anything without Jax," Airiella informed the Creator. "Jax, come here." Airiella looked back at him. She released Stolas's hand and stood, sliding Jax's shirt up to his chest. "Look, no mark. The rest have it here." Airiella tapped Jax's chest.

The creator smiled and gestured for Jax to turn around, which he did, the shirt bunching up in Airiella's hand, and Stolas saw it. His heart stopped beating at the words, "There is no greater love," appearing right below the giant wings tattooed on Jax's back.

Lucifer gasped and glared at the Creator with malice, sliding a look at Stolas. They both knew what that meant, and neither had the heart to say it out loud. Probably for different reasons, Stolas admitted to himself.

Airiella traced the words on Jax's back with her finger, clearly having a conversation with Jax in her head. There was a subtle change to Airiella's demeanor, and Stolas understood that Airiella knew what it meant on some level. In the bible, it was in the book of John: "There is no greater love than to lay down one's life for one's friends."

"Follow your heart Airiella, but always check to make sure that it's message is real and not simply a reaction to something you don't like." With those parting words, the Creator disappeared as a knock sounded at the door.

Chapter Twenty-Five

When everyone had left, Stolas dropped on to the couch, hanging his head low. Lucifer had been oddly silent the rest of the night, only giving Stolas a look of concern before he left. Kalisha sat down next to Stolas and rubbed his back.

"Someone will die, won't they?"

"I don't know, Kalisha. I don't. All of us have the potential to die in this. I think it all comes down to choices that Airiella makes." Stolas let out a string of curses. "I have no idea how I am supposed to guide Airiella, given the promises I've made."

"Let's not pick it apart. It will drive us both crazy." Kalisha chewed on her bottom lip.

"Seir!" Stolas yelled.

"What the fuck? Why are you yelling?" Seir appeared, looking somewhat drunk.

"When you work the guys on their skills, push them hard. Get them honed in and test them in stress situations," Stolas barked out. He didn't know what else to do. Stolas had no idea if one of them was going to die, or if it was Airiella, or himself, or all of them. Stolas had it narrowed down to a small group. If he had to lay money on it, it would be him, Airiella, or Jax. They all had different marks. That meant something.

"You called me here for that?"

"It's important, Seir," Kalisha spoke up softly. "You just missed the Creator being here."

That stopped Seir's ranting fast. "Here?"

Stolas looked at Seir, fear in his eyes. "Here. With them, Airiella, and Lucifer."

"Shit, Lucifer, and the Creator in the same room?"

"With Airiella between them," Stolas ground out. "I should have asked if they could cross into Hell. Training with Lucifer's guards would be excellent."

Seir choked on a cough. "You want them to train with Lucifer's guards? Are you trying to get them killed?"

"Can you think of a better way for the guys to learn how to fight demons that want them to die?"

Seir narrowed his eyes. "What's truly going on here? Why are you so tense right now?"

"Jax's mark is different from all the others," Kalisha told Seir.

"So is the one Stolas has."

"It's part of a quote. There is no greater love, it says, right below a tattoo of Airiella's wings," Kalisha explained.

"Well shit, call Lucifer back then." Seir looked sad. "Never mind, I'll do it. Lucifer," Seir called out.

Stolas just sat there. No matter how Stolas looked at it, he couldn't come to any other conclusion. "You have to train them hard, Seir."

"Yeah, I get it. I doubt the guys can cross, though."

"What is it, Seir?" Lucifer appeared.

"Can you bring a battalion of guards to our training spot tomorrow? I'd like to use them to help train their team."

"Consider it done," Lucifer said blandly. "Lassie, don't lose hope. Most of all, don't lose your life." Lucifer disappeared.

"After that ball of great news, I'm going to sleep. Tomorrow looks to be a hard day. I take it they are doing the physical workout with us before we go to the mountains?"

"I would assume so. The same schedule as today as far as I know," Stolas said, weariness creeping into his tone.

"Sleep, Stolas. We all are going to need it." Seir patted Stolas on the shoulder and disappeared.

"I'm going to go shower. Want to join me?" Kalisha asked him.

"Sure." Stolas's movements were wooden, and everything seemed to take a lot more effort. Mentally he checked out, only going through the motions of everything. As Stolas settled into bed with Kalisha, the only thing that brought him some measure of comfort was wrapping himself around her.

Stolas drifted in and out of sleep. *Hey,* Airiella's voice came into his head.

Stolas sat up quickly and flipped the light next to the bed on; Airiella wasn't in the room with him. Had she just talked to him telepathically?

Yes, it really happened. It turns out one of these smaller strands of energy contained that ability. It looks like you aren't rid of me even this way.

Love, Stolas turned out the light, so he didn't wake

Kalisha and lay back down. *We should talk about today.*

No, Stolas. I can't. Not about what you want to talk to me about, not right now.

Stolas felt tears sting his eyes. He didn't need Airiella's empath skills to know what she was feeling. *I haven't forgotten my promise.*

I said no. Stop now.

You contacted me, remember?

Because I was trying this out; not for any other reason than that!

How was Stolas supposed to be Airiella's advisor when she wouldn't talk to him? *Why are you playing with those powers right now anyway? Shouldn't you be sleeping?*

I tried. Why aren't you asleep?

How do you know I wasn't? Stolas reasoned with Airiella.

I know because your thoughts are as loud as mine are.

Love, stay out of my head if you don't want to talk about it.

I wasn't in your head. I grabbed the energy, and your thoughts are what hit me. So either this is my ability to talk this way to all demons, or it's specifically for you.

Do you feel like a puppet whose strings are getting pulled, too? Stolas asked her suddenly.

All the time; was Airiella's instant reply. *Jax told me he wants to be the one to fight Stone.*

Stolas sighed. *Lucifer is bringing his guards up for training tomorrow to train with them.*

Is that a good idea?

Yes. It will give the guys a chance to use their

magic against demons trying to attack them.

Stolas could hear the fear in Airiella's voice as she asked him, *Non-lethally, right?*

Seir will be with them. There were so many things Stolas wanted to tell Airiella, ways they could interpret the words, but she didn't want to hear it. It also felt like giving her false hope, something Stolas honestly didn't want to do.

I still love you, Stolas. No matter what happens.

The tone she said it in, struck a chord of fear deep inside Stolas. It had a ring of finality to it. *And I, you, love.* Stolas heard nothing else from Airiella, and after five minutes of silence, he figured Airiella had cut the connection off.

Morning came too soon, and the spotty sleep Stolas had gotten had done nothing to help his state of mind. Exhaustion pulled at him, and Stolas's temper was short. The workout Ronnie put them through helped with the irritability, but not the rest.

Stolas pushed Airiella hard, just as hard as he was sure Lucifer's guards were pushing the rest of the team. Airiella didn't complain; despite the fatigue she showed, she kept going, which made Stolas feel worse. When they finished, there was minimal conversation between any of them, including Seir.

Back at the hotel, Airiella reminded them Ronnie's wedding was in two days and then went to her room. They had a location to film the next day, on top of training. At the rate they were going, none of them would have the energy to fight.

Stolas went to his pack and pulled out some of the herbs to make a sleep tonic, then distributed it to each of them, extracting promises they would all drink. Airiella extracted the same commitment from Stolas, and he wasn't going to argue. He drank one down and collapsed on the bed, not even waiting for Kalisha to finish showering.

Chapter Twenty-Six

Stolas took his raven form and followed the paranormal crew to their location. Kalisha was staying behind with the other spouses. Something had spooked Kalisha, and she was sticking to the kids like glue. Airiella's raven settled next to Stolas, her eyes glowing with that amber light Jax called angel eyes.

There's a danger here, Stolas. I can feel it singing through my veins.

Startled, Stolas looked back at the raven who was staring at him still. *I don't see anything, love.*

That doesn't mean it's not here. It's dark and menacing.

Stolas took flight and circled the old hospital ruins before moving to the part where they were all gathered. Stolas didn't see anything at all. *I'm flying and looking; I still don't see anything at all. Can you tell me a direction?*

All around me, it's coming from everywhere.

Tell the guys to all stay together for this one then. No one goes off alone, that means you stay with them. If you can manage it, go invisible. The thought hit Stolas then. What if another demon had that same power that

Airiella did? Stolas wouldn't be able to see them. *Are you using your soul sight?*

I am now. Nothing is standing out, but it's here.

I believe you, love. I'm staying close.

Out of nowhere, Airiella's raven dive-bombed Stolas, slamming into his raven's body, causing Stolas to swoop down and almost hit a tree. Stolas looked back and saw a mist hovering in the air where he had been. A shadow. Airiella's raven flew back up beside him, herding Stolas away, towards Airiella.

Taklishim is under attack! Airiella yelled into his mind.

I'm sending Seir; you can't leave them!

Go! Go, help him! Airiella screamed.

I can't leave you, love. Stolas called out for Seir and landed as Seir appeared below him.

"The warrior is under attack. Get some guards from Lucifer and go help him!"

Seir nodded and disappeared. *Love, tell him Seir and some of Lucifer's guards are coming to help, don't attack them.*

Done. Can't I go and help Taklishim? You can stay here with these guys. Airiella pleaded, her voice desperate.

No love, you are stronger together, and you can do things I can't do.

Then I'll bring all of us! I can't leave Taklishim to fight this alone!

Stolas fought back a sigh and tried again. *Are you willing to take all this crew and put them in the middle of a fight right now?*

The entire group of them appeared out the front door. "We will go as one and come back and finish our job,

Stolas. Tak has always fought for us. For us to not be there when his family is on the line is wrong," Jax called out.

Airiella let her wings out, and Stolas flew down and transformed in front of them. "Let's go then."

Airiella popped them over, and Stolas changed and took to flight to get an aerial view and saw demons overrunning this small town; the warrior and his crew were vastly outnumbered. Below, Jax, Ronnie, Aedan, and Smitty took up fighting positions around Airiella, who was gathering power to her.

Wait! Your friends do not have stones to protect them! If you unleash that demon magic, you could hurt them! Stolas warned Airiella. *And all the innocent people trapped in this middle of this.*

They are protected, Taklishim assured me.

Whatever energy Airiella was gathering was something Stolas wasn't familiar with yet. Airiella was using some innate ability she was born with and unleashed a wave mixed of light and dark magic. Stolas could see the shock wave of it rolling through the town like a tidal wave cutting down every demon in its path. Except one.

The dark mage, Stone, still stood, protected by something. Stone was facing off with the warrior, Taklishim. Stolas directed Airiella to where they were, warning her of the protection around Stone. The guys were following closely, Ronnie and Jax, on either side of their angel.

Seir and Lucifer's guards appeared behind Taklishim. "Raven! Get out of here! That's what they wanted!" Taklishim yelled at Airiella.

Stone's going to track you, love. You need to leave a false path. Do as the warrior says, Stolas pleaded with

Airiella. *Seir and the guards will help him.*

Airiella ignored them both and threw up a wall of flames between the warrior and Stone and took a running dive at the mage, Airiella's wings wrapped around her as she crashed into Stone's legs, knocking him down. Airiella threw a flurry of punches and kicks, distracting Stone enough for Taklishim to get a few good hits in with his shadows. Airiella was a blur of motion, living proof of Ronnie's excellent training.

None of it mattered. Stone just disappeared, leaving a panting Airiella and stunned Taklishim in his wake. Airiella threw herself into the warrior's arms, murmuring words Stolas was too far away to hear. Stolas was able to see the mark on his chest, though, when the warrior lifted his shirt to show Airiella. It looked precisely like Ronnie's did. Airiella touched it briefly, embraced him again, then called Stolas to her so they could go back.

As they reappeared on the location, Airiella put her wings away and called out to him. Stolas transformed and approached.

"Love, that was a foolish move. What happens if they track you here?" Stolas whispered angrily.

"Then, I kill them here. I can't risk Tak's new babies and Onida, who is going to pop hers out soon."

"What was that you did? How did you mix the two magic's?" Stolas reached out and ran his hand up the scrape on Airiella's arm. Stolas pulled out one of the salves from his pocket and started to rub it on the abraded skin.

"I didn't know that I did mix them. I was so intent on just sending out a killing blast that I just did what felt right." Airiella looked down at her arm. "Thanks, that feels better."

"It worked, whatever you did. It was like a wave that took out anyone in its path. Ash, all of them. Except for Stone." Stolas put the container away, glad he had thought to bring it with him.

"Stone's protection didn't work against physical attacks," Airiella pointed out.

"Yes, but if that were your goal, you would have been better off sending in Ronnie or Jax." Stolas couldn't help but point it out.

"You should have heard them in my head," Airiella admitted with a small smile. "You all are probably right."

"Let us all help you, love."

Airiella gave Stolas a sheepish look. "Sorry."

Stolas sighed in frustration. "I'm not a very good advisor; it seems."

"Stop it. That had nothing to do with you. It was pure instinct that took over. All the people out there fighting could have probably handled it; they were all shifters and strong in their own rights. I'd just rather have them still in fighting shape rather than exhausted and injured."

Stolas shoved his hands in his pockets, so he didn't grab Airiella and shake her like he wanted to. "Love, it's their nature to do that. They were made for it."

"Maybe, but that happened because of me. The demons were looking for me and trying to draw me out. It worked, they got me there, but it also failed, because they are all dead."

"Stone isn't."

"He will be. I'll figure out how to take Stone down," Airiella promised menacingly.

"That's not the point!" Stolas almost shouted.

"The ease in which you took out an entire legion of demons in a matter of seconds frightens me," Lucifer said behind Stolas, making him jump.

Airiella started to glow, and Stolas jumped in. "Love, they are filming. If you are glowing, they will start too. Don't want that on camera, calm down. Lucy won't hurt you."

"I'm not doing it on purpose," Airiella argued.

"Didn't mean to startle either of you," Lucifer grinned. "It's just a bonus. Call it payback for scaring me the other day. I came here to say I've found out that Stone is supposed to be the anti-angel. Stone doesn't have even close to the same amount of abilities and skills that the angel does. From what I have gathered, Stone has Moloch and Bael's magic in him as we suspected."

"They tried to create a dark version of Airiella to defeat her?" Stolas was dumbfounded.

"Tried being key here," Lucifer sneered. "There *is* supposed to be an opposite to her. There's a different prophecy about that. However, it's not Stone."

"I'm not all light," Airiella argued.

"No, you're not. You wouldn't be able to see the darkness in others if you didn't recognize it in yourself. The difference is you don't feed it." Lucifer looked at Airiella closely. "If you did, we'd be having a different conversation right now. I'll admit the creator chose well with you. I also think you'd drive me batshit crazy if you ended up down there, so just don't."

Stolas snorted and tried to cover it with a cough, but Airiella heard it anyway and glared at him. "Lucifer's not wrong, but that doesn't mean you get to laugh about it."

Stolas held up his hands in surrender and turned

back to Lucifer. "Thanks for sending guards to help out."

"Don't know why I bothered. One little blast from this girl, and she obliterated them all. At least they showed up after that, or they would have become ash too."

A stricken look appeared on Airiella's face at that. "I didn't even think of that! I'm so sorry."

It was Lucifer's turn to snort. "And this is why I'm not too worried about you ending up down there to be my headache." Lucifer grinned at the scowl on Airiella's face. "Time for me to go."

Stolas waited until Lucifer was gone and stepped closer to Airiella. "Go join the others; I'll go back to watching over things."

"Wait. If Stone got created to be like me and Jax wants to be the one to take Stone out, how much danger does that put Jax in?"

"Love, stop. You need to get over this and let us all help. You heard the same things I did. Jax isn't helpless, none of them are. Respect Jax's decisions and talk with them all about it. Cover your bases and accept their input. You keep failing to understand that they stand to lose just as much as you do in this." Stolas pulled Airiella's arm out and pointed to her cancer tattoo. "No one fights alone, remember?"

"Low blow, Stolas." Airiella yanked her arm away, and as his words sunk in, she stood on her tiptoes and kissed his cheek. "Point taken." Stolas watched until Airiella was back inside with the others.

Stolas turned to transform and was face to face with Lucifer again. "Lassie, I have a bad feeling about this."

"What do you mean?" Stolas frowned.

"I have this nagging suspicion that Airiella's going

to make a wrong choice. You and I both know what that mark on Jax means. One of you won't survive this, and with the way she loves you all, finding the right path through that grief won't be easy for her."

"Airiella won't talk about it with me. You can always deny her entrance." Stolas grasped at any straw he could.

"Truly, I do like the angel, and surprisingly, she doesn't dislike me. You and I both know I can only deny some things. Airiella's going to need you to guide her, Lassie. It's not going to be easy, and I'm sorry my friend, but I sincerely hope it isn't you that will be the one lost."

"I don't think Airiella dislikes anyone. Trust is another issue entirely. I'm working on it, Lucy, getting through her fears over everyone is a big challenge. Airiella even protected you."

Lucifer laughed. "That was surprising and a little uncomfortable." Lucifer patted Stolas on the arm. "I think it was wrong of the Creator to put this burden on her, and in turn, you. It makes me furious in a way I can't explain, I see it as selfish of the Creator. That's supposed to be my role, the selfish one. Take care, my friend."

Chapter Twenty-Seven

K alisha, are you ready?" Stolas called into the bathroom.

"No, I need five more minutes," was the answer that came back to him.

"We are going to be late," Stolas warned.

"Fine, but if I look hideous, it's your fault," Kalisha casually remarked as she came out of the bathroom. Stolas felt like someone had sucker-punched him; she was so breathtakingly beautiful.

"My love," Stolas whispered. "I've never seen beauty like this before."

Kalisha twirled for him. The simple pale blue dress complimented her dark skin tone and flared around Kalisha's legs, hugging every delicious curve of her body as it settled down around her. She'd put on light makeup around her eyes, highlighting the unique color, and painted her lips a soft pink that was just begging Stolas to kiss her. "Don't even think about it." Kalisha laughed as Stolas moved towards her. "If you mess it up, I'll only have to take time to do it again."

"I find it hard to care if I'm late now," Stolas replied,

his tone low and husky.

Kalisha had pulled her long dreadlocks up and splayed the ends out, and Stolas wanted nothing more than to mess it all up while undressing her. "Come on, let's go." Kalisha tugged his hand as she walked past him.

Stolas obediently followed, raking his eyes over her, mentally undressing Kalisha and worshipping every inch of her. The lascivious thoughts made him hard as a rock. "I don't think I want to go now."

Kalisha laughed and turned to Stolas. "I can feel how turned you are. I like it, but we have to go. Airiella put a lot of work into making this special for Chrissie with not a whole lot of time between everything else that has been going on."

Stolas grunted his reply and popped them to where he felt Airiella. It was a beautiful location overlooking the water. Flowers lined the room as well as candles; the scent in the room was of blooming roses. The large picture window was facing the sea, the sun sparkling like thousands of little diamonds, romance heavy on the air.

"It's beautiful," Kalisha breathed out. "How did Airiella manage this?"

"I'm betting Airiella had the help of those two ladies right there." Stolas pointed at Mags and Jillian.

"Actually, I did this part myself," Airiella said from behind Stolas.

Stolas turned, and his breath caught yet again. Airiella was radiant in a sunset orange colored dress; the color set off her skin tone exquisitely. Her curly hair loose around her face, and her jewelry was stunning pieces of gemstones. Airiella was wearing makeup too; something Stolas wasn't used to seeing with Airiella. "You look beautiful, love. I was kind of hoping to see that tie-dye dress."

"Kalisha! Wow! You are gorgeous!" Airiella exclaimed, pulling her in for a hug while shooting Stolas a not-amused look over her shoulder.

"Wow! Yeah, she is," Jax agreed, sliding up behind Airiella and grinning at Stolas.

"I'm lucky, that's for sure," Stolas softly said as he gazed down at Kalisha. "This isn't a usual wedding color." Stolas pointed at Airiella's dress.

"No, but luckily Chrissie picked it because I can pull it off, and she loves this color."

"It's a color I always associate with Ells. When the sun hits her eyes, they glow like the sunset; this splendid burst of color comes from her eyes." Jax looked at Airiella. Jax spoke with such love and adoration that it made Stolas's heartbeat erratic at the thought that Airiella could lose Jax or any others.

Their bond was something you could feel being around them, and Stolas had to pull himself away before he did something stupid. "Let's go sit down." Stolas pulled at Kalisha, noticing she was caught up in the thrall as well.

"They have something extraordinary." Kalisha looked back at them as they took their seats.

"They do," Stolas agreed. "We do too, my love. As does each of the people here."

Father Roarke beamed from the front of the room as the ceremony got underway, Jax and Airiella leading the procession with Chrissie's boys being the ring bearers, and Jace carrying Angel as the flower girl.

Ronnie came next, his face splitting wide with a smile that brought tears to Stolas's eyes. Ronnie was so happy and in love. Stolas looked back in time to see Chrissie enter, stunning in her own right. Her blonde hair swept back from her delicate face; her makeup artfully done, highlighting her dainty features. Chrissie's dress was made of lace and form-fitting, her flowers a mix of the color of Airiella's dress and white.

Kalisha sniffled. "She's beautiful."

Stolas felt like an ass. Their ceremony had been nothing special, and he wondered if Kalisha felt cheated that she didn't get to have this for herself. Stolas questioned if he would be able to pull something like this off. Not that Hell was the best place to have a wedding, but they could do it here. He made a mental note to talk to Airiella about it.

You are such a man. Naturally, Kalisha wants something like this. You clearly love her just as much as Ronnie loves Chrissie. I'll talk with the girls later, and we'll work something out for you.

I don't deserve you; Stolas told Airiella.

The ceremony was simple and traditional, with Chrissie being more faith-based than Airiella, and it was what she wanted. Ronnie had never looked happier than he did at the moment, and Chrissie's boys were just as thrilled. It was just what they all needed to see as a reminder of what they were fighting for, a reminder that love and beauty still exist amidst the rampant hate the media portrayed daily.

Stolas had offered up the credit card from Lucifer to Airiella to pay for the reception afterward, and she'd accepted it without an argument for once. The food was delicious and the cake the best Stolas had ever tasted. They did all the traditional wedding rites, the first dance, the garter throwing, which coincidently had been thrown directly to Stolas, and the bouquet to Kalisha. Airiella wasn't subtle.

At the end of it all, the boys were split between Aedan and Smitty to give Ronnie and Chrissie a night to themselves while Airiella and Jax cleaned up and stayed with Kalisha and Stolas. The music was still playing, and Stolas paused in helping clean up to dance once more with Kalisha.

Stolas pulled Kalisha tight to him and swayed around the floor with her in his arms. Jax and Airiella, doing the same thing. "Now that the party is over, I am going to mess up those perfectly pink lips of yours," Stolas said softly in warning before capturing her lips in a deep kiss that left them both breathless. "I love you," Stolas whispered into Kalisha's ear.

"Maybe his tattoo simply means that there is no greater love than the one that they share," Kalisha murmured, her eyes watching Jax. "Did you consider that?"

"No," Stolas admitted. "I didn't. What made you think of that?"

"You telling me that you love me, and how you show me every chance you can. It's what Jax does for Airiella as well." Kalisha looked back at Stolas. "To me, it's obvious. When you saw Jax's tattoo, did you notice Airiella's name and the words love wins?"

"No." Stolas stared into Kalisha's eyes. "You didn't miss much looking at Jax, did you?"

Kalisha chuckled lightly. "Jealous?"

"Maybe."

"Don't be. Jax is beautiful to look at, but a blind person could see Jax only has eyes for Airiella. My eyes were drawn to the tattoo of Airiella's wings; it's magnificent art. Airiella told me Jax drew them. Anyway, that thought just popped into my head. You all have been so focused on the bad side of things; I figured I would point out the other side."

"You amaze me constantly." Stolas smiled and kissed Kalisha again. "I hope that is what it means."

Airiella walked up to them, Jax holding her hand. "Should we go train some more?" Airiella asked wearily.

"No, love. Take the night to celebrate love. It's a good reminder for us all." Stolas smiled softly.

"That is a great idea. Ells, listen to your advisor." Jax grinned lasciviously.

Airiella blushed. "No arguments here. You look fucking hot in that suit, and I can't wait to take you out of it."

Kalisha laughed. "Go. I have my own plans to put in action."

"I hope so!" Airiella giggled. "Stolas looks pretty hot too. All the men that were here pull off this formal look well."

"That they do," Kalisha agreed, a glint in her eyes that made Stolas blush. "We'll talk in the morning."

"Don't go anywhere alone. Don't leave the hotel," Stolas warned, his tone brokering no argument. At Airiella's slight nod, Stolas popped Kalisha and himself back into their room, where he immediately proceeded to mess up her carefully put-together look.

"Leave your clothes on," Kalisha panted at Stolas, a wicked smile on her face.

Stolas gave Kalisha a slow perusal, her disheveled state heightening his arousal. He lowered her to the floor in front of the fireplace. "My love, I'll do anything you ask you me to." Stolas nipped at her neck.

Kalisha reached for him, unzipping his pants and pulling Stolas free, stroking her hand up and down the length of him. Stolas shuddered in pleasure, a low moan catching in the back of his throat. He pulled out of Kalisha's reach and settled between her legs.

"No, not this time. If you get to use your mouth, I do too," Kalisha stated, pushing Stolas over to his back. Momentarily taken aback, Stolas watched amazed as she settled herself over his face. He happily licked up into Kalisha and then jolted as he felt her mouth close around him.

Between the taste of Kalisha on his tongue, her smell surrounding him, and the feel of her mouth on him, Stolas lost focus. His hips jerked up off the floor as she sucked him down, and Stolas gripped her hips, pulling Kalisha down tighter on his mouth and did his best to distract her the way she was distracting him.

Every moan from her wrung sensations through Stolas almost sending him plunging over the edge of the abyss they teetered on. He couldn't hold back any longer, her skillful tongue and hands causing him to explode as Kalisha ground herself down against his mouth, jumping off the edge with him. Kalisha pulled herself off him when she couldn't bear anymore and curled into Stolas.

"Pace yourself, Stolas, I'm not done with you yet." Kalisha stuck a finger between the buttons of his shirt and traced it over his chest.

"What gave you the impression that I was finished with you?" Stolas kissed the soft spot between her shoulder and neck.

"As long as we are on the same page, it's all good." Kalisha's smile was slow and sent heat rushing through him. "Even an eternity with you might not be long enough to ease this need in me I have for you."

Her words washed over Stolas, and love pooled deep in his heart. He dipped his head and kissed Kalisha with all the passion he could, needing her to feel that he felt the same way. "I hope it's never eased. Call me selfish."

"I want to tie you up and torture you with my tongue until you are helpless against me." Kalisha bit at his chin as his body again went rock hard.

"My love, I'm already helpless against you. If tying me up is what you want, then do it. I am yours to command," Stolas told her hotly. "You burn through my veins hotter than any hellfire I have ever experienced."

Kalisha pulled back and studied his face. "Do you mean that?"

"I do. You have only to ask, and I'll do whatever you want, my love."

Kalisha stood up and held a hand out to Stolas and pulled him to his feet. "I've always wanted to do this. It's even better now that it will be with you," she said, her eyes glowing with need. "I love you."

Chapter Twenty-Eight

Stolas felt torn between watching the sunrise or Kalisha sleeping peacefully. He had enjoyed getting tied up more than he thought he would. There had been something freeing in it, in having no control over what she was going to do to him, and when she would do it.

Kalisha had thoroughly explored every inch of his body, and Stolas felt destroyed by the amount of pleasure she'd given him. Finally, free from restraints, he'd slowly made love to her until they'd both collapsed from exhaustion.

Stolas would still be sleeping next to the beauty if he hadn't been woken from a dead sleep by the sounds of Airiella's screams echoing in his head. Those haunting screams Stolas had hoped to never hear from her again. He glanced back at the sunrise and dismally acknowledged that Jax's comparison with Airiella's eyes had been accurate, whether the sun was rising or setting. At least when Airiella had that glow to them from the light powers inside her, otherwise they were an intriguing shade of brown.

Stolas stepped out on the balcony after putting his

279

pants on, not zipping or buttoning them, not bothering with a shirt. It was unlikely anyone was up this early anyway. Stolas leaned on the railing with his elbows and hung his head down, trying to figure out the best way for them all to get through a war intact.

"Couldn't sleep?" came the quiet question from the object of his current thoughts.

"I could ask the same thing, love. Was that a nightmare?" Stolas didn't lookup. He knew Airiella heard him.

"I hope that's all it was," Airiella said quietly.

"Where's Jax?"

"He finally fell back asleep. I came out here to watch the sunrise. Not often I get to see it like this."

Stolas stood up and faced Airiella, pausing when her eyes went wide, and her jaw dropped slightly open. "Are you okay, love?" Stolas asked in concern.

"Shit. Stolas, you are fucking sexy as all get out right now. Damn. I almost want to climb this balcony and touch you to see if you are real."

Faintly embarrassed, Stolas blushed and realized Airiella had never seen him this undressed before. Truthfully, the first time she'd ever seen his chest had been when Airiella made Stolas show his mark. Stolas went to fasten up his pants that were riding low on his hips, but Airiella shook her head no at him.

"I like looking. I won't touch, though." Airiella smiled.

"There was a time I would have begged you to," Stolas admitted and glanced back through the door at Kalisha, sprawled out naked on the bed. "It's still nice to hear."

"Walk around like that, and you'll hear it often and not only from me." Airiella chuckled.

"I think I need to thank you again for opening my mind to the possibility that there was someone out there for me. I don't believe I would have entertained it if you hadn't told me. Now, I can't imagine not having Kalisha in my life."

Airiella gave him a tired smile. "I hope you never have to." Airiella brushed a stray tear from her eye when she thought Stolas wasn't looking, and it suddenly made sense to him.

Airiella's nightmare had been about losing Jax. Not even considering his state of undress, Stolas jumped across the gap between the balconies and pulled Airiella in for a hug, resting his cheek on her head as she clung to him, sobbing silently. Stolas didn't know what else to do. If the situation were reversed, Stolas wouldn't leave Kalisha's side for even a second.

"Love, we don't know what will happen. Make every moment count; that's all any of us can do at any given time." Stolas steered her back towards Jax.

"Let it be me," Airiella begged, "not him."

Jax must have picked up on Airiella's emotions because he woke up and was first startled by the lack of clothes Stolas had on, but Jax's expression shifted to one of understanding, and he crossed the room and had Airiella in his arms in seconds.

Stolas left the room quietly and went back across the balconies to his room and lay back down next to Kalisha, his chest wet from Airiella's tears and his heart breaking at the anguish in her voice with her plea to any being who would listen to her cries.

STOLAS

The unfairness of it all struck Stolas hard. Everything she'd already been through, how Airiella healed everyone she came into contact with, even if she didn't know it. The selfless way Airiella helped others at a high cost to herself and all she freely gave with no expectations in return.

In a flash of clarity, Stolas understood all those things could be what tipped Airiella over the edge to the dark side just as easily as they could be what kept her in the light. She was the balance and unfairly, it all hinged on Airiella, consequently, Stolas as well, as her advisor if she ever chose to listen to him. If Airiella fell, all of them will lose everything.

Stolas had understood it before, but it took seeing that moment with Airiella, and now being here with Kalisha in the aftermath that it all sunk in. All aspects of it. It wasn't just Airiella's burden, it was all of theirs, and it now weighed heavily on Stolas as he looked at the woman he loved, sleeping peacefully unaware of the turmoil inside him.

Stolas needed to talk to them all. There was no more time for them to skirt the issue or fears they were harboring. If he was going to be Airiella's advisor, then Stolas had to advise. That started with himself. No more accepting Airiella shying away from things she was afraid to talk about; if they were to find a way through it, they had to face it or lose everything.

Stolas looked at Kalisha, realizing that tears were falling as the vision of her blurred. He kissed her bare shoulder, his heart constricting with the thought of being without Kalisha. *I understand, love. Kalisha is worth more than my life. We can't avoid this anymore; we all need to talk if we want to get through whatever is coming.*

I can't, Stolas. I can't give it voice.

You have to, love. We all do. It's not just you that carries this, we all do. Every one of us that has this mark carries this burden with you. Stolas kept his voice firm. *I'll go around you if I have to, this is too important to ignore.*

Fine. Don't expect me to be happy about it.

I don't expect that at all. I understand why you feel the way you do. If I'm supposed to get you through this and advise you on courses of action, we have to be upfront about all possibilities and how we get through them. I wouldn't push this on you if it weren't necessary, love. I don't like it any more than you do; breakfast in my room. All the team needs to be there, spouses included. I also think your warrior and all that family need to be present too.

Are you forgetting that they are in another country?

No, Seir and I can get them and bring them back. Essentially, anyone that bears your mark needs to be here for this talk.

Fine. Airiella's tone sounded broken, and Stolas was the reason for it.

Airiella went silent, and Stolas didn't push her anymore. There wasn't a point to it. Stolas needed to mentally prepare for how hard this was going to be for all of them. There was certainly going to be fallout. Even though Stolas wanted to think this through, Airiella's plea kept echoing in his head that it be her and not Jax.

Stolas fought back the tears again, the stinging sensation in his eyes bordering on unbearable all due to that plea. There were so many cracks in his heart right now, because of all of this. Stolas feared he was just as much at risk for breaking as Airiella was.

"I think waking up and seeing you next to me might be one of the best experiences of my life, living or dead," Kalisha murmured sleepily. "But the anxiety you are feeling is a little overwhelming, what's wrong, Stolas?"

"I've forced a breakfast meeting with everyone to put everything out on the table. I can't let Airiella avoid talking about it because it scares her."

Kalisha appeared wide awake then. "Did something else happen?"

"I woke up, hearing Airiella's screams in my head. Figured it was another nightmare, and eventually, I made my way to the balcony to watch the sunrise, and Airiella was on hers. I don't think it was a nightmare; I think it was one of her precog dreams. If my hunches are right, it was about losing Jax."

Kalisha bolted upright. "You are going to make Airiella talk about that?"

"We have to, my love."

Kalisha nodded slowly. "I know you are right, but be gentle about it. Even talking about it has the power to cause deep hurt and rifts where there should be none."

"I'm learning that," Stolas told her softly. "It hit me hard when Airiella broke down out there. I put myself in her place and found it unbearable like my heart and soul were dividing. To beat it, we have to face it."

Chapter Twenty-Nine

I t seemed that none of the crew were able to sleep, and there was a knock at Stolas's door at eight, and they all filed in and sat. Stolas called Seir and asked that he get the others and drop the children off to sit with the shifters while they talked. When they showed up, Stolas was hanging up the phone from ordering room service.

Taklishim came over and shook Stolas's hand solemnly. "Raven told me that you straddle the dark and the light, the same as she does. Thank you for sending people to help us."

Stolas only nodded at Taklishim, not sure that words were necessary for the wary peace suddenly between them. Seir settled himself next to Kalisha but kept giving Airiella side looks, a look of concern on Seir's face.

"No boss for this meeting, Stolas?" Seir asked Stolas quietly.

"No. Lucifer's not necessary for this."

Seir stood and walked over to Airiella and knelt in front of her and exposed his chest, showing Airiella the mark Seir wore. "I wanted to tell you before now, but I didn't want to do it in front of Lucifer as I don't know how he would take it."

"You didn't need to tell me, I already knew. I can feel you differently now." Airiella smiled gently at Seir. "I don't think you'd have received a mark if you weren't able to be trusted."

Stolas was surprised, even if Airiella wasn't. Onida stood up and rubbed her back, Degataga, immediately at her side. "Do you believe the prophecy?" Onida asked Stolas.

"I do now," Stolas admitted reluctantly. "Before, I never put much thought into any of them. Too many parts of this one have proven to be true, which is why we all needed to be here for this, including you all. We have no idea where this war is going to happen or when, just that it will. It's not a matter of fighting on the side of Hell; it's a matter of fighting on the side of humanity. That's what we stand to lose if we can't get through this."

"Airiella said that she met the Creator," Tama spoke up. "We can all see how much more power she has right now, so it is true that Airiella is stronger than both the Creator and the Devil?"

"It is. Airiella can end them both. There isn't a being that exists that is stronger than her." Stolas stood and started to pace. "That doesn't mean any fight will be easy, nor does it mean Airiella can't be hurt, or even die. I do believe if she dies, she will come' back. Piecing together carefully crafted words from the Creator and the innuendo's behind them lead me to believe that."

"Moloch is here on this plane?" Taklishim asked, his voice bordering on aggressive.

"Moloch is, with legions. And your ex-council member Stone is with him, as you saw. Moloch and Bael tried to create a version of Airiella with Stone, one that can be Airiella's equal and battle her. Stone is no longer Stone. He's a twisted version of who he used to be that is ruled by hate now. Stone has powers, but compared to Airiella, he has nothing. Stone is still highly dangerous to the rest of us."

"And it's true that you are second in power to Lucifer?" Onida jumped back in.

"That is also correct. We'll get to all that. I had a moment of clarity earlier after being with Airiella this morning. I kept thinking of this as a burden *she* had to bear. I was wrong; this burden is shared by *all* of us. We received marks for a reason, which means we all have a role to play."

"We aren't just soldiers." Taklishim stood straighter. It wasn't a question, and Stolas saw from the look in the warrior's eyes that he understood what Stolas was getting it.

"No, we aren't. We are tasked with keeping Airiella on her path. Yes, we will have to fight, but our biggest challenge will come in helping Airiella. The choices she will have to make is what decides the outcome of all of this. Airiella chooses who lives and dies. If we guide her the wrong way, the consequences for all of us are devastating. This revelation was what hadn't sunk in for me before today. Logically, I understood it, but the implications of it all hit hard this morning. If this goes the way of Moloch and his goals, we lose everyone in this room."

Stolas stopped and let that sink in. Taklishim unmistakably had a strategic mind as he stepped in. "That doesn't mean we lose everyone at the same time. Moloch will draw it out, hit where it hurts the most, and the end game is still the same. We all die." Taklishim stopped and knelt before Airiella. "Sacrifices are never easy, Raven."

"Love, there isn't one person in this room that doesn't stand to lose everything. There also isn't one person in this room who thinks it's acceptable for them to lose you. You need to accept that every person here is going to do their best to keep you safe. If you take that away from them, you are taking their free will. That falls on the side of the darkness. Lucifer *really* doesn't want you down there. Lucifer sees the bigger picture and the role you play in the future. If you make too many choices on the wrong side of the line, Lucifer won't be able to deny you access to Hell if you die," Stolas explained gently.

"Raven, look at me." Taklishim still knelt before Airiella. "We are all in this whether you want us to be or not. You have to let us help. I don't want to miss my children growing up, but don't think for one second that I wouldn't sacrifice myself to make sure that they *have* the chance to grow up."

It was too much for Airiella, and she bolted to her feet. "If I can keep that from happening, then I will! Isn't that that reason for my creation?" she shouted. "If I can keep you safe, I should."

"Not if the cost of keeping us safe puts you and the outcome of this at risk," Tama said softly. "You can't save one, and lose the world, because you didn't truly save one if they are going to suffer and die anyway."

"That's not a choice I can make," Airiella cried, her body shaking violently.

"You aren't, love. We are. It's our choice to make; it's part of our role in this. You need to trust us to do the right thing." Stolas gentled his tone farther.

"I can't watch that," she said and tears streamed down Airiella's face.

"Love, every person in this room has heard your death screams, has witnessed you dying because you are saving one of us. How many of them do you think wanted to see that? To hear that?"

"Stolas's right, baby girl. That still haunts me." Smitty reached out for Airiella, but she shied away.

"Angel, as much as I hate to say it, Stolas has a point that we've all wanted to say but have been too afraid to." Ronnie tried to reach Airiella, but she'd made herself a standalone island they couldn't breach.

If Stolas could feel the pain radiating off her, he knew they all could. "Baby, whatever you are doing to keep us away, can you stop, please? I need to be touching you right now," Jax tried to plead with her.

Taklishim looked at Stolas. "You are the only one who can breach that. It's not the same as Airiella's usual powers. It has a slight taste of you to it."

Stolas knew precisely what power Airiella was using, and Taklishim was right, Stolas could get through it. It was a risk, and not one he was willing to take right now. "I won't do it, love. You obviously don't want to be touched, but you will listen to me."

Stolas stepped into Airiella's line of sight and held her gaze until he was sure she wouldn't look away. "There's only one of you, and every person here is afraid to lose you the same way you don't want to lose them. You've healed every person in here. You represent something to them." Stolas looked over to Smitty. "You were the first, right?"

Smitty stepped over next to Stolas. "I was. Please look at me, baby girl." Smitty's voice cracked.

Stolas put a hand on Smitty's arm. "You showed Smitty what it felt like to be immersed in emotion, not just fact. You helped him bridge a gap in his relationship with Jillian. Without you coming into the picture, these two wouldn't be where they are right now." Airiella slid her eyes back to Stolas. "You know how I know this?" Airiella shook her head at Stolas.

"These gifts that you shared with those who wear your mark, well mine is the ability to see things I couldn't see before. Call it sight, or whatever you want. I can see right into them; I can see the link you share with them all, and I can see what it's construction."

"That's a demon power," Airiella answered him.

"Pulling out their memories to dissect their life is a demon power, that's not what I'm talking about with this. I can see how you've changed them, your impact, where your touch is."

Smitty drew Airiella's attention back to him. "Regardless, what Stolas is saying is true. He's not telling you something you didn't already know."

Jillian stepped up and joined Smitty. "I wouldn't have shown up and been a bitch to you if I hadn't sensed the change in Art. Because of your impact on them, I chose to make this real between us; now we have a baby on the way."

Mags came and stood next to Jillian. "Not only did you make a sexual fantasy come true for me, but you also brought me even closer to the love of my life, and you healed something inside me that allowed me to have Aedan's babies."

Aedan came and stood beside Smitty, his face full of pain. "You healed me in so many ways, Airiella, I don't even know where to start. I saw that magic existed beyond the realm of possibility. I believed in faith, something I couldn't see. I learned to understand my emotions and let them run freely through me. I wouldn't have my children if it weren't for you."

Ronnie came and stood next to Aedan. "Angel, do you honestly want me a crying and sobbing mess in front of you right now? You know exactly how you healed me. I don't need to tell you."

"I do." Jax stood next to Ronnie, and the pain that slammed into Stolas was staggering. Airiella was losing control. "You died for me. More than once. So many times. You told me that sometimes all you wanted was for someone to save you for once instead of you doing it for them, but you won't let me. You loved me despite the shit that I grew inside of myself. You heal me every day. I would be dead right now if it weren't for you."

Stolas stopped Chrissie before she joined in and shattered Airiella. "Please, let me. Love, you bleed emotions everywhere you go. You bleed love; you bleed color, you bleed life. You bleed for everyone. No one is asking you to watch them die; they are asking you for a chance to give back to you. We are all in this together. You are stronger than Moloch, but you are still able to die; Moloch can to suck all the power from your soul. If Moloch does that, we all die. Every one of us."

Stolas could see Jax starting to crack under the weight of the pain rolling off Airiella. She was pale and shaking, her eyes clouded with tears, the empath in her at maximum capacity. To Stolas's utter astonishment, Chrissie pushed them all out of the way and breached the invisible barrier no one else could pass. Chrissie wrapped

Airiella up in her arms and murmured something in her ear.

Stolas saw Airiella's knees start to buckle, but before he could move, Jax had Airiella, and they were both encased in a circle of blue flames that none of them could see through. Kalisha came up to Stolas. "You got through to Airiella, give her a minute. That pain you feel is only a small percent of what is going through her."

"Is there something that I missed?" Taklishim looked at Stolas. "The prophecy didn't say Airiella would lose one of them."

"There's a lot that it did say, and didn't say both," Kalisha answered for Stolas.

Chapter Thirty

The blue flames disappeared, and Jax stood there with Airiella wrapped around him. "I've had too much time to think, and it's destroying me. I can feel myself slipping away." Airiella slid her legs down from around Jax's waist, pulled up the back of his shirt, and showed Taklishim Jax's mark.

Taklishim's fury was evident on his face. "I refuse to accept that."

Airiella laughed darkly, her voice thick with tears. "I've been trying to do exactly that."

"Airiella." Kalisha stepped forward and put a hand on her arm. "I've thought a lot about it too. It could mean just what it says. It could be referencing the love that you two share. It might not mean what you think."

Airiella choked on another sob, and Jax pulled her head into his chest. "Tell them, Ells."

Airiella reached into her pocket and drew her hand out, holding it to Kalisha. Kalisha looked at Airiella in confusion and held her hand under Airiella's accepting whatever was in it. When Airiella released her hand, all

Stolas saw were pieces of broken rock and dust. "What is that?"

"That's what remains of the stone Kalisha gave me to help keep nightmares at bay. That's what happened this morning with the nightmare; at least I was telling myself it was a nightmare. I think it was one of those vision dreams."

"That shouldn't be possible." Kalisha stared at the rocky dust in her hand. "What was the dream?"

"Jax dying," was all Airiella said, her eyes shut. When she opened them and looked at Stolas, his knees buckled under the weight of the stare. Ronnie stabilized Stolas.

"Maybe you misinterpreted it," Ronnie tried.

"She didn't. I saw it too." Jax kissed Airiella on the forehead. "I can't run from this any more than you can, Ells."

"That's why Stolas called this meeting," Kalisha spoke up when she saw the stricken look on Stolas's face. "If we are to get through it, we need to face it. Stolas told me he thought it could be three people."

"Four," Stolas changed his mind. "If she dreamed it, then it's possible Jax is the leading contender. If that was just pure fear causing it, then the runner ups are me, Ronnie and Taklishim."

"Why?" Smitty asked, shaken.

"Jax and I because our marks are different. Ronnie and Taklishim because they are closer to her than the rest. That is not said to belittle any of your bonds. The bond Ronnie and Taklishim share with Airiella is different than the others, and since I know, for a fact Moloch, is going for maximum pain, he will go for whatever will hurt her the most. Airiella is the number one obstacle in his way to getting what he wants."

A sob tore through Aedan's chest, and he dropped to his knees, Mags immediately going to his side as he punched the floor in anger. Jax held Airiella up as Aedan's emotions tried to take her down, and Stolas saw the look of devastation on Aedan's face when he finally looked up at Airiella. "There's a part of this you didn't mention," he said, his voice quaking, Aedan met the eyes of everyone in the room. "It's also the most obvious answer, and one none of us want to contemplate any more than we want to contemplate losing Jax. Though I can tell you right now, Airiella, I understand why Jax would do it, and I would do the same."

"Aedan," Airiella whispered.

"No. Let me finish." Aedan looked at Stolas. "Those words on Jax's back are probably exactly what you think they mean, one of us dies. You didn't mention Airiella. The most obvious answer to me considering she's done it over and over again. How many times has Airiella given up her life for us? Every single time. From the start, she has, before Airiella even met Jax. It fucking kills each of us inside when she does it and fills us with the greatest love we could ever know. Maybe those words are a simple reminder of that. It wouldn't surprise anyone in this room if Airiella were to give up her life yet again to save us. To save everyone in this selfish fucking world we live in, that doesn't deserve her. What if that is the meaning of those words? What if those words are telling us as a reminder? Maybe Airiella won't come back this time. If you are going to make her face the idea of losing Jax, then you need to make each of us face the fucking idea of permanently losing Airiella."

Jax sagged at Aedan's words, and Ronnie dove to catch Jax before he went down, taking Airiella with him. "Fucking shit!" Ronnie cursed at the thought.

"If Aedan hadn't said it, I would have," Seir finally spoke. "It was also something I had been thinking about, as well. I haven't seen it all as you have, I'm usually coming in after the fact, but I see it all the same."

Taklishim took in a ragged breath. "Me too. Aedan's right. No one here wants to contemplate it, Stolas, but if we are looking at all angles, we need to plan for that one too."

"If Airiella dies, we all do," Stolas told them flatly. He was trying his best to hide his absolute fear at the words Aedan had spewed out. Stolas couldn't tolerate losing Airiella any more than he could tolerate losing Kalisha.

"Not necessarily, Stolas." Kalisha took his hand. "Airiella could die defeating Moloch. She could die after saving everyone and everything. We believe Airiella will come back, but we have no way of knowing for certain. If you truly want to share this burden with Airiella, then you need to consider that as well instead of shoving the pain of losing Jax down her throat."

Ronnie led Jax and Airiella back to the couch, then dropped to his knees in front of both of them and sobbed. Chrissie slid to the floor, trying to remain stoic, but Stolas was able to see under the carefully crafted façade. Fear choked Stolas as the truth of what they were pointing out, sunk into his bones.

Degataga cleared his throat. "Let's just accept that there will be loss, as there is in any war. All situations presented are plausible, and the cost will be high no matter who it is."

Onida and Tama stood, and together they both

spoke, "We are all family. Together."

"This room holds the most powerful people, and love binds us." Taklishim looked at Airiella, deep pain in his eyes. "You've shown us time and time again that love wins. I have no reason not to believe that now."

Stolas saw Kalisha nod at Jillian, Chrissie, and Mags. "In the time I've been spending with these lovely ladies and the children, I have been teaching them to use the powers they now hold, the same as you've been working with the guys." Kalisha nodded at Seir. "That said, since Moloch is looking for children, I don't think they should be a part of the physical fight if it comes down to it. I think they need to be taken away or out of reach, at least. They will know enough to keep themselves safe as well as the children."

Airiella finally found her voice. "I agree, Kalisha. Train them as well as you can. Chrissie, Jillian, and Mags are strong on their own, but those kids and unborn babies need to stay protected. Onida, Tama that goes for you."

"Onida, yes; me, I can fight," Tama told Airiella.

"Not if Taklishim is," Airiella argued. "There is no way I am letting those children become orphans because of me."

"It's not because of you, Raven," Taklishim growled. "I don't like it either, but I respect Tama enough to let her make her own decision."

"Let go of the guilt, Airiella," Tama said quietly. "If I choose to be there, it's to ensure that my children have a future. If both Tak and I die, Onida will care for my babies; I do not doubt that."

"What if I can't live with that?" Airiella started trembling again.

"Then buck up, and let's figure out how to defeat the bastard," Onida said bluntly.

Stolas had the sense to know he was in the presence of truly remarkable people who were now rallying around the one who needed to see she wasn't alone. There was so much love in the air Stolas was almost drowning in it. For all Airiella's strength, she still didn't see that all the connections in the room went back to her. It was up to Stolas to show her.

Chapter Thirty-One

id you consider that Airiella might be telling the truth when she said that if Jax dies, we lose her?"

"Yes. I think that right there will be the hardest battle if it comes to that. If anything tips Airiella over the edge, it will be that," Stolas answered softly, his tone sad.

"They have the deepest bond I've ever seen," Kalisha remarked.

"They do. I saw it before Airiella and Jax were even a thing, and it's one of the reasons I backed off on trying to become more to Airiella. Their bond helped me see that I craved her because of what she represents to me. Yes, I'm in love with her, but not for the same reasons I'm in love with you."

"I don't question that, Stolas. I can see the truth in your eyes when you look at me, feel it in your touch when our skin meets. I do worry about how either of them will react if the other dies. If what Aedan said comes to pass, I don't know they will recover."

"They will, Airiella's made sure of it. She's tied them all together with a strength not seen in my time. Didn't you feel the love in that room? When one falters, one of the others, or all of them, step in to make sure they don't hit the ground. If they can't stop them from hitting the ground, they join them."

Kalisha ran her fingers up and down Stolas's arm. "I'm worried about Chrissie. When we've practiced, I haven't seen any signs of elemental abilities come out in her. Only once, when Mags fell over and twisted her ankle, Chrissie rushed over to her and wrapped her hands around it, trying to steady it for her. Mags was fine after that. What if Chrissie can heal? Nothing else?"

"That doesn't make sense, Airiella isn't a healer."

"Isn't she? Airiella comes back from the dead. She's not tried to heal anyone herself, has she? Empath's by nature are healers."

Stolas thought about it. "Maybe. I'll think about it. Do you think we should bring Chrissie to a training session with the guys? She can try to heal injuries sustained while training."

"I more thought Chrissie could train with Onida and Degataga before Seir brings the kids back home."

"Kalisha, you are brilliant. That's an excellent idea." Stolas leaned forward to kiss her. "They would know right off the bat if she can do it."

"Empath's are healers. Keep it in mind while you work with Airiella. You, yourself, pointed out how she's healed them," Kalisha reminded Stolas.

"I'm still debating the thought of bringing Airiella down to Hell to fight against Lucifer." Stolas soaked in the feel of Kalisha touching him.

"It's a solid plan. You know Lucifer won't permanently hurt her, nor Airiella him."

"Still, accidents happen, and if word gets out an angel is down there fighting with Lucifer, things could get out of hand fast." Stolas shuddered, then smiled despite the ugly thought. "Airiella's reflexes are art in motion; I sometimes find myself distracted, simply watching how she reacts."

Kalisha laughed. "You better get over that. Airiella will make your life miserable if you get hurt because you weren't paying attention."

"She's threatened me with that plenty. I just feel like we are missing something in all this."

"I do find it curious that Lucifer is willing to send his guards and legion to help Airiella with this battle, but the Creator hasn't made the same offer."

"That crossed my mind, as well. I haven't come up with a good answer for it either." Stolas still felt in the dark about most of it.

"You don't have to solve everything, Stolas. Some of it the group needs to work through themselves. That's why they asked for a few hours alone. It's hard to fathom that they might lose someone from their group; they need to be together. It hurts me to think about it, and I'm not part of their group."

"How can you even think that?" Stolas looked at Kalisha, stunned. "You are very much a part of the group. How do you think that mark came about? It's *not* because you are attached to me. Airiella knew you before she knew me. Airiella grieved for you when you died; she threatened me when she thought I forced you into a union. Airiella loves you. They all love you."

"I didn't think of it that way. I apologize. You are correct." Kalisha's eyes were deep pools of sorrow. "I love them all too."

"We are now part of the most elite group on the

planet. Kind of scary when you think about it. It baffles me that Moloch even thinks he has a chance of beating Airiella." Stolas fingered one of Kalisha's dreadlocks that fell over her shoulder.

"Moloch does, though, doesn't he?"

Stolas shrugged. "I can't say it isn't possible. It's not likely unless Moloch gets ahold of one of Airiella's team. All bets are off the table then. The power surges when Airiella loses control are off the charts. That's why I want the guys to train so hard. The more confident they are in their abilities, the better off Airiella is."

"Will you allow me to be a part of this fight?"

Stolas winced at the wording. "I don't own you, my love. I would prefer you to be out of the line of fire, but I will have to take the same stance that Taklishim did. I respect you enough to make that decision for yourself."

"Thank you, Stolas."

"Don't thank me yet. I may be an ass about it later due to fear for you." Stolas dropped his head back on to the pillow and stared at the ceiling. "I'm missing something. I can just feel it," he said again.

"Stop thinking about it. The more you dwell on it, the harder it will be to see it."

"I know. How are you doing with your powers?" Stolas changed the subject.

"I'm fine with them. Jillian has taken easily to hers, Mags as well. Chrissie does well with the physical part of it, thanks to Ronnie, but magic wise, she's defenseless. Mags can do the energy blasts, and her control is superb. Jillian has taken to fire like she was born from it."

Stolas chuckled. "Jillian has the attitude for it." Stolas thought about Chrissie and grew concerned.

"Chrissie has no control over any of the elements?"

"Not that I have seen."

"Could it be a focus issue?" Stolas wondered aloud.

"Out of the three of them, Chrissie's focus is laser-sharp."

"What goes along with healing then? There has to be something else." That Chrissie would get nothing didn't make sense to Stolas at all. Chrissie was her oldest friend.

"Empath. I suspect she was already one, but not to the degree that Airiella is. Maybe not even the same degree Jax is. Chrissie's adept at reading the other women, or even the room. She's definitely in tune with Airiella."

"That's not a good measure; we all are in tune with Airiella. You may be on to something. Are you going to talk to Onida and Degataga about working with Chrissie, or should I?"

"I'll do it. I have a history with Onida and Dega."

"Do you miss your old life?" Stolas propped himself up on an elbow to look at Kalisha.

"Sometimes. I think what I miss the most is the camaraderie I had with those council members. We were able to bounce ideas off each other to get to the heart of a problem and solve it. I never had to hide who I was with them as I did in general. My day to day life, no, I don't miss that. What I have with you is so much better. Before Airiella came into the picture, the council was boring stuff that Stone tried to make about him. Tak, Dega, Tama, Oni, myself, and Father Roarke would often meet outside council sessions or over video chat to work on things that came up outside of that. Jax and Aedan would occasionally send me emails asking for information about something they'd find in an investigation."

"Working with them again must feel good for you then." Stolas slid his hand over Kalisha's hip, needing to feel her.

"It does and it doesn't. It feels good to be with the team again, but not in such serious circumstances. It was a little different when the focus was on Jax and Airiella alone. Now the danger is present for everyone, and I find looking at the broader picture a lot more disturbing knowing that loss is inevitable."

"You don't regret claiming me?" Stolas whispered fearfully.

"Not one little iota. Despite the turmoil we find ourselves in, being with you has been the most natural thing. I always wondered why I didn't move on from the spirit world, and now I know it's because I was waiting for you. Do you have regrets?"

"Never about you. You were this perfect storm that blew into my head and cleared away the shit clogging up my brain. When I saw you clearly, my heart knew what the rest of me took a bit to catch up to."

"What did your heart know?"

"That I belonged to you. It's never been you belonging to me. We only had to say it that way because I am a prince. It's always been me belonging to you," Stolas replied reverently.

"That's quite romantic for a man of science." Kalisha brushed her lips across his. "How about we just say we belong together. I don't like the thought of ownership; my ancestors were forced into slavery." She kissed Stolas again.

"If you can find out who did that, I will make them suffer in the lowest pits of Hell," Stolas promised Kalisha.

Let's do this. It's not going to get any easier, and the longer I sit here wondering which of my loved ones will die, the harder it is for me to maintain control.

As you wish, love.

"Time to go, my love. Airiella is getting restless, and that's not a good thing."

Kalisha laughed. "Probably not, but sometimes the results are amusing. Airiella called Taklishim, Gandalf; Tama, Cat woman; and Onida, Hawkeye, during her interview when she was out of patience. Airiella also called out Stone and yanked that darkness from him brutally in an incredible display of power. So, if she's getting restless, then I agree, it's time to go." Kalisha stood and held out her hand to Stolas.

Chapter Thirty-Two

Please tell the master we are here," Stolas told Dakota.

"He's been expecting you." Dakota bowed slightly, his eyes never leaving Airiella. "He's in the study."

"Tell me again why we just didn't appear there?" Airiella asked in frustration.

"Surprising Lucifer like you did before isn't a good thing." Stolas led Airiella down the hallway.

"Yet bringing me here to fight with the Devil is? Why couldn't I just fight with you?"

"I can't make myself aggressive towards you, love. Even knowing it's practice." Stolas gripped Airiella's hand. "It's not that I don't want to help you prepare, it just hurts, and I'm trying to avoid that. Me losing control isn't any better than you losing control."

"Fine. Be all logical about it. Don't get pissy with me if I hurt your friend, though."

Stolas chuckled. "Lucifer's response was the same thing."

He knocked on the door, and at Lucifer's command to enter, Stolas burst out laughing seeing, Lucifer standing there wearing what looked like umpire pads for baseball. Even Airiella grinned. "You are worried about me kicking your ass?"

"I'd be foolish not to be worried about it. I did this, though, to make Stolas laugh. He's been a bit tense lately." Lucifer waved his hands, and the gear disappeared.

"When you say things like that, you make it hard to dislike you." Airiella crossed her arms and cocked her hip out sideways.

"Oddly enough, I, too, find myself quite liking you. Are you sure you both want to do this?" Lucifer asked sincerely.

"Yes," Airiella answered. "You aren't the first demon I've fought, but you might be the most powerful, and I need to learn if I can react to the unexpected."

"Are you carrying one of Kalisha's stones?"

"I am, are you?" Airiella fired back in a challenge.

"I am as well. Smart to keep them on us, it will at least dampen the magic from either of us." Lucifer strode forward to stand before Airiella. "I hope you can at least believe me when I tell you that I don't wish to harm you. I understand your presence in the world, and I even agree with it."

"Thank you." Airiella softened her tone. "I don't want to hurt you either. Mainly because you mean so much to Stolas, but also a little because you aren't as nasty evil as some legends about you say you are. Plus, you are really pretty."

"Oh, child, I am evil. Just not to those who don't deserve it. It would be good for you to remember that. I accept the compliment on being pretty." Lucifer winked.

Stolas shifted uncomfortably. "Is the area secure?"

"Yes, no one will know the angel is here other than Dakota. Shit, Stolas, relax. I won't hurt your angel."

Stolas didn't even bother correcting him, neither did Airiella, she just looked at him, her face unreadable for once. *He truly loves you; you know that, right?*

I do, love. I'm probably the only person that could claim that as well.

Not true, Lucifer loves the Creator too, but there are lines of anger running through that.

"Are you quite done reading my fucking emotions, angel?" Lucifer snapped.

"Yes, for the moment. Thank you for your cooperation. Please fasten your seatbelts and enjoy your flight." Airiella smiled and blasted Lucifer with air to knock him off his feet.

"Love, wait until we are outside." Stolas bit back a smile. It hadn't passed his attention that Lucifer was smiling as well.

"I apologize, lead the way, oh nasty one." Airiella bowed slightly.

Lucifer laughed. "This is going to be fun."

"How does this thing between you two work?" Airiella asked as they walked down the hall.

"Day to day, Stolas has free reign to do what he wants under loose parameters I've laid out. If I issue a formal command, because Stolas swore himself to me, he'd have to obey it. If he didn't, the vow breaks, and his life would be forfeit."

Airiella's step faltered. "The Creator said Stolas was welcome there, so how does that work?"

"I change the vow, essentially. I haven't done it yet, but I would never make Stolas choose."

"It's not a choice, Lucy," Stolas reminded Lucifer.

"Maybe for you, but for me, I can alter the vow so you can have both worlds and not receive punishment for it."

Stolas felt his head swim with the thought. "We'll talk about it later. Right now, we need to focus on making sure Airiella can do what she needs to do."

Lucifer studied Stolas coolly. "I'll do exactly as I see fit. It would be best if we both were to fight her at the same time."

"I agree," Airiella responded immediately.

"I can't," Stolas argued.

"If Big Bad orders you to, you can," Airiella pointed out.

Stolas swore and glared at Airiella. "Why don't we just start with one on one and see how you do with Lucifer before adding me to the mix."

"Chicken shit. Fine, I'll play it your way for now, but I reserve the right to request Big Bad to order you to participate." Airiella glowered at Stolas.

"Deal," Lucifer agreed, grinning evilly at Stolas. "The angel's got balls."

"Damn right, I do, or I wouldn't be fighting your battles for you," Airiella snarled.

"Bael might have been for me, and I didn't know about it until after the fact. This one, well, it's not only for me but for the world. I'm no happier about that mark on your soul mate than you are. It's why I agreed to this and agreed to use my guards to help them train."

"Thank you." Airiella looked around where they stood. "I can see your protection around this place."

Airiella suddenly ducked and pushed Stolas out of

the way as a stream of fire sailed over her head, singing the ends of her hair as Stolas landed flat on his back. Lucifer wasn't holding back much, that fire had been deadly, and aimed for both of them. Lucifer had played on her need to protect Stolas while leaving herself open.

Lucifer didn't know how good Airiella's reactions were. No sooner had Airiella rolled back to her feet, then she sent Lucifer flying backward with a hurricane-force blast of air. Airiella went invisible, and Lucifer paused before moving cautiously. He'd taken two steps when the ground shifted, and Lucifer's feet were held in place, holding him immobile.

Stolas felt the energy build, and as he shot to his feet, he was encircled in blue flames as a blast of energy tore through the area. Stolas heard the oomph of air Airiella expelled as she hit the ground, and the fire dropped. Lucifer had freed himself of the earth and was stalking towards Airiella aggressively.

Everything in Stolas wanted to call out to Airiella, to warn her, but he couldn't. Lucifer was too close to her, and his skin prickled with fear. Airiella swung her body around, dropping smoothly into a kick that swept Lucifer's legs out from under him. With speed Stolas hadn't seen her show before Airiella pummeled him with her fists before Lucifer even hit the ground.

Ronnie would have been proud. Airiella went invisible again, and Stolas felt another wave of energy building, hers this time. No flames erupted around Stolas as Airiella directed the stream only towards Lucifer, her control exceptional.

It knocked Lucifer right back to the ground and thirty feet away. Airiella's body started to glow, making his glow as well. Electricity sparked off her skin, one of the ways Stolas was positive she felt like she was in danger, but Airiella didn't strike Lucifer down. She stood there, immovable as Lucifer strode towards her again.

With a jolt of fear, Stolas realized Lucifer had frozen Airiella. Her skin glowed until she was pure light, Lucifer unable to get closer to her without hurting himself. With a tremendous roar from the ground, Airiella broke free and soared into the air on a gust of wind, her wings spread gloriously behind her.

Airiella landed behind Lucifer and planted a swift kick right in his ass. "That was fucking low. You could have hurt yourself with that move, asshole."

Stolas needed to relax. Airiella was under control. While Lucifer might be playing dirty with some of his moves, Stolas knew it was for Airiella's benefit. Moloch wouldn't play nice. Lucifer was a bit slower getting up this time and held out his hand.

"Give me a moment, please. I'm sincere about that request. It did hurt."

Stolas moved towards Lucifer then, concerned for his friend. A heartbeat later, Stolas was flying through the air with that blue glow around him as a cushion. Stolas hadn't even felt the energy build, and he knew Lucifer hadn't held back at all with that one.

When Stolas landed, it was hard, but somehow, Airiella had protected him and stood in the same spot she had been before the blast hit. It hadn't affected Airiella at all, but she was once again pure light, and Lucifer was halfway across the field.

"Did you honestly think I trusted you?" Airiella called out.

"No, but your reaction was perfect. Lassie, can you help me, please?" Lucifer's voice was weak.

"Shit. I hurt you." Airiella raced towards Lucifer, dropping to her knees. Her movements so fast that the knees of her jeans ripped open and knees skinned. "Is touching your skin going to hurt either of us?" Stolas heard Airiella ask as he finally got to them.

"I don't know. In case it does, let Stolas look," Lucifer answered honestly. "If you are still glowing, don't touch me, Lassie."

"Shit. I am. Pull your shirt up, Lucy," Stolas demanded without touching Lucifer.

Ariella gasped. "I didn't even touch you."

"No, but when you light up that way, it's like radiation to me," Lucifer groaned. "What hurts more is that none of my strikes have even come close to doing more than knocking you off your feet."

"Your pride hurts more than that?" Airiella gave Lucifer a look of pure sarcasm. "That's a third-degree burn. And now I'm tempted to touch it and see how you like it."

"Mercy," Lucifer pleaded. "This training is obviously not working. She needs to be training with guards as well as me."

"Lucy, no." Stolas pulled a container from his pocket and handed it to Lucifer. "Put that on. I'll get some stuff from home before we leave."

"Don't worry about it. I have a healer in the house." Lucifer smeared the mix over the burn, wincing.

"Was that the best you have? What you hit me with?" Airiella asked Lucifer.

"That last blast that you mirrored back at me was one of the strongest I could have sent. No, it wasn't the best

I can do, but seeing as I'm not trying to be lethal, that was the max power I could use."

"Then maybe don't hold back," Airiella suggested.

"Airiella, no." Stolas put his foot down.

"Hear her out, Stolas," Lucifer growled. "Did you not just see what happened? Airiella didn't even strike out at me; all she did was mirror it back to me, her energy infused with it."

"That's my point, Lucy. If you sent a lethal strike at her and she mirrors it back, what do you think will happen to you?" Stolas ground out.

Airiella looked shaken and crossed her arms again; something Stolas was coming to see was an emotionally defensive move for her. "I'm sorry."

"Don't be. If anything, you've given me a healthy level of fear of you. You didn't even expend much effort to do that either." Lucifer looked at Stolas. "She needs to test herself against more than just me. She won't only be facing Moloch; she'll be facing whoever is along with him."

"Are your guards expendable?" Stolas asked Lucifer point-blank.

"No, but we can always bring in a legion of the un-loyal," Lucifer offered.

"I'd rather not. The legion isn't brattle-trained, nor will those demons hold back." Stolas hated the thought.

"I don't *want* them to hold back. If you want to see what I'm truly capable of, you need to test me. If there are what you consider traitors or demons that are disposable, then why not? Would you rather join your friend in fighting against me?"

"Fuck, Stolas, she's got you nailed to the wall," Lucifer grinned.

"Love, you'd be facing an entire legion on your own." Stolas tried to reason with Airiella.

"I'm aware. Do you think I can't handle it?" Airiella's volatile temper came flaring to the surface.

"That's not it at all. I'm worried I won't be able to handle it if you get hurt." Stolas felt like a child throwing a tantrum.

"Get over it. If I can't protect everyone, then neither can you. Besides, if things go sideways, both of you are here to help stop it, right?"

"I have to say I rather like seeing Mr. Know-It-All put in his place every once in a while. She's using your own logic against you."

"I'm right here, I can hear Airiella." Stolas glared. "Lay down the rules for me then, love. I need to know when you want me to intervene."

"If I'm losing. That's when you intervene."

"You are by far my favorite angel of all time," Lucifer said gleefully.

"Does Jax know what you are planning?" Stolas played his last card.

"He does now," Airiella informed Stolas. "Would you like to go back and ask him? I'll wait right here watching over your boss whose ass I just kicked without trying."

"Ouch, that part may not have been necessary to verbalize," Lucifer grumbled.

"Shut up, you already said it."

"Fine. Lucifer, what legion are you planning to bring in?" Stolas switched his glare to Lucifer.

"One of Bael's that has been particularly disruptive since his demise. It was one I would have punished anyway.

If she kills them, it's no loss."

Stolas swore again. "Jax has no issue with this?"

"I didn't say Jax didn't have an issue with it. I said he knew. Jax doesn't like the idea, but Jax also understands the reasoning, and I let him look through my eyes and showed him your boss laying here injured, to which Jax laughed. Jax trusts me to do what I feel is best; he trusts *you* that you will keep me alive. Stop trying to guilt-trip me with Jax; it was your idea to come here and do this. Your options are either you and your BFF tag team me and don't hold back, or bring in your hellions for me to do away with."

"Lassie, I wouldn't suggest it if I thought she would be seriously hurt. She may take a blow or two, but she's not going to lose."

"Funny, Jax said the same thing. Ronnie, on the other hand, is fuming and may try to kick your ass later, just a heads up." Airiella reached over and took Stolas's hand. "You asked me to trust you; now you need to trust me. Wouldn't you rather me jump into this headfirst knowing that you've seen firsthand that I can take on a legion?"

"Shit, love, I have. You took out the ones that were attacking your friends."

"Yes, but not like this. I'll give you this guarantee, if I start to feel overwhelmed, I'll take these out the same way I did those."

"That's not a guarantee, that wasn't an entire legion, it was only part of one." Stolas kissed the back of Airiella's hand, then released it and scraped his fingers through his hair. "Fine, do it. But you have to keep Ronnie away from me."

Airiella laughed. "I'll do my best."

"Dakota," Lucifer called out.

"Yes, sir." Dakota appeared in front of them. "Sir, are you okay?" Dakota looked alarmed.

"I'm fine. Be discreet but get Bael's entire eighth legion here to this field as quickly as possible."

Dakota gulped. "The entire legion, sir?"

"Yes. Breathe not one word of this to another." Lucifer waited until Dakota left. "That invisibility trick will come in handy right about now."

"I'd have to touch you," Airiella warned.

"Not necessarily," Stolas told Airiella, putting himself between the two. "Touch me, and I'll touch Lucifer. I'm not glowing anymore."

Airiella did, and they went invisible. "How long can you hold this?" Lucifer asked.

"We haven't tested length of time, but it's not draining my energy."

"Dakota will issue a demand, won't he?" Stolas asked Lucifer.

"He will. I've repeatedly warned them that I will punish them, so this won't come as a surprise. An added benefit is it frees up space, helps the balance, and enforces my message to the rest."

"Are these bad demons?" Airiella asked quietly.

"Yes," Stolas answered firmly, not wanting to give Airiella details on the crimes committed to get them here.

"Oh, the air pressure is changing," Airiella commented right before a few appeared in the field before them.

Negativity rolled off them in spades, and Stolas heard Airiella gasp as it hit her. "Wow, their souls are black," she said softly.

"They all have magic, they are all bad," Stolas warned Airiella. "The second they see you, they will attack, and they will be nasty about it. Keep control of your emotions until the rest appear and try not to glow yet. I have no idea if your invisibility will keep us hidden if you are glowing."

"They'll see both of you as soon as I let go of you," Airiella cautioned.

"I don't care," Lucifer replied. "They won't make it out of here alive anyway. Whether it's you that kills them or me."

"Will they come after you guys?"

"Most likely." Stolas wasn't going to lie to Airiella.

"Then I'll protect you." Airiella's tone let Stolas know it wasn't worth arguing. Even Lucifer heard it.

"Can you at least make it a wide circle around us, so I don't burn anymore?" Lucifer requested.

"Sure."

"If I tell you to drop the flames, you'll listen to me?" Stolas squeezed Airiella's hand.

"I'll listen as long as you aren't just reacting to me getting knocked around," Airiella clarified.

Another large group appeared, and Dakota appeared a moment later, looking confused. "I'm here, Dakota." Lucifer spoke just loud enough for Dakota to hear him. "Go back in the house and activate a protection charm. Keep all staff inside."

"Yes, sir." Dakota looked around again and disappeared.

"Shit, this is overwhelming," Airiella snapped.

"Put your damn walls up." Stolas squeezed Airiella's

hand again.

"Thanks for the reminder," Airiella told him and let go of his hand.

Instantly the focus of the field was on Airiella. There were at least one hundred demon's intent on her death. Airiella moved away from Stolas and Lucifer casually, her very presence here astounding them. She started to glow, the electricity coming off Airiella intense.

Your shield is in place; it's invisible, so none of them think you are working with me. Even though they won't make it out of here alive, I'd feel better protecting your reputation.

Stolas snorted and repeated the information to Lucifer. "She's tricky. By doing that, not only is she protecting us, but we can't see where the barrier is. It effectively keeps us in place."

Stolas swore again. "Why couldn't I see that?"

"Because you are more worried about your angel than either of us." Lucifer patted Stolas's arm. "Truly, Stolas, this isn't a fair fight. The legion doesn't stand a chance against Airiella even if she doesn't rip their souls out. I also completely understand your devotion to her."

Stolas nodded tightly, closely watching as Airiella sent several mighty bolts of lightning into the field, electrifying the very ground they were standing on. Clouds of ash went flying into the air immediately.

Stolas tensed as they started to charge her, and Airiella went gracefully into fighting mode, every touch of her skin on them turning them to ash instantly with each punch, kick, block she made. They started to slow down around Airiella and moved out of her reach as they realized how lethal a physical attack would be.

"As cliché as it sounds, the angel is poetry in motion," Lucifer commented, his pose relaxed as he leaned back on his elbows to watch.

It wasn't long before they started flinging magical blasts at Airiella that, at best, moved her back a couple of inches. None of them touched her, and Airiella wasn't expending a lot of energy from what Stolas could tell. The sounds of fighting and battling filled the air around them as plumes of ash randomly exploded as Airiella took them out.

Stolas also saw that the ones at the back of the field weren't attacking either; they were plotting and watching what Airiella did. Those were the ones that worried Stolas. These lower-level stupid ones weren't the issue.

Airiella used the air to gather up a group on her left and sent an energy blast of light into it, sending ash swirling in a tornado around the field. Another group, believing she was distracted, attacked from the right, while another tried to flank Airiella from behind.

Those senses that amazed Stolas so much in practice flared to life, and lightning took both groups out simultaneously. Airiella used earth to grab hold of the ones in front of her, she blasted them with energy, and soon all that was left were the ones in the back that watched it all.

"It's child's play for her." Lucifer sat forward and shifted. "What's Airiella doing?"

Stolas felt the same thing Lucifer did. "She's ending it. Airiella's going to rip their souls."

"It feels different," Lucifer said thoughtfully.

"Airiella combines the light and dark in her. She does the same thing with some of the energy blasts. Even with Kalisha's stone, Seir said it felt like a million shards of flaming glass tore through him, and Seir wasn't even close to Airiella."

"That sounds unpleasant. But what is the angel waiting for?"

"I don't think Airiella likes doing it," Stolas answered carefully.

"That I can understand. I don't either."

The subtle shift of pressure in the air told Stolas she wasn't going to rip their souls, Airiella was still waiting, doing nothing. Stolas didn't feel tempted to intervene like he thought he would be, she'd quickly taken care of the larger horde of them as if it were nothing.

"They are attacking," Lucifer warned Stolas, his senses sharper than Stolas's. "The angel's frozen, that's why she isn't moving."

"How can you tell?" Stolas was searching out energy signatures, but there were too many for him to narrow down.

"I know how it feels. It's cooler energy, and it sits flush against the ground if you are looking for it."

Stolas switched his focus and tried to seek it out. Stolas thought he found it and followed it back to a relatively higher-level demon at the back. The beast was sitting there with a smug look on his face as if he'd beaten her already.

"She's fine, Lassie. Airiella broke my hold on her, and it was far stronger than this one." Lucifer glanced off to the side suddenly, his head swiveling left and right. "This will be her real test. They are trying to surround her."

"She's not glowing," Stolas growled, leaping to his feet.

"Son of a bitch! Drop the flames!" Lucifer yelled to Airiella.

"What's going on?" Stolas demanded, stepping forward five feet before he felt the burn of the invisible flames.

"Get the angel to drop the flames, Lassie. I can't help her if she doesn't. My magic doesn't work inside here. There are two behind us."

Stolas spun around but didn't see anything; *Love, let us go.* Airiella didn't respond. *Please, love. If Lucifer is worried, this isn't good.*

"If Airiella's stronger than you, why wouldn't she be safe?" Stolas asked his emotions all over the place.

"These are higher-level demons, there are at least fourteen of them, and they aren't going for the angel, they are coming for us. Without magic, all that is between them and us is this flame. Their combined power is stronger than mine. Individually, I could take them out. I could take them out even as a group, but I need my power to do it."

"Shit. When Airiella's frozen like that, can she access her power?"

"She can, but Airiella's stuck in a trance. Most likely, her biggest fear is playing out in her mind."

"Fuck!" Stolas screamed as a blast of energy tore through them, slamming them into the invisible shield and the ground. The pain came from the flames, not the magic that hit Stolas, the flames filtered out that.

Lucifer groaned as he rolled over. "You've got to get through to her, or we are going to die in here."

Love, hear me, you need to snap out of it. Whatever is happening isn't real. Listen to me, please. Lucifer is hurt; there are demons attacking us from behind. Let us free, love. Please.

Another wave slammed into them, and Stolas

managed not to go flying this time and held Lucifer in place, his body starting to glow. "Let go of me, Lassie," Lucifer begged him. Stolas snatched his hand back as soon as he realized he was burning his friend.

Stolas tapped into the power that made him glow and looking around slowly, finally spotted the two demons blending into a tree in the back corner. It wasn't soon enough, and another wave hit, Lucifer managing to grab ahold of Stolas's pant leg to keep from hitting the flames.

"Lassie, you're bleeding," Lucifer panted. "Your ears."

Stolas put his hand to his ear and felt the trickle of blood dripping out of it. The ground under his feet shook and trembled with the force of a massive earthquake knocking Stolas off balance as the field rolled like an ocean wave.

A piercing scream tore through the air that would have made Stolas's ears bleed if they hadn't been already, and his eyes desperately sought out Airiella, who was pure light now. Stolas couldn't even see the shape of her body anymore, and his retinas were burning.

Whatever was happening to Airiella had pushed her limit, and she was losing control. The flames around them crackled with a fierce electrical hum that made Lucifer whimper in pain, and a blast of energy tore through them again, more potent than Stolas had ever felt come from Airiella; he tasted blood in his mouth.

The earth shook again, and this time Stolas could hear Airiella breaking free, the ground crumbling beneath her feet as it obeyed her command to release her. The flames around them dropped, and Stolas opened his eyes to see Lucifer in awful shape, pale and trembling.

"Dakota!" Stolas screamed.

"Yes, sir?" Dakota appeared, shaken and scared.

"Get the healer out here now!" Stolas barked, unable to touch his friend without hurting Lucifer worse.

Dakota disappeared, and Stolas looked up to see Airiella running past him towards the two demons that had attacked them. Blind rage ripping across her face as she fired lightning directly into them, sending their ashes plummeting back to the ground.

Airiella dropped to her knees, tears streaming from her eyes. "I'm so sorry, Stolas."

"Go," Lucifer mumbled through the blood seeping from his lips. "Calm her."

Stolas shot to his feet and crossed over to Airiella, gathering her in his arms as another wave of energy rocked them back. A sickening crack echoed in Stolas's ears, and Airiella's warbled cry made it through the buzzing in his head. Stolas couldn't see anything.

Wings; Stolas found himself wrapped in her wings. Airiella had protected him and taken the hit. Frantically Stolas tried to find out where she was hurt, but he couldn't move out of Airiella's hold. Stolas felt the energy build, and with an awful cry, Airiella unleashed the power she had been reluctant to earlier and ripped the soul from the remaining demon Stolas hadn't seen.

Airiella sagged against Stolas as her wings fell from around them, revealing her face a bloody mess. The crack Stolas heard had been Airiella's cheekbone hitting a rock when they fell. "Shit, love. Hold on; the healer is here."

Airiella's eyes were vacant, and fear slashed through Stolas with force. He lifted her and ran over to Lucifer, who was gritting his teeth against the pain of the healer. "Damn it, wait." Stolas pulled out the container of pain salve. "Where is the pain?" Stolas barked at Lucifer, glaring at the healer.

"Inside. Ribs," Lucifer bit out.

Stolas tore open Lucifer's shirt and rubbed the salve over the burns and his ribs until the pain eased from Lucifer's face. "Thanks, friend."

"Finish." Stolas shot another look at the healer and turned back to Airiella. "Love? Can you hear me?" Stolas put some of the salves on his fingers and gently rubbed it into Airiella's face. "Please, love, answer me. If you don't, I'm pretty sure Ronnie will not only kick my ass but try to kill me. I can't keep my promise if I'm dead."

"What the fuck is happening?" Seir yelled, popping in. "The guys went ape shit crazy up there and damn near killed all the guards. We've got some major injuries up there." Seir took in the scene around him. "Did the war happen?"

"Jax," Airiella whispered.

"Jax is fine, but they are seriously angry right now," Seir said gently, dropping next to Airiella. "What happened to your beautiful face?"

"Airiella protected Stolas from a demon we all missed. Stolas would be dead if she hadn't," Lucifer said, his tone quiet.

"Why were there demons here? I thought she was practicing with you?" Seir looked over at Lucifer, trying to put it together.

"Love, look at me please," Stolas pleaded as the healer pushed Stolas out of the way. "You better make this painless, or I'm going to rip your arms from your body and beat you with them."

"Bad threat," Airiella whispered. "Should have threatened him with me, I'm scarier than you."

Insane laughter bubbled from Stolas's lips at the look on the healer's face proving Airiella right. "Sir, let me fix you first, it will be easier."

"Do it," Airiella told the healer, only one of her eyes looking at Stolas and the blood dripping down his face. "I'm sorry I didn't get to you in time."

"Seir, can you bring my broken guards back to me please so we can get them fixed up? Also tell the angel's people she's okay, maybe not mention the face thing. I already almost lost Stolas once today, don't need it happening again."

Seir chuckled. "You nailed that one. Ronnie is spitting nails."

"Ronnie knows I'm fine, they all do," Airiella whispered.

"I'll be back with the guards, then maybe someone can fill me in on what happened here."

Stolas looked back at Airiella, noting she was going into shock. "We need one of Airiella's medicine people."

"No, make me good enough to get back, don't bring them here," Airiella told Stolas.

"Tell me what happened, love. Not even Lucifer made you freeze that way." Stolas brushed Airiella's hair out of her face.

"One of them locked me in the nightmare that woke me up. I kept watching Jax die, over and over." Airiella's voice broke, and she ground her teeth against the pain as her bones slid back into place. "I smelled your blood, heard your voice over the screams in my head, and I lost control."

"If you hadn't, we'd both be dead," Lucifer told

Airiella gently, his hand hovering over her like he wanted to caress her face. "Your power both protected us and held us as prisoners."

"I'm sorry," Airiella groaned and closed her one eye.

"You also just saved the life of my best friend while single-handedly defeating an entire legion that had more powerful demons than I was aware of, sadly. The one thing I would say to work on would be to not fall for the tricks of the mind. They know the others are your weakness. They *don't* know you can overcome it."

"I almost didn't. I had to smell Stolas's blood to understand what was happening." Airiella sat up as the healer finished and winced. "Something else is broken somewhere."

"Find it," Stolas snapped at the healer.

"No." Airiella put a gentle hand on Stolas. "Taklishim or one of the others will fix me up. Thank you for fixing my cheek," Airiella told the healer, who still looked utterly terrified of her. "I'm not going to hurt you."

Lucifer dismissed him to heal the guards and gave Airiella a look Stolas had never seen on his friend's face. It was one of tenderness. "I'm no longer concerned you can't defeat Moloch or his army. You shouldn't be either."

Seir came back with twenty guards in varying states of injuries and came over to Airiella. "The rest are back at the hotel, and the medicine people are waiting with Jax in your room."

"How did humans manage to do this to guards?" Lucifer chuckled lightly.

"They started to glow, and they went wild. I've never seen anything quite like it from these guys before. They aren't just humans, sir. That was some next-level shit from those guys."

"Clearly. Were any of the angel's team hurt?" Lucifer asked, a wary eye on Airiella.

"Minor injuries. Once they started to glow, they had an entirely different level of strength to them."

Stolas looked at Airiella thoughtfully. "I told you they'd be harder to kill now."

"Want to tell me what happened here that set them off?"

"Lucifer suggested testing her against a legion since she kicked his ass." Stolas shot Seir a look. "Airiella, of course, agreed to it."

"An entire legion? Who's was it?"

"Bael's; his eighth," Lucifer supplied, and Seir's eyes widened.

"Did they get you with fear?" Seir touched Airiella's leg, and Stolas irrationally wanted to rip Seir's hand off his body.

"Yep. I'm guessing when I lost control, so did the guys." Airiella tried to stand but faltered. Stolas scooped her up. "Take me back, please."

Chapter Thirty-Three

Stolas managed to escape injury, but just barely. Once Airiella convinced Ronnie it was her idea and Stolas had tried to talk her out of it, Ronnie calmed down. Onida checked Stolas over for injuries at Airiella's insistence even though he knew he had none.

Kalisha rested her head on his chest while Stolas related the story. "Airiella's magic is Lucifer's kryptonite."

"It would appear so," Stolas agreed. "I don't think Lucifer would have sustained as much damage as he did if Airiella's flames hadn't burned him."

"Do they burn you?"

"When she turns them up, they do. Not like they do, Lucifer. They react with the dark powers in me. I think I am more immune than Lucifer because of the mark and the light." Stolas hugged Kalish tight to him for a moment, then eased up.

"Airiella will be fine, Stolas. Stop worrying. Today should have proven that to you."

"It did in a manner. Airiella's vulnerabilities were also quite pronounced. I can't even imagine the horror of watching you die over and over again and not being able to do anything about it, frozen in limbo."

Kalisha stroked her fingers over his cheek. "Jax is with her. Between Jax, Ronnie, and Taklishim Airiella is well taken care of at the moment."

"What happened with Chrissie?" Stolas remembered to ask.

"Chrissie is a healer. Onida spotted it right away, and they worked with her quite a bit. Chrissie is feeling much better now that she doesn't think she's worthless."

"She never was worthless." Stolas was angry.

"It's harder to convince someone of that when they are watching their friends easily perform acts that she felt like she was supposed to be doing as well. Why do you think Chrissie's different than the others?"

"Hard to say. There's no one closer to Airiella than Chrissie, well, perhaps Jax, but you know what I mean."

"It's a possibility I hadn't considered. Regardless, Chrissie's doing much better now."

"Good, I like her." Stolas had worried about Chrissie since the kidnapping with Rafe had happened.

"I do too. Chrissie is quite special. I also sense something about the baby she's carrying." Kalisha turned to look at Stolas.

"Something bad?" Stolas searched Kalisha's gaze.

"No. It's too soon to tell what it is. It gives me a sense of Airiella."

"That wouldn't surprise me. Airiella's bond with Ronnie is quite strong. For a while, I thought Airiella was going to end up with Ronnie despite the pull Jax had on her," Stolas reminisced.

"I never doubted what I saw between Jax and Airiella. From the start, Jax couldn't look away from her no matter how hard he tried, and believe me, Jax tried to ignore her. It makes me think of how I was when I first saw you. I don't even think you knew I existed then."

"I've always known you existed, my love. I just didn't think you would even consider looking in my direction. I'm a demon." Stolas smoothed his hand down the back of Kalisha's head.

"Stop saying that. You are more than a demon, and the Creator said it himself." Kalisha shifted against Stolas. "Why am I suddenly so exhausted that my brain won't think straight?"

"A lot of magic use in a short period of time, probably. Let's rest, my love. I, too, am tired."

Stolas felt his mind go foggy as he slipped into a restless sleep, the words of the prophecy running through his head along with disjointed visions of chaos and death. Screams of pain and terror echoed in his ears as Stolas bolted awake, a cold sweat dripping down his face.

Stolas's senses told him he wasn't alone, and as Stolas scanned the dark room, Kalisha woke next to him, her breathing stilled. "It's just me." Airiella's voice sounded from the couch. "Your nightmares were loud and too like my own. I wanted to check on you both to make sure you were okay."

"Stolas," Kalisha whispered to him, "go to her." Kalisha nudged Stolas hard, and he stumbled out of bed. "Airiella wouldn't be here if she didn't think she needed to be."

Stolas froze as he heard sniffling. He swore and started feeling around for his pants as Kalisha flew past him. Stolas found them and pulled them on before he switched on a lamp in the room, the faint light glowing a soft warm yellow that showed him Kalisha rocking Airiella in her arms.

"It didn't break you, that's all that matters," Kalisha was softly murmuring.

A quiet knock sounded on the door, and Stolas figured it was Jax coming to take Airiella back, but as he opened the door, a distraught Ronnie stood there. Stolas pulled the door open wider so he could see Airiella, and Ronnie muttered a quiet thank you and strode in the room, his large body dwarfing Kalisha as Ronnie knelt before them.

Stolas still wasn't sure what was happening. "Love, what's wrong?"

Airiella had moved from Kalisha's arms to Ronnie's, who had wrapped himself protectively around her as if his presence alone could keep anything from getting to her. "Angel, we are going to figure this out," Ronnie told Airiella as he dropped kisses on her forehead.

Stolas finally got a good look at Airiella as Ronnie moved to lean back against the couch. Her face was still swollen, but the bruising was gone thanks to Taklishim and Degataga. But the haunted look in Airiella's eyes was more pronounced, and Stolas could tell she was hanging on by a strand.

"Love, what did you mean my nightmares were loud?" Stolas tried again, sitting down in front of Ronnie and facing them.

"Our nightmares were the same, which tells me it's not a nightmare." Airiella's voice broke as the words tumbled out. "Then my brain kept playing on repeat that damn scene with Jax, and I started to lose my shit. I was worried you weren't okay because of the nightmare, so I came here."

"I'm tuned into Airiella when things go sideways and when I saw she wasn't with Jax, I came here," Ronnie offered his explanation.

"Does Jax know you left?" Kalisha dropped to the floor next to them, putting her hand on Airiella's foot.

"He was still asleep," Airiella mumbled against Ronnie's arm as she buried her face in his shoulder.

"Jax won't wake up for a while, Tama put him out so he'd get a full night's rest," Ronnie informed them. "I saw Airiella's nightmare but didn't feel her distress right away. Chrissie did, and woke me up, told me she needed me."

"What if the Creator was wrong, and I'm not the right person to do all this?" Stolas heard Airiella's muffled words.

"I believe you are, Airiella. I believe you are so much more than you think you are," Kalisha consoled her. "When it comes to you, nothing is impossible. I've known this group for such a long time, and the changes in them were immediate when you came into their lives. Everyone you touch with this love inside of you begins to blossom in ways that no one expected."

"What do I do if I lose Jax?" Airiella turned her head slightly, and the raw pain in those eyes sucked the oxygen from Stolas's lungs.

"We figure it out together, love," was all Stolas could manage to say.

"Come on, angel." Ronnie stood and lifted Airiella effortlessly. "I don't know about you, but I need to be with you both right now, can we do that?"

Airiella nodded, and Kalisha stepped in to kiss her

cheek. "Don't give up, Airiella. There's something in this whole thing we don't see yet."

Kalisha's admission shocked Stolas, who had been thinking the same thing since it all started to happen. She'd accepted his words, but this was the first that Kalisha had spoken that she agreed with them. "I'm doing my best to figure it out, love."

Kalisha wrapped her arms around Stolas and then watched Ronnie carry her out. "What happens if Jax dies?" Kalisha looked at Stolas.

"What do you mean?" Stolas looked down into Kalisha's deep-set eyes.

"With us, you said I would feel it if something happened to you. Will she?"

"Yes, with as connected as they are, Airiella would know immediately and probably be in excruciating pain from it. Physical pain, as well as mental and emotional. From what I've seen with Jax and Ronnie, it physically hurts them when she goes through it."

"There's nothing we can do to ease that, is there?"

"No, my love. No amount of magic can ease that kind of hurt." Stolas kissed the top of Kalisha's head.

Chapter Thirty-Four

The group didn't need more training. They needed a day of rest more than anything, but they still went to the morning workout that Ronnie led them in. It gave the team a sense of normalcy in the middle of the turmoil.

They stuck together after that, no one wanting anyone to be alone for long periods. "This isn't healthy," Kalisha whispered to him. "They are all acting as if Jax is going to die, and they are waiting for the funeral."

"I see it. I can't change it, though. Nor can I go to the team and tell them to stop grieving. Grief is the price of love." Stolas tipped Kalisha's chin up and softly kissed her.

Stolas and Kalisha sat back and watched as the others played games with the kids, and eventually, they all left together to spend more time outdoors. They were winding up a tour at a glass blowing place when Seir popped in looking frantic.

"I think it's happening." Seir's eyes were wide and wild looking.

"What?" Stolas stepped in front of Kalisha as if he were protecting her.

"Come, Kalisha, stay here with them." Seir grabbed Stolas by the arm and disregarding the public around them popped them out to one of the populated squares where Stolas saw flames erupting across merchant's booths. Screams of panic tore through the air, and crowds were running around trying to flee.

Stolas felt power rising in him and looked around, trying to spot what had caused the fires, smoke was starting to get thick in the air around them, the sounds of sirens getting closer. Finally, Stolas looked up when a breeze cleared the smoke for a second and saw Moloch on top of one of the buildings lining the square and Stolas's heart started slamming into his ribs. Seir was right; it was beginning.

"Take us back." Stolas grimaced at how Seir snatched his arm painfully and then appeared back in the studio. "Get the kids, Chrissie, Jillian, and Mags to the warrior and bring back the others that are coming."

Airiella looked at Stolas, her eyes understanding what was happening before anyone else caught on. Airiella pushed Chrissie to Seir, catching Mags's eyes and nodding. The guys gathered around Airiella and made their way towards Stolas as Seir disappeared.

"Moloch has attacked the public in one of the squares. Moloch is doing this to draw you out, love. We have to answer, or he will randomly kill all these people for no other reason than he can," Stolas quietly told Airiella.

"Is Moloch there?" Jax asked.

"Yes, I found him on top of one of the buildings," Stolas confirmed.

"That means Airiella has to fight in public, she'll be outed," Ronnie whispered furiously.

"I'd rather be outed than have a ton of deaths happen because I was trying to hide. It's fine, Ronnie." Airiella cupped his cheek.

"Do you all have the stones I gave you?" Kalisha's tone was all business as she checked each of them and started distributing ones that held attacking spells.

Seir popped back in with Taklishim and Tama. "Ready?" Seir asked, waiting for everyone to touch. As soon as they did, Seir brought them to the middle of the square.

Thick black smoke billowed up darkening the sky, and hot red unnatural flames lapped at booths, merchandise, and a few people. Firefighters were working furiously to put out the fires with little success, and police were herding the crowds away, only be to trapped as more fires broke out.

"Stay within sight of each other," Stolas barked out as they all turned to face outwards, looking for demons. "This is hellfire, more dangerous than normal flames."

Panicked screams filled his ears as Stolas saw the first demon. "I can't see through all this smoke," Smitty called out.

Stolas felt the air around them start to move as Airiella called to it and funneled the smoke out. The screams around them reached an ear-shattering pitch, and Stolas realized they were screaming at them; they were now all glowing blue.

Airiella stepped away and took a deep breath before speaking as if her voice were coming from hundreds of speakers throughout the square. "We are here to help, and if you see someone glowing like I am, they are not your enemy." Airiella pointed across the square at the demon slowly stalking towards her, smoke rolling off him and his eyes burning red. "The ones that look like that are the enemy."

The screams quieted as some began to realize that what they were seeing was something extraordinary and terrifying both. People were translating the message in various languages throughout the crowd. Their realities had been shattered by the hidden world rarely seen or understood by the masses.

The sky that had been a brilliant blue began to fill with daunting clouds as Airiella started working with the elements. Fat, heavy raindrops started to fall, helping the firefighters try to quench the flames destroying everything around them, using the air to suck the oxygen from the fire.

It was all Airiella could do right now with all the people running around. Smitty stepped out and started directing people to get under cover of one of the buildings behind them where no fires had broken out. There were no booths there; it was just a stone building.

People started catching on and heading that way while police stared at them with their mouths hanging open, not sure what to do. Stolas began looking around more trying to spot Stone since Stolas knew that was who Jax would go after first, and Jax was high on Stolas's list of people to keep safe.

Airiella had caught the attention of three more demons and had all of them now slowly heading towards her. "Do I need to go get Lucifer's guards?" Seir asked Stolas.

"No, not yet. I don't know if this is the big showdown or not." Stolas kept scanning as he talked. Moloch still hadn't moved from his spot on top of the building, but the evil smile on Moloch's face was chilling, and his eyes locked on Airiella.

Dead bodies lay across the square, some burned badly, others with blood pooled under them while their loved ones knelt by them, wailing helplessly. Stolas didn't miss the look Airiella sent at him; this was the nightmare they both had last night.

Airiella started to walk towards the demons who were in the way of the people left out in the square. Her fury was evident by the intensity of her glow and the way she walked. Stolas could feel the demons feeding off the fear, and as much as Stolas wanted to help Airiella, he needed to stay close to Jax and Ronnie.

Taklishim had gone into his warrior mode and Tama had changed into her cougar, her cat eyes following the demons' movement. Ronnie was shifting his weight back and forth, and Aedan and Jax were scanning the area as Stolas had been. Smitty was finishing rounding the people up, including the firefighters and police officers.

Behind the booth directly in front of me is another group of black souls, Airiella told Stolas.

One of the demons broke into a run and sent magic flying at Airiella. She quickly blocked it and dropped into another sweeping kick and, in a blur, made ash out of it and took off for the others that were advancing at her. With a speed that was almost too hard to track, Airiella struck physical blows using no magic of her own and dispatched the other demons.

There is no safe way to get these people out of here, Airiella broadcast to all of them. *All the exits are teeming with demons. There are scattered innocent souls intermixed with them as if they are holding them hostage, so I can't just blast them with magic and not hurt these people. I see Moloch on the roof, as well.*

Stolas couldn't talk to them all, so he spoke to Airiella only. *No sign of Stone. I know he has to be here somewhere.*

Airiella turned back to face them, and Stolas saw a wall of blue flames erupt out of the ground in front of the crowds of people gathered there. "Please do not be alarmed," Airiella called out, "those fires are to keep you safe."

I have no idea if they understand me, Airiella said frustrated. *Fucking bastard, why is Moloch hiding up there?*

A flaming spear embedded itself in the ground in front of Airiella, inches from her body. She had to have known it was coming because Airiella stopped moving before it had struck, and she was staring coldly up at Moloch.

Stolas watched in fascination as Airiella reached out and pulled it out of the ground, the flames not affecting her at all. Airiella broke it in half, then half again. The flames snuffing out as she dropped it on the ground and moved, checking on the bodies lying on the ground.

Her head was sadly shaking as Airiella confirmed each one was no longer among the living, tears streaming from her eyes as she came to a lady, clearly pregnant, clinging to life barely.

"Tak! I need help! She's alive!"

Taklishim ran across the square, knelt in front of the lady, speaking to Airiella, his words too soft for Stolas to hear. Somewhere behind him, a man was screaming hysterically, and Stolas figured that had to have been his wife.

"Jax, you can get through these flames, right?" Stolas asked him.

"I can. Do you think that man is related to the woman?"

"I do, can you bring him out?" Stolas's heart was breaking at the emotions rolling off Airiella. He didn't know how Airiella's team didn't buckle under them.

"I'll try." Jax moved, and Stolas stuck close to him, keeping his eye on Moloch, who was still watching Airiella with glee.

Jax brought the man out, and Tama herded him to the lady, standing behind while Airiella talked to them softly. Taklishim pulled off his shirt, and Stolas stared in horror as Taklishim cut the woman open, pulled the baby out, cut the bloody cord, and wrapped the baby up, handing it to the man who was sobbing uncontrollably.

She was too far gone, Airiella's voice came in Stolas's head, crackling with emotion. *Tak waited until she passed before taking the baby out. Please have Jax get them back to safety before that asshole tries to kill the baby, and I lose every bit of control I am trying to hold on to in front of all these people.*

Stolas relayed the information, and Jax ran over to the man, Stolas, behind him until the man was safely behind the flames. Hordes of demons swamped the square, separating Airiella from the rest of them. They were everywhere, and the silent fear of the crowd was once again panicked screams.

Chapter Thirty-Five

L ucifer, it's time," Stolas called out as a bright ball of light appeared before them, and Stolas was looking at a group of angels, the ones that had come before Airiella. They looked coldly at Stolas, derision on their faces.

"We're here to help her," one called Samuel told him. Stolas remembered Samuel well; this wasn't the time for discord.

Lucifer appeared on Stolas's other side with his guards behind him, thousands of demons around them. The angels reacted badly to Lucifer and went to attack when suddenly flames erupted around all of them, and Airiella appeared before Stolas.

"If the Creator sent you to help me, then help me." Airiella pointed at Lucifer and his guards. "They are not to be harmed by you or any of those with you. They are here helping me as well. Understood?" Airiella's tone was hard and angry.

"They are demons," Samuel ground out, spitting.

"I'm well aware of what they are. We are fighting a common enemy. Lucifer and his crew are not to harm any of you." Airiella looked back at Lucifer for his confirmation on that, and at Lucifer's nod, Airiella looked back at the angels. "Understood?"

Samuel didn't respond, just looked at Lucifer with unbridled hate in his eyes. "Samuel, you wouldn't be here if the Creator didn't think you would follow directions, do you even know what Airiella is?" Stolas tried to interrupt.

"Stolas, don't. Samuel, is it?" At the angel's curt nod, Airiella went on. "I don't give a flying fuck if you don't like him or not. If you harm any of them that are here to help me, I will end you. The reverse is also true. The shitstorm of demons around us is our targets. If you can't follow my directive on this, then either leave or wait for me to prove to you I mean what I say."

"Understood," was Samuel's terse reply. The flames around them eased as Moloch dropped down into the middle of his army, manically laughing. Chills went up Stolas's spine as the deadly gaze turned on Airiella.

"You can't even get them to follow directions, and you think you can beat me? Not one person will be left standing when I finish with this. I will devour them all; you included as you watch those you love die first. Their lives are meaningless, a way for me to get to you."

Stolas expected more flames as the threat against them became verbalized. Instead, Airiella calmly turned and faced Moloch. "Nothing is redeeming in your soul, Moloch. Why is it you think you will survive this? I won't allow it. Simple as that."

Lucifer moved to stand next to Stolas. "Did Airiella just defend my guards and me to her kind?"

"Yes, as well as threaten you and guards if you hurt them," Stolas reminded Lucifer.

"I have no intention of harming them. I had no idea Moloch's army was this large, though."

Neither did Stolas. The legion Airiella had taken on was nothing compared to this. There were demons of all levels here. "Any idea where Stone is?" Stolas still hadn't found him.

Fighting had broken out around them as another wall of blue flames enveloped them, and Stolas felt the energy getting drawn to Airiella. "Shit, this is going to hurt," Lucifer growled. He stepped into the middle of his guards to try to help alleviate the blow that would hit.

The flames absorbed it. In one attack, Airiella had taken down over half of the demons that had surrounded them. The rest of the power that hadn't materialized before, now firmly in place. The flames dropped, and the real fight had started at Moloch's furious bellow of pain and rage. It was all-out chaos.

Airiella's team all had their weapons in hand and began to use their physical training, fists flying as they all engaged. Stolas could hear the cougar ripping through demons and cries of pain all around him. Stolas tried to keep his eye on Jax, Ronnie, and Taklishim but lost sight of them almost immediately. Airiella was nothing more than a blur of movement as she kicked, hit, stabbed, ducked, and moved around the demons.

Stolas couldn't even see Lucifer anymore. Kalisha was next to him throwing her stones and using magic at a rapid pace and Stolas followed her lead, he was more confident with his magic than he was his fists, even after all the training. Explosions were tearing through the square all around them as Kalisha's stones did her bidding.

For each demon they took out, two more appeared.

The only way Stolas knew where Airiella was, was because of the electricity crackling from her. Moloch's screams were echoing in the square with every blow she landed. They fought on until they were standing on piles of ash, exhaustion pulling heavy at Stolas's bones.

Stolas had no idea how much longer they could go on like this. Their movements had all slowed drastically, and his energy was starting to wane. Ronnie was the closest to Stolas, and he was panting hard, his hands braced on his knees for seconds while Ronnie tried to catch his breath before having to fend off the next attack. Bruises and blood were covering him enough that Stolas couldn't tell if it was his blood or those that Ronnie slew.

Stolas hadn't even found Stone yet. The roar coming from Tama's cougar followed by a high-pitched yowl chilled his blood, and Stolas's heart raced in his chest as he started to look for her frantically. His skin started to glow brighter, and Stolas worked his way through demons slashing at them as he pushed through, ash coating the blood sticking to his skin like some sick form of armor.

Stolas saw Taklishim out of the corner of his eye, and he turned that way, letting off another blast of energy to clear the way. Tama lay at Taklishim's feet, blood pouring from a wound on her side, deep from its looks.

I need flames around me, love. Tama is injured. Airiella didn't respond, but not too much time had passed, and flames erupted around him and Taklishim. Stolas pulled out the salve's container that would clean the demon poison from Tama's wounds and applied it liberally while Taklishim worked on healing the wound.

"Do you want me to have Seir get you out of here?" Stolas asked Tama.

"No, I'll be fine," Tama said wearily. She didn't look okay, even as the wounds healed, Stolas could see the fatigue in Tama's face, in the way she held her body.

"I won't argue with her," Taklishim told Stolas tightly.

Let me out, love, Stolas requested as Tama changed back into a cougar.

The ground beneath Stolas started to shake, and the air was whipping around his face. The flames dropped, and he scanned to see what was causing the reaction and found Smitty and Aedan locked in with a couple of higher-level demons. They had reverted to magic to fight, using the earth to hold them in place and the air to keep others away while Smitty tried to stab at them with his knife.

Stolas's heart stopped as Aedan went flying through the air and slammed into a stone pillar over a hundred feet away. Stolas didn't even stop, just fired off a couple of fireballs, taking the demons out as he ran to check on Aedan. Stolas saw Aedan get to his feet and stumble before righting himself, Stolas slowing to a stop as he looked Aedan over.

"I'm fine. Just bruised," Aedan told Stolas. "I don't have a lot left in me, though."

"Together, let's band together," Stolas told Aedan, cutting a path through towards where he had been with Taklishim, grabbing Smitty on the way. Stolas found Kalisha near Ronnie and corralled them, searching for Jax. "Stay together," Stolas told them again.

Before Stolas could move, flames erupted around him again as Ariella let loose another blast of energy that tore through most of what remained, leaving a handful of the stronger ones standing, Moloch and Stone, who squared-off against Jax.

Stuck behind the flames, Stolas couldn't get to Jax until she dropped them. *Let me go, love. I can't help him if I'm stuck here,* Stolas pleaded with Airiella.

Moloch was severely injured but still standing, hulking over Airiella as he looked around at the ruins of his army. Moloch's rage was palpable, and as he spotted Lucifer among the blue flames, being protected by Airiella, he brought a flaming chain down that wrapped around Airiella's legs. He sent her careening into the building that got in the way of her trajectory.

Stolas felt the bolt of pain at the impact and was helpless to do anything. The only bright side, if Stolas could look at it that way, was that the rest were protected, and Stolas didn't have to track them. It also meant Airiella was going to take the fall, again, sacrifice herself. She landed in a heap next to another of the angels who were able to walk in and out of her flames, and he helped her up, a white light flaring from his hands as Airiella's broken wing mended itself, along with an assortment of other injuries.

Moloch was headed directly for Lucifer, thinking Airiella was still down, which was his mistake for underestimating Airiella. She let out another blast of light energy that dropped Moloch to his knees. He roared a string of curse words in a demonic language Airiella wouldn't understand, but it was enough to distract Moloch away from Lucifer, which was her goal, and Airiella dropped the flames around them as Moloch focused back on her.

Stolas glanced once at Lucifer to make sure he was okay before beelining towards Jax, who was using a combination of physical and magic attacks against Stone.

Stolas saw the strike coming the minute Stone moved, and time stood still as Jax took the hit a split second before Stolas got to him. Blade and magic slicing right into Jax.

Blue flames shrouded them all as Stolas bowled into Jax's body, Moloch's laughter mixed with the scream that tore through Airiella's throat the moment Jax received the injury. The dark magic was tearing Jax up, and there wasn't a damn thing Stolas could do to stop it.

Airiella's scream echoing in his mind, the pain she felt making Stolas cry out and the blast of energy that tore through the square again, taking out the remaining demons, leaving Moloch and Stone. Jax's life was bleeding out of him in Stolas's arms. Jax's body was shuddering with the pain as the dark magic ripped at his soul.

Stolas felt Airiella call on the dark magic, and she tore Stone's soul from his body in the most violent way Stolas had ever seen before. Stolas could hear the threads of it ripping from Stone's body, Airiella's emotions leeching into the act, the pain she was feeling bleeding into every strand that snapped so Stone felt the same pain she did. The divine justice in Airiella was burning and obliterating the soul as she ripped it out, piece by piece. The vision Airiella presented was both beautiful and terrifying. Airiella's hair was floating around her head, dancing with electricity. Her wings were shining like armor radiating all that was good in her. Airiella's skin wasn't glowing blue, though; it was now a violent purple color and lethal. Stolas swallowed thickly, Jax clawing at his arm as he tried to speak.

"Don't let her fall," Jax was saying.

Love, let me go, Stolas begged Airiella. *I can't help you here.*

You promised! Airiella's jagged voice ripped through Stolas's mind, sounding fractured in a way that wasn't good for anyone.

I can't help either of you if I'm stuck. Listen to me, love. Please hear me. I have never steered you wrong; you have to let me up. Damn it, Airiella, drop these fucking flames!

"Lassie." Lucifer's voice carried to Stolas. "Airiella's in a dangerous place, get her to listen to you, she's at my door."

Moloch continued to laugh, not caring that Stone was painfully obliterated, turned to ash, wiped from existence, and then offered the one thing that would break Airiella's resolve. "I can give him back to you. Join me, and he will live."

Stolas felt the waver in Airiella's power, her emotions wild with anguish as Moloch dangled the one thing Airiella said she couldn't live without in front of her face. Moloch didn't even try to get close to her, as the power coming off Airiella would have sent Moloch to ash at one touch of her skin. Moloch poked at her from a distance, his voice cruel and calculating.

Trade me, love. Offer me as a trade. Let me up; let me help you. Please don't accept Moloch's offer; he will kill you. Moloch can have me. Love, please, let me up. Stolas rambled, desperate to get through. *Remember what I told you about not accepting deals with Lucifer? It stands for Moloch as well. What you get back might not be Jax. Drop the flames, love. Please.*

Airiella collapsed to the ground with another heartbreaking scream as blood bubbled from Jax's lips. Stolas let out a cry of his own as the worst-case scenario played out. Stolas's heart shattered with hers as Airiella now faced a decision that she should never have had to make, her greatest love dead in Stolas's arms. If he thought the emotions Airiella released that day Stolas saw her at the beach were astounding, this was a pale comparison to the intensity of what ripped through every person in the square as she lost Jax, dropping them all in one fell swoop.

Hear my voice, love. I love you enough to give my life for this. I have no regrets, don't accept Moloch's offer. Listen to me, please; remember every word of the prophecy. Ride my wings, love; follow me through this dark. Let me go. Let me help you. I'm with you, always.

Moloch swung the chain again, sensing the weakness in her, the crack in Airiella's soul at losing Jax. Stolas was helpless with fright as Airiella looked directly at Moloch and told him to do it. "Kill me, fucker."

Stolas felt a cry of rage tear through his throat as the chain bore down on Airiella with a sickening crack, then it shattered to pieces in Moloch's hand, the damage to Airiella done and her power destroying the weapon used on her. The flames around Stolas went out the moment the chain hit her, and Taklishim and Ronnie raced towards Jax as Stolas ran to Airiella.

"You promised me," Airiella cried, her voice thin and reedy. "I still love you, remember that. I know it's not your fault," she said and her voice weak with pain as Stolas felt her intention to give up settle over him. "Goodbye, Stolas."

"Get up!" Stolas yelled at Airiella, his voice harsh and anger ripping at his heart. "Get your ass up and fight!" Airiella stared at Stolas in shock and tried to move her broken body. "Those hard decisions you have to make are here and now. Let Jax die for nothing, or finish what you need to do. Avenge Jax. Fucking get up right now!"

Never had Stolas felt like more of an asshole then he did at that moment. He was using Airiella's pain against her as if it didn't matter like it was trivial. Stolas didn't know how to get through to her; the pain was all Airiella felt. Half of her soul was dead with Jax, the void in Airiella easy to see, and terrible to experience.

Moloch chose that moment to make another move on Stolas and sent a crushing blow into his back so hard that Stolas heard his spine crack. An intense moment of pain and then Stolas lost all feeling in his body. Thankful, he wouldn't at least feel the landing.

"No!" Airiella screamed, purple light filling the square as she released a wave of air that caught Stolas, lowering him to the ground. "No!" Airiella repeated, louder, her voice colored by the rage that was now rolling through the square in uncontrolled waves. Airiella had lost control. "You don't get me; you don't get to claim any more lives, you get to destroy nothing else. This fight ends here, asshole! You lay one more finger on any of these innocent people, and I'll make you suffer before I end you."

"Stolas isn't an innocent," Moloch sneered. "Killing Stolas is doing the world a favor."

The mix of Airiella's light and dark, creating the purple glowing energy that sparked off her in violent waves, was serenely beautiful. Tama reached Stolas, her hands settling on his back as Tama used what precious energy she had left to heal him. Stolas didn't think it was possible. That single blow held all of the rage that Moloch had in him, and the damage was extensive. Stolas didn't care; all that mattered was Airiella not falling.

Instead of putting flames up around everyone, Airiella encased herself and Moloch inside a small ring of fire that burned intense and purple. Stolas could feel the lethal energy it gave off from across the square. He could no longer hear what Airiella was saying, but Stolas felt her. He experienced everything inside Airiella, the anguish, and angst that was trying to tear her apart. Airiella's desire to give in to Moloch's offer, the physical pain that wracked her body in the ways the emotional pain wasn't. The fight in Airiella was desperately clinging to the light in her soul. The endless pit of anger at the hurt inflicted on Stolas and the others in her circle.

This storm of emotion was what Stolas meant when Airiella bled life. Airiella was suffering for all of them, literally and figuratively. The colors of her feelings were spectacular and mesmerizing as Stolas heard Airiella clearly say, "You should have killed me, not Jax." The sound of the chaos around Stolas, the frightened screams of the people Airiella had been protecting all fading to nothing as her power grew and spiraled in a pattern that could only mean Airiella's control had snapped completely.

The explosion that happened threw them all, scattering them in different directions. Stolas's ears were ringing with a pain he shouldn't be feeling. His whole body ached, and somewhere in his mind Stolas understood that Tama had healed his injuries enough to give him movement and feeling back. Stolas's nerves flared to life in time to receive the crushing pain of the energy blowback from the blast Airiella had sent out. The flames protecting the crowd of people were gone, and pillars were crumbling to the ground as the earth shook and trembled in response to Airiella. The statue in the middle of the square toppled as if it hadn't been standing there for centuries.

Ash swirled through the air in multiple funnel clouds as Airiella lost control again, and Stolas's vision went black, everyone and everything blocked from sight except the clouds of ash. Stolas felt the soul ripping power tear through what remained of the square with, heavy pressure. Bolts of purple lighting rained down in muted flashes through the dark where Stolas assumed Airiella stood, in a thunderous cacophony of sounds that covered the screams of every living soul left, leaving Stolas feeling deaf.

When the dust settled, Stolas saw Airiella's ravaged face. Black and bloody with tear tracks clearing paths down her cheeks. Not one sign of Moloch left. The only clue Airiella was still breathing was her heaving chest that rose up and down with the silent sobs as she gave in to the emotions flooding through her. Each tear sliding down Airiella's face felt like a rainstorm on Stolas.

Lucifer appeared in Stolas's line of sight. "Talk to her," it sounded like Lucifer was saying. "She can bring him back."

"What?" Stolas could hardly hear through the ringing in his ears.

"Talk to her, Lassie; she needs to go to him. She can bring him back. Remember the prophecy. She's still at my door." Lucifer's face mirrored the pain in Airiella's, her emotions sparing no one.

Stolas stared blankly at Lucifer, certain he heard wrong. It had sounded like Lucifer had told Stolas that Airiella could bring Jax back. He rolled to his side, every bone in his body feeling broken.

"You are not stupid, Lassie, you heard me. Get your

miserable ass up and fix this. Airiella can give life."

With a flash, Stolas understood, and it made sense. This revelation was what Stolas had been missing the whole time. It wasn't Airiella helping people get pregnant, though that might be part of it. Stolas allowed Lucifer to lift him to his feet as Stolas staggered over to Airiella, pushing through Ronnie until Stolas looked into Airiella's eyes, seeing them dull with pain, the fight has gone out of her. Stolas wasn't going to get through that way.

This fight isn't over. You can heal Jax, love. Get up; finish this. Bring your mate back. Airiella, I know you can hear me. You listened to me before, even though I let you down. It's not finished; I'm still your advisor, and I need you to get up now and bring him back. The love in you isn't dead. Feel it.

I can't heal, Stolas. I've never been able to. The sound of Airiella's defeated voice in his head almost broke Stolas's will to push her.

You can take life as well as give it. Go to Jax. Put your damn bloody hands on your love and fill Jax with the power inside you. Remember, you make the decision who lives or dies. Don't choose Jax to be dead. Laying here and ignoring me is admitting Jax is gone. Jax is not gone if you don't want him to be. Choices, love. Make a choice. I'm trying to save Jax right now, and you aren't listening to me. The prophecy said you could take life as well as give it. Fucking listen to me. Damn it, please, love. You made the right choices; I believe this is what the prophecy meant.

Around Stolas, time stood still, frozen in place except for Stolas and Airiella. He didn't know if Airiella had done it, or the Creator had, but Stolas took the opportunity.

Did I ever tell you about the first time I saw you?

No, Airiella closed her eyes, the pain in her heart heavy enough to drown Stolas in sorrow for the rest of his damned life.

It was in California, I felt you. From across the miles, I felt your love. I hadn't felt love like that in at least a thousand years if not more. I had no choice but to follow it, and I saw you. A hint of your wings was visible, and I was stunned because all those that came before you had white wings. There you were, bleeding love like there was a never-ending supply of it with wings half-black and half-white that weren't there. Ronnie was sitting behind you, watching you. I didn't know who Ronnie was, and I didn't care. All I knew at that moment was that you would change my life. I watched you for hours, my raven sitting in the trees behind Ronnie. I felt the pain in you break free, and I wept with you. I knew I wanted you; I craved you. I didn't understand that what I was feeling was love, not until I pulled you away from Bael. It took me that long to realize it was love. I watched you fall in love with each member of your crew, and I felt jealousy like never before. I wanted to crush them all. Then when you and Jax came together, my heart broke, and I lost hope. I knew then what that all-consuming love looked like, and I knew you weren't mine, but that I loved you anyway and would do anything I could to keep that love in you alive. Even if it was me that couldn't have you.

Jax's gone Stolas. There is no me without Jax.

Jax is not gone love. He's still here, waiting for you to bring him back to you. I can feel it. Please trust me on this. I wouldn't give you false hope. Time around them came back to life with ear-shattering sounds.

Something akin to hope flared in Airiella's eyes then died out just as fast. *I can't get up, Stolas. I have nothing left.*

Stolas swore and bent over, almost falling on top of Airiella, but Taklishim steadied Stolas, and he pulled Airiella to her feet and dragged her over to Jax. *Fight for it. For once, love, please don't fucking argue with me. Just put your hands on Jax. Believe in yourself as I do.*

"This better work, Lucy," Stolas muttered as Airiella put her hands on Jax's chest. Her tears were falling on Jax's ash-covered face, leaving tracks that matched hers, whispering words of love to Jax.

Taklishim pulled Stolas away. "If what you say is true, give Airiella space. The pain of losing a mate is indescribable, and no matter who you are, healing is hard, harder still when dealing with all that Airiella is."

Stolas glanced over at Taklishim's mate, Tama, sitting there, injured, bloody and naked. Stolas pulled his shirt off, handed it to Taklishim, and nodded at Tama. Stolas stood there waiting and watching Airiella, his own emotions wildly out of control and raw. It was taking Airiella way too long, in his personal opinion, until Stolas saw a warm glow emitting from her hands.

"It's out of our hands now, Lassie. She's no longer knocking at my door," Lucifer told Stolas gently.

"What is the cost of Airiella doing this?" Stolas looked at Lucifer. "And why do you think it will work?

"I think Airiella has paid whatever cost there is." Lucifer nodded at the crowd congregating around them. "The world will know who the angel is now, what she's capable of, and that she protected the Devil. That's a heavy price for her. As for why, think about it carefully, Stolas. As soon as I saw him die, I knew she could bring him back. His soul is still here, waiting for her, I know you saw it. Shit, I think everyone could see it."

Stolas didn't care about the crowd; he only cared that Airiella got Jax back. It was all that mattered to Stolas at the moment. Airiella may not have crossed to the dark side, but if Jax didn't come back, the world wouldn't have her as she'd said. Stolas had seen the crack in Airiella at Jax's death, felt the fight go out of her. If it had been Kalisha, Stolas couldn't say he would have handled it differently, even knowing the things he did.

Tama slowly walked over to Stolas, limping and holding her side still. "Thanks for the shirt. I don't think Airiella has enough energy to do this, Stolas; she's almost on empty."

"It has to work," Stolas said softly, unwilling to believe anything else.

Stolas heard steps behind him and turned to see Seir, guiding a shaking Chrissie with him. "Help her," Stolas told Chrissie, who ran clumsily to Airiella, dropping beside Airiella and fighting to keep her emotions in check. Chrissie's hands joined with Airiella's on Jax's lifeless body. The glow grew a bit brighter.

Stolas looked at Tama's grim face and Taklishim's stoic one, both fighting back the tears. "Chrissie's not strong enough to help Airiella, is she?"

Taklishim shook his head sadly. Stolas looked over at Ronnie, trembling, his arms around both Smitty and Aedan's shoulders as Ronnie stood between them, both men holding Ronnie upright, his injuries keeping him from standing on his own. Stolas had an idea and walked over to them, whispering in Smitty's ear.

Taklishim sidled up next to Stolas. "I don't know if it will work, Airiella might be too drained, the connection might not be able to help." Taklishim had understood what Stolas was doing.

"It's worth a chance. I'm not giving up," Stolas told the warrior firmly and watched as the three men helped each other to their broken angel and laid their hands on Airiella. "Is Airiella in danger?"

Taklishim nodded. "When you look at Airiella, see beyond the light of her soul, straight to her heart and that barely flickering light deep within is Airiella's energy. What she pulled off here today is nothing short of a miracle. We helped, but in comparison to what Airiella did, we did nothing. The amount of energy Airiella used was tremendous, far more than she has ever shown. Now, Airiella is literally pushing her life force into Jax. I don't know what will happen if she gives it all. We could lose her."

Stolas looked at Airiella the way Taklishim described and saw what he was talking about, saw how dim the light was and how quickly it was fading. But Stolas also saw the connection between them all, and the one to Jax was not out. It was still glowing, even if it was barely discernable. That was all Stolas needed to see.

I love you so much, Airiella, Stolas told her. To his amazement, that little light in Airiella's heart got brighter.

Stolas looked over at Taklishim and Tama and idea forming in his mind. "Use your link to Airiella, tell her how you feel about her." At the odd looks they both gave Stolas, he explained what he had done and seen and looked back at her as Taklishim got a thoughtful look on his face.

"Seir, can you bring back Degataga? There are some

people here that need healing," Stolas told Seir quietly, whose own face was sad. "Tell them both to use their links and start telling Airiella how they feel about her. The women too," Stolas added. If love was the key to this, Stolas was going to make sure she got flooded with it.

"The priest is coming." Seir nodded to the back of the crowd and disappeared. The gasp of the crowd reminding Stolas they had an audience. If it were up to Stolas, he'd out them all. As it stood, Stolas didn't care what they saw anymore. Some things were more important than appearances and things that could be explained.

Father Roarke approached his face filled with anguish as he stopped next to Stolas. "Tell Airiella how you feel about her. I think love is the key to this. Airiella feels like love has died, let's remind her it hasn't," Stolas demanded.

Kalisha heard Stolas and called out loudly, "Airiella Raven, I love you, you beautiful angel."

"Stolas, please tell your boss to leave. Associates of mine are coming, and since Airiella publicly declared him off-limits to the angels, they aren't happy. It was all aired thanks to technology. They see no distinction between Lucifer and the ones that aided the fight and the ones that died. I'd rather not give Airiella another reason to hurt," the priest told Stolas quietly.

Stolas quickly stepped over to Lucifer and relayed the message to him, who agreed and left just as fast to spare Airiella any more trauma. Seir came back with Degataga, who immediately set about healing the people not helping Airiella.

Stolas waved Degataga away as he made his way over to him, intent on healing his injuries before the others.

"Don't worry about me; take care of the others first."

"You have quite a few injuries, Stolas," Degataga told Stolas.

"I'm aware of every one of them too." Stolas moved his lips in what he hoped passed for a smile.

"Seir is coming back with Onida," Degataga told Stolas before moving on.

That's just what happened too. Onida showed up and silenced Stolas with a look as she healed him. "There will be no martyr's today. Kali is my friend, and she loves you. So does Airiella. The pain of losing a mate, especially one connected as they are, is felt by all connected to her. This loss isn't on you, Stolas. The very fact Airiella knows you are suffering is holding her back."

At Ronnie's wail, it took everything Stolas had not to shove the woman away as he felt the connection he had with Airiella sever, knowing what it meant. The power built up in him again at the unfettered anger that boiled over with Airiella's loss, and Kalisha forced him to look at her as she reached Stolas, shaking her head at him and holding his chin in her hand.

"Stay with me, Stolas. Jax is alive, Airiella achieved her goal. She isn't gone, her energy is; we can help Airiella," Kalisha reminded Stolas, grounding him in the present.

Onida, Degataga, Taklishim, and Tama all worked on healing Jax enough to stabilize him before they turned and put their hands on Airiella; Stolas, Seir, Kalisha, and Father Roarke joining in. Airiella's body began to vibrate under their hands, and with a pop, she disappeared from their sight.

Chapter Thirty-Six

J ax was rushed to the hospital, along with the rest of the team, to assess their injuries. Father Roarke stayed behind for damage control with the crowd as the Vatican team arrived, followed by massive amounts of news crews.

Stolas had managed to get the salve for the demon poison applied on Jax before the ambulance carted him away. The rest had all agreed that they couldn't feel their connection with Airiella anymore either when Stolas had asked them. Stolas couldn't accept it, and deep in his heart, he knew she was alive. He just didn't know where.

Seir brought them back to the hotel, and Stolas and Kalisha showered together to keep each other standing. The bottom of the tub stained pink and black with the blood and ash washing off them. Stolas didn't know how she did it, but Kalisha got him cleaned up, dried, and sitting on the bed.

Despair washing over him the same way the water from the shower washed Stolas clean. Kalisha pushed him back and lifted his legs on the bed, crawled over him, curved her naked body into his, and pulled the sheets over them.

"She's not gone, Stolas. Please don't give up on her now," Kalisha whispered. "We came so close to losing every one of Airiella's team tonight, including you. But we didn't. That means something."

"Where is she, then?" Stolas's whisper broke, and his arms tightened around his love, remembering how Airiella had felt when she lost Jax.

"I don't have that answer, Stolas. I only know I can feel life when I think of her. Seir bringing Chrissie back was a stroke of genius that probably saved Jax. Just as you having everyone tell Airiella, they loved her was."

"I failed Airiella, my love. I failed at the one thing I promised her." Stolas broke under the onslaught of the emotions besieging him.

"Stolas, are you so vain to think that you can beat something that was prophesied before you were alive? You were no more capable of changing that outcome than anyone else. It all came down to Airiella and the choices she made. She made the right ones, letting Jax's sacrifice stand to do what needed doing."

Stolas let go of the emotions he'd been keeping in check and sobbed into Kalisha's hair, her scent filling his senses as the pain of the night worked its way through him. Kalisha held him tight. When Stolas started shaking violently, Kalisha got up, put some clothes on him, and covered them both back up. Stolas fell asleep, mumbling how he hoped he never felt the pain Airiella did, that he couldn't stand to lose Kalisha like that.

Stolas's dreams were nightmares, scenes from the fight replaying in his mind. Jax dying, Airiella giving up, guilt eating him alive, remorse filling his every cell. Stolas visualized himself back with the Creator for a moment, and when Stolas felt the air around him change, he was there.

The Creator smiled. "I've been waiting for you. Airiella's not awake yet, but I've patched her up."

Stolas stared at the Creator. "Am I dreaming?"

"Not at all. Follow me," the Creator said and held out a hand to Stolas, and he took it, allowing himself to be led like a child. A door that hadn't been there before appeared in front of Stolas and opened. There she was, lying peacefully in a soft bed, the smell of jasmine filling the room.

"Airiella?" Stolas whispered, his weary body slumping over the bed as Stolas embraced her sleeping form.

"She's in a healing sleep, she can't hear you, but she can feel your presence," the Creator said softly.

"How did she get here?" Stolas asked without taking his eyes off Airiella, afraid she would disappear again.

"I brought her here."

"Is she dead?" Stolas was almost afraid to ask.

"No, but Airiella wouldn't have been left alone enough back there to heal the way she needs to."

Stolas guessed that made sense. "What about Jax?"

"Airiella sacrificed everything in her to bring him back. Jax will be fine."

"Will she be fine too?" Maybe Airiella would get her wish and no longer have these powers that burdened her with problems she shouldn't have to be fixing.

"Of course, she will. Airiella faced down the worst thing she could think of, losing Jax. It doesn't get harder than that. She selflessly gave the power I gifted her to bring him back. Every choice I believed she would make, she made, including protecting your friend. I have yet to be disappointed with this one. Her language is more colorful than most others, but it works for her. Airiella even brought Samuel back."

"Samuel died?" Stolas hadn't seen that.

"He did, pretty quickly too. I don't think Airiella was aware she brought him back, but she did."

"I'm afraid to ask what happens next," Stolas admitted.

"Airiella goes on. That one battle restored the balance in a way I couldn't have hoped for."

"What do you mean?" Stolas ran his fingers over Airiella's cheek. Her skin soft under his fingers, warm and alive.

"The setting for that battle was not ideal. I would have rather not had Airiella exposed as she was. It worked, though. Those that saw what happened have a renewed faith in love and humanity. That, combined with Moloch's death, restored the balance in a way I didn't expect. She risked everything, saving that unborn baby from Moloch first, putting herself right in his line of fire without a thought or care. Maybe above anything else, that alone had a profound effect on people. I didn't foresee that, and I should have. This girl's love should be a lesson for everyone."

"Are you finished with her services?" Stolas forced himself to ask as his brain filed away that information to look at later when he would pick everything apart with Kalisha trying to learn where he could have been better.

"Oh, heavens, no. What she was, she still is. You and Kalisha are free to roam as you please. I believe Lucifer has a new vow for you to take. My foolish old heart knows well enough that you won't leave your friend, and he and I have agreed to share you both. If you'd like that is. You still have free will, Stolas, I won't force you to take sides, neither will Lucifer."

Something broke loose in Stolas with those words, and more tears came flowing from his eyes. "I don't deserve that, but Kalisha does."

"Oh, my child, you do. You aren't to blame for what happened. It would have ended quite differently if you hadn't been there, reminding Airiella who she is. Reminding her who she is *without* the burden I laid upon her, that is. Her spirit was always one of a fighter, filled with a love like no other. Those words on Jax may have been prophetic, but they are also true in the definition that Kalisha gave them."

Stolas choked on a sob that stuck in his throat. "I promised Airiella."

"Stolas, you delivered. Jax was protecting you, Airiella, and Taklishim from Stone. You were Stone's targets. Jax knew what he was doing. If you hadn't reminded Airiella who she was, she wouldn't have brought Jax back. It was that which saved him. She also saved you from trading your life for Jax's. In turn, you all gave back to her when she gave it all for Jax. Excuse me for a moment; I need to speak to your soul mate who has woken and found you gone. Kalisha's a little distressed. Please take a moment with Airiella and allow me to speak with Kalisha."

Stolas nodded, silently apologizing to Kalisha for his absence, and moved, lying next to Airiella on the soft, cushiony bed. His mind flooded with thoughts, and Stolas silenced them all, allowing himself a moment to just be with her, this creature that changed his life so drastically in such a short time.

"Love, there aren't words I can find to express how much I love you and how much you give for all of us all the time. Please, accept my sincerest apology for what you have been through and my deepest gratitude for the love you brought to me."

"Stop apologizing, Stolas. I told you, I don't blame you." Airiella's hoarse voice broke through as those angel eyes looked at him. "I feel like shit, but this bed is amazing."

Stolas felt a laugh rumbling deep in him, Airiella was fine. She was her. "I'd kiss you, but I think your first kiss should be with Jax." Stolas leaned his head against hers. "You did it. You saved everyone."

Airiella's breath had gone still at the mention of Jax. "Is Jax okay?"

"Jax was alive when the ambulance took him and the others. I was able to get the poison salve on him. The Creator said Jax was fine."

"Is that where I am? In Heaven?"

"Yes, love. No, you aren't dead, the Creator brought you here to heal," Stolas answered the unasked question. Airiella shook in his arms as tears pooled in her eyes but didn't fall.

"I healed him?"

"You and Chrissie both. The others gave you their energy to keep you going." Stolas let his tears fall again.

"Why can't I feel anyone?" there was fear in Airiella's voice.

"I don't think you are all the way healed yet. You might not have the energy to open the connection. Why don't you go back to sleep? I can go back and tell them you are fine."

"No, stay with me, please. I feel better with you here." Airiella relaxed back into the bed and turned into Stolas, clutching his hand. "Thanks for getting me through that, Stolas. I almost gave in. The thought of life without Jax had one foot over the edge."

"I know, love. I'm glad you finally listened to me. Hush now, rest. I'll stay right here with you," Stolas promised, his voice filled with the love Airiella brought out in him.

"You always have, Stolas," Airiella murmured. She turned and wrapped her arm around Stolas. "Love you more."

Warmth filled Stolas's chest as he held the precious angel against him and drifted to sleep next to her. Peace finally settling in his brain.

Chapter Thirty-Seven

Stolas woke several hours later to find Airiella staring at him, a goofy look on her face. "You were talking in your sleep," Airiella informed him.

"About what?" Stolas tried to clear the sleepiness out of his mind.

"Kalisha. How good Kalisha tastes," Airiella giggled. "It was rather sweet."

Stolas blushed and sat up. "I should get back to Kalisha."

"You should, Kalisha's worried about you. And I want to see Jax."

"Ah, you both are awake," the Creator said and walked in. "Not quite healed yet, the both of you, but well enough to handle the storm down there."

"What storm?" Airiella asked. "Do I have clothes to wear?"

Stolas pulled off his shirt and handed it to Airiella. "Yum, you smell good, look good like that, too." Airiella slipped the shirt on and stood up, her legs wobbly. Stolas grabbed Airiella around the waist to steady her as he swung his legs around.

"I'm afraid the world knows about you now, Airiella," the Creator broke the news. "It's a bit chaotic down there, but support is in overwhelming favor of you."

"Shit." Airiella covered her mouth with a hand and looked wide-eyed at the creator. "Sorry."

"No worries, child. I knew what I was getting with you. Stolas can take you both back," the Creator said and touched Stolas's hand and knew exactly where to go in the hospital to bring Airiella directly to Jax. "Jax is awake, go on now."

Airiella threw her arms around the Creator. "Thank you."

"My child, I should be thanking you. You've restored balance. Now you have to maintain it."

Airiella grimaced. "No normal life for me, then?"

"You weren't born for normal, but I daresay it will be much easier now for a while. You'll know when you are needed, the light in you will tell you. Go on, your group is waiting for you." The Creator smiled, and Stolas brought them back without a second thought.

Kalisha launched herself at Stolas the moment they appeared, as Airiella flung herself at Jax. Tears of joy on all their faces. "My love, I wasn't expecting you to be here."

"I got told to wait for you here," Kalisha told Stolas, raining kisses over his face.

"Does he need to be here?" Airiella asked, gesturing at Jax through her tears. "Can we go home?"

The door burst open, and the rest of the team flooded in at hearing Airiella's voice, relief evident across all their faces at seeing both Jax and Airiella alive and well. Father Roarke pushed through. "As Onida declared herself your doctor, she can release you. The Vatican will fly you home for your protection. There's a bit of a crowd outside the hospital, I'm afraid. And at the hotel."

Seir chimed in from the back, "I'll take Onida and Degataga back home after she signs you out. I know Onida can't fly so close to her due date."

"Let's just wait a minute," Jax spoke softly, his voice not fully back yet. "This may be our only chance to relax, and I want to enjoy a minute with Airiella before everyone else demands her time again. Who else can say they spent their honeymoon working with ghosts and fighting a demon to save the world and dying for it?"

Ronnie stepped forward and shoved Jax back into a laying position as Ronnie took up the other side of Airiella, stretching his arm across them both. "Not funny. I'm sick of watching both of you die all the time. Can we cut this shit out of lives for a while?" Ronnie's face wrought with worry.

Stolas herded everyone out of the room, leaving Chrissie in there with Airiella and Ronnie while they took up positions outside the door to keep people away. Taklishim settled on the other side of Stolas, handing him a scrub top to put on. "Thank you for what you did. You've earned my respect and gratitude."

Stolas held his hand out to Taklishim, who took it and shook it firmly. "The same to you."

"Where was she?" Taklishim asked as Stolas pulled the top on.

"The Creator had Airiella. Grabbed her, thinking she would heal better without being in the middle of all this," Stolas said with a dry chuckle.

"That's the truth." Tama sighed. "I'm afraid all of our secrets are out; we've become international phenomena."

"Is it possible that it will be better this way?" Kalisha asked them softly.

"I can see both sides of that issue," Stolas answered diplomatically. "My gut says it's better Airiella is out, maybe not so good for the rest of us."

"Airiella won't see it that way. She values her privacy," Taklishim pointed out.

"As do I." Stolas shook his head in frustration. "Have they put a name to us yet?"

"I kind of yelled Airiella's," Kalisha grimaced, "so they have hers, and of course the crew of Shadow Seekers."

"The rest of us?" Stolas prodded.

"They are working on it," Taklishim confirmed. "The Vatican knows more than we'd like them too, but they aren't too keen on sharing secrets either." Taklishim leaned back against the wall and looked directly into Stolas's eyes. "Is Airiella, still Airiella?"

"Yes. Airiella's supposed to maintain the balance she brought about. I think Airiella was hoping it would have gone away, but all that she was remains inside her." Stolas hoped that things remained calm for a long while.

"That baby she had us save," Tama swallowed before going on, "has become a media sensation. There seem to be a few haters among the crowd wanting to know why Airiella didn't save the lady as well as the baby but brought back her husband."

"They are calling her selfish," Taklishim added, shooting a look at Stolas that he didn't understand. "I didn't feel comfortable answering any questions."

"That's ridiculous," Kalisha sputtered. "Airiella saved angels, humans, and demons alike. She doesn't even know she did it. She thinks the only one she saved was Jax."

"Not true, the Creator told Airiella she saved Samuel," Stolas told them. "But yes, essentially, as far as she knows, those are the only two." Stolas ran his hands through his hair and sighed deeply. "This doesn't surprise me, and it shouldn't for you either. There will always be those that see things differently, that's the balance she is supposed to maintain. There's even a balance among all the rulers, the Creator and Lucifer, most of all. Legends all paint them differently, the Creator being benevolent and all good, and Lucifer being all dark and bad. Hopefully, you all know that is not true and have seen it for yourselves."

"There is more truth to that than I'm comfortable admitting," Taklishim agreed. "Lucifer not once went after a human or an angel, or any of us, and neither did the demons he brought with him. While at the same time, the angels were aggressive towards all of them, even after Airiella stepped in."

"I know you both are right, and I know Airiella can handle the negative part of this, I just don't like it," Tama stated. "By the way, what are you, Stolas? We can't exactly call you a demon."

"I guess I'm a hybrid: half-angel, half-demon. Airiella would be my boss. Don't tell her that."

Ronnie and Chrissie walked out of the room then, their faces streaked with tears, but underneath was a relief. Chrissie walked up to Stolas and hugged him tightly. "Thank you so much for taking care of all of us. I know none of us made it easy on you."

"Before you argue that you didn't uphold your end of things, you should know Airiella made me promise to kick your ass up and down the hallway if you said that."

Ronnie held his hand out to Stolas, and he shook it, grateful he could call this man a friend.

Kalisha laughed aloud as Chrissie embraced her as well. "Of course, she did."

"Onida is checking them out. She said Taklishim and Tama could take care of the rest when they got home. Degataga is waiting downstairs to take us back to the hotel to pack everything up," Ronnie told the others.

"What about the media camped out down there?" Tama asked, concerned.

"Better they follow us than follow Airiella," Smitty answered, his arm around Jillian. "Seir will take Onida and Dega home from the hotel, and we'll be going with a Vatican escort and guard to the private airfield," Smitty recited, tapping his head to let them know he was repeating what was getting told to him.

Mags grinned. "Since they are going home that way, I guess that means Dega gets to babysit all the kids?"

Stolas laughed. "I'm betting that Seir brings the kids back with him. He's fair like that."

Chapter Thirty-Eight

Stolas was wrong. Degataga offered to babysit while they flew back. Stolas settled back into the comfortable seat on the plane as they prepared for takeoff. A Vatican representative joined them as well, trying to get as near to Airiella as possible.

It was laughable to think the guy would succeed; the entire team kept Jax and Airiella in their middle. Father Roarke sat across from Stolas and Kalisha; he turned on the TV while they waited and put the news on so they could all see what was being said and aired.

"We are getting word, right now, that this mysterious group of people has boarded a plane owned by the Vatican on a private airfield. So far, the woman known as Airiella Raven has been unavailable for comment since disappearing into thin air after bringing her husband back to life. There have been unconfirmed reports that she is back here and with her husband, Jax Walker."

"Connie, we did receive word that Jax Walker is alive and well, but we haven't been able to make contact with him either. The Vatican is keeping things tightly

under wraps as usual. The most we have been able to confirm is that they do indeed believe that Airiella Raven is an angel and that the battle that took place was against demons."

"Chris, we've seen footage of wings sprouting from her back, that doesn't come as a surprise to anyone. The number of miracles we have seen from the various grainy cell phone videos shows several people we have yet to identify as aiding her in this fight, all in ways that defy logic and belief."

The priest changed the channel. *"The father of the baby cut from its dead mother has told us that he isn't interested in doing any more interviews. As far as he is concerned, he was given a gift by an angel and her helpers. He asks that people please respect his privacy and grief. The video has gone viral of the grisly scene, and viewer discretion is advised."*

"Please prepare for takeoff," a flight attendant came out and announced, turning the TV off. "You can turn the TV back on after we reach cruising altitude."

"Just as well, I suppose," the Vatican mouthpiece started. "I'd like to take an opportunity to speak with Airiella and the rest of you, if I may. My name is Father Montoya."

"Well, Father Montoya," Stolas interrupted the priest, "if you are about to pitch a political agenda, please reconsider. Since both Airiella and myself had personal conversations with the one you consider your boss," Stolas pointed to the sky, "that is who created her; we already know what is expected of her."

Airiella snickered quietly. "If it's not political, then, by all means, Father Montoya, please go on."

Father Roarke belted out a loud laugh. "I told you, son. She answers directly to a higher power than the Vatican."

Airiella cleared her throat. "Actually, if you want to get right down to the nitty-gritty, I have more power than either the Creator or Lucifer, and I can choose to remove either from their position if I feel that the balance will be maintained by doing so. In a roundabout way, I answer to both the Creator and Lucifer and those you see here on the plane with me follow my lead. Please make no mistakes, Father Montoya, I just want to be clear about this, I have no political agenda. The powers granted to me are an awful burden I wouldn't wish on anyone. I conform to no religion, no belief system. What is just, right, and on the side of love, is where you will find me, and often that is a gray area. I will not denounce Lucifer publicly, just as I will not claim God as my savior, they both have equally important roles. The truth of my grace, as people are calling it, is the people on this plane saved me, many times, and in different ways. I've faced more bad shit in my life than most people and have clawed my way up from rock bottom several times. While I appreciate the ride home, in style, I'll add, I won't serve the Vatican any more than I will serve any other institution that asks me to. I am not singling out the Vatican."

Stolas was absurdly proud of Airiella. He wound his fingers through Kalisha's and leaned his head back against the seat as the plane taxied down the runway and started to lift off. Father Montoya didn't speak again until they were in the air and climbing.

"I thank you for your honesty, Ms. Raven."

"Mrs. Walker, if you want to be formal," Airiella

replied with a smile, Jax kissing her cheek. "Or you can just call me Airiella, as many do."

"Thank you, Airiella. I have a few questions I was wondering if you could answer about what happened in that square?"

"I'll do my best, but I will also defer to what my advisor thinks is necessary to share; that would be Stolas."

Stolas smiled at that and couldn't help his reply of, "What? Now you choose to listen?" Stolas shook his head at Airiella and rolled his eyes. "Go ahead and ask Father."

"Well, um, what was that?" Father Montoya asked simply.

"A demon war," Stolas answered for Airiella. "Moloch was one of the princes of Hell. He wanted to take over for Lucifer, kill the other princes, take their power, and eliminate Airiella for the power she holds. If that had happened, the earth would have become a realm of Hell. A breeding ground for demons and evil the likes of which you have never imagined. It was precisely this war why Airiella was created, granted the powers of both Heaven and Hell. She alone had the power to decide who lives and dies, including your God, and the Devil. Airiella is the balance when those two can't work things out for themselves."

Airiella looked at him, stunned. "Yep, what Stolas said, though I'm kinda shocked that he told you."

"It's unheard of that one exists that has more power than God," Father Montoya began to argue.

"He's one of the learned priests," Father Roarke explained. "All book learning."

Stolas nodded his understanding. "Books were written by man, Father Montoya. Based on stories passed down by man. While there is some truth to it, it's rarely the entire story."

"It might be unheard of," Airiella added, "yet, here I sit as living proof."

"You sit here, yes, but to me, that is not proof that you are more powerful than God."

Airiella shrugged. "You are allowed to believe what you want, Father. I'm not going to argue it. I've learned along this journey that if I am to be the balance, both sides of the equation must exist. Also, all that shit you guys preach about Lucifer is wrong. He's not at all like what you make him out to be."

Stolas snorted at hearing Airiella defend Lucifer to a Vatican ordained priest. "She's correct in that."

"Stolas, is it? How would you know this?" Father Montoya's face was red with anger now, splotchy, with beads of sweat popping up along his brow.

"I'm a prince of Hell as well. To be more accurate, I am half-angel, half-demon, and I walk the same line of balance that Airiella does. I always have, as an angel and as a demon. I've known Lucifer since we were children, I chose to fall to maintain that friendship and follow him. I have lived well over two thousand years, and I know a lot more than your books will ever tell you. I also have the power to bind you to keep from repeating any of this to another living soul. Do you understand that?"

"Yes?" the priest looked very uncomfortable with Stolas's admission.

"Is that a question or an answer, Father?" Airiella leaned forward, allowing electricity to crackle under her skin.

"An answer," Father Montoya replied quickly. "Why do you have a demon as an advisor?"

"He's more than a demon. You'd do well to remember that," Airiella snapped, jumping to Stolas's defense. "I don't take kindly to people insulting those that just helped me save the world. More so, I don't like people I love being spoken to like that. This kind of behavior is why the world is as bad off as it is. I also have Father Roarke here as an advisor, as well as the rest of my crew. Are there any of the others you'd like to insult as well?"

Father Roarke laughed again. "I told you, son, this would not be a conversation that would go as you thought it would. Now, please give your word that if these fine people wish for you not to share anything that they have told you that you won't."

"Is there a part of this that you wish for me not to share?" Father Montoya automatically asked.

"Please leave any information about me or Kalisha out of your report," Stolas demanded, using the demon magic in him to make it binding.

"As you wish, Stolas. I will not include you or Kalisha in any reports I make," Father Montoya obediently said, sealing the vow he didn't know he made.

"Any other questions, Father?" Jax asked as he stroked Airiella's hand.

"Why did you bring back demons?" Father Montoya added.

"I did?" Airiella looked over at Stolas.

Stolas nodded at her. "Airiella brought back demons, humans, and angels, Father. Though she wasn't aware she was doing it, this is the natural justice in her soul, which consists of pure love. The gift of life passed down from angels that roamed the earth before Airiella; and from the Creator. Those that came back wouldn't have come back if she didn't think they deserved to be alive. Airiella can see the very soul of a person and is adept at reading them to see if they deserve to continue."

"I brought back more than Jax and Samuel?" Airiella stunned question had Jax pulling her closer.

"You did, love." Stolas unbuckled his seat belt, not caring if the flight attendant got upset or not. Stolas moved to kneel in front of Airiella. "You were incredible, love. If you had taken my offer to trade my life for Jax's, I would have died knowing that I had seen history like never before being made. You were beautiful, terrifying, and absolutely justified in every action you performed. Toeing that line, but not once crossing it. You stayed true to your heart. Yes, you scared me, and I thought I lost you a couple of times. When Jax died, and half of your soul went with him, you took part of mine with you. And through it all, the love that makes you who you are never faltered. You put everyone else before you."

Jax looked at Airiella with eyes that shine with love, brighter than any other Stolas had seen in a human in all his years. "I'd do it all over again for you, Ells."

"Please don't, that was awful," Airiella choked out while Stolas sat back next to the woman who held the rest of his soul.

"Raven, Stolas is right. If someone came back, they were supposed to be here; if they didn't, it isn't your fault. You struck fear in the hearts of those that meant harm and showed them exactly what happens when they give in to it. You showed love and mercy to those who became caught in the crossfire, and even when you lost the person that means most to you and were offered his life as a bargaining chip, you stayed true; and protected us while doing it,"

Taklishim told Airiella.

"Does that answer your questions, Father?" Tama asked, leaning forward to look past Taklishim.

"Almost, I am unsure of what your roles are in this? We saw some unexplainable things on those videos," Father Montoya pushed. "Things relating to you both."

"They'll remain unexplainable," Stolas broke in. "Do you agree to that?" Stolas let his demon magic flare again.

"Yes, sir. They will not be included in my report, either."

"It's kind of sexy when you do that," Airiella joked.

"I think so too." Kalisha smiled at Airiella, stroking Stolas's face.

Jax, Ronnie, Aedan, and Smitty laughed while the women were all nodding in agreement. Stolas blushed again and looked down at his hand, holding Kalisha's. "Show no weakness, dude," Ronnie told Stolas, chuckling. "These women will eat you up."

"Let's recap, shall we?" Stolas changed the subject. "Demon war, Moloch, Airiella is the balance and will be judge, jury, and executioner when needed and holds the power of Heaven and Hell. Any questions?"

"The last one, these people here, they are your team?"

"Yes. As well as some others that are at home," Airiella confirmed. "I will lay my life down for any of them."

"As we will for her," Stolas added with a frown at Airiella. "Airiella's already laid her life down numerous times and paid a cost that your very Jesus would have been unable to pay."

"Yes, well, Jax demonstrated part of that already, I'd rather not have anyone else do the same. It was a little stressful." Airiella ignored the rest of Stolas's statement as Father Montoya wrote furiously.

"Holy hell, angel, I love you." Ronnie laughed at Airiella's expression. "It's still true, Father Montoya. She's the center of our world and the glue that holds us together. Airiella's biggest superpower is love."

"Your wives are what hold you together," Airiella corrected him. "I just keep it interesting."

After the laughter died down about Airiella keeping it interesting, Father Roarke said, "The rest of your burning questions can remain a secret, Father Montoya. Since Airiella just called me an advisor of hers, if you have further questions, you can run them through me. I'll make myself available to you should the need arise. Stolas, can you make that binding?" Father Roarke asked with a smile.

Once again, Stolas let the demon magic loose and asked the priest, "Do you agree to the terms that Father Roarke presented you?"

"Yes, that sounds fine to me," Father Montoya answered distractedly as he wrote things down on his pad of paper. Stolas held back another laugh and spotted the priest writing "superpower = love, keeps things interesting."

Chapter Thirty-Nine

I wouldn't ask if it weren't important, Lassie," Lucifer pleaded with Stolas. He'd been home less than a week and finally felt rested and recovered. "Kalisha, do you see why I need this?"

"I can see you *think* you do, but I'm going to side with Stolas on this. Whatever he thinks is best, I will support it. Stolas has not once done the wrong thing when it comes to Airiella and guiding her. She's as much a part of him as I am."

Love, are you busy? Stolas kept his eye firmly on Lucifer while he asked.

I'm currently sitting on the beach with Jax and have no plans to move from here. Why?

Lucifer wants you to come here for a meeting with the princes. He wants to use you as a way to keep them in line.

And you are okay with Big Bad using me? Stolas could hear the skepticism in Airiella's voice.

No. I'm okay with Lucifer having you at the meeting. He doesn't plan to reveal my role in this, but I will be there as one of the princes. Most of them are not believing you are what they have heard. My advice is come but make no deals agree to nothing, the standard line I gave you last time.

Fine, when?

"When, Lucy?" Stolas finally spoke.

"I can have them here in minutes if your angel is available." Lucifer looked relieved.

If you want to get it out of the way, we can do it now.

What about Jax? I don't want to leave him. I'm not over watching him die yet.

Me neither, love. Let me see if Lucifer can grant Jax a one-time passage.

"She doesn't want to leave Jax. Will you allow Jax in and out with Airiella?"

"He will stay with her and go nowhere else?" Lucifer asked in his binding tone.

"Don't pull that shit with Stolas," Kalisha bit out. "Jax goes where Airiella goes."

Lucifer laughed, delighted. "I'll agree to safe passage for Jax in and out."

"That means it was already something Jax had, wasn't it, because of who he is to Airiella?" Stolas had wondered about that.

"Maybe," was all Lucifer would say about that.

Jax will be safe as long as he is with you. You already know I won't allow anything to happen to him, and Lucifer won't either, he's terrified of you; probably half in love with you as well.

Stolas didn't get a response, and he sat there looking at Lucifer, who was studying Stolas carefully, assuming he was still talking with Airiella. "Come on, Lassie. I'm trying to prevent another war like that one from happening again."

Stolas felt Airiella's presence and held back the laugh that threatened to come out when all the papers on Lucifer's desk flew around the room. Kalisha didn't try to hold it back; she just burst out laughing.

"The angel's here already, isn't she?" Lucifer looked around and gave a cry of alarm when his body lifted in the air. "Shit, angel girl, let me down. I almost pissed myself."

Airiella appeared with Jax holding her hand. "That would have been funny." Airiella took a seat next to Stolas. "Let's do this and get it over with."

Lucifer let loose his summoning power, and Stolas felt the pull even though he was already there. "I just want them to see you and understand if they cross a line I have clearly drawn, that they will be facing you. I've made my rules clear. If they are topside where you reside, my rules still stand, though they alone are accountable for their actions, and I will not protect them."

"Fine. If demons harm innocent people, the demons answer to me," Airiella informed Lucifer.

"Yes, that is one of the lines I am making clear to them," Lucifer agreed. "If necessary, will you show your power?"

"Without actually going all the way," Stolas interrupted to make sure Lucifer knew Airiella was not a pawn for Lucifer to use to kill his wayward princes.

"Before I answer that, did you redo the oath that Stolas made to you?"

Lucifer chuckled. "Damn it, I truly like you. It's not many that challenge me as you do. Yes, I did."

"Are you happy with it, Stolas?" Airiella looked at Stolas, concern in her eyes.

"I am, love. They are arriving; please go stand over near Lucy since he doesn't want our relationship known."

"Isn't it already after all that shit aired on TV?"

"No, they only know I was there, but so was Lucifer. As far as they know, I was there at his request."

Airiella moved and stood close to Lucifer, Jax trying to put himself between them, but she wouldn't allow it. Kalisha squeezed Stolas's hand as Airiella crossed her arms. The softness and love that surrounded Airiella presented a deep contrast to the look on her face and the power that came to life just under her skin.

Don't glow; Stolas warned Airiella.

No shit.

Dakota opened the door, and the princes filed in, those with partners taking up positions against the wall as the other stood in front of them; Lucifer, behind his desk with Airiella and Jax off to the side. The room's tension was thick as Seir took a seat next to Stolas, a questioning look on his face as he glanced at Airiella and Jax.

"What is the meaning of this disgusting creature being here?" Azrael shouted, one of the princes that had been close to Moloch.

"Silence," Lucifer roared, allowing his power free, demanding obedience.

It was a strange sensation for Stolas not to tremble under the commands to submit to Lucifer's will anymore. His new oath of loyalty encompassing the Creator and Airiella. Stolas didn't have to obey anyone, other than

Airiella if she demanded it. He knew she never would unless it came to the mortality of someone Airiella loved.

Once Lucifer was sure they were all under his control, he looked at Airiella. "This being is not disgusting, I do not want to hear anything less than respect when speaking to her, or about her. I will punish whoever disobeys this. Understood?"

Lucifer waited for confirmation from everyone in the room before continuing, all of them realizing that was a binding command. "The angel is justice. She is the most powerful being alive. She is above myself and the Creator. This angel is who you will face should you disobey my rules outside of Hell. The angel has defeated Bael and Moloch. Wiped out entire legions as if they were nothing."

"She had the help of her friends," Azrael spoke out again, pushing the boundaries.

Lucifer gave Stolas a look that he understood without needing the words. Lucifer wanted Airiella to prove her power.

Pull their souls, love, all of them, just partially as you did with Lucifer.

Happily, my skin feels like it's about to combust.

Stolas winced as the room's power became almost intolerable as Airiella grasped all their souls and pulled them halfway out, Stolas's new abilities allowing him to see this easily. He didn't need to see it to view the fear on their faces as they realized exactly what Airiella could do.

Seeing the very slight nod from Lucifer, Stolas told her to let them go.

It was kind of fun. Wonder how many demons shit themselves?

Stolas bit his lip to keep from laughing as Lucifer

made them each renew their vow to him and agree to the punishment Airiella saw fit if they were to disobey. Once done and they all left, Lucifer dropped back into his chair.

"Damn, woman. You are terrifying. Was that power display necessary?" Lucifer yanked up his sleeve and looked at the blisters on his arms.

Stolas reached in his pocket and threw the salve to Lucifer, who started rubbing it on liberally. "Don't complain, you wanted it."

"It wasn't my intent to do that. I think it's just the way you react to me. The power surge was because of how many demons were around me, and that was me keeping it contained."

"Thank you for your assistance. I don't anticipate any demons stepping out of line, and I can guarantee that that the punishment will be severe if someone does. Not only do the legions answer to me over their prince, but if one of their legions goes off track, the prince will have to answer for it. I did this to try and give you the normal life you crave and rightly deserve. I had no hidden agenda, and I will continue to be honest with you."

"That's not to say Lucy won't still try and trap you given a chance, so keep me between you two," Stolas added.

"Easy enough," Airiella said, walking over to kiss Stolas's cheek, then Kalisha's. "See you soon." She popped back out with Jax, leaving him sitting there confused.

"Am I missing something?" Stolas asked Kalisha.

"How would I know? I just assumed it was something you had planned." Kalisha shrugged. "Are we done here?"

Lucifer was grinning, but he nodded. "You're done. Go on."

Stolas stood up and looked over his shoulder at his friend as they walked out the door. Lucifer was up to something.

Chapter Forty

Stolas bolted awake at Chrissie's cry. Kalisha seconds after him. "What was that?"

"I think Chrissie is calling us." Stolas shook the fog from his head.

"Stolas! Kalisha! Come help! I need you!" came the cry again a minute later.

They jumped out of bed, throwing clothes on frantically as Stolas tuned in to Chrissie's signature and brought them up to her. "What's the matter?" Stolas looked around as Kalisha put her back to his protecting him from behind.

Chrissie giggled. "I can't believe that worked."

Kalisha, hearing the laughter, relaxed and turned around. "You aren't in danger?"

"I was only going to be in danger if you didn't show up," Chrissie said, smiling. "Ells would have kicked my ass."

"What's going on?" Stolas demanded, trying to control his erratically beating heart.

"Come with me, dude." Ronnie appeared from inside the house. "Don't argue; it's safer that way."

"You, Kalisha, come with me." Chrissie grabbed Kalisha's arm and pulled her towards Aedan's house.

Stolas looked at Ronnie. "I'm not moving until you tell me what's going on. I was asleep!"

"It's three in the afternoon!" Ronnie scolded Stolas and moved behind him and started to push him physically towards the house. "Don't make me pick you up and carry you."

"Time moves differently here than it does in Heaven or Hell; it was the middle of the night. And you wouldn't dare." Stolas took a few steps on his own, wondering if Ronnie really would carry through on his threat.

"Ronnie won't have to if you don't do what he says, I'll do it for him." Airiella poked her head over the balcony. "Shut up and do it."

Ronnie shrugged. "I told you it was safer not to argue."

Stolas looked back in the direction Kalisha had gone, mildly feeling unsettled at being away from her and not knowing why. "Talk to me, Ronnie."

Jax walked out his face bearing a gentle smile. "Chrissie wanted to throw a real wedding for you and Kalisha, so we made it happen."

"Should have just trusted me." Ronnie grinned at Stolas's shock.

"Your friend gave us this credit card to use, and well, we did. Now you need to get ready." Jax joined Ronnie, pushing Stolas into the house.

"Lucy knew about this?" Stolas muttered and allowed them to direct him to a room where he found a tuxedo waiting for him.

"He did." Jax broke out in laughter. "He was too afraid of Airiella to argue with her that you wouldn't like the attention."

Stolas finally laughed. "Okay, that I can see. Lucifer's right, but when it comes to Kalisha, I will do anything she wants."

"You'd do it for Ells too." Jax smiled. "Don't disappoint the women. They really want to do this for you." Jax handed him a jewelry box. "Get dressed. I'll wait in the hall."

Stolas opened the box and saw a stunning ring for Kalisha and a band for himself. Both with matching stones that portrayed black, white, and gray. The gray stone was the centerpiece. Stolas felt his emotions well up inside him and jumped as Lucifer popped in.

"You knew about this?" Stolas whispered.

"I knew about the surprise wedding, not that they had these stunning things made." Lucifer looked at the rings in the box. "I also knew they'd allow me to be here. Well, to be more accurate, I was threatened that I had better be here for my best friend."

"Never hurt these people, Lucy," Stolas muttered quietly, setting the rings down on the bed as he started to undress and put the tuxedo on.

"Hold on there, my friend. Go shower first." Lucifer pushed Stolas to the bathroom. "Your hair is frightening. And for your peace of mind, I don't plan on hurting them."

Showered, Stolas dressed in the tuxedo and used magic to dry his hair, Lucifer fussing with it in a prissy way. Stolas pushed him away, annoyed. "It's fine."

"If you hold still for a minute, it will be. Don't piss

off your angel; she scares me."

Stolas held still while Lucifer messed with his hair and then finally opened the door to see Jax, Ronnie, Smitty, and Aedan standing there, drinks in their hands. Aedan handed Stolas one, and Smitty gave one to Lucifer.

"Guess I can cross drinks with the Devil off my bucket list," Smitty joked.

"I can't believe this is happening." Stolas gulped down the drink.

"Do you not want it to?" Ronnie sounded concerned.

"He does, I think Stolas is just in shock," Lucifer answered for him. "Today, I am not the Devil. I'm just his friend."

Stolas let them lead him out to the backyard where the other weddings had taken place. Thankfully it was absent of all the people except the ones that knew both Kalisha and himself. To Stolas's surprise, Taklishim, Tama, Onida, and Degataga were there.

They bristled at the presence of Lucifer but remained calm and even friendly. Stolas looked around for Airiella, but along with the rest of the women, she was absent. Father Roarke approached him. "They asked me to do this, Stolas. What I'd like to know is how you would like me to go about it?"

"What? What do you mean? Are there different ways to get married?" Stolas was seriously confused.

Lucifer and Smitty bust out laughing. "The priest means for vows and religion, Lassie," Lucifer told him quietly. "I do love you, my friend."

"Don't choke on your amusement of my naiveté, Lucy," Stolas murmured back at Lucifer.

"I wouldn't dream of it," Lucifer replied with a smile.

"I'm from both worlds, Father," Stolas told the priest. "I'd rather have something that focuses on neither though. Just love."

"I never thought I'd see the day you'd be a full-fledged romantic. Be still my heart," Lucifer droned on dramatically to the amusement of the rest of the guys.

Lucifer is picking on me, and I might start a war of my own if this doesn't get moving soon, love.

To Stolas's utter enjoyment, Airiella popped in front of Lucifer, and her skin crackled lightly. "I hear you are making fun of the groom. Do you honestly think that is fair of you when he knew nothing about this?"

Lucifer was startled enough to back up a few steps, and then a grin split his face. "Still scary, I see. I happen to know that since Stolas loves me, and you love Stolas, you won't hurt me."

"You have that wrong, bucko. I won't kill you. I never agreed to not hurting you," Airiella fired back.

Stolas laughed at the look on Lucifer's face. "Okay, I think he gets it. I owe you one."

"Hell yeah, you do!" Ronnie crowed. "I got a picture of his face!"

Stolas laughed even harder at that as Airiella disappeared again. "Don't get too cocky, Lucifer," Smitty told him slyly. "Airiella loves and adores Taklishim, and she zapped him when he annoyed Tama."

Lucifer schooled his face into a fake calm as he digested those words, and at Jax's confirmation of the facts, settled down. Stolas hadn't felt this lighthearted and happy in a long time. He let the guys lead him around, had pictures taken, then they went serious.

"It's time," Jax said, guiding Stolas up the aisle. "Just stand here and do what either Airiella or Father Roarke tells you to do. It's easier that way. I'll be taking pictures."

Lucifer stood off to the side out of deference to the rest of the guests, though the only ones Lucifer bothered were the medicine people, and even then, it was only Taklishim that reacted the most.

Mags, Jillian, and Chrissie came down the aisle and took their seats, Chrissie grinning at Stolas as Ronnie put an arm around her. "Thank you," Stolas mouthed to her.

Airiella came into sight next, and next to her, Kalisha. Stolas's face went slack at the sight of Kalisha. Chrissie had outdone herself this time. Kalisha's dark skin was glowing against the stark white of the dress, and as she moved, the lowering sun glinted off the silver and black beads woven through the fabric. Kalisha was stunning.

Her dreadlocks were peppered with small white flowers and held above her head by something he couldn't see. Kalisha's earrings matched the stones in the rings Jax had given Stolas, and each movement she made, she shimmered in the sunlight.

Stolas almost ran to her. It was only Airiella's voice in his head that stopped him in his tracks. *Don't you dare move. Kalisha asked me to walk her down the aisle, and that's what I am going to do. Behave and wait right there. Oh, and close your mouth.*

Stolas snapped his mouth closed and heard Lucifer laughing behind him. Fighting the urge to turn and glare, Stolas instead watched his precious love walk towards him as if she were floating. When they finally reached the end of the aisle, Airiella turned and kissed Kalisha's cheek and went to sit beside Ronnie and Chrissie.

Stolas had no idea what happened next. He lost himself in the beauty that stood before him, mesmerized by the vision Kalisha presented to him. He repeated what he was supposed to when told and continued to stare at Kalisha.

Kalisha, Stolas, Stolas jolted as Airiella's voice broke into both of their heads. *With the powers given to me, I'd like to use them to bind you two together in a way as close as I can. I know you took vows under Lucifer, but this will be a bit different. Take each other's hands when Father Roarke tells you to.*

Stolas had to force himself to listen to the priest, and when he told Stolas to take Kalisha's hands, he didn't hesitate. Stolas felt the swell of magic rise in the air, the heady combination of the light and dark mixing as it only did for Airiella.

Kalisha gasped as she felt her soul move. Stolas went utterly still, his trust in Airiella complete. *Together, I merge what love has shown me to be absolute, into one. Nothing will be able to break this bond you share, and it will fulfill all your needs in each other. When one of you feels lost, the other is your guide. Trust in the love, in the bond, in each other. Love will always win.*

Tears swam in Stolas's eyes as he felt his soul merge in a way he didn't know was possible. Everything Kalisha was, her very essence filled him, and a line from her heart to his was visible between them. Airiella had gifted them a connection.

My love, Stolas whispered in his mind.

And you are my love, Kalisha whispered back.

"The rings, please," Father Roarke asked, and Stolas felt Lucifer slip the box into his hand. "We can skip straight to the I do's."

"I do," both Kalisha and Stolas said at the same time.

Stolas pulled the ring out of the box and slid it on to Kalisha's finger as she gasped at the gorgeous stones. Stolas handed her the band to put on his, and she slid it on, tears sliding down her cheeks. "Kiss the bride, Stolas," Father Roarke laughed.

If you don't kiss her, I will! Airiella warned Stolas when he just stood there staring at his wife.

Stolas grinned and swept Kalisha off her feet, locking his lips on hers with the silent promise no one else heard but them that he would always be there to catch her if she fell. The group cheered behind him as Stolas set Kalisha gently down on the ground.

"There better be food," Lucifer growled at Airiella as they walked back towards the house.

"Stuff it, Big Bad. Of course, there's food. And cake." Airiella grinned over at Lucifer. "Devil's food."

Stolas howled in laughter at the look on Lucifer's face, once again, put there by the most unlikely friend he'd ever had. Airiella goaded Lucifer at every opportunity she could, and Stolas loved every bit of it. For a short time, Airiella had taken the Hell right out of the Devil himself and let Lucifer have fun.

They spent hours talking, dancing, eating, and listening to stories, even Lucifer divulging antics he'd gotten up to as a child. Before they left, Jax came out of the house, a gift in his hand, handing it to Kalisha, telling her to open it when they got home.

Airiella air-kissed Lucifer, giggling as he winced at the closeness of their skin, and then kissed both Kalisha and Stolas before sending them on their way. Stolas bid farewell to Lucifer, and he took his bride home. Bride, Stolas had a bride now.

"You had no idea they were up to that?" Kalisha asked Stolas as she sank into a chair.

"None whatsoever. Was it too much? Did you not like it?" Stolas worried.

"Stolas, it was fantastic. I couldn't have dreamed a more perfect wedding, or dress, or a drop-dead sexy husband. And these rings, wow!" Kalisha stared at her hand. "What are these stones?"

"Diamonds," he told her. "Black diamonds, white diamonds, and the gray color in the center diamonds are astounding. I have no idea how they managed it." Stolas looked at the smaller stones inlaid into his band. "They are perfect."

Kalisha held the gift out to Stolas. "Open it."

Stolas pulled the paper off to reveal a photo album. The cover of the album was when Stolas was kissing Kalisha. Jax had incredible talent with a camera. Stolas ran his fingers over the picture. He scooped Kalisha up and sat in the chair, settling her on his lap as they went through the album.

The pages were filled with pictures of Kalisha and him that Stolas hadn't even known had been taken. Along with the photos of the wedding. Stolas had wondered why Jax wasn't out there with them, now he understood. As they came to the end of the album, there was a sealed envelope with his name.

Stolas pulled it open, his heart clenching as he read:

Stolas,

I don't know how time stopped, I'm glad it did, but I do remember the story of you seeing me for the first time. Somehow, it was that story that brought me back from the brink to you. I also remember every time we've ever met, everything you've ever told me. I've never been as excited to share a vision with someone as I was with you. While I had no idea that it would be Kalisha, I couldn't be happier that it is her. Together you two are perfect.

You deserve the kind of love that I have with Jax, and Kalisha will give you that; I know you love her the same way. I also know how much finding that meant to you. I can feel it being around you both. The Creator told me how to merge your souls; it's the closest thing to what Jax and I have with our connection that I could do, aside from sharing the vision to open you to the possibility you could have it. It's the way angels bond, or so I was told. Despite what you think, you've always been an angel, fallen or not, redeemed or not.

I can only assume why you knew so much about me, why you were drawn to me. The darkness in each of us recognized each other. You've never let me down. I have so many things to thank you for, so much I owe you, that this is the only thing I could think to do. You'll never have to crave love or miss it again. It took some serious digging on my part, something I promised myself I wouldn't do. I hope you'll forgive me for that, for the intrusion.

You've saved me from me, from Bael, and Moloch. You've guided me, taught me, and loved me even when I pushed you away. You've promised me things that *are impossible and tried to make it possible anyway. Knowing now that you've been watching over me this whole time, it makes sense that even when I felt alone, I knew I wasn't.*

I know your heart, Stolas. I know those deepest parts of you that you don't want to admit. I know Kalisha's as well. I see you. I see her. Emotions never lie, even when you try to hide them, I still see them. Without you, I wouldn't have the man that I can guarantee is holding me close to him as you read this. The man that gives me a reason to keep going. I've learned a lot about prophecy, more than I ever wanted to know, and I understand the layers that make it up now, the double meanings.

My gift to you isn't this album, though, with Jax as the photographer, I am sure it's spectacular. It's not this letter or a wedding. My gift to you is life. Do me a favor when you finish reading this, put the letter down, hug your wife, and listen. Listen in the same way you looked for my energy. I'm a part of you both now, and I know you'll hear it. When you do, you'll understand my gift. (If you don't, you're in for a hell of a surprise!)

Stolas, you might just be closer to me than anyone, other than Jax, that is. Please believe that. I love you both with a love that will never die.

Love,

Airiella

Stolas put the letter down and unquestioningly did exactly as Airiella had asked. He hugged Kalisha to him, held her tightly, allowing the love they shared to wash over him and quiet everything around them. Kalisha's arms wound around his neck as they both listened. Stolas calmed his mind, closed his eyes, and tried to hear beyond the silence.

In that silence and stillness, only feeling love, Stolas heard a little beat. Rhythmic and steady like a distant drum. His eyes flew open and widened as he pulled back and looked at Kalisha. She hadn't understood it yet, but she'd heard it. "What is it, Stolas? I don't follow."

"It's life, love. Life." Stolas put his hand over Kalisha's belly. "Life. Us." Stolas didn't know how it was possible, or how she'd done it, but Airiella had seen directly into the deepest most sacred parts of his heart and given Stolas something that by all rights shouldn't be possible. Something he'd always wanted and never told a single soul.

Kalisha gasped as she finally grasped the meaning, her mouth crashing over his in a desperate kiss. "I love you."

Stolas let the emotion take over him as pesky tears pooled in his eyes again. "There is nothing more important to me than you, and now this. I don't know how Airiella knew, but I'll be forever grateful, and I'll do my damn best to prove it to you every day."

Airiella had bled life for him once again, and the tiny sound filled his ears. *Thank you, love.*

Just keeping things interesting, Airiella replied with a laugh.

Not ready to say goodbye to these characters yet? Don't worry, they make an appearance in the series following this one. Thank you for sticking with me through this series. I hope you enjoyed the journey.

-MICHELLE LEE

www.ingramcontent.com/pod-product-compliance
Lightning Source LLC
Chambersburg PA
CBHW060307100726
47907CB00002B/320